The Silver Rose

The Silver

A NOVEL

Rose

SUSAN CARROLL

BALLANTINE BOOKS · NEW YORK

A Ballantine Books Trade Paperback Original

Copyright © 2006 by Susan Carroll

Published in the United States by Ballantine Books, an imprint of The Random House Publishing Group, a division of Random House, Inc., New York.

BALLANTINE and colophon are registered trademarks of Random House, Inc.

Library of Congress Cataloging-in-Publication Data

Carroll, Susan.
The silver rose : a novel / Susan Carroll.
p.   cm.
ISBN 0-345-48251-4
1. Catherine de Médicis, Queen, consort of Henry II,
King of France, 1519–1589—Fiction.   2. France—History—
Henry II, 1547–1559—Fiction.   I. Title.

PS3553.A7654S56 2006
813'.54—dc22   2005055544

Printed in the United States of America

www.ballantinebooks.com

2 4 6 8 9 7 5 3

Book design by Susan Turner

To my son Ricky;
wherever your journey leads you,
always remember I love you.

And to my enthusiastic fan,
Patricia Ann Cute,
the lady who holds my brother's heart.

Acknowledgment

The completion of each book marks the end of another journey. I could not have found my way to the end of this road without the help, encouragement, and sage advice of so many people: my agent, Andrea Cirillo, my editor, Charlotte Herscher, her assistant, Signe Pike, and my copy editor, Martha Trachtenberg. I am greatly indebted to Gina Centrello, Linda Marrow, and the entire Ballantine production staff.

For their continuing support, I also have to thank the ladies of my local RWA chapter, Jan Steffens, Elizabeth Bare, Leslie Thompson, and Teresa Davis. My friends: Julie Kistler for her aid with plot and research, and Stephanie Wilson and Kay Krewer for helping me understand the mysterious ways of horses.

And as always my heartfelt love and gratitude to my dearest friend and critique partner, Kim Cates, for taking this long and difficult journey with me and especially for seeing me down that last long mile. I couldn't have made it without you, Frodo.

The Silver Rose

Prologue

THE SUN SLIPPED BELOW THE HORIZON, THE LAST OF THE light fading like smoke from a snuffed-out candle. Darkness descended over the cliff side and the line of trees, turning the rugged Breton coastline into the kind of land Simon Aristide understood best. A land of night and shadow.

His hands encased in leather gloves, the witch-hunter gripped the reins of his mount. Like her master, the spirited ebony mare blended with the darkness. Aristide's shoulder-length hair was as black as the horse's mane and just as wild in the brisk wind blowing leeward. He was likewise garbed all in black from his thick boots to his leather jerkin. His beard-shadowed face cast no pale gleam to alert his enemies, his skin toughened from many days spent in the saddle, weathering the elements.

Simon had an angular countenance, the set of his mouth hard and uncompromising, rarely softened by a smile. His left eye was as dark as the rest of him, glinting with a piercing intelligence. His ravaged right eye he usually kept concealed beneath a black patch. A heavy scar, the result of a duel, bisected his forehead, disappearing beneath the patch only to emerge in a thin crease that marred his cheek. He was an intimidating figure, tall, with sinewy limbs. Anyone would have to be mad to attack him.

But Simon had concluded that the creatures stalking him *were* mad or else imbued with evil and malice to a chilling degree. On a night like this, alone, isolated from any signs of human habitation, he preferred to think his pursuers were merely insane. It was more comforting than the alternative.

As the shadows deepened around him, Simon resisted the urge to nudge Elle into a gallop. The barest pressure of his knees and they'd both be off like the wind. But it would be far too dangerous, the cliff path narrow and treacherous even in the full light of day. A full-out gallop in the dark would be pure suicide. An easier road beckoned to him through the trees that rimmed the cliffs, but the gnarled trunks, the thicket of shrubs and undergrowth offered far too many places for concealment.

Simon kept the mare to a sedate walk. He heard nothing beyond the steady clop of Elle's hoofbeats, the wind rustling through the trees, the surf battering the rocks far below, and yet the back of his neck tingled with the awareness that he was not alone out here in the darkness. *They were here.* At least one of them. Perhaps the one he had sensed dogging him in the last village he had passed through.

Or perhaps exhaustion and only a few snatched hours of troubled sleep were starting to get the better of him. But he didn't think so. Elle's behavior told him otherwise. The mare had been twitchy the past mile or so, skittering, tossing her head, her ears pricked.

Simon reached down to pat her neck when the sound carried to his ears. At first he thought he imagined the faint wail of an infant. It could be no more than the wind keening over the rocky headland. Simon's gut knotted with dread all the same.

Around the next bend, the land leveled off and the cries became louder and more plaintive. Simon drew Elle to a halt, tensely scanning the distance. Barely one hundred yards ahead, moonlight flooded an object abandoned perilously near the edge of the cliff. Anyone else might have mistaken it for a blanket roll left behind by a careless shepherd. But Simon had seen such bundles before, with one difference this time.

This one was still alive, the infant's cries borne to him clearly on the wind. Simon's heartbeat quickened, his first impulse to charge forward. But he'd narrowly avoided ambush too many times to be that rash.

He slid from Elle's back and drew the mare into a stand of trees, tethering her to the trunk of a sturdy but pliant beech. Elle's eyes did not roll in terror, but she was blowing and stamping. She shifted her sleek powerful chest and shoulders as though to block him from leaving the grove.

Simon stroked the horse to soothe her. He lingered in the shadow of the trees, his gaze tracking the path to the jutting of the cliff. The plateau where the child had been abandoned offered no place of concealment, no cover for anyone attempting to hide. It would not offer Simon any, either, if some assassin lurked farther down the path or even in the trees, preparing to lodge an arrow in his back.

But that was not his enemy's usual mode of attack and the cries of the infant overrode his caution. They were growing weaker by the moment. It was just possible that they had never counted on Simon being here this soon.

Easing past Elle, Simon drew his sword and started forward. He could barely hear the child now, only one final whimper and then a terrible silence. All stealth and wariness forgotten, he ran, dislodging a hail of pebbles beneath his boots.

He hurtled toward the small bundle on the edge of the cliff, dropping to his knees beside it. The wind stirred the edge of the coarse blanket, but there was no movement from the tiny figure. Simon set down his sword and stripped off his gloves. He gathered the swathed infant into his arms with a gentleness that was as rare as his prayers.

Please. Please let me have arrived in time. Just this once.

He peeled back the flap of the blanket, his breath hitching sharply. The doll's glass button eyes fixed him with an empty stare, the jagged mouth stitched onto the canvas face sneering at him. *Tricked.*

He scarcely had time to register that fact before he heard the snap of a twig on his blind side. He jerked toward the sound and realized that there was a hollow in the ground below the place where he knelt. He caught the barest blur before the woman crouching there sprang at him.

Her teeth bared in a snarl, she launched into him,

knocking him onto his back. Moonlight glinted off the weapon in her hand as she thrust at his neck. Simon deflected the blow with the doll and bucked upward, hurling his attacker off of him. She hit the ground with a furious screech. By the time he had regained his feet, she had also scrambled to hers. And she was between him and his sword. With a contemptuous smile, she kicked it farther out of his reach.

She was clad in baggy breeches and a peasant's tunic, her dark hair unkempt, her eyes manic, her mouth cruel and cunning. Simon kept a knife hidden inside his boot, but he made no move to go for it.

"Keep back, woman," he said. "I have no desire to harm you. Drop your weapon and I am willing to spare you if you answer my questions."

The creature threw back her head, emitting an eerie imitation of an infant's mewling cry. "What's your question?" she mocked. "Where's the babe? There is none, witch-hunter. Not this time. And that is the only answer you'll get from me. Aside from this." She brandished her weapon, circling in closer.

"No desire to harm me. Bah." She spat in Simon's direction, the spittle landing inches from his boot. "I know how you witch-hunters ask your questions. With the rack and the branding iron."

"That is not my way," he said, "If you attack me again, I will have to kill you."

"What does that matter? I am not afraid to die. The Silver Rose will resurrect me."

With a bloodcurdling screech, she leaped and was on

him again. Simon caught her wrists to hold her back. No mere woman should have been so strong. Whatever madness or evil surged through her veins, it was all Simon could do to keep her at bay. He felt the heat of her breath, heard the gnash of her teeth as she came within an inch of tearing open his cheek.

He was more concerned with the strange weapon she clutched in her right hand. She stabbed at him, the tip tearing through his jerkin. Simon twisted her wrist until she cried out and dropped the weapon. She went into a fury, kicking, snapping, and trying to bite. When nothing else availed, she butted the top of her head beneath his chin. Simon reeled, his jaw exploding with pain. He lost his grip on her and staggered back, barely managing to stop himself from plunging over the edge of the cliff.

His attacker rushed at him in an effort to drive him over. He dodged her charge and it was she who teetered, the ground giving way beneath her. She fell, scrabbling wildly for purchase. Simon flung himself to the ground and caught her arm. She dangled below him, her legs and free arm flailing, her face white with rage. Her weight strained the muscles in his arm until they burned with pain.

"Who sent you?" he growled. "Who is this Silver Rose that you serve?"

"Go to hell," she shrieked.

"Tell me what I want to know or—" Simon gasped as she clawed at his hand, digging her nails in so viciously, his grip slackened.

He felt her start to slip, made another desperate grab for her arm. But it was too late. She hurtled into the darkness, his last view her face gloating with insane triumph. He heard the thud of her body as it struck the cliff side on the way down and then a splash. The sea was like a dark, hungry beast, frothing at the mouth as it devoured the witch's broken body and all the answers he so desperately sought along with her.

What demon possessed you, woman? Where does your coven hide when all of you are not out spreading terror and trying to kill me? And who is this she-devil you call the Silver Rose? This sorceress you all worship so much you are willing to die for her, believing she has the power to raise you from the dead.

And what if she could?

The thought sent a chill through Simon that had nothing to do with the wind whipping in from the sea. With a low groan, he retreated from the edge and rolled onto his back, seeking to recover his breath. He sat up slowly, brushing the tangle of hair from his face. He winced at the throb of his hand where the witch had lacerated him with her nails. The salty taste of blood filled his mouth. He had bitten his cheek when she had butted him with her head.

He worked his jaw carefully. It hurt like the devil, but she hadn't managed to dislocate it or loosen any of his teeth. His injuries could have been a great deal worse, he reflected as his gaze fell upon the strange weapon he had forced from her hand. He had encountered such a hellish device before, witnessed the witch blade's lethal power. But he had never managed to gain possession of one to study it more closely.

Simon picked it up carefully. At first glance the weapon

looked like nothing more than a very thin stiletto with a needle-sharp tip. But once the stiletto punctured the skin, the hilt could be pushed, sending a poisonous liquid through the blade. Simon had no idea exactly how the witch blade worked, but he'd seen the results. The wound was small, looking far from mortal, but the death that it wrought was slow and agonizing.

Simon set the weapon down, seeking some safe way of transporting it. He found the discarded doll and stripped the blanket away. Out of its swaddling, the doll was a crude semblance of a child. No more than a cloth head and body carefully weighted with something to give it just the right feel of a small infant when wrapped in the blanket.

Simon seized the doll and hurled it off the cliff. His anger was tempered with relief, that that was all it had been this time—a fake. He'd witnessed more cruelty, death, and evil in the span of his twenty-eight years than most men twice his age. But he was not certain he could endure the sight of one more dead child. He'd lain awake far too many nights, picturing the torment of those helpless babes he'd been too late to save. Left exposed in some remote locale where their cries would go unheard, abandoned to perish slowly of hunger and neglect.

What kind of woman could command others to commit such horrors? The same woman who could craft a weapon like that poisonous stiletto, the strange silver flower that was her emblem arrogantly engraved on the hilt. No matter what it took, Simon intended to find the witch and put a stop to her ungodly crimes. Unless the Silver Rose got him first.

That was more than likely if he behaved as stupidly as

he'd done tonight. Five years ago, even two, he would never have fallen for such a trap. But his lone crusade was wearing him so thin, he was surprised he still cast a shadow.

He wrapped the blanket around the stiletto. Retrieving his sword and gloves, he trudged back to where he had left Elle. She stamped, tossing her head and yanking on the lead, spooked by his battle with the witch. It took much soothing on his part before she settled down. He rested his forehead against the velvet softness of her nose.

"Lord, Elle, I'm so tired of all this. So damned tired."

She whickered, her dark eye gleaming softly in the moonlight. She nuzzled his hair and lipped at the neckline of his shirt as though to comfort him. As absurd as it seemed, Simon sometimes thought the mare understood him.

Except Miri Cheney would not have thought it absurd. She would have said . . . Simon's breath snagged in his throat as her image stole into his mind, so clear even after all these years. The memory of a young girl with hair pale as moonlight, a face as ethereal as an angel's, eyes that could be the soft hue of morning mist or the dark color of a storm at sea. Fey eyes that could make a man forget who he was, what he needed to do. Or worse still, forget who she was. A daughter of the earth, a wise woman. That was how Miri had always referred to herself. No matter what she chose to call herself, a witch was still a witch. And yet, there had been something different about Miri.

Despite her unfortunate family background of sorcery, she had been more misguided than tainted by evil. The girl had possessed an innocence, a shining faith in the ultimate goodness of the world, a hope for the best in people. Girl?

No, she'd be a mature woman by now and that light of hers had probably dimmed since her family had been forced to abandon their home on Faire Isle, driven into exile. Simon was in large part responsible for that.

Rumors had reached him this past year that one of the Cheney sisters had dared return to the island and was living there in quiet seclusion, a woman possessing an almost supernatural ability to cure any sick or wounded creature she came across. There was only one person that could be . . . Miri.

Simon tightened his grip on Elle's bridle as he sought to banish the woman from his mind. Remembrance of her loosed upon him far too painful regrets. But Miri had been invading his thoughts more of late and he could no longer keep the gates of his mind barred against her. His enemies were gathering strength to an alarming degree. He was alone. He was exhausted. He was desperate. Each day inched him closer to the conclusion he stubbornly resisted. There was only one way he was going to defeat the Sisterhood of the Silver Rose.

He needed the help of another witch.

Chapter One

THE STORM HOVERED IN THE DISTANCE, THE GATHERING clouds like a herd of wild gray stallions about to rampage through Port Corsair and steal away the serenity of the summer afternoon. As Miri cantered her pony into the small harbor town, she straightened in the saddle, her nostrils flaring as she scented the air. The storm was one, perhaps two hours away at most by her reckoning. The rocky coast of Faire Isle usually took the brunt of the tempests hurled from the sea, but not even the heart of the small island would be immune to the force of this one.

The brisk wind blowing leeward threatened to wreak havoc with her hair, but her pale blond tresses were tightly bound in a braid that fell to the small of her back. Hair so severely confined might have left another woman's face too harshly exposed, but it only served to emphasize the striking mold of her cheekbones. There was something a little fey in her expression, the reflection of a woman who kept mostly to herself, more comfortable with the creatures of the forest than she was with her own kind.

Tall and thin, she wore a belted, ankle-length gown, the soft gray hue adding to the ethereal illusion that she was a lady who could easily vanish in a puff of mist. Her skirts and petticoats bunched uncomfortably about her knees as she rode astride. The fashion for sidesaddles had never been adopted by the practical women of Faire Isle. Miri would as soon have dispensed with a saddle altogether and donned a comfortable pair of masculine breeches as she had been wont to do as a child. But she feared that she already created enough of a stir when she ventured into town these days.

As Miri slowed her pony to a walk, she braced herself for the familiar onslaught of faces peering at her over cottage fences. Some simply stared; others nodded their heads in uneasy recognition. An apple-cheeked woman weeding her garden ventured to wave, but as Miri went by, the woman immediately turned to whisper to her daughter.

Miri held her head high, but the whispers, the stares thrust her back through the years to another gloom-ridden summer day . . .

The drum beat out a relentless tattoo and her heart seemed to thud in tempo as she was dragged toward the town square by the grim-faced witch-hunters in their black robes. The halter they had fastened about her neck abraded her skin raw, but she tried to keep her chin up, remember who she was, the daughter of the brave Chevalier Louis

Cheney and the Lady Evangeline, one of the wisest women Faire Isle had ever known. But she shrank from all those staring eyes, the faces of people she'd believed were friends and neighbors.

She was a true daughter of the earth. How could they think that she was a witch who had made an unholy pact with the devil? Why would anyone want to hurt her? She twisted her head and directed a pleading glance toward the youngest of the witch-hunters. Although he swallowed hard, his dark eyes growing moist, Simon kept marching and doggedly beat the drum . . .

Miri shuddered and thrust the memory back into the dark recesses of her past where it belonged. She was no longer that frightened and bewildered child, but a woman of six and twenty, all too familiar with the ignorance and cruelty to be found in the world. So much had changed in her life since that dark summer day she'd survived her arrest for witchcraft, except perhaps for one thing. Many still suspected her of practicing sorcery.

"Filthy little witch!"

Miri flinched in spite of herself at the shrill cry. She shifted in the saddle, glancing about her for the source of the angry outcry only to realize that the epithet had not been hurled at her.

A group of some half-dozen women was clustered near the common well, engaged in a heated conflict. Miri's first instinct was to ride swiftly on by. She hated altercations of any sort and Ariane had warned Miri when she had returned to Faire Isle six months ago. On the morning they had parted, Ariane had cupped Miri's face between her hands, her sister's rich gray eyes worried and solemn.

"I know how badly you need to return home, but oh, please be careful, Miri. You were never convicted of treason and witchcraft as Gabrielle and I were. Give them no excuse to do so now. Live quietly on Faire Isle. Remember that even after all this time, our family still has powerful enemies."

Enemies like Catherine de Medici, the dowager queen of France, but far better known as the Dark Queen and a suspected sorceress, and her son, Henry, the present king of France, an irrational and vindictive man. But the enemy uppermost in Ariane's mind had been the one they did not speak of, the mere mention of his name enough to afford Miri pain. The witch-hunter, Aristide.

Just as Miri was no longer that innocent child, Simon was no longer that tenderhearted boy, apprenticed to the terrifying Vachel Le Vis, a fanatical witch-hunter. Over the years Simon had grown into a hardened and dangerous adversary, far more to be dreaded than his long-dead master who had first arrested Miri.

Hugging Ariane fiercely, Miri had pledged to do her best to heed her advice.

"Do nothing to draw undue attention to yourself, dearest."

"I won't, Ariane. I swear it."

Recalling that promise, Miri nudged Willow away from the square, trying to blot out the sound of the furious, upraised voices. But out of the corner of her eye, she caught a glimpse of the victim of this wrath, a sandy-haired girl, who looked not much older than fourteen. She clutched the ends of a shawl about her frail shoulders, the cloth a bright weaving of many dyed hues like the biblical Joseph's coat of many colors. Her freckled face blazed defiance although she held her other hand protectively in front of her abdomen. Miri drew rein, shocked as she realized the reason for the gesture. The girl was heavy with child, her thin frame appearing far too frail to bear the burden swelling beneath her gown.

Her chief opponent appeared to be an angular woman, sleeves shoved up to reveal red, work-roughened arms. Miri recognized Josephine Alain, the local potter's wife. She advanced toward the girl, shrieking, "Slut! We've warned you for the last time. We don't want you showing your face in our town ever again."

Madame Alain was reinforced by an irate chorus of agreement from her neighbors, only timid little Madame Greves appearing to make an appeal for calm. The girl muttered some furious retort, her face streaked with defiant tears.

Madame Alain stepped closer, spluttering more insults, shaking her finger under the girl's nose. The girl stumbled back a step and struck Madame Alain's hand away. To Miri's horror, the woman set upon the pregnant girl, slapping her and pulling her hair.

Forgetting all she had promised her sister, Miri scrambled off of Willow. Seizing the pony's bridle, she peered directly into one of his large soft eyes.

"*Wait,*" she commanded, then raced toward the group of women.

By the time Miri reached the conflict, the girl had sought refuge at the base of the statue in the square. She curled herself in a protective ball with her multicolored shawl drawn over her head as Madame Alain pummeled her back.

The other women crowded about, urging her on, only Madame Greves holding back, wringing her hands in her apron.

Miri charged in, shoving women out of her way. She locked her arm about Madame Alain's neck and hauled her back from the fallen girl.

"Stop it," Miri grated in the woman's ear. "Have you completely lost your mind?"

Madame Alain grunted, fighting to break free of Miri's grip. Miri spun the woman about with a strength born of desperation and hurled her away. The woman staggered and landed hard on her rump. Spitting furious curses, she fought her tangled skirts in an effort to rise.

Although her heart thudded hard in her chest, Miri stepped in front of the sandy-haired girl, clenching her fists. "Stay back. All of you. The next person who lays a hand on this child will answer to me."

Josephine Alain regained her feet, ready to launch herself at Miri but she was restrained by two of her neighbors.

"Great heaven, Josephine. Don't you see who that is? The Cheney woman."

Miri's name buzzed through the cluster of women, their faces reflecting varying amounts of fear, wariness, and awe. Although Madame Alain shrugged free of the hands restraining her, even she hung back, glaring.

Miri found the sudden silence unnerving. She was relieved when Madame Greves found enough courage to come forward to help. Taking the girl gently by the elbow, Madame Greves aided her to her feet. As soon as the girl had regained her balance, she thrust the woman's hands away.

"Leave me alone, damn you. I'm fine."

Madame Greves's eyes rounded in shock and she beat a hasty retreat. The girl looked shaken, but otherwise unharmed. Miri blew out a deep breath. Having thrust herself into the middle of this situation, she was uncertain what to do next. She was painfully aware of having neither Ariane's calming aura nor her other sister Gabrielle's regal manner.

She was more disquieted by the prospect of addressing this crowd of hostile women than she had been battling her way through them. Folding her arms defensively in front of herself, she demanded, in what she hoped was an authoritative tone, "Would someone care to explain to me what is going on here?"

"It is no concern of yours, Miribelle Cheney." Strands of gray hair escaped from Madame Alain's chignon, the wind blowing them about a face that had once been pretty. Bitterness had soured her visage into a shrewish expression.

"I am afraid I must make it my concern, when grown women run mad enough to attack an innocent girl. One moreover who is far gone with child."

"Innocent?" Madame Alain snorted. "Carole Moreau is nothing but a little whore, spreading her legs for every sailor who comes into port."

"Oh, are you worried I won't leave any for you?" Carole snapped.

"Why, you—you *salope.*" Madame Alain lunged at her again, but Miri blocked her path, stopping her with a fierce look.

Madame Alain shouted at the girl past Miri's shoulder. "We have warned you time and again not to come around here, flaunting that bastard growing in your belly before decent women."

"I have as much right to be here as anyone else," Carole blazed, but her lip quivered.

"You ought to stay at home, keep your shame hidden away."

"I would say the shame belongs more to the men who took advantage of such a young girl," Miri said icily.

"Oh, no, Mistress Cheney," another woman piped up, a buxom blonde. "Carole truly is a wicked creature. Always muttering curses against us. She made my milk curdle the other day. Her eyes radiate pure evil."

Several of the other women nodded in agreement and crossed themselves.

Miri shook her head at them incredulously. "Since when did the women of Faire Isle start believing in such nonsense as evil eyes? My God! I have seen my share of folly and cruelty in the rest of the world. But this island was once a place of refuge, especially for women who met with misunderstanding and abuse elsewhere. We were wont to treat each other with respect. What has happened to your kindness, your compassion?"

Miri appealed to each woman in turn, peering deep into their eyes. Most hung their heads or looked away. Only Madame Alain spoke up.

"You have been gone a long time, Miri Cheney. Nothing has gone right for this island since the raids of Le Balafre and his witch-hunters. People from the mainland fear to come here anymore, our trade has fallen off to nothing. My own family has been particularly hard hit, our pottery business failed, and my husband dead of grief, leaving me six children to keep from starving. And it is all the fault of your sisters for bringing the wrath of that accursed witch-hunter and the French king down upon our heads."

Miri felt the heat rise in her cheeks, but she replied calmly, "My sisters are neither traitors nor witches. I am deeply sorry for your troubles, madame, but if you want to blame anyone, blame me. It was my fault for placing too much faith in the wrong man, for not stopping Le Balafre when I had the chance."

Although Miri despised herself for it, even now she could not think of him as the dreaded Le Balafre, but only as Simon . . . Simon Aristide.

"Oh, I do blame you," Madame Alain said. Although the other women stole wary looks at Miri, and Madame Greves tried to hush her friend, Madame Alain stepped closer. Miri could feel the animosity pouring off the woman like a hot, dark wave.

"Though no one else here has the courage to tell you this, you are no more welcome on this island than that little slut you are protecting."

"I regret that you feel that way, madame. But Faire Isle is my home as it is Mademoiselle Moreau's. Neither of us is going anywhere." Miri met the woman's glare without flinching.

Madame Alain was the first to look away, muttering. "We'll see about *that.*" She stalked off across the green, the other women trailing after her.

Only Madame Greves lingered. Tugging at her kerchief strings, she gazed earnestly up at Miri. "You must not mind Josephine, milady. She has had a hard time of it and she often says things she doesn't mean."

"Madame Alain only said what everyone else is thinking."

"Not everyone." Madame Greves ventured to touch Miri's sleeve. "You probably believe that we have all forgotten the good that your family once brought to Faire Isle. But many of us remember the old days and we rejoice to have our lady back amongst us."

"Oh, no, madame," Miri cried. "I am not the Lady of Faire Isle. That was my sister, Ariane."

"I know that, my dear. Such a kind and wise woman, the Lady Ariane, a true healer. I pray she might someday be restored to us. But your gift for curing the poor beasts is just as great as hers for helping ailing folk. We have all heard how you brought the Pomfreys' cow back from the dead."

"No, no! It wasn't dead, only very ill. It—it was—"

"A miracle!" Madame Greves beamed at her. "You have a very powerful magic. Your reputation is spreading even as far as the mainland." The little woman whispered in a conspiratorial tone. "We have taken to calling you our Lady of the Wood."

Miri's heart sank in dismay. *The Lady of the Wood?* Oh, wonderful. So much for her promise to Ariane to draw no attention to herself and she'd barely been home six months. Before she could attempt to convince Madame Greves that her curing of the cow had been nothing more than sensible animal husbandry, they were interrupted by Madame Alain's shrill voice ringing across the green.

"Laurette!"

Having noticed her friend's defection, she beckoned imperiously. Madame Greves drew back from Miri, sketching a deep curtsy. "Well, I—I just wanted you to know all that, milady."

"Thank you, madame. But I am not *milady*. I am only—"

But Madame Greves was already gone, scurrying after the other women. Miri sighed. Despite Laurette Greves's kindness, she was not sorry to see her go, as uncomfortable with the woman's adoration as she had been with Madame Alain's hostility.

Now that the confrontation was over, Miri experienced the inevitable aftermath she always felt in the wake of any rage or violence. A tremor coursed through her, her nerve endings feeling like the delicate strings of a harp that had been plucked with rough hands, forced into playing discordant notes.

She wrapped her arms about herself, gazing toward where Willow peacefully cropped some grass. She longed to fling herself on the pony's back and retreat to the solitude of her woods until she regained her sense of harmony. She had all but forgotten Carole's presence until she heard the girl grumbling beside her.

"Good riddance to the lot of those old harpies. They nearly ripped my shawl and my *grand-mère* made it special just for me before she died. If I could pox the lot of those wretches, I'd do it in a heartbeat, make them grow warts on their noses and carbuncles on their fat arses."

Carole's lip quivered as she brushed a smudge of dirt from the end of the beloved shawl. But when she realized that Miri had turned to look at her, she swirled the shawl about her shoulders and lifted her chin to a truculent angle. Her freckles stood out in sharp contrast to her pale skin, a bruise forming beneath one eye, her cheeks still streaked with the tracks of her tears. Her face was heartbreakingly young, the expression in her fierce blue eyes far too old.

"I suppose you expect me to thank you for coming to my defense," she said grudgingly. "But it wasn't necessary. I can look out for myself."

"I am sure you can, mademoiselle." Another woman might have been taken aback by the girl's truculence. Miri was too accustomed to being growled at by injured creatures in the wild, the bared teeth that masked hurt and fear. Long experience had taught Miri when it was safe to touch, when best to hold back. She plucked her handkerchief from her belt and extended it instead.

Carole eyed the scrap of linen suspiciously. "What's that for? I am not crying." She mopped the back of her hand across her damp cheeks.

"Of course you are not, but you are bleeding. You have cut your lip."

Carole thrust out her tongue, wincing as she tested the corner of her mouth. She reluctantly took the handkerchief from Miri and dabbed it to her lip.

"I am not a slut, either. No matter what Madame Alain says."

"I never thought that you were," Miri said gently.

"There were not many sailors, only one. And Raoul said he loved me and would marry me and buy me a fine blue gown." Her thin throat worked as she swallowed hard. "And then he sailed away and never came back and—and the devil take him. I've laid a curse on him and hope he falls in the sea and sharks tear him to bits."

The girl tossed her head defiantly. "There! Now I suppose you will tell me how wicked I am, that it is evil to say such things."

"No, it is perfectly understandable that you should feel that way." Miri's response earned her a wary look from the girl. Carole cocked her head to one side as though uncertain what to make of Miri.

"Are you sure you are all right?" Miri asked anxiously. "Perhaps you should go home and let your Maman—"

"My mother died last winter. I live with my aunt and uncle now, but only because they've never been able to have children of their own. If I have a boy, they'll adopt him and let me stay on."

"And—and if it's a girl?"

"Oh, I expect they mean to toss us both out." Carole gave a brittle shrug as though trying to pretend the outcome did not matter much to her, either way.

Miri was hard-pressed to conceal her shock and dismay, unable to conceive of the callousness of these people who should have been looking out for this young girl, soothing her fears, reassuring her. Miri's own family had always been so warm, so caring. She could not imagine anything she could do bad enough to ever put herself beyond the pale of their love and forgiveness.

Her heart went out to Carole, but Miri had always found it difficult to reach out to strangers. She said almost shyly, "Carole, I—I confess I know more about breeding mares than I do about a young girl about to foal. If there is anything at all I could do, I would like to help you. My—my name is Miri Cheney."

Tentatively, Miri extended her hand. A wistful expression crossed Carole's face. Miri doubted that the girl had experienced many gestures of kindness in her life, at least not lately. She gazed into Miri's eyes for a long moment, only to blink and draw back, her youthful features hardening.

"Oh, everyone on Faire Isle knows who you are, my Lady of the Wood. Thank you for your offer, but I don't have any ailing cow or sick bunny that needs tending. I have been told all about *you,* a half-witch too afraid to use her real power and knowledge."

"I don't know who has been telling you such things, but I don't consider myself a witch at all. I am a daughter of the earth, nothing less and nothing more."

"That is exactly what I mean." Carole sneered. "No, Mistress Cheney, I need no help from the likes of you or anyone else on this miserable island. I have friends, very powerful friends who will look out for me."

Miri wished that might be the case, but she feared it was only the empty boast of a girl, clinging to her last scrap of pride.

"Carole—" Miri began, but the girl cast a scornful look and walked away. Despite her awkward gait, she moved rapidly across the green.

Miri started to go after her, only to draw up short, not knowing what else she could do or say. Trying to reach the heart of a wounded girl was much more complicated than setting the broken leg of an injured fox or badger. Miri watched helplessly as Carole disappeared down one of the lanes. She wished fervently that Ariane was here. Her older sister was so gifted at calming troubled waters and pouring balm into aching souls.

Even Gabrielle would have known better how to handle Carole. There was something about the girl that reminded Miri poignantly of what Gabrielle had been like when she was young, so quick to hide her hurts beneath a tough façade, shoving away anyone who would comfort her. But Gabrielle was as far off as Ariane, Miri's family scattered in opposite directions, miles from the island that had once been their home.

It struck Miri as an inexplicable and cruel trick of nature that Carole Moreau should be burdened with an unwanted babe while Ariane, who had so longed for a child, remained barren. But her sister had put a brave face on it, genuinely rejoicing each time that she successfully delivered another woman of a babe, especially when it had been Gabrielle.

Happily wed to her Captain Remy, Gabrielle had spent these past years ripe and blooming with creation, three daughters so far, producing babes almost as easily as she did the paintings and sculpture that were Gabrielle's own special brand of magic.

Ariane had resigned herself to her childless fate. Taking deep comfort in the love of her husband, Renard, she was content.

She tried not to dwell on thoughts of her sisters. Her heart ached for them too much. It had been her own choice to come back to Faire Isle, but Miri was starting to feel it was the biggest mistake she'd ever made—next to trusting Simon.

Faire Isle still looked much as she remembered it, the rocky harbor where she'd once stood and waited hopefully for her father's ship to return, the same deep, dark woods where she'd hunted for fairies. Port Corsair was still the same with its lumbering old inn, row of timber-framed shops, and dusty lanes where she'd trailed shyly after her older sisters.

But those lanes she recalled as bustling with activity and women toting their market baskets, gossiping and laughing, stood mostly empty this summer afternoon and not just because of the threatening weather. So many familiar faces were absent: Mistress Paletot, the gifted sword maker; old Madame Jehan, the apothecary; the Jourdaine sisters, skilled weavers. All talented and clever women, charged with sorcery, either condemned or obliged to flee for their lives as Ariane and Gabrielle had done.

What women remained kept more to themselves, minding their own families and tending their gardens. Miri did not know what she had expected to find on Faire Isle after an absence of ten years, but certainly not this atmosphere of fear and mistrust. It was as though a bottle had been uncorked, releasing a dark miasma that had stolen away the spirit of the island itself.

Faire Isle had always been populated mostly by women, the wives of fishermen and sailors gone at sea. But there were widows and maidens as well who found Faire Isle a refuge, a unique place they could prosper and ply trades forbidden to their sex elsewhere. And yet Miri was not naïve enough to recall the island as being idyllic. No, women being women, they had known their share of bickering and squabbling. But nothing like the ugly scene Miri had witnessed this afternoon. It was ironic that such violence should have taken place before the statue that commemorated the best traits of a woman, wisdom, compassion, healing.

Miri gazed up at the monument depicting a gentle lady in flowing robes, her arms extended. One of the hands had been broken off, the face smashed beyond all recognition. Miri's breath hitched in her chest. She did not know if the vandalism had been the work of witch-hunters, the king's soldiers, or even embittered townsfolk. The pedestal that used to be decked with floral offerings was now overgrown with weeds.

"I should have done something about this long ago," she thought guiltily. But she had steadfastly avoided this part of the town square ever since her return, the sight of the defaced statue far too painful.

She knelt down now and doggedly tugged up clumps of weeds, clearing the inscription at the base. *Evangeline . . . Our Lady of Faire Isle.*

"Maman," Miri whispered. With a heavy heart, she traced her fingers across the worn lettering. She had only been eleven years old when her mother had died and the island people had erected this monument to Evangeline's memory. Evangeline's knowledge of the old ways and her skill in brewing medicines had saved the entire island from the ravages of the plague.

But the statue also honored the generations of wise women who had gone before her. There had always been a Lady of Faire Isle, counseling, protecting, and healing with her gentle magic. At least until Ariane had been forced into exile.

Ariane's husband, the former Comte de Renard, had ever been wont to say, *"There is a fine line between a woman being proclaimed a saint or a witch."*

Her mighty brother-in-law had been proved right on more than one occasion. Just as Ariane had been when she had counseled Miri not to return to Faire Isle.

"I should have listened to you, Ari," Miri murmured.

Miri was still rather surprised that Ariane had not done more to prevent her return. Ariane had always been notoriously protective of her younger sisters. Exile had been hard on all of them, but Miri felt as though she was the only one never able to adjust to the change.

She was like one of those small white wildflowers that grew on the far side of the island, unable to successfully take root elsewhere. They clung to life, the shoots still green, but the petals never blossomed again. She had tried to conceal her unhappiness, but there had never been any deceiving Ariane. The Lady of Faire Isle was far too gifted at the wise women's ancient art of reading eyes.

Whatever she had read in Miri's eyes, Ariane had finally consented to her return to the island. As she had handed Miri into the boat, she had attempted to smile through her tears.

"Godspeed, little sister. And whatever you are looking for, I hope you find it."

"I am not looking for anything, Ariane," Miri had protested. *"I only want to go home."*

Home . . . A hard lump rose in Miri's throat. As she cleared the last of the weeds from her mother's monument, she wondered if there was such a place anymore. Not with her mother dead and her sisters far away. As for her father, all hopes for Louis Cheney's return had ended a year ago when she had received word that his ship had been wrecked off the coast of Brazil. The *Evangeline* had sunk during a storm, taking with her all hands.

With her family gone, the island was a bleak and lonely place. But if Miri didn't belong here on Faire Isle, then she didn't belong anywhere. She felt as though she was nothing but a ghost drifting through a land that should have been so familiar to her but no longer was. The feeling might have been quite unendurable except for one small consolation.

She was not the only phantom haunting Faire Isle.

ʕʕʕʕ

THE CONVENT OF ST. ANNE'S was situated above the town on a gentle rise of hill. But the bells calling the sisters to prayer had long ago been silenced, the stately stone buildings bleak and empty beneath the lowering gray skies. The convent had been closed many years ago, the sisters dispersed to other orders—at least those who had been fortunate enough not to be charged with heresy and witchcraft.

The only sign of habitation was the smoke curling from the caretaker's cottage nestled in the shadow of the convent walls. It was there that the other ghost of Faire Isle dwelt—Marie Claire Abingdon, once the formidable abbess of the convent and closest friend of Evangeline Cheney.

The cottage was rather humble surroundings for a woman who had wielded such power, the daughter of a powerful aristocratic family, accustomed to command the elegancies of life. But Marie Claire had managed to make the place her own, colorful braided rugs scattered over the rough stone floor, the shelves that should have held a peasant's crockery laden with her books. A large cage occupied one corner of the room where her two pet ravens croaked and preened their glossy feathers.

A cozy fire and a branch of candles did much to dispel

the gloom of the day. Although the wind whistled and rat-
tled the slate tiles of the roof, Miri felt safe and comforted,
seated at Marie Claire's small table near the hearth. Like
Ariane, Marie Claire possessed a calming aura, although it
still gave Miri a jolt to see the woman no longer wearing
her habit.

The absence of her flowing robes and wimple made
Marie Claire seem somehow diminished, more vulnerable.
Her advancing years were beginning to tell upon her, her
soft white hair thinning, her posture a little bowed, but her
countenance still bore those marks of strength that had
made one exasperated bishop label her "far too willful for
a nun."

As Marie Claire fetched a simple repast of bread and
cheese from her cupboard, Miri regaled her with the grim
happenings in the square that morning. Marie Claire listened gravely but an odd smile played about the woman's
mouth when Miri said, ". . . and those women were so
angry, so beyond reason, especially Madame Alain. I have
nothing like Ariane's manner of authority. I have no idea
how I persuaded them to relent."

"Don't you?" Marie Claire threw her a fond glance.
"It's those fey eyes of yours, child. They shine a fierce light
into the darkest corner of a person's soul. Make one feel
mighty ashamed, want to do better."

Miri shook her head at what she could only think of as
pure nonsense. "However it happened, I was relieved to
save Carole from a severe beating." She added ruefully,
"Although that was all I was able to do for her."

"Yes, she's rather a belligerent little creature," Marie
Claire said as she carried the food over to the table.

Miri eyed the amount of bread and cheese Marie Claire had heaped on her plate, doubting she could consume the half of it. She never seemed to have much appetite these days. But to please Marie Claire, she nibbled at a piece of bread.

As Marie Claire filled two pewter cups with a robust red wine, she remarked, "I have warned Carole myself many times. She would do far better to remain quietly at home and mind that sharp tongue of hers."

"Is that what the daughters of the earth have come to on this island?" Miri asked sadly. "Living quietly, minding their tongues, trying to be invisible? You surprise me, Marie. That was never how you behaved."

"No and look where it got me."

"You now regret how you lived your life?"

"A woman can't get to be my age and not have some regrets, child." Marie Claire sighed as she settled herself into the chair opposite Miri. "I fear I was always too strong-willed. First rebelling against my parents' efforts to marry me off to some aristocratic dolt. Then as abbess, defying the archbishop, insisting on running St. Anne's on my own terms, reading books the church had clearly forbidden. Am I sorry that I didn't make more effort to curb my intellect, to be more meek and biddable?"

Marie Claire's mouth crooked in a wry smile. "No, not entirely, though I think I could have learned to be a trifle more—er, diplomatic and discreet. That is all that I tried to counsel Carole. That sometimes a little caution is best."

She trained her shrewd gaze upon Miri. "The same advice I would give to you, my Lady of the Wood."

Miri had raised her glass to take a sip, but she set it

back down with a sharp click. "Oh, lord, you heard about that. You must have been speaking with Madame Greves."

"Madame Greves and quite a few others. You set most of the island abuzz when you brought the Pomfreys' cow back to life."

"I did no such thing. The cow was indeed unconscious, but bringing it round was no great matter."

"No great matter! Miri, I am told the poor beast suffered from milk fever, which is well known to be an incurable disease."

"It wouldn't be," Miri said indignantly, "if the world had not become such a superstitious and ignorant place that people have become afraid to consult the ancient texts wise women compiled centuries ago. But no, I perform a simple procedure and am suspected of being a witch."

She spread her hands in appeal. "But what else could I have done, Marie? The Pomfreys are poor folk. They could not afford to lose that cow. Should I have just refused to help, let that poor animal perish? And her with a newborn calf."

Marie Claire sighed. "No, you could no more deny aid to a sick creature than Ariane could turn her back on an ailing child. Just be as careful as you can and remember, you still have powerful enemies."

"If you mean the Dark Queen, her battles were with Ariane and Gabrielle. I doubt she even remembers the existence of a third Cheney sister."

"Trust me, my dear, Catherine de Medici has a long memory. She never forgets anyone or anything that might prove a threat to her power."

"That hardly describes me. The Dark Queen would

have far more reason to be wary of *you*, Marie. You were the one who was able to plant a spy in her very court."

"That was a long time ago. Now I am an old woman of no power or consequence. Most of the world believes me long dead."

"Forgive me, Marie," Miri said hesitantly. "But I doubt your pretense has really fooled anyone. At least not here on Faire Isle."

"No, most of the local people are quite aware of who I am, but they tolerate my presence. Even Father Benedict says nothing when I creep into his church to hear the mass. But he is a kind young man, a good shepherd who would rather coax a wayward lamb back into the fold than see it slaughtered for straying."

Marie Claire smiled and took a long swallow of wine, but there was clearly something else weighing on her mind, something that filled Miri with an inexplicable sense of apprehension.

Marie Claire ran her finger over the rim of her cup, silent for a long moment. "Miri . . . I have been reluctant to tell you this until I was sure. But I have had another message from a friend of mine, a wise woman living in Saint-Malo."

Marie Claire paused, released a long breath before saying, "He is back."

There was no need for Miri to ask who Marie Claire meant by *he*. Her stomach clenched so hard it hurt. She wrapped her arms across her middle.

"S-simon Aristide?" she faltered. "But he has not been heard from in years."

"Nonetheless, he has been spotted prowling about Brit-

tany. Le Balafre is far too distinctive a figure to be mistaken.
He appears to be traveling alone, no army of witch-hunters
at his back, but that does not make him any less dangerous."

"You need hardly tell *me* that." Miri shot to her feet,
struggling to conceal her agitation. She paced over to the
cage and thrust crumbs of her bread through the bars. With
a flutter of wings, the ravens descended from their perch
and pecked greedily at the crusts with their long beaks.

Wolf birds . . . that was the other name for Marie
Claire's beloved pets. Predators.

Just like Simon.

Except that that had not always been true. Miri's mind
swept her back to a long-ago midnight upon a rugged
cliff amidst the towering circle of stone giants and the flare
of torchlight. The night winds had teased the dark curls
spilling over Simon's brow, a startling contrast to his milk-
white skin . . . the most beautiful boy she had ever seen.

"I thought all witch-hunters were old and ugly," she
had said in dazed accents and Simon had flashed his irre-
pressible smile.

"Odd. I have always believed the same about witches."

"But I am not a witch."

"I never said you were," he had responded in a gentler
tone.

And Simon hadn't . . . at least not then. Becoming
aware that Marie Claire was addressing her, Miri thrust
aside her troubling memories of the past.

". . . and perhaps now you will understand why I am so
concerned about the reputation you are getting as this Lady
of the Wood. I fear that Simon Aristide has never given up

searching for your family since you all fled Faire Isle. Not
that I am afraid he would harm *you*. He always harbored a
certain tenderness where you were concerned."

"Tenderness? The man is not capable of such an emotion, although once . . ." Miri trailed off. Once she had believed that there was so much good to be found in Simon,
that he was merely lost, misguided, wounded. If she could
have coaxed him out of his darkness, she could have
healed him. But her experience of injured animals in the
wild had led her to the painful understanding that some
creatures were damaged beyond even her ability to help, a
flat empty look in their eyes. She had seen that look in
Simon's face. The man no longer had a soul.

As she fed the last of her bread to the eager ravens,
Miri was struck by the full import of Marie Claire's words.
She spun about to regard the older woman intently. "If you
are not worried that Simon would harm me, then what *are*
you afraid of?"

Marie Claire shifted uncomfortably, avoiding Miri's
eyes, but Miri read her silence all too well. She felt the
blood rush into her cheeks, a hot sting of guilt and shame.

"You fear that if our paths crossed, I'd be weak enough
to trust Simon again. Perfectly understandable. I put my
family, you, this entire island at risk because I believed in
him." She swallowed hard. "I—I was even foolish enough
to fancy that I loved him."

"Oh, my dear." Marie Claire crossed the room and
caught Miri's hands in a gentle grasp. "That was not foolish. There is a great virtue in trying to find the best in people. No one is entirely black of heart, not even Aristide."

"How can you speak one word in his defense?" Miri

cried. "After all that he cost you, the closing of the abbey, your position, almost your life?"

"That was not entirely Aristide's doing. The church never cared for uppity women and I am afraid the sisters of St. Anne's were always too independent for the archbishop. His Eminence had long wanted to disband our order."

"And Simon's witch-hunting gave him an excuse."

"His Eminence never really needed one. And as for Aristide, rather than threatening my life, he saved it."

"What do you mean?"

"Did you never wonder how I managed to escape from St. Anne's with the place surrounded by witch-hunters and the king's soldiers? It was only because Aristide allowed it, calling off the guard long enough for me to get away."

Miri blinked, a little stunned by Marie Claire's revelation of this softening on Simon's part. She scowled, struggling to dismiss it. "It was just a careless mistake on his part."

"Monsieur Le Balafre is not a man given to carelessness."

"Then—then he must have been hoping that if he let you go, you would lead him to the rest of us."

"Then why did he make no effort to follow me?" Marie Claire countered.

"I don't know," Miri replied miserably, drawing away from her. She had already wasted far too much time and heartache trying to sort out the contradictions of her acquaintance with Simon Aristide. The boy who had been so kind and gentle with her, who had seemed like her friend. The arrogant young man who had intimidated and threatened her, warning her that he meant to destroy her brother-in-law, that he would be just as ruthless to her if she sought to prevent him. Simon had always hated the Comte de Renard, suspected him of the worst kind of sorcery. But when he had had his opportunity to kill Renard, Simon had deflected the shot because Miri had been in the way.

Gabrielle had always been wont to complain, *"Why can't the blasted man make up his mind to act like a proper villain and be done with it?"*

Miri entirely agreed with her. It would have made despising Simon so much easier and far less painful.

As though determined to compound Miri's confusion, Marie Claire went on, "To give the devil his due, there is one other thing that I will always be grateful for. When the writs of arrests were sworn out, he took great care that your name should never appear."

Miri stiffened. Marie Claire might be grateful for that, Ariane and Gabrielle as well. But it was one of Simon's actions that Miri found most unforgivable.

"You'll never know how much I resent him for that," Miri choked. "That my sisters, my good brother-in-law Renard, you and so many other women on this island should have been charged with sorcery, while I alone was spared because of some whim of Simon's."

Miri tried to fight her anger, the emotion poisonous to her, but it coursed through her like a dark tide. "I hate him," she said with fierce intensity as though trying to convince herself as much as Marie Claire. "I have never hated anyone else in my life, but Simon forced me to loathe him. I hate him for what he did to my family, my friends, and most of all, for what he did to this island. There used to be a wild sweet spirit that lived here and Simon destroyed it. I should have shot him that night in Paris but I was too weak. But believe me, if I ever get another chance, I'll know how to deal with the villain."

"Oh, hush, child." Marie Claire cradled Miri's face between her hands, a deeply troubled look creasing the older woman's brow. "This kind of talk is not like you."

"Isn't it?" Miri whispered, wondering how well Marie Claire knew her, wondering how well she knew herself anymore. "I suppose I do sound like young Carole, cursing her former lover. This is what Simon Aristide has reduced me to, these horrible black emotions that tear me up inside."

Tears burned Miri's eyes and she blinked them back fiercely. "That—that is why I try never to think of him."

"Then I am sorry for ever mentioning the man's name. I only thought that you should be warned. I shall pray very hard that your paths never cross again." Marie Claire gently brushed aside the sole tear that had escaped to trickle down Miri's cheek. "But I really do feel you should leave Faire Isle."

"Because of Simon?"

"No, because you should have never come back here in the first place."

Miri gave a tremulous smile, attempted to jest. "What! Are you so tired of my company already, Marie?"

Marie Claire's eyes clouded with a look full of such wistfulness, such loneliness, it pulled at Miri's heart. "No, child. Having you here has meant the world to me. But this island is no longer any place for you. It holds nothing but memories of a time that is gone forever."

"The same is true of you," Miri protested, but Marie Claire only shook her head with a sad smile.

"I am an old woman. Memories are all that are left to

me. But you are too young to dwell in the past." Marie Claire stroked back a stray wisp of Miri's hair in a tender, motherly gesture. "You may not have asked for my advice, but I am giving it to you. Leave Faire Isle, go back to Bearn, and marry that young man who adores you."

Miri felt herself blush. "You sound like Gabrielle. No doubt she has been writing and complaining to you about my folly."

Unlike Ariane, Gabrielle had not been nearly as resigned or understanding when Miri had mentioned her desire to return to Faire Isle. It had been the one remark that had been able to snap Gabrielle's attention from the latest canvas she'd been working on.

"Are you completely insane, Miribelle Cheney?" In her agitation, Gabrielle had waved her brush, scattering stray flecks of paint about the room. "Why would you want to go back to a place where you'll be lonely and miserable, to say nothing of possibly being in danger? When you could stay right here and marry the man who has been your devoted slave ever since he met you? Wolf has been so patient, but neither of you is getting any younger, my dear sister. You clearly love the man, so what in heaven's name are you waiting for?"

Miri had been completely unable to answer that question. She reached inside the neckline of her gown and drew forth a large oval locket suspended from a silver chain, her mind filling with the image of the man who had given it to her. A bold, sable-haired rogue with piercing green eyes and blade-sharp features . . . Martin le Loup, as he liked to call himself. Miri was one of the few people who used his given name of Martin instead of Wolf.

She had never accepted a present from any man other than her father and she had been reluctant to allow Martin to fasten the costly locket about her neck. Martin had a flair for drama and could be given to making flamboyant, impassioned speeches. But he had completely disarmed Miri this time with a pleading glance and by uttering a single soft word.

"Please . . ."

Rather shyly, Miri displayed the locket to Marie Claire. "Martin gave this to me the day we parted."

The surface of the locket was etched with the likeness of a wolf baying at the moon. Miri fumbled with the catch, opening it to reveal the miniature clock encased inside.

Marie Claire squinted at the words etched on the other half of the locket. "Forgive me, my dear, but my eyesight is not what it used to be."

"It says *Yours until time ends.*"

"Ah! A very romantic fellow, this Martin of yours."

Miri's lips twisted ruefully. "Oh, yes, Martin is indeed that. Romantic, passionate, and—and full of such vigor at times it can be quite exhausting. Life with him would always be a grand adventure and I do care for him, very deeply."

Marie Claire regarded her quizzically. "And so?"

Miri closed the locket and tucked it back into the bodice of her gown with a deep sigh. "I've already had far more adventure in my life than I ever wanted. I crave quiet, Marie. Sometimes I don't think I am suited to be any man's wife." She gave a wry uncertain laugh. "Gabrielle always said she was afraid I would end up an eccentric old woman, living alone with dozens of cats. No doubt she is right."

"Speaking of cats!" Marie Claire gasped, straightening sharply as she stared at a point past Miri's shoulder.

When Miri twisted around to see what had so startled the older woman, she spied a familiar black cat perched on the ledge outside the window, back arched in displeasure as the wind ruffled its fur.

"Necromancer!" Miri exclaimed. She rushed over and forced open the casement, allowing her cat to leap inside. Necromancer landed gracefully on four snowy-white paws, the only part of him that was not dark as midnight. The cat's arrival sent Marie Claire's birds into an uproar, flapping and squawking so loudly she was obliged to fling a cover over their cage.

Despite her familiarity with Miri's cat, Marie Claire appeared a little disconcerted. "Bless me! How did that creature get here, all the way from your cottage in the wood? And however did he manage to find you?"

Miri closed the window and shrugged. She had given up wondering a long time ago how Necromancer managed anything. Even to a woman like herself who respected the intelligence and unusual abilities animals often displayed, Necromancer was uncanny. He was old, well past the age of fifteen in human years. He was no longer as swift as he used to be and his fur was thinning in patches near his ears, but he still possessed an eerie skill to track Miri wherever she was. She supposed the superstitious would call the cat her familiar. To Miri, he was simply a much-needed friend.

"You old fool," she scolded fondly, bending to gather the cat in her arms. "You are growing much too ancient to go prowling so far—"

She checked abruptly as Necromancer skittered away from her. Fur standing on end, he emitted a furious hiss.

"Merciful heavens," Marie Claire cried. "Whatever is wrong with the beast?"

Miri didn't reply, her attention riveted on Necromancer. She experienced a strange empathy with all creatures of the earth, but never had her ability to communicate been as marked as it was with this one small cat. Necromancer had alerted her to approaching danger on many occasions, saving her life.

She crouched down, her gaze locking with the cat's great golden eyes, her thoughts melding with his. The warning that he sent caused Miri's heart to still.

"You are in great peril, daughter of the earth. The one whom you have long dreaded has returned to your isle. The witch-hunter, Aristide."

Miri tried to draw in a lungful of air and found she couldn't. Her mind reeled with disbelief.

"You—you are certain of this, Necromancer?" Miri thought desperately. *"You have seen him?"*

The cat's golden eyes blinked in confirmation. Miri sank back on her haunches, feeling the blood drain from her face. So much for Marie Claire's hope of praying the man away. Miri reflected how right she had been all these years to avoid talking about Simon. It was as though merely by uttering his name aloud this afternoon, she had conjured up the devil.

But why? Why had Simon come back to Faire Isle? Surely he had done enough damage to the women of this island. What more could he possibly want?

"You," was Necromancer's alarming reply to her thought. *"This time the witch-hunter has come looking for you."*

Miri closed her eyes, realizing what must have drawn Simon down on her, made him reconsider sparing her from charges of witchcraft. The gossip that was spreading about her, the reputation she had gleaned as this Lady of the Wood. And all because she had broken her promise to Ariane to live quietly. Well, she would have time enough to castigate herself for that later. At least she hoped that she would.

She jumped when she felt Marie Claire's hand rest on her shoulder. The woman's uneasy gaze darted between Miri and her cat.

"Miri? What is going on? What is wrong?"

Miri parted her lips to speak, only to clamp her mouth closed, reconsidering what she had been about to say. If Simon was coming for Miri, there was no reason to alarm Marie Claire or get her involved. The old woman would only seek to protect Miri, end up placing herself in harm's way.

Struggling to her feet, Miri corraled Necromancer and scooped him into her arms. "N-nothing is wrong. Necromancer is only worried because—because of the weather. Storms always upset him. I need to get him home, Marie."

"But surely it would be better if you both remained here, waited for the storm to blow over."

"I don't think this one is going to do that," Miri said grimly, but she managed to paste on a brittle smile. "I— I have other animals back at the cottage. My pigeons, the rabbits. S-so much to do. I really *must* be going. I will— will visit you again in a few days."

She hoped her stammered explanation would be enough to fool Marie Claire. The former abbess had never been quite as good at reading eyes as Ariane. Not giving Marie Claire a chance to question her further, Miri brushed a kiss against the older woman's cheek and ducked out the cottage door into a world where the sky seemed to have grown that much darker, the wind even sharper.

Clutching Necromancer to her, she raced toward the shed behind the cottage where she had stabled Willow. The wind tangled stray wisps about her eyes and she paused just inside the shelter of the doorway to catch her breath. A part of her had always known she was fated to cross swords with Simon Aristide again one day. She had believed that when the time came she would be able to face him, tough and unflinching.

But with the prospect looming before her, her heart raced. She felt as though the scarred tissue of an old wound had split open, leaving her raw and vulnerable. Necromancer twisted in her arms, stretching up a paw to pat urgently at her chin.

"You have no time to waste, daughter of the earth. You must hide yourself. Aristide may be a great predator, but he does not possess the skill necessary to track you."

That was perfectly true, Miri thought. She was familiar with every glade, every rock, and every cove of this island. There were at least a dozen places she could secrete herself where she would never be found. She could flee just as she and her sisters had done all those years ago.

The reflection left a bitter taste in Miri's mouth and something inside her revolted. No! She'd be damned if she'd go to ground like a terrified rabbit. This was *her* island, *her* home. She would not be driven out a second time.

Miri's mind worked furiously, trying to calculate how much time she had. Simon could not know where she now lived, but he would find someone to betray her. He was infernally good at that. The witch-hunter would track her to her little cottage tucked deep in the woods.

And then . . . Miri's mouth set in a grim line. This time she would be waiting and give Simon Aristide exactly the kind of reception he deserved.

Chapter Two

THE DEVIL HAD RETURNED TO FAIRE ISLE.

Doors slammed closed, frightened mothers herded their children inside, and alarmed faces peered out through cottage windows as Simon cantered Elle through the lanes of Port Corsair. He was accustomed to the fear he engendered, had once done his best to inspire such terror, a useful tool of his trade. Now it only left him feeling tired and isolated.

They obviously remembered him well on Faire Isle, despite how much his appearance had altered. Strange, because he felt so removed from the young man who had invaded this island years ago. So arrogant, so infernally self-righteous, believing that he knew all about the nature of evil, only to discover that he knew very little about the darkness that could lurk in the human heart, least of all his own.

Le Balafre, they had called him in hushed whispers, the Scarred One, and Simon had reveled in the fearsome title, young fool that he was. He had stormed onto Faire Isle with an army at his back, determined to find the legendary *Book of Shadows* and bring the sorcerer Renard to justice.

Justice? Or had it merely been revenge? Even after all this time, Simon wasn't sure. Either way, he doubted it made much difference to the women of Faire Isle. All around him, he could still see the scars he'd left on this small community. Shops that had been burned to the ground and never rebuilt, cottages with gaping doorways and windows. A litter of rubble, broken hopes, and disrupted lives. The towers of the abandoned convent at the top of the hill loomed over him, all the more stark and bleak because of the keening winds and lowering skies.

Simon stared up at the empty buildings, feeling as though he was passing through a graveyard of every mistake he'd ever made, all those regrets he scarce dared examine for fear his entire life would unravel in his hands.

He guided Elle onto the road that led into the woods, leaving Port Corsair and its silent reproach far behind him. The overburdened clouds looked ready to unleash a furious hail of rain at any moment. He might have done better to bide his time at the harbor inn and wait for the storm to pass.

But time was against him. The Sisterhood of the Silver Rose waxed stronger and more cunning by the hour. Simon believed the witches' next attack would finish him. It was damnably hard to swallow his pride and come seeking aid from a woman he'd once betrayed. But delay would not make facing Miri Cheney any easier.

As the forest closed around him, Simon reined Elle to a walk. Thunder boomed, lightning flaring down the road ahead like the ordnance of some distant battle. Not the best place to be during a storm, although in Simon's view, these woods were not a good place to linger at any time.

The moss-covered trees were like towering giants, their roots sunk deep in the dark secret places of the earth. Gnarled branches swayed in the wind, their leaves whispering of ancient mysteries, druids, fairy folk, and sorcery. The perfect place for a witch to dwell.

Simon leaned forward to give Elle's neck a pat, more for his comfort than for hers. The eerie aspect of the wood should have rendered the mare nervous. Although Elle was restive, he could have sworn it was more the eager excitement of a horse scenting journey's end.

Strange as that notion struck him, Elle seemed at home here. Any tension, any unease was all his. Perhaps it was because for the last quarter mile, he kept remembering the last time he'd stood face-to-face with Miri Cheney. Her silvery-blue eyes as cold as a winter sky, she had aimed a pistol directly at his heart when fate had intervened in the form of an explosion, throwing them both to the ground. Would Miri have really pulled the trigger? Had she learned to hate him that much?

He would soon have his answer . . .

The thick canopy of trees and the storm-ridden sky robbed the afternoon of much of its light. As the road narrowed, Simon squinted to discern the way ahead, trying to compare what he saw with the directions he had been given.

Knowing that Miri's former home, Belle Haven, was lost to her, Simon had made inquiries at the inn regarding her present whereabouts. The Passing Stranger was the sole male bastion on this island populated by petticoats. Although the men were not as frightened of him as the women, the habitués of the taproom regarded him with dour suspicion.

Simon had always found that if he scattered enough coin, he could loosen someone's tongue. The one who had finally betrayed Miri to him was not one of the rough-hewn seamen or fisher lads, but another woman. She'd come creeping into the taproom with a shawl flung over her head, a faded creature with hard, shrewish features. Although she had trembled with fear, she had dared to seek Simon out.

"I—I hear you are looking for the Lady of the Wood," *she said in such a quavering voice he had to bend closer to hear her.*

Simon nodded.

"And—and you are paying?"

Simon had been hard-pressed to conceal his astonishment. His memory of the women of this island was that they were doggedly loyal to one another and especially to their beloved Lady of Faire Isle and her family. As he pressed several coins into Madame Alain's eager work-reddened hands, he felt a curious mingling of contempt and pity for the woman. That had not stopped him from acquiring her information.

"Just follow the road through the forest. Eventually

you'll see a path split off leading deeper into the wood it-self. Just follow that path and it'll take you straight to her cottage." His money clutched tight in her fist, Madame Alain had stifled a sob and bolted, although Simon was not certain what she was running from, him or her own guilt.

As he neared the track Miri's betrayer had spoken of, Simon realized there was one fact the woman had failed to mention. There was not one path, but two forking off from the road in completely opposite directions. As Simon reined in, hesitating over which way to go, he was startled to discover that his horse had definite opinions on the subject.

Elle tossed her head, pulling toward the least likely of the paths, the one that was less traveled and more over-grown. Simon did all he could to hold her back as lightning lit up the wood again. He spied something so astonishing he thought if he had been a horse, he would have reared back.

Elle merely strained at the bit, redoubling her effort to surge down the path. Simon barked out a sharp command, hauling back on the reins in a way that demonstrated he'd tolerate no more of her nonsense. When he finally settled the mare, he peered down at the creature he'd spotted, still unable to credit his eyes.

There was something almost supernatural about the cat squatting calmly at the fork in the paths, in this wild place, upon this wild afternoon. Its wind-ruffled fur was as black as ink except for the snowy white of its paws. Simon blinked, half-expecting the creature to vanish. But the cat's amber eyes blinked back at him, stirring in him a memory of a long-ago night upon a windswept hill at the far side of this very island.

Simon had charged forward, his heart thudding with the fear and eagerness of his very first raid, hoping to catch a coven of witches in the act of performing their satanic rites amidst the towering circle of standing stones. What he'd found was a beleaguered Miri fiercely fighting off the other girls in her effort to save the cat slated for sacrifice.

The brazen young hussies had scattered in terror at the sight of Simon, but Miri had determinedly stood her ground, freeing the small black cat bound to the stone altar. That had been the first time he and Miri Cheney had ever clapped eyes upon each other. The witch-hunter and the witch.

No, Simon thought ruefully. They had not been that to each other, not way back then. He had only been a boy with so much yet to learn and she had been little more than an appealing child with fey eyes and a winsome smile.

This creature staring at him surely could not be the same cat Miri had rescued that night, not after all these years, could it? Simon cocked his head, studying the cat intently. Although he felt like a perfect fool, he called uncertainly, "Necromancer?"

The cat meowed for all the world as though it acknowledged its name, then with a saucy flit of its tail, it vanished up the path. When Elle strained to follow, Simon made no effort to stop her. If that was indeed Miri's cat, and why else would such a tame creature be out here in these woods, then it was undoubtedly streaking for home.

But the track that the cat led them down was scarcely worthy of the name. The trees closed rapidly around them, branches and leaves slashing at both Simon and his horse. The ground became too treacherous with thick roots and hidden chuckholes to make riding safe any longer.

Simon dismounted and led Elle, shoving back limbs to clear the path. From time to time he caught the rustle of bushes, the glimpse of a shadow that was the cat. The little black devil was either leading him toward Miri's abode or else to some dark center of the forest where he would be hopelessly lost.

Either way, it was too late to turn back. The sky grumbled and Simon felt the first cold splash of rain upon his cheek. He needed to find shelter for himself and Elle and find it soon.

Just when the path seemed in danger of disappearing entirely, he was heartened to spy a clearing in the distance. Smoke curled in wisps from the chimney of a small stone cottage. He'd lost sight of the cat, but this had to be the place. Who else but Miri would live in such a godforsaken place with only the beasts and birds of the wood for neighbors?

Leading Elle past the thick trunk of an oak tree, Simon strode forward only to feel the ground shift. He lost his grip on the reins as he was swept roughly off his feet, the world rushing past him in a dizzying blur.

Stunned by the unexpected assault, it took a moment to comprehend what had happened. He was entangled in the rough cords of a thick net, swaying yards off the ground, trapped like any witless rabbit blundering into a hunter's snare. The taut ropes of the net gouged his face and arms. Simon might have experienced a grudging admiration for

Miri's ingenuity in arranging this little surprise if he had not been so alarmed for Elle.

The mare had been spooked when he'd been caught in the trap. As he twisted to look for her, one of his boots ripped through the mesh of the net. He saw no sign of Elle. If she had taken off in panic, plunging blindly through the woods, it would be a miracle if she didn't end up breaking a leg. The sword Simon might have used to cut himself loose was strapped to her saddle.

As for his knife, it was tucked in the boot that now dangled through the hole in the net. As Simon struggled to work his foot free so he could reach the weapon, the branch of the tree that held him creaked ominously.

He swore roundly, not knowing how the situation could possibly get any worse. That was when the clouds opened up and it started to pour.

※※※

MIRI HUDDLED IN THE DOORWAY of her cottage, heedless of the wind and rain lashing inside. She eyed the dark figure trapped in the net high above the ground with a mingling of grim satisfaction and awe.

With his wild mane of dark hair, massive body, and fierce cursing, Simon Aristide seemed more ferocious beast than man. She could not make out his face from where she stood, but he must have been able to perceive her hovering upon the threshold of the cottage.

"Miri!"

Her name was borne back to her on the wind like the

infuriated roar of a dragon. Even though the witch-hunter was in no position to be a menace to her, she shrank back involuntarily. She started when Necromancer brushed up against her ankles, the cat taking shelter beneath the hem of her skirts.

"I got him," Miri said somewhat breathlessly.

The cat glared up at her. *"Wonderful. Now close the door. I am getting soaked."*

Necromancer slipped past her, retreating deeper inside the cottage. Miri hesitated, despite the rain that spattered her face and dampened the front of her gown. A deafening clap of thunder sounded, followed by a jagged flash of lightning, heightening the peril of Simon's predicament. She ought to just slam the door closed, leave him to his fate.

But she fretted her lower lip and fingered the hilt of the knife sheathed in her belt, the blade sharp enough to easily cut him free . . .

"Miri!" Simon bellowed out her name again. "I know you are there. Get out here right now and cut me down or I swear I will—"

He choked off into impotent fury, but the implied threat was enough to harden Miri's resolve. She backed up, starting to close the door when his voice roared out again.

"For the love of God, woman. At least go find my horse."

His horse? Miri froze, horrified that she had overlooked a detail so important. Alerted by Necromancer, she had watched from the cottage for Simon's approach, her attention fully focused on the witch-hunter, waiting as he had walked right into her trap.

She had never seen his mount, but she should have had the wit to realize he hadn't marched all the way here on foot. He must have been leading his horse and now the poor beast, bewildered and terrified by the fate of its rider, had torn off in a panic. Miri bolted out into the rain, not even taking time to snatch up a cloak.

She crossed the clearing, keeping a wary distance between herself and the figure thrashing in the net high above her. If Simon noticed her, he ventured no remark other than a grunt as he struggled to free his boot from a hole in the net.

Miri darted toward the track that led to the glade. Simon's frightened horse could be anywhere by this time. She was relieved to discover that the mare had not strayed that far. She had no idea what could have curbed the horse's natural instinct to take flight in the face of danger. The mare waited only a few yards down the path, looking very wet and forlorn, trembling, with no idea where to go or what to do.

Miri approached cautiously. Although the mare's eyes were dark with fear and misery, she made no effort to pull back when Miri took hold of the bit beneath the bridle. Miri comforted the creature as best she could with the low crooning song that had ever been her own special brand of magic.

She shivered, already soaked to the skin, her braid a sodden weight dangling down her back. Ignoring her own discomfort, she murmured reassurance to the horse as she sought to lead the mare back to the clearing.

"Everything is all right," she cooed. "I am here to help you. Let me take you to someplace where you will be safe and dry."

For the first time, the horse offered resistance, rolling its eyes back, one word emerging from the jumbled chaos of its thoughts. *"Free . . . free."*

"Of course, you will be free. I've liberated many of your brethren from cruel or careless masters. You are bound to serve that horrid witch-hunter no longer."

The mare gave an impatient stamp of her hoof, her urgent thought communicating to Miri more clearly. *"Free . . . him. Free him!"*

Miri was so astounded she nearly released the bridle. The mare was not afraid *of* Simon, but *for* him. Frightened, confused by the trap, the horse had not known how to help her rider, but she had been unwilling to desert him either.

Miri shook the rainwater from her face, not knowing how to respond to the mare's desperate plea. The sharp crack of a branch carried to her ears above the wind and the steady drum of the rain.

Miri spun about, her heart leaping into her throat at the sight of the towering figure crashing through the break in the clearing. She had no need to think of a response to the mare's plea to free Simon. He had somehow managed to do that himself.

Silhouetted by another flash of lightning, the witch-hunter was a figure of nightmare, dark clothing plastered to the hard contours of his body, his black hair snarled in wet tangles across his ravaged face, rain dripping from his beard, his mouth set in a taut white line.

Miri dropped the reins and snatched the knife from her belt. "Keep back or I swear I will—will—"

"Will what? Kill me?"

It was like a horrible echo from the past, hurtling Miri

back through years to that night in Paris, that moment in the Charters Inn when she had held Simon at bay with her pistol. His response now was the same as it had been then. He kept coming.

"You want to plunge that knife into me? Go ahead. I won't try to stop you. Look! I'm not even wearing my mail coat." He tore open his jerkin and shirt, baring a slash of his hard-muscled chest, the dark mat of hair glistening against his rain-soaked skin.

She stumbled back, slamming up against the rough bark of a tree, the solid elm allowing her no further retreat. She raised the knife, tightening her grip on the hilt.

"Stay back, Aristide! I mean it!"

Simon closed the distance between them in one long stride, drawing so near the tip of her blade rested over the region of his heart. His hand came up and Miri braced herself, expecting him to wrestle the knife from her grasp.

To her astonishment, he laid his palm alongside her cheek.

"Go ahead and do it," he said in a voice ragged with weariness. "Someone's going to finish me off sooner or later. It might as well be you."

Miri swallowed hard, fighting to cling to her anger and resentment, to remember all that Simon had cost her, the loss of her trust, her home, her family, the destruction he had brought to Faire Isle. But another flare of lightning afforded her a glimpse of his face, of Simon Aristide, the man she had convinced herself no longer had a soul. And yet she could see the loneliness, the torment, the exhaustion of his spirit, trapped in the depths of that single dark eye.

He was not merely goading her as he had done that time

in Paris. Some part of Simon truly did not care whether he lived or died. Miri wondered despairingly how they had come to this, that innocent boy and girl who had first met on a midnight hillside. Simon, who had learned to hold life so cheap, including his own, and her not much better, a daughter of the earth threatening to kill.

A tremor coursed through her and she lowered her hand, allowing the knife to slip from her fingers and thud to the ground. Twisting away from him, she closed her eyes, assailed by that strong rush of emotion Simon had always inflicted upon her, anger and sorrow, hurt and a frustrated longing for what might have been.

"Damn you to hell," she cried, hot tears trickling from her eyes to mingle with the cold rain.

"Too late."

"W-what?"

She started when he touched her cheek, brushing away the moisture with the rough pad of his thumb. "Your curse, my dear. It comes far too late. I've been in hell for quite some time."

Miri trembled so badly, her knees might have given way if Simon had not braced her by grasping her shoulders. She stiffened, resisting, but he drew her gently, inexorably into his arms. No matter how she despised herself for it, she was weak enough to rest her brow against his shoulder. His large hand engulfed the back of her head as he stroked her hair, murmuring something about it being all right.

"All right?" she choked. "Do you realize I've never held a weapon in my hand, never tried to hurt anyone until you came along?"

"I know. I'm sorry."

Damn him for sounding as though he meant that, Miri thought. So much for all of her fierce boasting to Marie Claire, that she would know how to deal with Simon the next time she encountered him.

How appalled Marie Claire would be to see her cradled in the witch-hunter's arms. To say nothing of how Ariane and Gabrielle would react. It was the thought of her sisters that gave Miri the strength to draw back, shove Simon away from her.

Mopping tears and rain from her face, she fought through her confused jumble of feelings, focusing on the only thing that made sense to her, the mare that stood trembling nearby.

"Your horse is cold and frightened," she informed Simon tersely. "We need to get her in out of the rain."

※※※

THE SMALL BARN behind the cottage was snug and dry, the air redolent with scents that Miri had long found soothing and familiar, sweet hay and warm horse. Shivering in her wet clothes, Miri gestured toward the only empty stall. Simon eased his nervous mount inside. It was a strange aftermath to their conflict, this working in silent harmony to look after the mare Simon called Elle. But Miri suspected that they both found it easier to deal with the horse's needs than each other.

Willow thrust his head over the door of his stall and whickered softly, the stolid pony more curious than alarmed by the intruders in his barn. But the pigeons that roosted in the rafters had gone silent. Miri could sense them up there in the shadows, watching warily with their beady eyes. Her birds were fully as disturbed as she was by the invasion of Simon Aristide.

As Miri rummaged about through her tack box for some towels, she studied Simon out of the corner of her eye. He seemed like a stranger, fitting none of her memories of him, neither the handsome boy who had once figured in her dreams nor the dreaded Le Balafre who had formed her nightmares.

He looked older, wearier, his wet hair slicked back from his brow, throwing his beard-coarsened jaw and scarred face into sharp relief. When she had last seen Simon, he had been shaved bald, determined to look as grim as possible, to intimidate everyone who crossed his path, including her.

But nothing could have been gentler than the way Simon handled his horse. The mare was still spooked, blowing and trembling.

"Easy now. Easy, my beautiful lady," he crooned, caressing the mare's neck with long firm strokes. "It's all over. You're all right now."

Miri watched him with a kind of wonder. Never had she known Aristide to display such affection to anyone.

You know that is not true, the voice of memory whispered in her ear, recalling a stolen moment in a secluded cove so long ago, the breeze from the channel stirring the black curls of Simon's hair, his handsome young face as smooth as her own.

Simon leaned forward and Miri's heart missed a beat

when she realized what he intended to do. She shyly tipped up her face, closing her eyes. Simon touched his mouth to hers, so lightly, but the kiss seemed to blossom inside her, sweet and warm.

Her very first kiss . . . Simon had been so tender, as tender as he was being now. Miri caught her breath, cutting off the thought.

"Don't start doing that again. Looking for things in Simon that aren't there," she adjured herself. Miri carried the towels over to him, taking great care to keep an arm's length away.

"There now, Elle. You are safe. You have nothing to fear." As the mare calmed beneath his hands, Simon turned to Miri. *"You* have nothing to be afraid of either."

"That is a strange assurance to come from someone who once did his best to terrorize me and my entire family."

"That was a long time ago, almost ten years. I—I have many regrets about that summer."

"And perhaps your chief one is that you never charged me with witchcraft. So is that why you are here? To finally remedy your error."

"No." Simon frowned as he loosened the straps of Elle's saddle. "After all this time, I hoped you would have realized I never wanted to hurt *you.*"

Miri regarded him incredulously. "Thanks to you, the king of France attainted my entire family for sorcery and treason. We had to flee into exile while the crown confiscated Renard's estates on the mainland. They even took Belle Haven, my family home that was handed down through generations of daughters of the earth, the land that was never any man's to take. And I can't even begin to describe what you did to Faire Isle itself, turning it into a place I don't even recognize anymore.

"God help me, Simon, if you ever did decide you *wanted* to hurt me."

"Miri, I—" He broke off, apparently realizing the futility of anything he could say. But his face was shadowed with regret as he stripped off Elle's saddle.

"You might as well have charged me with witchcraft, too," she persisted. "Why didn't you?"

Simon propped Elle's saddle up in a corner. "Because I believed you were innocent."

"No more innocent than many other women you perse-cuted, including my own sisters. So why did you always insist upon sparing me?"

"I don't know." Simon's lips quirked into a rueful half-smile. "Perhaps because you have always been my one weakness."

Just as Miri feared he had always been hers, but she was not about to admit that to him. She thrust one of the towels into his hand. Thunder boomed outside but to Miri, it seemed as nothing compared to the tension crackling in-side the barn. As Simon began to rub down Elle's flanks, Miri tried to towel off the animal's neck, but the horse shied back in alarm, nearly stepping on Simon.

"Whoa," he called, patting the mare reassuringly. "What's the matter, Elle?"

Peering into the mare's wide brown eye, Miri could tell at once.

"She's afraid of me now," Miri said in a small voice. "Because she saw me try to hurt you."

Simon stroked the mare until she calmed again. "My poor Elle," he murmured "She ought to be used to people attempting to kill me."

"It—it happens that often?"

"Often enough," came his wry reply.

The information provided her with a disturbing glimpse into what Simon had become, the object of hatred, isolation. Why did he travel alone? Why was he no longer surrounded by an army of men to protect him? Miri fiercely reminded herself that it was none of her concern. The last thing she wanted was to feel any interest or empathy with the man.

When he went back to toweling Elle down, she approached the horse with more caution, gradually winning back her trust, until she was able to dry off the mare's powerful chest. Miri knew she'd be better off not knowing, but she could not stop herself from asking. "So how did you know where to find me? Who did you bribe?"

"Some sour-faced creature. Madame Elan was her name, I believe."

"Madame Alain," Miri corrected, more saddened than angered. "Of course it would be Josephine. I only hope you paid her well. She has a large family to support and things have not prospered on Faire Isle. People from the mainland have been afraid to come here since your raids and our trade has fallen off badly."

Simon paused in his vigorous toweling to peer gravely at her. "The lack of trade has nothing to do with what happened ten years ago, Miri. People have little goods or money to barter. Have you been to the mainland recently? Crops are failing because of the drought, livestock dropping in the fields. Gangs of desperate people rove the lanes, ready to attack each other for a crust of bread. Faire Isle is not the only place enduring hard times. This island is no different from the rest of France."

Miri frowned as she bent to tend to the mare's forelegs. "I am sorry to hear of such troubles, but there is one thing you have never understood, Simon. Faire Isle *is* different from the mainland or at least it was. This island was always a special place of peace and healing, a refuge that you destroyed. The women who fled have never returned and those who remain are cowed, their spirits withered like Josephine Alain."

Simon rested one arm across Elle's back and blew out a wearied sigh. "I know you're not going to believe this, but I do truly regret much of what happened on Faire Isle. When I rode out here to find you, it—it disturbed me to see so many shops still abandoned, so many homes that have never been rebuilt."

"I am not just talking about burned-out cottages and empty shops. There was a gentle spirit on this island, a magic that you crushed beneath your boot heel."

Her lips thinned in a bitter smile. "But you are a witch-hunter. I always seem to forget that. Destroying magic is your mission, your sole purpose in life, is it not?"

Although Simon flushed, his jaw jutted to a stubborn angle. "You seem to have forgotten why I was obliged to come here to Faire Isle. I was the king's appointed representative to investigate charges of sorcery. Your family attacked me and my men, burned down the inn where we were staying."

"Because you had charged Gabrielle with witchcraft

and were holding her hostage to trap my brother-in-law. You were going to hang Renard without even trying him first."

Simon scowled at the reminder but he was quick to counter, "Perhaps that was wrong, but a trial seemed an unnecessary waste of time. The Comte was clearly guilty. He was caught possessing the *Book of Shadows*. And your sister wasn't exactly innocent either. Gabrielle admitted to consorting with Cassandra Lascelles, a noted practitioner of black magic."

Miri felt the heat rush into her cheeks, her anger compounded by the frustration of not being able to defend her loved ones as indignantly as she would have wished. Because Simon was right, blast him. Renard was a good man, but he had inherited an unfortunate fascination with the darker side of magic from his wicked old grandmother, Melusine. And Miri herself had been nervous of Gabrielle's friendship with Cassandra, a sorceress skilled in necromancy and crafting amulets of alarming power.

The *Book of Shadows* had only tempted Renard because he had hoped to ease his wife's heartache, find some safe way for Ariane to bear a child. And Gabrielle had only been seeking a way to protect her beloved Captain Remy, not understanding the true evil of Cass's amulets until it was too late.

But Miri knew it would be useless trying to explain any of that to Simon, especially about Renard. Simon had long ago convinced himself that the Comte was a sorcercer. It was far easier to remind Simon of his own inequities instead.

"You told me that all you wanted was to see the *Book*

of Shadows destroyed," she accused. "You said that if I persuaded Renard to surrender that evil book, you would let both him and Gabrielle go free and like a fool, I believed you. But you continued to hound my family long after that night. You had the *Book of Shadows*. Why couldn't you just get rid of it and leave us alone?"

"Because I never got the chance to destroy the cursed thing." The color in his face heightened as he admitted reluctantly, "It—it disappeared."

"What!"

"At some point during the chaos of the fire, someone stole the book."

"You mean that terrible *Book* is still out there for someone to make use of, to decipher all those hideous spells?"

Simon nodded grimly.

"Oh, that's marvelous." Miri threw up her hands and paced past the stalls in her agitation, ignoring Willow's playful attempt to nip at her. "Well done, Simon. You persecute my innocent family to the ends of the earth while you let one of the greatest evils of all time slip through your fingers. So that is why you tore this island apart. You thought one of us still had that *Book*."

Simon followed her out of the stall and locked his arms across his chest. "Perhaps one of you still does."

"You mean Renard, I suppose. I can tell you with certainty that he doesn't."

"You never believed he had it the first time," Simon replied coolly, but when Miri halted and glared at him, he flung up one hand. "Truce. I didn't come here to rake up the past or quarrel with you."

"Then I wish you would come to the point and tell me exactly why you are here."

"I am beginning to wonder that myself." He grimaced, but as his gaze rested on her, something softened in his face. "Perhaps it is partly because when I heard you had returned to Faire Isle, I—I just wanted to see you again, to know how you were faring."

"Now you've seen me and I'm just fine," Miri snapped. "So what's the other part of your reason?"

He moved toward Elle, burying his fingers in the horse's mane. At last he said as though the words were wrung from him. "I—I need your help."

Miri stared at him, too stunned to say anything for a moment. She finally gave a mirthless laugh. "You are completely unbelievable, Simon Aristide. Twice in the past I trusted you, even mistook you for a friend. But all you were doing was using me to destroy my sister's husband. Is that what you are after again? I couldn't help you with that even if you tortured me. Since I returned to Faire Isle, I—I have lost track of Ariane and Renard. I have no idea where they are or Gabrielle and Remy either."

Miri bumped up her chin defiantly, daring him to call her a liar. Simon likely knew she wasn't telling the truth, but he chose not to challenge her.

"I am not after Renard," he said. "I once believed the comte the most wicked being I had ever encountered, but I've learned better. Until recently, I had no idea what real evil could be. I have struck up against an enemy too powerful, too clever in the dark ways for one man to defeat."

"So why come to me? Why not go to your patron the

king? You and he once made a pact, didn't you, to rid France of all sorcery?"

"The king unfortunately lost interest in our campaign and moved on to other pursuits. He has proved a weak and volatile man who has mismanaged France so badly he can barely hold his throne safe from the rising power of his nobles."

"Well . . . well, what about your fellow witch-hunters?"

"I have not employed mercenaries for a long time, not since the raid on Faire Isle. My men slipped completely out of my control, looting and burning. I suffered from delusions of grandeur in those days, imagining that I could command the obedience of such battle-hardened men when I was little more than a stripling myself." Simon's lip curled in an expression of self-derision. "What an arrogant young ass I was, so infernally sure of myself."

Miri eyed him doubtfully. Yes, he certainly had been arrogant, obstinate, and inflexible. She would have thought him incapable of ever admitting he could be wrong about anything.

"And just what are you now, Simon?" she asked.

Simon raked his hand back through his damp hair and gave a ragged laugh. "Now I am sure of nothing. All I am is very tired . . . and alone."

He scarcely needed to tell her that. She could see that soul-deep weariness in his gaze, feel the pull of his loneliness like a dark tide threatening to draw her in. She had to lock her arms tightly about her middle to steel herself against it.

"So what do you want from me?"

"I know I have no right to expect anything from you.

All I am asking is that you listen to my tale. If you choose not to believe anything I tell you, I swear I'll leave you in peace. You'll never set eyes on me again."

He took a step toward her. When she tensed, he stopped, coming no closer. He offered his hand instead. "Is it a bargain?"

Miri stared at those strong, blunt fingers, feeling more torn than she had ever been in her life. Given her history with Simon, she would have to be six kinds of fool to accede to his demand.

Except that that was the problem. Simon wasn't demanding. He was asking, and far more humbly than she would have imagined possible. All that he requested was a hearing. It seemed so unreasonable to refuse him.

But she could almost hear Gabrielle's voice scolding in her head.

"Have you lost your mind, Miri? After all this man has done, you are worried about treating him unreasonably. I vow you'd give the devil himself a second chance."

And it could well be the devil standing before her. Miri glanced up at Simon, but his face provided her no answers, his dark gaze steady but unreadable. Although she ignored his outstretched hand and brushed past Simon, she conceded in a low voice, "All right. Come to the cottage as soon as you are done looking after your horse."

"Thank you," Simon said gruffly, but he doubted that Miri even heard him as she slipped out the barn door and vanished into the rain and darkness.

But her image remained with him as he set about the task of feeding Elle, ladling oats into a feed bucket. For so long, the memory of Miri had been frozen in his mind, a girl just blossoming into womanhood, lithe and willowy, her features so serene, so ethereal, she did not seem like she'd been fashioned out of the same clay as the rest of the world. More like she'd been born of air, light, and spirit.

She was no longer that girl. What curves he could make out beneath that soaked gown were definitely those of a woman. Her face was thinner, paler than he'd remembered. The openness, the wonder that had once sparkled in Miri's eyes had dimmed, the shadows beneath them deep. He was responsible for that. If he were damned for nothing else he'd done, he would be for the havoc he had wreaked on this one gentle, trusting heart.

As Elle blissfully plunged her nose into the feed bucket, Simon rubbed his knuckles between her eyes, a caress that the mare was particularly fond of.

"Ah, the devil take me, Elle," he murmured. "I've inflicted enough pain on that woman. I should never have come here."

Time and again he had betrayed Miri's trust, used her in his quest to rid the world of witches. The damnable thing was he might well end up hurting her again. If he possessed any scrap of decency, he would simply wait out the storm, saddle up Elle, and ride away, find some other way to defeat the Silver Rose and leave Miri in peace.

But Simon sighed, knowing that he would not. Because he was every inch the bastard that Miri Cheney thought he was.

Chapter Three

SIMON PLUNGED THROUGH THE POURING RAIN, HIS SADDLE-bag flung over his shoulder. By the time he reached Miri's doorstep, any drying out he'd achieved in the barn was lost. He was dripping wet, his streaming hair snarled across his face. He hammered against the door with his fist, the rough wood abrading his knuckles. He was astonished when it yielded, creaking open. Darting inside, he slammed the door closed.

As he slicked back the wet hair from his face, Simon saw the reason that it had opened so readily. Miri had neither iron lock nor wooden bar upon her door. He ought to have been grateful for it and it was after all none of his affair. But it alarmed him to discover that the woman was still that trusting.

The cottage was a far cry from Miri's former home, Belle Haven, with its beautiful tapestries and multiple bed-chambers. The dwelling place consisted of one large room, with a ladder leading to a loft above, the outline of a simple box bed barely visible. The rest of the furnishings below were likewise simple, a pine table, a few stools and chairs, a cupboard, and a cypress chest, but the cottage still managed to convey an aura of cheerful disorder. A blue shawl was draped over the back of a chair, the contents of a sewing box were strewn across the table, drying herbs and baskets hung haphazardly from hooks mounted in the beams of the ceiling. A cluster of baby rabbits huddled together in a wire cage bedded with straw, no doubt some orphaned creatures Miri was seeking to rescue.

Shutters were battened across the windows, muting the wind and the lash of the rain. The soft glow of candles and the logs crackling on the hearth made the place seem like a haven of warmth and light. Or was that more owing to the woman who stood drying her hair before the fire?

Miri had removed her wet clothes, her gown and underpinnings hanging from a rope she had strung from a hook on the hearth to a peg imbedded in the wall. She was clad only in a shift, and the firelight silhouetted her womanly figure through the thin fabric. Simon could clearly make out the dusky aureole of her nipples, the soft curve of her hips, the shadowy delta at the cusp of her legs. His breath hitched in his throat.

Miri froze at his entrance, her comb tangled halfway down a long skein of her hair. Obviously she had not been expecting him to finish up in the barn so soon. Simon shuffled his feet. It was damned strange. He had kicked in more doors, forced his way into more homes than he could count, but never had he felt so much like an intruder.

"Er—I am sorry. I tried to knock. Should I go back out until you—you—"

Miri tugged the comb from her hair and clutched it in her hands. "Don't be foolish. You are already soaked. Just take off your boots. They're muddy."

Simon nodded, trying not to stare at her as he eased his saddlebag to the floor. He was bruised. He was tired. He was soaked to the skin and still he was amazed to feel heat course through him. For so long he had thought himself numb to any feelings that were not directly related to his needs for survival. His body announced otherwise, the flash of desire that sizzled through him as unexpected as being struck by lightning.

Miri tensed like a doe suddenly aware of the hungry gaze of a wolf. She stalked over to the shawl she had left abandoned over the chair. She draped herself in the voluminous woolen folds, knotting the ends across her bosom. Her movements were unhurried and not in the least self-conscious. Rather than a woman modestly seeking to veil herself, it was more like having one slam the bedchamber door in one's face.

Plunking down on a three-legged stool, Simon struggled to work off his boots. It proved a difficult proposition, the leather slick with rain and mud. But the exertion allowed him time to recover from the wayward reaction of his body to the sight of hers. Matters between him and Miri Cheney were strained enough without the added complication of any carnal impulses.

Lining his boots up neatly by the door, Simon wiped

his hands clean on his breeches that were already a mess from his fall. He stepped hesitantly toward the hearth, feeling like some mongrel dog approaching a beckoning campfire and not at all sure what his reception would be.

Wordlessly, Miri handed him a linen towel and retreated to the opposite corner of the room to finish combing her hair. Simon found himself in sole possession of the blazing fire. Well, him and the cat. Necromancer curled up on a braided rug before the hearth, lazily eyeing Simon through narrowed slits.

Simon held out his hands to the welcome blaze of heat. A small cauldron of something steamed over the fire, emitting a fragrant spicy aroma. His back to Miri, Simon applied the towel first to his face, shifting aside his eye patch.

His leather patch had gotten wet in the rain, but Simon seldom removed it except when he was alone, self-conscious about the extent of his injury, even after all these years. When he'd finished drying his face, he replaced the patch, wincing at the feel of the damp leather settling back against his cheek.

As Simon worked to undo the laces of his doublet, he said, "You ought to have some sort of bar or lock on that door."

"Why?" Miri compressed her lips as she struggled with a particularly stubborn knot in her hair. "There is a reason I live way out here in the woods. My neighbors are ones I can trust, the four-legged kind."

"Unfortunately your address is also known to the sort that walk on two legs. If you insist upon the company of animals, at least you should surround yourself with useful ones. A pack of large fierce mastiffs would serve you far better than a basket of rabbits or this scrawny old cat."

In spite of his gruff words, Simon found the sleek softness of Necromancer's dark coat irresistible. He hunkered down to stroke the dozing feline. Necromancer went from sleeping cat to hissing fury in the bat of an eye. Lashing out, he scratched Simon's small finger, the same hand that already bore the claw marks from the witch who had tried to kill him two nights ago.

Simon jerked back, swearing while Necromancer stalked off in high dudgeon. With amazing agility for such an old cat, he scrambled up the ladder, disappearing into the darkness of the loft.

"Damn!" Simon muttered, sucking the streak of blood from his injured finger. "I'm glad he wasn't the one wielding the knife earlier."

Miri's lips twitched with the hint of a smile, but she was quick to suppress it. "Yes, you should be. That *scrawny old cat* was the one who lured you straight into my trap."

"Not a particularly effective trap. If you are going to rely on snares for protection, I can show you how to fashion a better one. A simple noose would have caught me around the ankle and left me hanging upside down and far more helpless. Or get an iron trap with the kind of teeth that can crush a man's ankle."

"Such traps would be far too dangerous. What if I caught some fox or poor little rabbit by mistake? I don't happen to like harming innocent creatures."

"Believe it or not, neither do I."

She clearly didn't believe it. Turning away from him,

Miri went back to combing her hair. Suppressing a tired sigh, Simon struggled out of his jerkin and draped it over the rope line Miri had fashioned. He spied a painting hanging on the wall, half-hidden by the drying clothes.

Simon pushed Miri's gown aside in order to obtain a better look, his face softening with recognition. Set in a gilt-edged frame was a unicorn cantering through the forest, a magnificent study in contrasts between the vivid details of the trees and the phantom aura of the unicorn. The longer one stared at it, the more one became unsure where myth ended and reality began.

Her sister, Gabrielle, had done the painting for Miri. When Simon had last seen it, it had been incomplete and seemed destined to remain that way. But it had been Miri's greatest treasure, so fixed had she been in her childlike belief in unicorns.

Simon smiled in spite of himself, the memory bittersweet. He felt ridiculously pleased that Gabrielle had finally finished the painting and that Miri still had it. He'd lain awake for too many sleepless nights when he realized that his actions had cost Miri Belle Haven. He was glad she still had some small part of her childhood home.

He heard the floorboard creak and realized Miri had crept up behind him. "So Gabrielle finally finished your unicorn?"

"Yes," she replied softly.

"I remember how you always used to insist there was one that roamed Faire Isle. Of course, I being naught but a lowly boy could never hope to see the creature."

"And I recall how you tugged on my braid and teased me, telling me I was too old to believe such things."

"And you told me most indignantly, 'The day I am too old to believe in unicorns is the day that I die, Simon Aristide.'"

Once more, she almost smiled at him, biting down on her lip to still its quiver.

"So do you still see the old boy in your rambles through the woods?"

Miri shook her head.

"Never tell me that you think I drove the unicorn away as well," Simon half-jested, determined to provoke a real smile from her. "I swear I never touched a single hair of his mane."

"No, the unicorn is probably still there. I simply stopped looking for him." Her face grew more pensive and sad, adding to the burden of guilt he already carried.

No doubt she was recalling what he should have had the tact and wit to remember himself. He'd only ever seen the unicorn painting because Miri had trusted him enough to allow him inside her home. Simon had used the opportunity to gather evidence against her brother-in-law, to steal the ring that would lure the Comte de Renard to Paris, where he could be arrested. It was the first time Simon had betrayed Miri's friendship in his zeal to bring the sorcerer to justice. Unfortunately, it had not been the last.

That was the trouble with even the best of the memories that they shared, Simon reflected ruefully. They would always be tainted with his many betrayals, shadowed by their vastly differing views of the world.

Miri twitched her gown back into place, blotting out the sight of the unicorn. She regarded him with a sudden frown. "You're bleeding."

Simon lifted his hand to find the angry-looking scratch still oozing blood, his finger smeared with it. Impatiently, he started to wipe it on his shirt when Miri intervened.

"Don't do that."

He was surprised when she seized hold of his hand. Snatching up the towel, she dabbed brusquely at the scratch, causing it to sting. When Simon sucked in his breath, she said, "Necromancer clawed you pretty good. You should never presume to touch any creature unless you are invited to do so."

"I'll try to remember that," Simon replied dryly.

As she finished cleaning his scratch, her hands grew gentler. It had been a long time since anyone had touched him with anything approaching kindness. Her gentleness was a far more dangerous seduction than the sight of her body had been. Simon's urge to draw back was immediate and instinctive. But he felt strangely helpless to move, rather bemused to find himself being tended by the woman who should have wanted him dead.

"So why didn't you do it, Miri?" he demanded.

"Do what?"

"Kill me when you had the chance. It was what I would have done in your place."

Although she continued to tend his scratch, she appeared disturbed by his question, a tiny furrow creasing her brow. "I am a daughter of the earth. I am meant to heal, not harm."

"And is that the only thing that stayed your hand?"

"N-no. I suppose it was also because I have endured enough grief over you. The thought of you dying, your blood spilling over my hands—" She shuddered.

"Then you don't completely despise me?"

"It would seem not." She glanced up at him and her smile broke free at last. The merest quirk of her lips but Simon felt as though a huge weight had been lifted from his heart.

He had almost forgotten the power of those fey eyes of hers. Like a clear white light drawing him in with all the force of the moon's pull upon the wayward sea, that inexplicable attraction that had always existed between him and Miri. What was more, he was certain she felt it, too.

She flushed and released his hand. "T-there. The bleeding has stopped. It looks as though Necromancer's attack won't prove fatal, but—" She peered closer, for the first time noticing the gouge marks above his knuckles.

"Good heavens, what happened there?" she teased. "Did you try to pet a bear?"

Simon drew back, self-consciously covering the scratches with his other hand. "No, it is only a memento from a dispute I had with a witch two nights ago."

"Oh?" Miri's light tone faltered. "And—and how did this *wise woman* fare from the encounter?"

"The *witch* is dead." When Miri paled, Simon silently cursed the bluntness of his own tongue.

"Not by my hand," he hastened to add, but Miri was already backing away from him.

The eyes that had been so soft a moment ago now pierced him with reproach. "You once boasted to me that when you suspected someone of being a witch, you immediately put her to the sword."

"That is all that it was, the boast of a swaggering young dolt who was trying to appear as ruthless as possible. I

have never behaved that arbitrarily." Honesty compelled
Simon to add. "At least I hope that I haven't.

"The woman plunged over the side of a cliff when she
was trying to kill *me*. I actually tried to pull her up to
safety, but she clawed my hand. She fell to the rocks below
and was swept out to sea. I assure you she was no *wise
woman*. She was most definitely a God-cursed witch, an
agent of the Silver Rose."

"The Silver Rose?"

"Yes, the enemy that I mentioned in the barn, the
sorceress that I have ridden so far to tell you about."

Except he feared she might no longer be willing to listen to him. She shrank from him, regarding him with troubled eyes. Simon wished to hell he had never mentioned
the dead witch, but he had promised himself he would be
truthful with Miri this time.

"Miri, please," he reminded her. "You agreed you would
hear me out."

He could clearly see her inner struggle mirrored in her
face. At last she gave an unhappy nod and gestured toward
one of the chairs pulled up to the table.

"You had better sit down and tell me everything."

"I'm still rather wet."

"That's all right." She flicked a nervous glance at him.
"I don't have any dry clothes to offer you, so I would just
as soon you didn't take anything else off."

"I wasn't going to. I am rather wary of exposing my
more tender parts to a sorceress or her cat." He attempted
to smile, but met with no answering response.

As Simon drew a chair closer to the fire and sat down,

Miri bustled over to her cupboard. Fetching two earthenware mugs, she tried to blot out the image of some unfortunate woman's body broken on the rocks. Not by my hand, Simon had insisted. How desperately Miri wanted to believe him.

But his tale had jarred her, effectively reminding her of who and what he was—a witch-hunter. Perhaps that was just as well, considering how dangerously close she had come to forgetting it when she had attended to his wound, allowing herself to be pulled a little too deeply into the velvet darkness of his gaze.

Simon leaned back in his chair, stretching his long legs across the hearth. When Miri approached, he drew them in to allow her access to the cauldron. His damp breeches and linen shirt clung to his frame, outlining the powerful contours of his body. The sight triggered in her a memory far different from the gentle sweetness of their first and only kiss. A memory of the time she had been alone with Simon in his bedchamber at the inn in Paris. He had prowled toward her, cornering her against the wall, leaning in so close, she could feel the heat of his breath. The hard barrier of his chest brushing up against the bodice of her gown, he had used his knife to ruthlessly claim a lock of hair, his voice a sensual purr, his gaze dark and predatory.

His intent had been to warn her to stay away from him, to alarm and intimidate her. He had certainly succeeded in that. But he had succeeded in something else as well, causing her blood to race with a longing that was lustier, earthier than anything she had ever experienced before. Her first taste of desire . . .

Her cheeks warmed with more than the heat from the fire. Miri fought to suppress the memory as she ladled the hot liquid into one of the mugs.

"Here," she said, extending the cup to Simon, determinedly keeping her gaze from roving any lower than the strong cords of his neck.

"What is this?" Simon asked as he took the cup from her hands.

"An herbal tea that Ariane taught me to brew. Very restorative and good for fending off the chill."

Simon held the mug beneath his nose and sniffed the rising steam with a wary look on his face.

"It is not poisoned, if that is what you are afraid of."

Simon shrugged. "I wouldn't much care if it was."

"Don't say such a dreadful thing."

When he glanced up at her in surprise, she continued earnestly, "It is like spitting in the face of God and scorning all the good spirits of the earth to have so little regard for yourself. Life is a precious gift."

"Even if one makes a miserable use of it?"

"It is never too late to change, Simon. Pursue a different path."

He made no reply. Blowing on his tea to cool it, he took a cautious sip. But as Miri filled her own mug from the cauldron, he admitted, "About two years ago, I did try something different. Back when I still enjoyed the king's favor, he gifted me with a small holding of land. I attempted to settle there, built a house and barn. I had some notion I might try breeding horses."

Miri twisted her head to regard him with surprise. "What happened?"

Simon cradled his mug in his large hands, staring pensively into his tea. "I was too used to being alone and when you spend your life fighting darkness, it finally gets inside of you. I have walked in the shadows for so long, I don't remember how to dwell in the light. I—I just didn't seem to fit, to belong anywhere."

Miri turned away quickly, his words striking in her a painful answering chord. Except for the part about the darkness, Simon might well have been speaking of her. She finished filling her mug and retreated to a seat near the table.

Simon took a swallow of his tea and continued, "Besides, it is hardly a propitious time for a witch-hunter to go into retirement when there is great evil abroad and I seem to be the only one aware of it."

He leveled a searching look at Miri. "I take it you have heard nothing? Not one rumor of the existence of this new coven of witches?"

"As I have told you so many times in the past, I know nothing of any witches," Miri replied, warming her hands with the heat pouring through her cup. "My only acquaintance is with wise women, other daughters of the earth."

"These women are more like daughters of darkness. They call themselves the Sisterhood of the Silver Rose. They use that flower as their emblem."

"Roses grow in many colors, Simon. Silver isn't one of them."

"These roses are like nothing you have ever seen. Leached of all color and scent, glittering as though encased in ice. If you ever find one, don't touch it. They are permeated with some sort of poison. A farm lad in Dieppe came across one, presented it to his sweetheart. Both he and the poor girl were cursed to a slow, lingering death."

Some of Miri's skepticism must have shown on her face, for Simon scowled at her over the rim of his mug. "What? You don't believe me?"

Miri delayed answering by sipping from her cup, the bitter and sweet of the brew mingling on her tongue. "The rose was likely blasted by frost and the farmer and his sweetheart merely taken ill. There are many contagious fevers and ailments that can strike suddenly, unfortunately beyond many an ignorant doctor's ability to cure. As for all this talk of a coven . . . That's what you used to call Ariane's council meetings and they were nothing more than gatherings to promote friendship and share learning of the healing arts."

"I may have been wrong about your sister," Simon conceded tersely. "But I am not about the Sisterhood of the Silver Rose. These women are pure evil."

"So what exactly do these sisters do? That is, when they are not cultivating poisonous roses and trying to kill you."

"Spread fear and destruction. Recruit new members to her order."

"Her?"

Simon waved one hand in an impatient gesture. "The Silver Rose. The sorceress. The leader of this sisterhood. I have never seen her or heard a whisper of what her true identity might be.

"In the beginning I suspected the Dark Queen might have something to do with this coven. She is certainly capable of wielding such destructive power. But from what I

have gleaned from the Silver Rose's followers, they consider Catherine de Medici as much of an enemy as they
do me."

Simon frowned and added, "What *little* I have gleaned.
These witches will kill themselves before betraying any of
the Rose's secrets. They have this fixed belief that she can
bring them back from the dead."

He shot Miri a troubled look. "Is such a thing possible?"

"How would I know? I don't practice black magic. Nor
do any of my family," Miri protested. After a pause, she
added reluctantly, "I have heard tell that those skilled in
necromancy can communicate with the dead, but to actually bring them back to life—no, that would be going against
the will of God and the laws of nature."

"And yet . . . I once saw your sister do just that. The
time the Comte de Renard threw my old master in the pond
and he drowned. The Lady of Faire Isle used her magic art
to breathe life back into Monsieur Le Vis." Simon's voice
was soft, but his eye pierced Miri with—with what? A faint
trace of accusation?

She stiffened with a mingling of alarm and indignation.
"Le Vis was not dead, only unconscious. Ariane merely re-
vived him using her healing skills." Miri smacked her cup
back down on the table so hard, liquid sloshed over the
rim. "Good lord, Simon Aristide. Never tell me you suspect my sister is this evil Silver Rose. Because if that is why
you have come to me—"

"No! No, of course not."

Miri would have been more reassured if Simon had
sounded more convinced. She went on fiercely, "Ariane is

the epitome of what a daughter of the earth should be, wise, healing, nurturing. She is not in the least mad, which is what any wise woman would have to be to try to bring someone back from the grave. It would be completely insane."

"No more insane than some of the other hellish practices the Rose encourages among her followers." Simon's fingers tightened on his cup, his mouth grim. "Human sacrifice. Babes, some scarce hours old, abandoned to die of hunger and neglect. I have found four of them in the past year."

"How—how terrible and sad," Miri replied in a low voice. "But that is not necessarily a sign of any satanic sacrifice. If things are as bad as you say on the mainland, many families must be driven to the brink of desperation by the prospect of another mouth to feed or—" Her mind filled with the image of Carole Moreau's tragic young face. "Or often young girls who conceive out of wedlock are cast off by their families, left with nowhere to turn, so they leave their babes on the doorsteps of abbeys or churches—"

"These infants weren't left near any church," Simon growled. "They were deserted where they would never be found until it was too late, on cliffs or remote hillsides, placed on the rocks like some pagan offering. No act of desperation, but the cold-blooded murder of helpless babes, and all of them male. Sons abandoned by their mothers on the orders of this infamous Silver Rose."

"I cannot believe any mother would willingly—"

"Of course you can't." Simon blew out an exasperated breath and levered himself to his feet. "You have never been willing to concede that *wise women,* as you persist in calling them, could ever do anything wrong, never been able to see the evil that surrounds you."

"And evil is all that you do see," Miri retorted. "You've been a witch-hunter for far too long. What do you think, Simon? That this Silver Rose is trying to unleash some biblical plague against firstborn sons? Or maybe she just wants to destroy all the men in the world."

"I don't know, damn it." Simon slapped his hands down on the mantel and braced his arms, bowing his head. "I don't know," he repeated in a wearier voice. "I have too many questions and no answers."

He angled his head enough to give Miri a searching glance. "Are you not crediting anything that I tell you? Or do you just think that too much witch-hunting has addled my brain?"

"No, but perhaps it has overstimulated your imagination, causing you to turn the actions of a few evil or demented women into some sort of unbelievable conspiracy."

"All right, then. Tell me if I have imagined this." Simon thrust himself away from the mantel and strode over to where he had left his saddlebag. Yanking it open, he dove inside and drew out some object wrapped in a linen cloth.

He stalked back to Miri and plunked it down on the table before her. As he carefully undid the small bundle, she leaned forward, watching with a mingling of curiosity and apprehension.

The cloth fell away to reveal what at first glance looked like a slender knife, the stiletto-like blade fitted into a hilt carved with the emblem of a rose.

"This is the diabolical weapon the Silver Rose has devised. I call it a witch blade. Note her symbol etched here."

Simon traced one finger over the flower. "Part of the hilt is actually hollow, a place for storing poison. When you push it down—" Simon lifted the weapon to demonstrate. "It acts like a plunger, forcing the poison down through the blade itself, which is also hollow."

But Miri scarce heeded his explanation, her eyes widening with awe as she recognized Simon's witch blade for what it actually was.

"Great heavens," she breathed. "It's a syringe."

"A what?"

"A *syringe,*" she repeated. "They have existed since the time of Galen."

"Who was she? Some sorceress?"

"No, *he* was an ancient Greek physician, a very wise and learned man."

As Miri reached for the syringe, Simon tensed and cautioned her. "Be careful. I have drained all the poison out and cleaned it, but the witch blade is still dangerous, the point quite sharp."

Miri took it from him gingerly, testing the plunger, studying the thick needle with wonder and fascination. The syringe that Galen had devised and wise women still employed was crude by comparison. Only a barrel and plunger with a blunt tip. One always had to have a blade handy to cut an incision through the skin.

"Wherever could the Silver Rose have learned to make this?" Miri murmured. "To fashion a hollow needle and attach it to a basic syringe . . . it—it is so clever and would make it so much easier to—"

"To kill people?" Simon cut in icily.

"No, to administer medicine to some poor creature who was too weak to swallow. Or—or a person even. How quickly and efficiently one could get a healing potion into the blood—"

"That is not what the damned thing is being used for," Simon snapped, snatching the syringe out of her grasp.

"Yes, but—" Miri halted when she saw the dark look on Simon's face. She had to bite down upon her lip to stifle her frustration as he whisked the fascinating instrument from her sight. She longed to have a chance to properly study it. But she could tell that her interest was only irritating Simon and rendering him uneasy. She stifled a deep sigh as he packed the syringe away in his saddlebag.

"All right," she said. "I concede that this mysterious Silver Rose of yours exists and that she is putting her knowledge to terrible use. But I don't know what I can do to help you unmask her. As you can see, I live very much out of the way here. Even if I did pay more heed to what was going on in the wider world, I don't possess enough power and influence among other daughters of the earth to help you track this woman down."

Simon closed the flap on his saddlebag. He avoided looking at Miri as he replied, "No. But the Lady of Faire Isle does."

A tingle of apprehension coursed through Miri. "W-what?"

"Your sister. Ariane." Simon tried to sound casual but the tension in his face told Miri that he understood full well the enormity of what he was about to ask of her. "If you could just send her a message—"

But Miri was already on her feet, too alarmed, too outraged by his request to even speak. All she could do was vehemently shake her head.

"Miri, I am certain that you have to know where she is. You and your sisters were so close. You would never remain out of touch with them for long. What is more, I also know how you communicate. With those birds you have bewitched to carry messages over long distances."

Miri found her voice enough to splutter. "*Trained,* blast you. My pigeons are trained to deliver messages."

"All right, all right." Simon flung up his hands in a placating gesture. "Could you please get word to Ariane with one of these *trained* creatures? I won't make any effort to follow the bird if that is what you are afraid of. I could hardly do so even if I tried.

"I don't even want to know where Ariane is, just to warn her about what is happening. Isn't the Lady of Faire Isle supposed to be a guardian, keeping other wise women from doing harm as well as protecting them?"

"Ariane always tried to do just that. But she is not the Lady anymore, thanks to you. Maybe if you hadn't driven Ariane away from Faire Isle, she would have found out about this Silver Rose and stopped her a long time ago. Did you ever think about that, Simon?"

"Yes, I have. You have no idea how often of late, I have regretted—" He checked himself, dragging one hand wearily through his hair. "But I can't undo the past, Miri. All I can do is try not to repeat it."

Stepping closer, he encircled her wrist, his fingers resting against the delicate skin above her pulse. "I need Ariane's help, her connection with the community of witch—

I mean wise women. No matter where she is, she is still the Lady of Faire Isle. Don't you think she would want to know about this rising menace?"

"I am certain she would and that is exactly why I have no intention of telling her." Miri pulled free of Simon's grasp and shrank back, uncertain which she found more dangerously seductive, his gentle touch or his pleading gaze.

"If Ariane heard of this trouble, she would think it her duty to return to Faire Isle in spite of any risk to herself. And where Ariane goes, Renard would follow. Both of them lured back into any trap you might be setting. You already seem to half-suspect that Ariane might be your Silver Rose."

"I told you that I don't. Your sister is fundamentally a good woman, although I confess I do find some of her skills and knowledge a bit, er, disconcerting. The thing I most fault her for is her choice in husbands. But if Ariane returns, I promise she will be safe from me." Simon added grudgingly, "And Monsieur le Comte, too."

"You'll have to pardon me if I don't believe you. The last time you induced me to trust you, you nearly succeeded in destroying everyone and everything that I love."

Simon opened his mouth to retort, only to close it, a myriad of emotions chasing across his face: sorrow, shame, regret.

"You are perfectly right. I have given you no reason to ever trust me again and every reason to go on hating me."

"And that is exactly the problem. I don't want to hate you, Simon. It hurts too much. I am so afraid that if you betray me again, the next time I might actually be able to use that knife."

She paced away from him, rubbing her arms for comfort. "If the danger was only to me, I might be willing to take a chance on trusting you again. But to put Ariane and Renard at risk . . . I can't do it. I *won't* do it. My answer to your request must be no. So unless you mean to force me to tell you where Ariane is or—"

"I would never do anything like that."

She peered at him over her shoulder, expecting to find him angry or wearing that cold, hardened expression. It was how he would have reacted in the past to her refusal to cooperate. But Simon merely looked defeated, his shoulders slumped like a man who had just seen his last hope burn and crumble to ash.

"I am sorry," Miri said in a softer tone.

"Don't be." Simon's mouth flickered in a sad semblance of a smile. "If anyone should be apologizing it is me. Given our past history, it was unreasonable for me to expect any different reply."

He fetched his jerkin from the line and shrugged back into it. Striding past her to the door, he sank down upon the stool, and reached for his boots.

"What—what are you doing?" Miri faltered.

"You kept your end of our bargain. You listened to what I had to say. Now I am keeping mine." Simon worked his foot back into the damp, mud-spattered leather. "I promised you I would leave you in peace."

That would undoubtedly be the best thing. For both of them. So why then was she beset with this sharp pang? She drifted closer as he struggled with his second boot, resisting a strange urge to snatch it away from him.

"It is still pouring rain and likely to continue for hours.

You look exhausted. I—I have no bed to offer you, but if you would like to stretch out on my hearth and—"

"I don't think that would be a good idea. Far better that I return to the lady who is accustomed to sharing my nights."

"Oh?" Miri was hard-pressed to conceal her dismay. Simon seemed so alone. It had never occurred to her he might have a woman waiting somewhere.

Simon levered himself to his feet with a smile as though he guessed exactly what she was thinking. "I meant Elle. She is the only lady in my life. I am used to bedding down in the stable with her."

"Oh." Miri was annoyed to feel herself blush. It was certainly no concern of hers if Simon had a woman or not. "That—that is good. Not that you have no other lady, but—but Elle . . . she will look out for you, warn you if danger approaches."

"So she has. More times than I can count."

Miri nodded. She and Simon stood only a foot apart, but already the distance seemed to yawn much greater. A long and awkward silence fell. All sounds of the storm had ceased, only the rain continuing to beat at the windows and roof of the cottage.

Strange. Miri had always found the sound of rain soothing, but this time it struck her as rather haunting and melancholy. Perhaps because she was so acutely aware that this might well be the last time she and Simon met. So how did one go about saying good-bye to a man who had once been both cherished friend and hated enemy, first love and lasting heartbreak?

Miri nervously entwined her fingers together. She wondered if she should offer him her hand or merely curtsy when Simon solved her dilemma by doing the last thing she would have expected.

He seized her about the waist and hauled her so hard against him, she emitted a soft gasp. Startled, she looked up at him, his face a dark blur. Before she could protest, his mouth descended upon hers, taking her in an embrace that drove the remaining breath from her body.

It was nothing like the gentle warmth of their first kiss. His beard abraded her skin as he devoured her with his lips, his embrace so fierce, it was as though he sought to claim a part of her very soul to carry away with him.

Miri felt helpless before the onslaught, her hands trapped between them, braced against the unyielding wall of his chest. She could feel the heat of his skin through the damp fabric of his shirt, the wild thunder of his heart. It echoed inside her, her own heart racing as Simon plundered her mouth and stirred her blood with a kiss born of heat and despair, desire and loneliness.

Simon's emotions threatened to engulf her like a dark tide. Miri's mind reeled, uncertain whether she wanted to fight or simply surrender, but once more Simon took the decision out of her hands.

He thrust her away, ending the kiss as abruptly as he'd begun. His chest rising and falling, he stared at her as though seeking to imprint her image upon his mind. Then without another word, he flung open the door and disappeared beneath the curtain of driving rain.

Chapter Four

*T*HE STAIRCASE WOUND UP AND UP INTO THE CLOUDS, THE
*risers twisting and turning at mad angles. Miri trudged step
after step, seeking to avoid trampling the lizards that
darted about her feet. Sleek, slippery, and cold, the salamanders brushed against her ankles. Just as she despaired
of ever reaching the top of the stair, she emerged into a
room laid out like a gigantic chessboard, the black and
white tiles lined with massive chess pieces carved of stone.*

*Miri froze as the black queen raised her scepter. She
bellowed out a guttural command that sent her pawns
marching forward. Miri cowered behind a white rook until
she realized they were not charging at her, but the white
knight astride his marble steed.*

She tried to shriek out a warning but her cry was lost in

the roar of the pawns' attack. Cudgels upraised, they rained blow after blow upon the knight, shattering his mount, reducing him to a broken heap of limbs and armor.

Miri rushed to the knight, horrified to realize it was not a chess piece at all, but a man that lay there broken and bleeding. His black hair fell across his face, obscuring his visage . . .

Miri's eyes flew open. Gasping, she bolted upright from her pillow, dislodging Necromancer, who was curled up on her chest. Oblivious to the cat's offended meow, she kicked aside the coverlet and shot out of bed, straightening so suddenly she nearly banged her head on the low ceiling of the loft.

She reeled with one urgent thought. Simon. She needed to find him and warn him at once. Her heart hammering, Miri scrambled halfway down the ladder before she remembered.

Simon was long gone. How many nights ago had it been—two? Or three since he had vanished into the rain, leaving her plagued with troubled dreams of abandoned babes and sinister women harvesting deadly roses. But of all her nightmares, this last, the attack upon the man had been by far the worst, too much like her old dreams, the ones that had haunted her girlhood, strange and inexplicable portents of things to come.

She climbed the rest of the way down the ladder and clung to the lower rung, trembling. She had thought herself long past the age of her night terrors, something she had offered up thanks to God she had finally outgrown. It had been years since she had had such a dream, so strong and urgent; she still wanted to track Simon down and tell him.

But tell him what exactly? Beware of salamanders? Avoid chessboards? That his life was in danger? That someone was out to destroy him? Scarcely anything that Simon didn't already know.

Sweeping her tangled hair out of her eyes, Miri stumbled out of the cottage, seeking the barrel she always left outside her door to gather the rain. Plunging her hands into the cold water, she splashed it over her face, welcoming its icy sting, hoping to shock away the last vestiges of her tormented sleep. She flung back her head and drew in a lungful of air, trying to breathe in the calm that blanketed the woods this morning.

Dawn . . . her favorite part of the day, when the world was newly washed with dew, the vivid greens of the forest soft and misty in the early morning light. On such a peaceful morn as this, the violent storm that had hurled Simon back into her life seemed like something that had never happened.

All traces of the man were gone, the net she had used to ensnare him removed from the tree, not a single one of his footprints or Elle's tracks remaining. She could almost imagine that Simon's visit had been no more than another dream except . . .

Miri ran her finger ruefully over her lower lip. Except for that kiss Simon had branded upon her mouth, so heated, so ruthless, her lips had been tender for a long time after he'd gone. Her mouth had recovered but her heart still felt bruised by the memory of Simon's fierce embrace.

Blast the man. Why couldn't he have just offered her his hand? Why had he had to seize her and kiss her as though . . . as though the sky was about to fall and the entire world come to an end? His embrace had not been merely the sad parting of a man who thought it unlikely their paths would ever cross again. No, more like the kind of desperate farewell a soldier bestows upon his sweetheart upon the eve of a battle he has no expectation of surviving. Simon didn't expect to live to see her again and he could well be right.

Miri shivered as the images of her dream crept back into her mind, the blows of the cudgels, the dark tide of blood. She wrapped her arms about herself and shook her head in denial. There was no reason to suppose the man in her nightmare had been Simon. She had not even been able to see his face.

There was no doubt that Simon did have many enemies. He had done his best to make himself a feared and hated man, but he had managed to survive this long, hadn't he? If only he hadn't seemed so exhausted and alone.

But that was not what worried Miri the most. It was that shadow she sensed that had fallen over his spirit, making him no longer care whether he lived or died. Her refusal to help him might well have been the final blow, but what else could she have done? She could not put her family at risk by trusting him again, especially when she was not sure how much she believed his stories of this Sisterhood of the Silver Rose. He had offered her no real proof other than that extraordinary syringe he had called a witch blade, but Miri could only reflect wistfully what a boon such an instrument would be to healers everywhere.

It had been far easier to credit Simon's sinister tales on a dark night with the wind and rain lashing at her windows. But in the clear light of day, the notion of a witch's coven hatching some dire conspiracy against mankind seemed utterly fantastic. The bitter truth was Simon had lied and deceived her far too many times.

Miri started when something silky brushed up against her ankles. Glancing down, she saw that Necromancer had followed her from the cottage. He prowled about her legs, rubbing his scent against her. With his uncanny instinct for knowing when she was troubled and the source of it, the cat blinked up at her.

"Forget him."

"I am trying." Miri sighed.

"Try harder."

"Glib advice coming from a feline whose memory extends no further than his last nap, monsieur," she retorted, giving the cat a playful nudge with her bare toes. But as she returned to the cottage to dress and tend to her morning chores, she made a concentrated effort to banish Simon back to the locked chamber of her mind where she had kept him for so long.

Once, such workaday tasks as milking her goat, feeding her pigeons, and currying her pony would have filled her with a simple contentment. But Miri completed her chores in a haze of distraction she could not entirely blame on Simon. She had felt restless and unsettled even before his visit.

Slinging a basket over her arm, she plunged into the forest to replenish the supply of wild roots and berries she used in brewing some of her elixirs. Necromancer prowled ahead of her, darting in and out of bushes, indulging his curiosity over some stray insect or butterfly he spotted.

She padded along after Necromancer, her toughened

soles inured to the bracken beneath her feet. Carefully parting branches that blocked her way, she caressed her fingertips over the rough bark of a stately elm. Once she had been able to feel the thrum of life that pulsed upward from roots buried deep in the earth, the heartbeat of the island itself. Had the ancient magic truly fled? Or had her fingers merely grown too clumsy to sense it?

She still possessed her ability to whisper through the woods, doing nothing to disturb the peace of the wildlife, a small brown squirrel regarding her quizzically from its perch, the cheerful twittering of the birds undisturbed by her presence. Miri often found it strange to think she had learned this silence of movement not from her daughter of the earth mother, but her far more flamboyant father. The Chevalier Louis Cheney was a knight as noted for his ready wit and booming laugh as he was his valor, a welcome figure in court circles. But Miri had known little of the dashing gallant who cut such a swath in Paris. Her childhood memories were forged of the tall handsome man who had been the center of her small world, her chief co-conspirator and playfellow.

During those precious summers that Papa had returned from court to visit their island home, how often had they rambled through the woods hunting for fairies or crouched low in the bushes breathlessly waiting for a glimpse of the unicorn.

"You must be very still, ma petite," he would whisper in her ear, his dark head bent close to hers. "Even such magical creatures develop a powerful thirst from roving about the island. Keep your eyes fixed there upon the

stream and you'll see him steal out from the trees for a drink."

Although Miri had shivered with excitement, she had been unable to refrain from expressing her doubts. "But Papa, neither Ariane nor Gabrielle have ever seen the unicorn. So how will I be able to? I am so much younger and—and littler."

"Ah, but out of all the daughters of the earth on this island, you are the one blessed with the gift for seeing what the rest of us poor mortals cannot. You are a bit of a fairy child yourself, my little Miri."

Miri wondered if her father had any idea of the impact his words had had upon her. Born before her time, she had been a fragile babe, a delicate child, for a long time small for her age. She had always felt so much weaker and less capable than her strong, clever sisters. It filled her small heart with a fierce pride to think there was at least one gift she possessed, one thing that she could do that Ariane and Gabrielle could not.

She could see the unicorn. Or had she merely been under the spell of her father's gift for telling tales, his ability to spin castles in the air with the mere power of his words?

Although Maman had always smiled at Miri's excited descriptions of their adventures in the woods, she knew it had worried her practical mother as well. Once when she had believed Miri out of earshot, she had gently admonished Papa.

"Do you really think it wise to fill Miri's head with so much fantasy, Louis? Between her beloved animals and

her imagination, the child dwells far too much in her own realm. I fear it will make her ill prepared to deal with the real world."

Papa had merely chuckled and replied, "A little fantasy never harmed anyone, my far too serious Lady of Faire Isle. The real world, as you call it, can be a damned unpleasant place. The child will learn that all too soon."

So she had, Miri thought sadly. She had been but nine years old when her father had set sail on his voyage to the new world, promising to fetch her all manner of extravagant presents from mysterious far-off lands.

"You just keep watch for my ship sailing home, petite. I'll be back before you know it. Wait for me . . ."

And wait she did, long after her sisters had given up hope. A part of her still longed for a time and place that could never come again. An enchanted world where fathers didn't perish at sea and mothers did not die young. Where sisters were not torn apart and the handsome boy one loved and trusted did not turn out to be a dangerous adversary.

Her woods were always haunted, but they seemed more so than usual this morning, misted with bittersweet memories. Marie Claire had warned Miri about dwelling too much in the past.

"This island is no longer any place for you. It holds nothing but memories of a time that is gone forever . . . Leave Faire Isle, go back to Bearn and marry that young man who adores you."

Her search for wild roots forgotten, Miri set down her basket. Leaning back against the broad trunk of a tree, she drew forth the locket tucked inside the bodice of her gown, tracing the etching of the wolf gazing longingly up at the moon. Her lips parted in a smile that was half tender, half sad as she thought of her own Wolf, Martin le Loup, with his roguish eyes, trim beard, and sable-colored hair. The last time she had seen him, they had been strolling through the gardens of Navarre's palace, Martin resplendent in his embroidered jerkin, a short cape swirling off one broad shoulder, like a peacock flaunting his feathers before his much more somber peahen. Overcoming her reluctance to accept the locket, he had fastened it about her neck.

"It is not as though it is a betrothal ring, Miri. Only a token of—of friendship, a trinket."

"A very expensive trinket," Miri murmured, nervously *fingering the braided chain, worrying how much of his hard-won coin Martin had spent. "It is pure silver."*

"Ah, but not as silvery as your eyes by moonlight. Now that is real treasure."

Miri cast him a wry glance. Her dear friend could be a notorious flirt, extravagant and honey-tongued with his compliments. Martin's hands lingered about her neck, but at Miri's look, he sighed and drew back.

Miri fumbled with the catch. When she opened the locket and saw the inscription and the timepiece set inside, she was even more dismayed.

"Martin, this—this timepiece was a gift to you from the king himself." A mark of Henry of Navarre's esteem and gratitude for the dangerous mission Martin had undertaken, spying upon the powerful forces of the Catholic League, who threatened the borders of the tiny Huguenot kingdom.

"I can't possibly accept this. If His Majesty were to discover you fashioned his gift into a necklace for me, he might well be offended." But when she tried to take off the locket, Martin closed his hands over hers.

"Navarre of all men would understand. He is a great romantic himself when it comes to wooing the ladies. There is only one difference between us. He has been true to many women, I only ever to one. Besides, for what reason does a knight errant strive to acquire such gifts from a king? Only to lay them at the feet of his lady fair, ever trying to prove his worth."

"You don't have to prove anything to me."

"Oh yes I do. Your knight has many more dragons to slay, many more quests to fill ere he deserves to win your heart, my lovely Lady of the Moon."

Miri smiled ruefully. *"Sometimes I think the knight enjoys his questing as much as the prospect of claiming his lady. Have you ever considered that the day you win her, your adventures would be over?"*

"No, that would be the happiest day of my life," Martin insisted, squeezing her hands. *"But in the meantime, I hope that at least my humble gift will insure you don't forget me."*

"As if I ever could."

"Couldn't you?" he asked wistfully. *"Sometimes I wonder."*

Miri tugged one hand free to touch his cheek. *"And sometimes I think you would be far better off if you forgot about me."*

Martin shook his head, his eyes darkening with a rare expression, tender and serious. *"It would take a mighty*

*spell to make me do that, milady. I have adored you since
the moment I first set eyes upon you. I—I know you have
suffered a great deal of heartbreak, that you don't feel
ready to become any man's bride—"*

"And I may never be," Miri tried to warn him as she
had done so many times before.

"It doesn't matter." Martin brushed a kiss against the
back of her hand. "I will wait for you forever . . ."

Forever. Miri tucked the locket back inside her gown,
feeling that Martin had already waited long enough for her
to emerge from her shadow world of regrets and memories. Despite his overly dramatic expressions, Miri had never
doubted his devotion to her, the truest friend she had ever
had. He loved her and yes, she believed she loved him. Perhaps Marie Claire was right. It was time for Miri to leave
the past behind her, to return to Bearn and bring an end to
Martin's questing. And her own.

"Miaow!"

The urgent cry from her cat roused Miri from her musings. She straightened away from the tree, realizing that
while she had been lost in her thoughts and memories, she
had lost track of Necromancer as well. Her aged cat, accustomed to considering himself a mighty hunter, often disre-
garded the fact that in these woods, he could end up prey
himself.

Glancing anxiously about her, trying to determine the
direction of his yowl, Miri called, "Necromancer?"

To her relief, the cat burst out of the underbrush, appearing unharmed and unpursued. He raced toward Miri
and scratched at her skirts, his thoughts barraging her in a
frantic and chaotic jumble.

"Daughter of the earth . . . must come. It needs your help. An orphan."

Miri frowned. *"Whatever is in trouble, I hope you have had nothing to do with orphaning it. If you have been after some poor titmouse again—"*

Necromancer's amber eyes glowered reproachfully. *"No foolish mouse or wretched rabbit this time. It is one of your kind. A human child."*

A child? Miri gaped at the cat, torn between consternation and disbelief. What would a child be doing out here alone in these woods? Before Miri could question him further, Necromancer streaked off again, urging her to follow.

"Hurry."

Miri ran after him as best she could, moving with none of her usual reverence for the woods, impatiently shoving branches out of her way. At least there was some semblance of a path, for Necromancer was leading her down the track to the stream that cut through a large portion of Faire Isle. Miri frequently made her way there to fill her buckets or wash clothes, sometimes just to stare absently into the sparkling waters as she remembered, grieved, and dreamed.

Necromancer had left her far behind by the time she emerged from the woods and scrambled down the embankment. She spied the cat waiting for her by the flat rock where she was wont to sun herself or lay out petticoats to dry.

Something else occupied the rock this morning, something bundled up in the folds of a brightly colored shawl. Miri came to an abrupt halt, her heart slamming up against her ribs, Simon's words returning to haunt her.

"Human sacrifice. Babes, some scarce hours old, aban-

doned to die of hunger and neglect. So small, so still and cold."

No. Miri could not believe anything so terrible could have happened. At least not here on Faire Isle. Despite her denial, her heart thudded with apprehension as she crept closer. Necromancer prowled nervously about her skirts as she loomed over the rock, but she scarce noticed him, her gaze riveted on the small bundle. So quiet and unmoving.

Miri's mouth went dry. Dreading what she might be about to find, her fingers trembled as she reached down to draw back the folds of the shawl. She choked out an anguished cry at the sight of the small face. The babe looked scarce hours old, some of the fluid that had sheltered it in its mother's womb crusted on the cap of its head.

Miri laid one finger on its small cheek. It was not stiff and cold as she had feared, but warm. The child was still alive. It stirred beneath her touch, emitting a thin cry.

Half-sobbing with relief, Miri bent down to gather the babe up into her arms. The shawl fell back enough to reveal that the child was male. Swathing the garment back snugly about the tiny boy, Miri cradled him close, her voice soothing him in a ragged whisper.

"There now, mon petit. You are safe now, but who could have done such a wicked thing, leaving you here all alone?"

But Miri already knew the answer to that question, recognizing the bright-colored shawl, having seen it recently gracing the shoulders of a defiant young girl heavy with child.

"Oh, Carole, what have you done?" Miri murmured. Or more accurately, what had the girl been persuaded to do?

Miri froze, her breath catching in her throat as she stared down at the object that had been concealed behind the infant, but now sparkled in the sunlight upon the rock. A flower whose petals should have appeared vibrant, velvety, and warm, but instead looked encased in frost, glittering deadly and cold.

A silver rose.

Chapter Five

Miri hastened away from Marie Claire's empty cottage, peering anxiously down the dusty lane. The entire town of Port Corsair seemed eerily deserted this morning. She balanced the infant in a makeshift sling fastened about her neck, fighting down a sensation akin to panic. She had been doing her best to quell her fears, keep her imagination from running riot, ever since she had stumbled across that deadly silver rose and realized Simon had been telling her the truth. The evil he had described was all too real and it had found its way to the shores of her island.

While she had dismissed his warning, the followers of the Silver Rose had already prowled Faire Isle, luring in young Carole Moreau. Miri winced now as she recalled the girl's boast, a remark Miri had paid little heed at the time.

"I have friends, very powerful friends who will look out for me."

No, not friends, Miri reflected grimly. *Witches.* Never in her life had she applied such a vile term to any woman, but she could not think what else to call creatures so depraved that they could prey upon the misery and desperation of a confused young girl, persuade her to do something as dreadful as sacrificing her own child.

Where was Carole now? And what of Simon? When he had left Faire Isle, had he had any inkling his enemies were so close by? Or was it possible he had been taken unaware and—?

Miri's chest tightened and she thrust her fears to the back of her mind. There was nothing she could do about Carole or Simon at the moment. Her immediate concern was the babe clutched in her arms. As near as she could tell the tiny boy had suffered no ill effects from his ordeal, but he needed care that Miri could not provide.

She had to find him a wet nurse and quickly. And she had to locate the child's kin, Carole Moreau's aunt and uncle. For both those things, Miri needed Marie Claire's help. But to Miri's dismay, the older woman was not at her cottage. She forced herself to remain calm, to think where Marie Claire was most likely to have gone.

Much as the former mother abbess had often chafed at the restrictions of the convent life, she missed the old routine of her days, the orderly round of devotions. Miri knew that Marie Claire often slipped off to the church to tell her ave beads and pray. Commanding Willow to stay, she left the pony cropping grass by Marie Claire's gate and dashed off down the lane.

As Miri approached the small stone cruciform structure that was St. Anne's, she sent up a silent prayer that Marie Claire would be there. She paused outside the heavy oak door to adjust the weight of the babe, the knot of the sling starting to chafe the back of Miri's neck.

Miraculously, the child had fallen asleep. Miri only hoped it was a natural one. She had rescued the foundlings of many creatures in the wild, but a human infant seemed disturbingly more fragile, more lacking in any sort of instinct for survival. Cradling the child close to her, Miri shouldered open the door to the church.

The interior of Saint Anne's felt dark and cool after the heat and brightness of the summer's day. Miri squinted as she searched the hollow emptiness of the nave, the main altar appearing solemn and deserted.

But a candle had been lit at the niche where the statue of St. Anne presided with gentle open arms. Someone had prostrated herself before the mother of the blessed virgin. As Miri approached, her heart sank as she realized it was not Marie Claire, but a much thinner woman, her brown hair flecked with gray.

Her thin arms were stretched out rigidly before her, her hands clasped in a posture of supplication. Miri had no difficulty recognizing the gaunt figure of Josephine Alain, even though her head was bowed. Miri started to beat a swift retreat, but the sound alerted Madame Alain to her presence.

Madame Alain's head snapped up. As she scrambled to her feet, Miri tensed, her arms tightening instinctively around the babe, hardly knowing what to expect from a woman who had hated her enough to betray her to a witch-hunter.

Madame Alain went white at the sight of Miri. "Dear God," she rasped. "I thought that—that you might be—be—"

"Captured by that witch-hunter you sent after me?" Miri filled in bluntly. "No, I regret to disappoint you, madame, but Simon Aristide had no interest in arresting me. He is long gone and I am still here."

"Oh!" Madame Alain's hand flew to her mouth. She sank back to her knees, crying, "Oh, thank you, God. Thank you."

Miri blinked. This was hardly the reaction she had been expecting from such an angry, vindictive woman. She crept closer. Tears tracked down Josephine's face as she wrung her hands together. She bore the haggard look of a woman who had not slept for days, dark hollows beneath her eyes. She shrank down as Miri approached, averting her head as though she could not bear to meet her gaze.

"I thought you had b-been taken by that man or you m-might even be dead," Josephine wept. "And I c-couldn't find the courage to tell anyone what I had done until this morning."

Her voice dropped to a broken whisper. "I—I am so ashamed. S-selling another woman out to a w-witch-hunter. Dear heaven, what kind of horrible person have I become? I have been praying to God that I may not burn in hell for it." Her shoulders shook with a suppressed sob. "No w-woman on this island will ever forgive me or s-speak to me again."

Despite all that Josephine had done, Miri was moved by the woman's miserable state. She rested her hand gently on Josephine's shoulder. "Of course, everyone will forgive you. *I* do."

Josephine risked a glance up, torn between wonder and disbelief. "You-you do? I cannot imagine why you s-should. There is nothing I can ever do to make you amends."

"I need no amends, only your friendship. And your help." Miri eased herself down beside Josephine and nudged back the edge of the blanket that had fallen across the infant's face.

Josephine sniffed and mopped the tears from her eyes. "Why—why, it's a babe."

"And a very hungry one, I fear," Miri said. Even in his sleep, the tiny boy sucked earnestly at his fist in a way that tugged at Miri's heart. "I tried to feed him a little goat's milk."

"Goat's milk!" Josephine exclaimed in horror. "That is far too harsh for a babe of this age. Surely he cannot be more than—than—"

"A day old, I think."

"Where on earth is his mother?"

"I don't know. I found him abandoned in the woods." Miri hesitated before adding. "He—he is very likely Carole Moreau's child. I am terribly worried about her, madame. I believe she may have fallen under an evil influence and I can't find Marie Claire either—"

"Then you have not heard?" Josephine interrupted.

The grave look on the other woman's face deepened Miri's sense of dread.

"Heard what? Has something happened to Marie?" she asked sharply.

"No, it's that wretched girl. Carole has gone missing and her aunt is nigh frantic. That is where Marie Claire has gone and much of the town to aid in the search. They are likely looking for you as well since—since I finally confessed what I did." Josephine flushed guiltily. "Did you see none of them on the road as you came into town?"

"I did not take the most direct way. I looped round behind the woods on the longer, but easier path, because of the child." Miri flinched, imagining what a jolt it must have been for Marie Claire to hear about Simon's visit to her cottage from someone else, how worried her friend must be.

"I have to find Marie at once," she said. "But what of Carole? Does no one have the least idea of where she has gone?"

"The only report comes from Sebastian, a fisherman who lives in a hut the other side of Luna Cove. But the old man spends more time in his cups than he does at his nets, so his word is not always reliable."

"What did he say?" Miri asked anxiously.

"He tells some wild tale of seeing Carole with two women, strangers to the island. One an elf and the other a veritable giantess." Josephine paused to roll her eyes. "Carole appeared to be terrified and she was crying, at least according to Sebastian. But as I said, most of the time the old man drinks himself half-blind."

Josephine touched the babe's cheek, her work-worn hand surprisingly gentle. "And you think this is Carole's son? No one even knew she had given birth. Her aunt and uncle meant to adopt the infant if it was a boy, give her a permanent home as well. This child would have been her salvation. Why would Carole just abandon him?"

Miri had not yet decided how much to reveal about the existence of the Silver Rose. She had no wish to raise more alarm among the women of Faire Isle, at least not until she had consulted Marie Claire.

"I don't know exactly how Carole came to abandon her child or go off with these strangers," she hedged. "Perhaps she was desperate, seeking the kindness and compassion she failed to find on Faire Isle."

"That rebuke is meant for me, I suppose."

"It applies to me as well. I made little more effort to reach out to Carole than anyone else did. But right now we must decide what is to be done with her little boy."

As Miri shifted the child in her arms, the babe stirred and began to cry. Josephine held out her hands diffidently, "May I?"

Miri eased the child out of the sling and handed him off a little awkwardly. Josephine drew the babe close, shushing and rocking him with a tenderness Miri would never have imagined the woman capable of. She envied the easy confidence with which Josephine handled the fragile infant, the experience of a woman who'd had six babes of her own.

Holding the child to her shoulder, Josephine rose to her feet, nodding to herself and saying, "Helene Crecy."

Miri followed suit, also rising. "I beg your pardon?"

"Helene had a child herself six months ago. She'll help with this wee one. The woman has breasts the size of melons, enough milk to feed an army of infants." Josephine's lips quirked. Her thin face still held a trace of her former prettiness when she allowed herself to smile. She strode back through the nave, making crooning noises to comfort the whimpering babe. Miri hastened after her. The woman paused at the church door long enough to glance back at Miri.

"I didn't keep the money that dreadful man gave me. I donated it to the church and, well—I—I wanted you to know that."

"Thank you," Miri began, but Josephine had already vanished out the door.

༈༈

MIRI PACED the confines of Marie Claire's cottage while the older woman carefully pulled back the ends of the linen towel Miri had wrapped around the poisonous rose. Its frosty petals glittered against the snowy white cloth as Marie Claire studied the strange flower through the lenses of her copper-framed spectacles.

She looked exhausted from the fright she had had regarding Miri's safety and from helping in the fruitless search for Carole Moreau. The girl was nowhere to be found. She and her mysterious companions, whoever they were, had vanished from the island, along with old Sebastian's battered fishing dinghy.

Carole appeared terrified and she was crying . . . that was what Sebastian had said. However the girl had first felt about these new friends of hers, Miri did not believe that Carole had departed with them willingly.

A chill swept through her despite the warmth of the

day. She wrapped her arms about herself, arms that felt strangely empty since she had surrendered Carole's child to the care of Josephine Alain. Miri felt a trifle guilty about that, as though by being left in her woods, the babe had somehow been entrusted to her. But she could do no better for the infant than turn him over to more capable hands.

When the other women had trudged home from the search for Carole, all exhaustion, all tension and enmity melted away at the sight of the helpless babe. Madame Crecy of the enormous breasts had immediately put the babe to suck while her neighbors crowded about cooing, offering up all manner of advice. Many of them were the same women who had joined with Josephine in persecuting Carole only days ago.

Perhaps like Josephine, they were stricken with remorse. Perhaps it was the innocence of the babe that had softened them. Or perhaps it was possible the gentler, kinder spirit that had once pervaded Faire Isle was not as dead as Miri believed. Grateful as Miri had been to witness it, she had felt shut outside that magic circle surrounding the babe. But it had been her own mind that had distanced her, carrying her far from the island to the man she had banished from her doorstep.

She had but to close her eyes and she could still see Simon's harrowed face as he vanished into the storm. And she had just let him go, determined to be willfully blind to the threat he had described. If she had paid more heed to what he had said, paid more heed to anything in the world outside her own snug cottage, could she have detected the evil that had invaded her shores and saved Carole from it?

Simon had been battling the forces of this Silver Rose

alone for months. Those witches had already tried to kill him several times. For all Miri knew, they might have succeeded by now. She was tormented by disturbing memories of her recent dream, her vision of the broken knight. The nightmare had been disjointed and vague, the face of the man unknown. It was only when the symbols in her prophetic dreams became crystal clear that they ran the danger of becoming true. Miri tried to draw some comfort from that thought.

A muttered exclamation from Marie Claire drew Miri's attention back to her friend.

"I'll be hanged if I ever saw the like of this cursed thing before," Marie Claire said, shoving back from the table. Although she had taken great care not to touch the flower, she crossed over to the ewer and basin and vigorously washed her hands.

Miri glanced down at the sparkling rose, which showed no signs of wilting. "It is so unnatural," she agreed. "This rose had to have been cut down a long time ago and transported a great distance. Yet the petals are not in the least dried or brown. Is it really possible for anyone to grow flowers that never fade or die?"

Marie Claire toweled her hands dry. "No, I think this was no more than an ordinary white rose. It is the dusting of this poison that acts as some sort of preservative."

"A truly strong and deadly poison if it can be absorbed through the skin."

"Not unlike the concoctions our dear Catherine has been known to use when handing out charming gifts like poisoned gloves."

Miri would have almost found it a relief to think

Catherine de Medici was behind all this. At least she was a known enemy, but Miri was obliged to demur. "No, Simon is certain that the Dark Queen is not involved."

Marie Claire peered over the rims of her spectacles, frowning at Miri. Miri blushed a little, realizing how intimately Simon's name had tripped from her tongue.

"I mean Monsieur Aristide," she amended. "Le Balafre."

She retreated to the open window, hoping the faint breeze from the garden would help cool the telltale fire of her cheeks. She had recounted for Marie Claire the details of Simon's visit, at least most of them. She had omitted that searing kiss he had planted upon her in parting.

Marie Claire joined her at the window. "I heard the rumors of Aristide's brief visit to Faire Isle. You are so adept at hiding in your woods, I foolishly allowed myself to believe he had come and gone without crossing your path. It never occurred to me you would seek to confront that dangerous man on your own. I should have known better." She sighed. "I won't pretend I am not hurt by the way you lied to me, choosing to keep me in the dark."

"I am sorry—" Miri began, but Marie Claire forestalled her with a wave of her hand.

"I understand you were only trying to protect me, but you were the one who most needed protecting."

"I already told you, Simon made not the slightest move to hurt me. In fact, it was quite the other way around and we should both be grateful that he came. If he hadn't, we would have no idea what had happened to Carole or know anything about the threat of the Silver Rose."

"True enough," Marie Claire conceded. "Although I am ashamed to admit, I was happier in my ignorance." She stripped off her spectacles, rubbing the bridge of her nose. "I hoped I would never have to deal with anything like this again in my lifetime. It was bad enough those days when we had Melusine running amok. You are far too young to remember. You weren't even born then."

"I have heard the tales," Miri said. "Not a great deal from Renard. My brother-in-law has always been reluctant to discuss his infamous grandmother. But the old apothecary Madame Jehan used to take a wicked delight in thrilling all the island children with accounts of Melusine's terrible exploits, how she poisoned crops and cursed livestock. I used to have nightmares about little lambs and colts foaming at the mouth and dropping down dead in the meadows."

Marie Claire grimaced. "Adelaide Jehan was a good old soul, but she was incorrigible when it came to spinning her wild yarns, and Melusine certainly gave her plenty of fodder. Renard's grandmother fomented rebellion among the peasants of Brittany, aiding them with her knowledge of the dark arts. She believed she was fighting for justice, freeing the downtrodden from the oppression of their masters. All she did was lead a great many innocent people to their death and blacken the reputation of wise women everywhere."

Marie Claire's eyes welled with sadness. "We are already a dying breed, the daughters of the earth. There are so few of us left to study the ancient wisdom, keep it alive for the next generation. Soon the only ones left with the courage to practice the old ways will be those who distort it for evil like this Silver Rose. If Monsieur Aristide is right and this madwoman truly is attempting to raise an army of witches, may God help us all."

Her shoulders slumped as though the full weight of her years were bearing down upon her, but she rallied, saying, "Well, the creature must be found and stopped. I can think of only one thing to do."

"What is that, Marie?" Miri asked.

But Marie Claire seemed to be talking to herself as much as Miri. When she strode purposefully toward her cupboard, Miri trailed after her. There amongst the old woman's crockery and books reposed a small wooden chest. As Marie Claire lifted it down, her wolf birds set up an excited squawking, fluttering about their cage as though they had anticipated what the old woman was about to do.

Marie Claire flung open the lid, revealing a store of writing materials, quills, ink, and parchment. As she reached for one of the quills, she said, "We need to send word to the Lady of Faire Isle immediately, apprise Ariane of these events."

"No," Miri cried.

"I don't like it any better than you do, my dear, but—"

"No, Marie," Miri said even more forcefully. "You know as well as I that Ariane and Renard would rush back to France, putting both their lives in danger."

"Ah!" Marie Claire arched one fine brow. "So despite the fact that you risked meeting with Monsieur Aristide alone, you don't trust this witch-hunter of yours."

Miri colored hotly. "He is not my witch-hunter. And . . . and no, I don't entirely trust Simon, at least not where Renard is concerned. But remember, my sister and her husband have other enemies, the Dark Queen and the king of France."

Marie Claire stroked the feathered tip of the quill through her fingers, her brow knit in a deep frown. "Then what about Gabrielle? She is alarmingly adept at intrigue, and she managed to hold her own in the court of the Dark Queen for over two years—"

But once more Miri shook her head. "Gabrielle has a husband and three little daughters to protect. Although their farm near Pau has remained safe thus far, they have always run the risk of being invaded by the Catholic League's army. Navarre has taken the brunt of these endless civil wars plaguing France. Gabrielle already has more than enough to contend with."

"But someone has got to deal with this Silver Rose," Marie Claire protested. "And unfortunately I have neither the power nor the vigor of youth that I once did. So who in heaven's name would you recommend we turn to?"

Miri plucked the quill from Marie Claire's grasp and returned it to the chest. "I am afraid there is only me," she said quietly.

"*You?*" Marie Claire's startled exclamation and doubtful look were hardly flattering, but no worse than the doubts Miri entertained about herself.

She smiled sadly. "I realize I am only a pale reflection of my sisters."

"I—I have never thought that," Marie Claire faltered. "But—but—"

"I am the last wise woman you would ever send to confront an evil sorceress," Miri finished wryly. "The foolish dreamer, always hiding in her woods. Maman worried that

I dwelt too much amongst my animals and the realms of my imagination, never facing up to the hardship and problems afflicting the rest of the world. She was right."

She bit down on her lip to still its quiver. "Maman would—would have expected better of me. I have not the wisdom of the Lady of Faire Isle, or anything like Gabrielle's fiery courage. But I am also a daughter of Evangeline Cheney. It is time that I remembered that and behaved in a way that would make her proud of me."

Marie Claire cupped Miri's face between her hands. "Oh, my dear, your mother would have been very proud of you. You are every bit as wise and brave as your older sisters. But I knew Evangeline well. Your mother was my closest friend, and I can tell you with dead certainty she would never have expected you to charge off to face some demented sorceress alone."

"I wouldn't be alone." Miri took a deep breath before confessing, "I intend to find Simon Aristide, seek his help."

Marie Claire's hands fell away from Miri, her jaw dropping open in dismay. "Have you completely lost your wits, Miribelle Cheney? To even think of venturing anywhere near that dangerous man—"

"You said only the other day that you didn't think Simon would ever hurt me."

"Not intentionally, no. While I concede Aristide has some good in him, he also has more shadows lurking in his heart than a graveyard at midnight."

"That might be true, and yet, Simon seems so different from the man who raided our island that summer."

When Marie Claire pursed her lips skeptically, Miri went on. "He is no longer as arrogant and inflexible as he used to be. You didn't see him on the night he turned up on my doorstep out of the storm, so wearied and defeated. It is rather ironic, isn't it?"

She gave a mirthless laugh. "When I finally succeeded in steeling myself against him, Simon was telling the truth and really did need help. And I just sent him away, possibly to—to die."

"That man's fate is not your responsibility," Marie Claire said sternly. "After all he has done, you owe him nothing."

"I know that, but Simon may well be our only hope for defeating this Silver Rose and rescuing Carole from her clutches."

"What on earth makes you think the girl wants to be rescued?"

"I don't believe Carole truly wanted to harm her child. The babe was wrapped in her favorite shawl, her most treasured possession, and she left him where I would be certain to find him. I never perceived any evil in the girl, only deep hurt and confusion. However she became involved with this coven, I don't think she understood what she was getting into until it was too late."

"You may well be right. Yet however sorry I might feel for Carole, I don't see why you should put yourself at risk to save her."

"Because I should have tried harder to reach out to that girl when I had the chance."

"And so should I and every other woman on this island," Marie Claire replied impatiently. "But even you must admit Carole was not the easiest girl to befriend."

"No, she wasn't." Miri smiled ruefully as she recalled

the girl's bristling defiance, more thorny than the roses that blossomed on the bushes outside Marie Claire's window. But just like those fragrant blossoms, Carole's thorns were a poor shield for her vulnerability.

Miri's smile faded. "If Carole had been a wounded fox or badger and snapped at me, I would never have backed off. But I let her drive me away, back to my little cottage, and forgot all about her. I have to find a way to save her and I am going to need Simon's help."

"But for a respectable daughter of the earth to get into bed with a witch-hunter. It simply isn't done, my dear child."

"Great heavens, Marie! I—I am only talking about a temporary alliance. I never thought of anything like—" *Bedding with Simon . . .* Miri's cheeks heated at the images that flashed through her mind.

"I was only speaking metaphorically. However, if it comes to that—"

"It won't. I assure you any warmer feelings I had for Simon died a long time ago."

When Marie Claire cast her a sharp look, Miri busied herself with carefully folding the linen cloth back over the poisonous rose. "My sisters are in exile. The council of wise women has long been disbanded. What other choice do I have besides to make use of Monsieur Aristide?"

"Just take care he doesn't end up using you, my girl," Marie Claire warned grimly. "And what about your Martin le Loup? What would he think of you roving about the countryside, pursuing this dangerous quest, putting yourself at risk? By what you have told me, the man is completely devoted to you, intrepid, resourceful, and skilled at intrigue to boot. Why not send for him?"

"Because there is no time, Marie, and I would not have the least idea how to reach Martin anyway. He—he is likely off on some reckless adventure of his own, another mission for the king of Navarre."

Miri's hand strayed to the locket hidden beneath her gown and she experienced a stab of guilt. Truth be told, she had scarce given Martin a single thought since this morning, when she had resolved to leave Faire Isle and marry him. But this morning seemed a lifetime ago and Martin felt very far away. Miri was ashamed of feeling glad of that fact.

Martin could be a trifle . . . volatile and impulsive. As passionately as he adored Miri, he had always loathed Simon with an equal measure of jealous detestation. The last thing Miri needed or wanted would be to have the two men crossing swords.

"Martin would hate what I am about to do," Miri admitted reluctantly. "Sometimes I think if the man had his way, he would keep me in a velvet-lined room, safe and protected while he fought all my battles for me. I hope that in time I can teach Martin what Renard has become wise enough to understand about Ariane. That a wise woman cannot always remain tamely by her own hearthside, no matter how much she might wish to do so."

And God help her, Miri did very much wish it. She drifted back to the window lest Marie Claire see, despite all her bold words, how far from calm and resolved Miri felt. She stared wistfully out at the garden, drinking in the bold mix of colors and textures, cabbages and marigolds, wild fennel, lavender and asters. But most of all the lush red roses, beautiful even in their imperfections of fallen petals and overladen stems. So different from that sterile rose enfolded in the linen cloth.

Beyond the garden was the dusty lane, leading back to the deep comforting shadows of her woods. Or on down to the harbor, the rocky causeway that stretched to the mainland and the uncertain future beyond.

Miri sighed, wondering who she was attempting to fool, Marie Claire or herself. The mere prospect of flinging harsh words at someone was enough to tie her stomach in knots. How did she ever imagine she would be able to destroy some unknown sorceress? And it could very well come to that. Unless the Silver Rose destroyed her first.

She was afraid of battling this Silver Rose, even more afraid of the consequences should she fail. And then there was Simon Aristide. Miri didn't know if she was afraid she would not be able to find him, or more afraid that she would. No matter how vehemently she insisted her feelings for him were dead, she knew that she risked arousing that dark attraction that pulsed between them, desires that would be a betrayal of Martin, of her entire family, all that she stood for and was . . . a daughter of the earth.

When Marie Claire stepped up beside her, Miri stiffened, anticipating that the woman meant to assail her with more arguments. But Marie Claire folded her hands, looking worn down and resigned.

"Very well, if you are determined upon this course, I am coming with you."

Miri was deeply touched by the offer, but she shook her head gently. "No, Marie."

Marie Claire bridled. "What? You are willing to consult a witch-hunter, but you are dismissing my help? You think me too old and useless?"

"What I think is that you have never been a good horsewoman and I am going to have to ride fast and hard, cover a lot of ground quickly to have any hope of catching up to Simon."

Marie Claire folded her arms stubbornly, but she apparently recognized the truth of Miri's argument because she grimaced.

"Besides," Miri went on. "You are needed here to keep watch over Faire Isle lest any of the Silver Rose's followers turn up here again. You can also aid me in other ways. I know you still have some contacts on the mainland. I can never make this journey on Willow. I need to find a swift horse with a great deal of stamina and you must tell me where I can find other wise women I can trust to help me on my way, offer me safe shelter for the night. I also have to find someone to look after my place while I am gone and there is one other task only a wise woman like you can manage."

Marie Claire eyed Miri warily as though she suspected Miri of trying to cozen her. "Humph! And just what might that be?"

"Necromancer." Miri smiled ruefully. "You must prevent my very wily, but ancient cat from trying to follow me."

❦❦❦

THREE DAYS LATER, the island was still unsettled by the disappearance of Carole Moreau and the equally mysterious departure of the Lady of the Wood. There was more visiting between cottages and traffic amongst the shops in Port Corsair than there had been in years. Women neglected their workaday tasks, gathering in small knots along the lane, to gossip, to exclaim, and to speculate. The only one who might know the full truth behind recent events was Marie Claire. But the former mother abbess kept more to herself than usual, spending increasing amounts of time at St. Anne's, praying for Miri's safe return.

On the third day after Miri's departure, Marie Claire knelt to perform a more earthbound task. Wincing at the stiffness in her joints and the state of her garden, she eased down onto her knees to attack the army of weeds that threatened to overrun her herb beds.

It was a soft morning, a light breeze tickling the strands of hair that escaped from beneath her linen cap. Sparrows twittered amongst the branches of her apple tree, the leaves making a pleasant rustling sound. Marie Claire might have found a momentary balm for her worries, had not the peace of the day been disrupted by the sounds emanating from her cottage. Even from here, she could hear the plaintive yowls of the cat caged in her kitchen.

"I hear you, my friend," Marie Claire murmured wearily. "But I can't let you out. I promised her."

She grimaced, realizing that over the past few days, she had begun to talk to that cat as much as Miri, although she was not able to understand Necromancer as well. And that, Marie Claire decided, was a very good thing, because she was convinced that at times, that little black devil was actually swearing at her, hissing bitter reproaches at her for ever letting Miri go.

Marie Claire paused in her weeding to brush some strands of hair out of her eyes with the back of her hand. Not that she hadn't heaped the same reproaches upon herself, she thought. But short of trying to cage Miri instead of the cat, Marie Claire had seen no way of stopping her. None of Evangeline's daughters had ever been tractable women. The Cheney sisters had inherited a full measure of their mother's stubborn strength.

Despite all her gentleness, Miri had an inner core of adamantine and this was not the first time Marie Claire had struck up against it. Years ago, Miri had done something very similar, run off alone to Paris, impelled by concern for her sister Gabrielle. That journey had been perilous enough, but not one tenth as dangerous as this one.

Before Miri had left, she had obliged Marie Claire again to promise she would not write to Ariane and tell her of her younger sister's doings. Never had she been so tempted to break a pledge. Not only was she terrified of the dangers Miri would face in confronting this unknown Silver Rose, but Marie Claire was just as troubled by the idea of Miri being alone with Simon Aristide.

"He has changed, Marie."

Did Miri have any notion how much her eyes softened when she said that, when she even pronounced the witch-hunter's name? How she blushed even as she insisted she harbored no tender feelings toward Aristide? Who was it that Miri was really rushing off to save from the Silver Rose, Carole Moreau or Simon Aristide? Marie Claire doubted that even Miri knew the answer to that question and that was what truly worried her. No matter what gentler feelings Aristide harbored for Miri, the man was far too much at war with the darker side of his own soul ever to be relied upon.

At least a dozen times each day, Marie Claire had reached for her quill, determined to write to Ariane. If Marie Claire maintained her silence and God forbid, anything happened to Miri, how could Marie Claire ever face Ariane again? And yet . . . how could she draw one dear friend into peril to insure the life of the other?

Besides, it would take time for her message to reach Ariane, even more precious time for the Lady of Faire Isle and her husband to return to France. By the time Ariane and Renard were able to go after Miri, it might already be far too late.

Marie Claire issued a tremulous sigh. Never had she felt so infernally old and useless. Glancing down at her hands, she realized that in her abstraction, she was pulling up clumps of rosemary along with the weeds. She bent back to her weeding, trying to keep her attention focused on her task when she was startled by a distant shout.

She glanced up to see a small figure come hurtling down the lane. Shading her eyes and squinting, Marie Claire recognized Helene Crecy's six-year-old daughter, Violette. Skirts flapping about her bare ankles, the girl ran, bellowing for her mother at the top of her lungs.

"Dear God in heaven, now what?" Marie Claire muttered, her chest tightening in apprehension. Pressing her hand to the small of her back, she struggled to her feet just as Madame Crecy burst out of her cottage, the Moreau infant clutched in her arms.

As she hurried out onto the lane to intercept her daughter, she was hard followed by Madame Alain and her own brood of children, Josephine's face pinched with alarm.

"Maman! Maman!"

As Violette skidded to a halt in front of the women, Helene balanced the babe against her shoulder and bent down to the little girl. Marie Claire could not hear Helene's anxious inquiries, but Violette's piping reply carried clearly.

"The prince has come to Faire Isle." The child shrieked and danced in her excitement. "Like the stories you tell me, Maman. You know, the handsome prince who kisses the poor girl and saves her from the witch's spell and then they live happily ever after. Well, the prince is *here* and maybe he'll kiss you. Only I expect Papa would not like that."

Helene straightened, giving vent to a relieved laugh. Marie Claire pressed her hand to her chest, overwhelmed with relief herself, not certain her heart could have taken the arrival of any more dire news or trouble. Even Josephine essayed a dry laugh, although she could not resist scolding Helene. Marie Claire caught snippets of something about *"unwise to be filling the girl's head with such nonsense."*

"It is not nonsense," Violette cried, stomping her small foot with indignation. "Look, here he comes."

She pointed one chubby finger at an approaching rider. As the man drew closer and Marie Claire was able to discern his figure more clearly, she thought the child could well be forgiven for mistaking him for a fairy-tale prince. Seldom had such a dashing gallant been seen on the shores of Faire Isle. Even from this distance, he gave the impression of being a handsome man, his deep brown hair smoothed back beneath a black velvet cap sporting a white plume. A short green cloak with a rose silk lining hung off one broad shoulder, his doublet and venetians appearing of as fine quality as his brown leather riding boots.

All along the lane, women peered out windows or hung over garden fences to gawk as the stranger trotted past, his sleek dapple-gray stallion moving with a jaunty step as his master smiled and nodded. It was as though the horse was as well aware as the man of what a swath they were cutting through town and both were mightily enjoying it.

Marie Claire wiped her hands on her apron, realizing that she was gaping as much as everyone else, but could not seem to help herself. She drifted closer to her garden gate, as the stranger reined to a halt not far from Helene Crecy, whose mouth was hanging open.

As he bent forward in the saddle, murmuring some greeting, Helene was all but knocked aside by Josephine's eldest daughter, Lysette, a buxom fourteen-year-old. Blushing and giggling, the girl sidled up to the stranger, but before they had a chance to exchange more than a few words, Josephine pounced like a mother tigress.

Roughly hauling her daughter back, Josephine stepped forward. Some low, brief conversation took place between her and the stranger. As hard as Marie Claire strained, she could not catch a word of it.

The stranger straightened in the saddle, looking considerably taken aback. As Josephine continued her harangue, he cast a disgruntled glance down the lane. His entire face seemed to light up. Ignoring Josephine, he smiled and bowed to the other women, then gigged his horse into motion.

Marie Claire scarce had time to realize he was heading

straight to her cottage until he was at her gate. Vaulting from his horse in one graceful, fluid motion, he looped the reins around a fence post. She saw that her first impression of him had been correct. He *was* handsome, the sharp angles of his face tamed somewhat by a neatly trimmed mustache and beard. But that was by far the only tame thing about him.

He had a rogue's eyes and a rogue's smile, the kind that would make most women lock up their daughters and then be unable to resist his charm themselves. Even Marie Claire was discomposed at the way her heart fluttered as he came through her gate.

She was further disconcerted when he dropped to one knee before her. Capturing one of her hands, he carried it reverently to his lips.

"Reverend Mother," he murmured.

"I beg your pardon, monsieur. But I am not— That is I am no longer—" Good Lord, Marie Claire thought in disgust. Was she actually blushing and stammering?

"To me you will always be Mother Abbess." He peered up at her through the thickness of his lashes, flashing her that devastating smile. "I could hardly have the sauce to call you Marie Claire."

"I believe you would have the sauce enough for anything, my son," Marie Claire said, finally coming to her senses. She drew her hand away, saying sternly. "Never mind about my name. I think you had best be telling me yours and right quickly."

He looked stunned for a moment, then sprang to his feet crying, "What! Never tell me you don't know me."

When Marie Claire regarded him in confusion, he

pressed his fingers to his chest. "Madame, surely you cannot have forgotten. It is me, Martin le Loup. Captain Nicholas Remy's friend, Mademoiselle Miri's devoted slave, and your most humble servant."

He doffed his cap, his cape swirling as he swept her a graceful bow. He smiled at her hopefully while Marie Claire blinked, feeling completely stupefied.

Martin le Loup? It couldn't be. She stared at him, racking the features of this tall, strapping man for some sign of the rangy youth who had trailed so worshipfully after Miri that long-ago summer, those last days of peace on Faire Isle before Aristide and his witch-hunters had descended.

Marie Claire thought she could scarce be blamed for not recognizing Martin. He had grown, changed like a fledgling duck transforming into a mighty-winged swan. But as she studied him, she caught a spark in the deep-set green eyes, a hint of mischief about the lips that put her in mind of the boy she'd once known.

"My heavens! Wolf. It—it is you." She pressed her hand to her mouth. Then she fell upon him with a glad cry.

Martin returned her embrace with rib-cracking enthusiasm, hefting her off her feet with an exuberance that left her giddy. She thumped his back saying, "There now, you rogue. That will do. Put me down at once.

"What a disrespectful way to treat an old woman," she complained, but she was laughing as Martin grinned at her and set her back on her feet. Her cap had gone askew. As she straightened, she noticed her neighbors watching with popping eyes. If Josephine craned her neck any harder, the woman was going to fall flat on her face.

Marie Claire laughed again and realized she had not

done so for days. After all the worry and tension, it felt mighty good. She beamed up at Martin.

"Oh my dear Wolf. I cannot tell you how glad I am to see you."

"And I you, Reverend Mother. Faire Isle is not a large place, nothing like Paris. A man could practically stuff this entire island in his purse and yet I had begun to despair of ever finding you or Miri. People here have always been a little stiff with strangers, but I vow they are worse than ever. Do you know what yon shrew said to me when I but made civil inquiry?" Martin gestured in Josephine's direction.

"She said I might as well save my breath, because no decent woman on the island would have aught to say to such a shifty-eyed varlet. Mon dieu!" He flung up his hands. "I have been accused of being many things by the ladies. A shocking flirt, a flattering rogue, too devilishly handsome for my own good. But I ask you. *Shifty-eyed?*"

His indignation might have amused Marie Claire under other circumstances, but she had sobered at the mention of Miri's name, knowing what she had to tell Martin, dreading it.

"Wolf, about Miri—" she began.

"And just where do I find my lovely Lady of the Moon?" Martin peered eagerly past her as though expecting Miri might emerge from the cottage at any moment. "If I know anything of her, I suppose she has taken up residence in some little hut somewhere, living among the squirrels, rabbits, and bears."

"We don't have bears on Faire Isle, but yes, she has a cottage far out in the woods—"

"Ah, I feared as much." He fetched a long-suffering sigh. "Well I hope to put an end to that."

"Wolf . . ." Marie Claire tried again, but he cut her off, smiling and pressing her shoulder.

"Wait until Miri sees what I have for her. The loveliest length of blue wool that I purchased when I was recently in England. If it were up to me, I would see my lady draped in nothing but the finest silks and brocades. But I thought this is more what Miri would prefer. What think you?"

"I am sure she will like it but—"

"Oh, I will admit when it comes to cuisine, the English leave much to be desired. As for that swill they call ale . . . pah!" Martin rolled his eyes. "But those people certainly know how to weave a good wool. This fabric is so fine, so soft, a woman might even be tempted to use it for her wedding—"

"Martin!" Marie Claire spoke up more forcibly. The sharpness of her tone seemed to get through to him at last.

Looking considerably crestfallen, he said, "I can guess what you are thinking. That I have no business to be talking of weddings where Miri is concerned and you are right. I am completely unworthy of her. I am a fool to even hope—"

"No, Martin." Marie Claire finally pressed her hand to his mouth to silence him. She gazed sadly up at him, her eyes filling with unexpected tears. "You are no fool, but what you might well be is the answer to an old woman's prayers."

He stared at her for a long moment, a frown creasing his brow. He caught hold of her hand, squeezing it.

"What is it, Reverend Mother? What is wrong?" he

asked gently and then in a sharper tone. "Is it Miri? Has something happened to her?"

Marie Claire stole a glance down the lane, realized they still had an interested audience and it was getting larger. Tugging Martin toward the cottage she said, "I have something of a very grave nature to tell you. But I think we had better go inside."

ﯓﯓﯓ

As she finished recounting the recent events that had shaken Faire Isle, Marie Claire inched her chair back, keeping well out of the way of the man who prowled her cottage, muttering fierce invectives. Even Necromancer crouched beneath the table as Martin paced and ranted, venting his anger, fear, and frustration.

"Damnation, how could Miri—? How could you let her—" He started to growl at Marie Claire, only to check himself. "No, I am sorry, Reverend Mother. There is only one person to blame for this situation—that God-cursed Aristide."

Martin flung his cap down and kicked a stool out of his path. When it crashed against the table leg, Necromancer bolted, seeking cover behind a basket on the hearth.

"How dare he!" Martin fumed. "After all that bastard has done, how dare he come seeking help from Miri? He calls himself a witch-hunter, but I swear he is more of a sorcerer, bewitching my lady, luring her to follow him into danger."

"To be entirely fair, I don't believe Monsieur Aristide lured her anywhere. It was Miri's own choice."

"Then why didn't she choose me? Christ's blood, she ought to know by now I'd do anything for her, fight a thousand witches if she asked me to. But no! She goes off in search of *him*." Martin dragged both hands back through his hair. "How many times will she let that villain betray her, break her heart before she is no longer willing to trust him? I thought she had finally grown past all that . . . past all thought of him."

His emotion spent, Martin finally stopped pacing and sank down upon the stool, dangling his hands despondently between his knees. Marie Claire's heart ached for him. In that moment, he seemed to dwindle, more resembling the boy he had been that summer he had trailed after Miri, performing any antic he could think of to get her to notice him, to coax her to smile, to laugh, to forget Simon Aristide.

Marie Claire shuffled to her feet and gently rested her hand on his shoulder. "Miri only went after Aristide because she believed there was no one else to turn to, to defeat the Silver Rose. If Miri had had any idea where you were, she would have sent for you instead."

Martin angled a doubtful look up at her. "Would she?"

"I am sure of it," Marie Claire said, silently begging God's pardon for lying because she was sure of no such thing.

Martin reached up to press Marie Claire's hand. Then he struck his thigh and rose briskly to his feet, saying. "Well, I am here now. I am sorry for raging about your cottage and bellowing like a wounded boar. The only thing that is of any importance is Miri's safety. How long has she been gone?"

"She left three days ago."

"Three days! Mon dieu," Martin exclaimed in dismay. "That gives her a considerable start. She could be anywhere by now."

"Well, I did receive word from a friend of mine, last evening. A wise woman from Saint-Malo. Miri arrived that far in safety and Hortense sent three of her servants to accompany Miri until she finds Aristide."

"Well, thank God for that much." Bending down to retrieve his cap, he brushed a speck of dirt from the crown. "At least that gives me someplace to start searching for my lady. With any luck, I will be able to overtake Miri before she joins up with that villain and fetch her back home."

"I don't believe Miri will allow you to do that. She is determined to rescue the Moreau girl and put a stop to the evil practices of the Silver Rose."

Martin shrugged, smoothing out the feather of his cap. "Oh, I'll take care of that."

Marie Claire might have been tempted to laugh at the man's nonchalant air. But for all his swagger and elegant apparel, she had noticed other things about Martin as well. His hands were not those of a courtier, but callused and tough like a man accustomed to wielding a rapier and handling the reins of a spirited stallion. The weapon strapped to his side was no showy blade, but a length of serviceable steel.

From what Miri had told her, Martin le Loup was not unacquainted with danger, having undertaken many secretive and perilous missions for the king of Navarre. But Marie Claire still felt the necessity to warn him.

"Martin, you do realize that going up against this Silver Rose will not be as simple as fighting off a troop of enemy soldiers or even a pack of ruthless bandits. This woman is a—a genuine witch."

"I understand that." His mouth tightened, a strange shadow seeming to pass across his features. He murmured, "But I have had to deal with a witch before. Yes, by God I have."

"That is right. I had forgotten. You were with Captain Remy that time when he tried to wrest the king of Navarre free of the Dark Queen."

Martin seemed to snap back from whatever dark remembrance of the past haunted him. "Er—yes, the Dark Queen."

Marie Claire ruefully shook her head. "I am afraid I place little faith in Aristide's opinion that the queen has had no hand in this affair. In my experience, if there is any dark mischief brewing, Catherine is bound to be involved somehow. I have been so worried—"

"Well, don't be." Martin strode toward her and gathered both of her hands within his own. "If she is, I will deal with that, too."

The man's confidence was as infectious as his smile. Despite all the fears pressing down upon her heart, Marie Claire found herself smiling back at him.

"I promise you, Reverend Mother, on my very life. I will keep Miri from harm, guard against the Dark Queen, and vanquish this Silver Rose. Then I will do something that I should have done years ago."

"And what is that, my dear?"

Martin's teeth flashed in a smile that was as wolfish as the glint in his eyes. "Why, I intend to kill that bastard of a witch-hunter."

Marie Claire's smile crumpled in dismay. "Oh, no, Martin. I don't think Miri would—"

But her protest was lost as Martin kissed her cheek and strode to fling open the door. Necromancer crept after him. Marie Claire leapt forward, barely managing to prevent the cat's escape. She scooped him up in her arms. Necromancer had never presumed to scratch her, but she felt the light prick of his claws through the fabric of her gown.

As she struggled with the cat, she tried to call out to Martin, but he was already astride his horse. Necromancer glared up at her and for once Marie Claire was able to discern his thoughts with startling clarity.

"What have you set into motion now, you silly old woman?"

"Bless me, I don't know," Marie Claire murmured. Gathering Necromancer closer, she sagged against the door jamb, watching Martin le Loup vanish down the lane.

Chapter Six

THE QUEEN MOTHER REPRESSED A SHUDDER AS SHE DEscended into the bowels of the Bastille, escorted by a contingent of guards and the governor of the prison. The walls were dank and moist as though the stones themselves had been tortured until they bled. The aspect was more cheerless seen through the black webbing of her veil, the dungeon thick with a gloom the blazing torches could not dispel, the air befouled with the stench of fear and pain.

But Catherine de Medici thought she could have taught the unfortunates immured in this place something about the endurance of pain. Each step she took was a torment, muscles and joints throbbing from another bout of sciatica, her ankles and hands swollen.

She was feeling every one of her sixty-six years this

morning, but she had learned a long time ago that a queen could not afford to display any infirmity. There were too many rivals for power ready to descend upon one like a pack of jackals at the first sign of weakness. Too many ene- mies, and she appeared to have acquired one more.

She thought of the remnants of the flower locked away in the cabinet in her bedchamber at the Louvre. The rose's strange silvery luster had finally begun to fade, its velvety petals now ashen in hue. But the flower had already ac- complished its deadly task.

Yesterday, Catherine had alighted from her carriage to attend the wedding mass of one of her courtiers at Notre Dame. The area outside the great cathedral was thronged with onlookers waiting for a glimpse of the bride and groom. A young woman had darted out of the crowd, try- ing to shove past the Swiss guards to offer Catherine a flower.

That in itself had been unusual enough to draw Cather- ine's attention. The mood in the city these days was so tense, so black with discontent, Parisians were far more likely to hurl rotted vegetables or mud clots at her than roses. And it had been such an extraordinary-looking rose, so icy white, it had appeared silvery. There was something odd about the girl too, far too fresh-scrubbed, pretty, and clean for a Paris street vendor, her slender hands encased in gloves.

Although the young guardsman had done his duty and kept the girl back, he had been won over by the petite blonde's pleading smile. Accepting the gift from the girl with a smart bow, the guard had broken ranks to fetch the flower to the queen. Some inexplicable instinct had prevented Catherine from touching it. She had wrapped the unusual rose in her handkerchief instead. As the flower vendor had prepared to disappear, the back of Catherine's neck prickled, her sense of unease deepening. She had commanded the guard to go after the girl and . . . not arrest her precisely. Merely detain her for questioning regarding the horticulture of her extraordinary flower.

And a mighty good thing she had done so because that same guard now lay dying in agony. Catherine might be able to save the young man if she tried, but not without revealing she knew a great deal too much about poisons and their antidotes.

Too many already suspected her of practicing witchcraft, but no one had ever dared charge her openly. She was not about to risk exposing her unique skills merely to save the life of a young guard, foolishly entranced by a pretty face.

The queen's escort drew to a halt outside the thick wooden door to one of the cells. As the jailer fumbled with his key, the governor turned to Catherine to make one last appeal to her. Monsieur de Varney had been appalled from the beginning by the notion of conducting a queen down into the worst passages of the fortress. A thin, nervous man, his enormous white ruff made him appear as though his head, with its peppery-gray beard, was being presented to Catherine upon a charger.

"Your Grace, I beg you to reconsider. There is no need for you to distress yourself further in this matter."

No need to distress herself? Catherine reflected grimly.

Oh, no, only the fact that there was someone lurking out there who wanted her dead and whose skill in poisons rivaled her own.

"This creature has confessed to her part in this infamous assassination plot," the governor continued. "It will only be a matter of time before she gives up the names of her confederates and—."

"Open the door, de Varney," Catherine cut him off softly. "And let me see her. Has the girl identified herself?"

"She says her name is Lucie Paillard. She claims to be the daughter of an innkeeper from a village in the Loire Valley."

"This innkeeper's daughter is a long way from home."

"She may be lying. We'll soon have the truth from her. These cellars are loathsome, plagued with vermin and disease. No place for a lady, let alone a queen. If Your Grace would just return to my quarters and—"

"The door, de Varney," Catherine commanded. *"Now."*

The governor vented a long-suffering sigh. He gestured toward the jailer to unlock the door. It creaked open, revealing a small, narrow cell, even more fetid than the outer hall. As the jailer lit Catherine's way inside, she pressed a scented handkerchief to her nose beneath her veil.

De Varney hovered behind Catherine. She took one look at the prisoner and understood why the governor was so nervous. Manacled to the wall, Lucie Paillard hung unconscious from her chains, no longer fresh-scrubbed, no longer clean, no longer pretty. Clad only in her shift, her white limbs were bruised and swollen from being racked, her legs burned raw from being scalded with boiling oil, the blisters on her skin beginning to fester.

"You cursed fool," Catherine hissed at de Varney. "You've killed her."

"N-no, Your Grace," the governor made haste to exclaim. "Torquet," he snapped at the guard. "Bring her round."

The guard complied by dashing a bucket of brackish water in the girl's face. When Lucie only tossed her head and moaned, he thrust a flask between her lips and forced some sort of cheap spirits down her throat.

As the girl choked and retched, Catherine stepped back in disgust, deploring these crude measures. None of this barbarity would have been necessary if her eyes were what they once had been. Catherine could have gained all the information she required from the girl with one piercing look. She had mastered the wise woman's art of reading the eyes with a skill that few had ever equaled. But like so much of the rest of her body, her vision had begun to fail her as well.

When Lucie finally roused, her eyes fluttering open, Catherine curtly ordered the guard to stand back. As she moved closer to the prisoner, the girl's head lolled to one side. She studied Catherine with pain-glazed eyes as the queen drew back her veil.

"Well, do you know me, Mistress Paillard?"

A spark of recognition flashed in those dull eyes. Lucie's dry, cracked lips stretched in a semblance of a smile.

"De Medici," she rasped. "Florentine shopkeeper's daughter."

Catherine heard the governor's sharp indrawn breath, but she remained unruffled. It was an epithet that had been hurled at her ever since she had first set foot in this country, the haughty French never considering a woman descended from Italian merchant princes good enough for their young king, despite the impressive dowry she brought.

Long inured to the insult, Catherine displayed no reaction until the girl added hoarsely, "Sorceress . . . Dark Queen . . . my enemy."

Catherine tensed. She ordered the guard and de Varney to retire from the cell. The governor made a faint effort to protest, but was silenced by a cold look from Catherine. At least her eyes still held that much power, she thought with satisfaction.

As soon as the men had retreated, Catherine cupped the girl's chin. Forcing Lucie's head up, Catherine probed her eyes, concentrating with all her will. But it was like trying to penetrate the surface of some murky stream. Catherine squinted until her own eyes watered and she was obliged to give up the attempt in frustration.

Forcing herself to speak to the girl in gentle accents, Catherine said, "How am I your enemy, child? I may well be your only friend. You have done a foolish thing by participating in this plot against my life. But I could be merciful if you tell me what I want to know. I alone have the power to save you—"

Catherine broke off in astonishment. Weak as she was, Lucie managed to pull free of her grasp and shake her head.

"No. You have . . . no power. Not like my mistress, my Silver Rose."

"And who might she be?"

"The one . . . who will destroy you." Lucie moistened her lips, barely able to whisper. Catherine had to lean closer in order to hear her.

"The revolution is coming. Silver Rose . . . will have your kingdom one day."

"Indeed," Catherine replied dryly. "And how does she propose to do that? Conquer France by barraging my armies with poisoned flowers?"

"She has more than . . . the roses. She has the—the *Book*."

"Book? What book?" Catherine asked sharply.

Lucie's breathing grew labored, her eyes filming over. Catherine gave her a brisk shake.

"What book?" she demanded more fiercely.

Lucie's mouth worked silently. Before her head slumped forward, she managed to whisper.

"Book . . . of Shadows."

✸✸✸

CATHERINE SLUMPED against the squabs of her carriage, seeking a more comfortable position for her aching joints as she was jostled back to the Louvre. Despite the stifling heat of the day, she had drawn the curtains across the windows, the glint of the sun unbearable, aggravating the stabbing pain behind her eyes. Another one of her cursed headaches brought on by more vexation.

And the Lord knows she already had enough of it. As her carriage lumbered through the streets, Catherine was keenly aware that the thin walls of the coach and an escort of Swiss guards were all that separated her from the malcontented populace. Like much of the rest of the country, Paris teemed with misery and unrest.

It had been an ill-fated spring, floods followed by

drought that ruined crops and decimated cattle. Food was scarce, prices were high, bellies were empty, and tempers were short. The civil war between Huguenots and Catholics that had plagued the country for the past two decades continued unabated, a constant drain upon the royal coffers.

Of course, she was blamed for it all, Catherine reflected bitterly, massaging the bridge of her nose. What had the latest round of scurrilous pamphlets being circulated around Paris called her? *"A serpent born of tainted parents in the charnel house of Italy . . . the most infamous she-devil ever to hold royal power."*

The fools didn't seem to realize that whatever stability France had known these past years was entirely owing to her efforts. Certainly not to her son, his most royal majesty, Henry III, by grace of God, king of France.

When Henry wasn't amusing himself in wild revels with other painted fops, he indulged in fits of religious zeal that involved lengthy retreats and flagellation. While he wasted time, prostrate on his knees before some marble statue, his kingdom was on the verge of disaster, his crown threatened by the rising power of his nobles, especially one in particular, the duc de Guise.

The duke had but to appear within the gates of the city for these wretched Parisians to rush after his horse crying, *"À Guise, à Guise."* Like he was the second coming of the Christ, their great Catholic hero, Catherine thought scornfully. Handsome, bold, and arrogant, the duke used piety as a thin mask for his ambitions, which reached as far as the throne itself.

As if all of that were not enough to plague her, she had this new threat to worry about, this—this Silver Rose, whoever the devil she was. But Catherine would learn nothing more from young Mistress Paillard.

The girl was dead, thanks to de Varney and his oafish warders. The governor had sweated and babbled excuses. Lucie Paillard must not have been as strong as she looked. Perhaps the girl had a weak heart or—or—

Catherine had silenced de Varney with a cold look. The plain truth was de Varney and his minions lacked finesse in the arts of torture. And now the Paillard girl had slipped into the dark arms of death, taking the rest of her secrets with her.

No wonder Catherine's head felt ready to split in twain. She had not even had the strength to properly rebuke de Varney for being so inept. Hobbling up from the dungeons, her one thought had been to escape before the governor or any of his minions realized how shaken she was. That there were words that could strike fear even into the heart of a Dark Queen.

"My Silver Rose will destroy you. She has the Book of Shadows.*"*

Could that wretched girl have possibly known what she was talking about or was it merely the ravings of someone tortured to the brink of madness? The *Book of Shadows* was the stuff of legends among daughters of the earth. Rumored to be a compendium of ancient knowledge long lost to the world, it contained magic of the most dangerous and wondrous kind. Descriptions of how to fashion weaponry that could decimate populations or destroy entire cities, potions and methods to keep one young, preserve life until one became all but immortal.

Many called the book a fable, but Catherine knew better. She had come so close to obtaining it once, or so she had believed. She closed her eyes, her mind drifting back to that summer night ten years ago when she had awaited the return of her spy from the Charters Inn, where the witch-hunter Le Balafre and his men were quartered in Paris.

A trade was supposed to take place between the Comte de Renard and Simon Aristide, a bargain made to save the life of Gabrielle Cheney. Catherine had little doubt it would prove to be some kind of trap. She knew what an arrogant and ruthless bastard young Aristide was and grudgingly admired him for it. Dealing with Le Balafre's treachery was a problem for the Lady of Faire Isle and her family. Catherine was only interested in the object of the trade, the mysterious book that the Comte had somehow managed to acquire.

As Catherine had paced her apartments, alarming reports reached her that something had gone terribly wrong at the Charters Inn. There had been a battle or some sort of an explosion. No one seemed able to tell her exactly what, only that the building had caught fire and likely would burn to the ground. As yet, there were no reports of any casualties, but the witch-hunter's prisoners had escaped and Monsieur Le Balafre was definitely still alive.

Catherine paid scant attention to those details. She had only wanted to know one thing . . . Where the devil was Bartolomy Verducci? She only prayed the old fool had not gotten himself blown to bits on the most important mission she'd ever given him—the acquisition of the *Book of Shadows*.

She had begun to consider the rash action of venturing forth to make some inquiries herself when one of her ladies-in-waiting brought her the welcome intelligence of the signor's return. When Verducci staggered into her antechamber, his breeches and jerkin were ashen with soot. His eyebrows had been singed off, likewise the ends of his beard. His head was wrapped in a thick bloodstained bandage that prevented him from donning his cap.

At any other occasion, Catherine would have rebuked him for appearing before her in such a state, but she wasted no time on pointless preliminaries, not even asking where he had been all this while.

"Well, sirrah, have you succeeded in your mission? Did you acquire it?" she had demanded anxiously.

Verducci held up a pouch that he attempted to present to her, but the scrawny little man collapsed at her feet. Catherine had snatched up the pouch, barely able to suppress her cry of triumph as she drew out the worn leather book. Her euphoria had lasted no more than the fleeting second it took her to crack open the cover. What she had held clutched so tightly in her hands was no *Book of Shadows.* Only a Huguenot Bible.

Catherine braced herself against the sway of the carriage, remembering the depth of her anger and disappointment. She had been sick with rage, nearly forgetting the regal bearing that had been drilled into her since childhood. She had wanted to throttle Verducci with her bare hands, only one thing staying her. The man was already at death's door and he held the only clue to what had gone wrong.

When she had nursed him back to consciousness, the signor had been devastated when he had learned of his failure. He had wept like a mewling infant.

"F-forgive me, Your Grace. But I did acquire the Book, *I swear it. In the chaos after the explosion, I managed to seize it all, the* Book, *the twin medallions, the r-ring you gave Mademoiselle Cheney. E-everything . . ."*

Catherine could not have cared less about the ring. She had no idea what medallions Verducci was nattering on about. All she had wanted to know was what had happened to the *Book of Shadows.*

Her powers had been so much stronger then. She had forced Verducci to lie still while she had pierced his gaze with her own, seeking to probe his memory. But it was like stumbling through the ash and debris of a cottage leveled by cannon fire. The old man's wits were permanently addled by the injuries he had sustained to his head.

The best Catherine could retrieve was a blurred memory of Verducci staggering away from the blazing inn, the pouch containing the precious book clutched to his chest. Blood trickled down his brow, his eyes streaming from the acrid sting of smoke, his throat raw and parched. And then there was someone, a woman, Catherine thought, but the person's face and form were lost in the haze of Verducci's damaged memory.

All he recollected were hands bandaging his head, a soothing voice urging him to drink from a flask. And then nothing more until he managed to drag himself up into the saddle for the long journey to Blois.

But it had taken no great mental leap on Catherine's part to fill in the gaps in Verducci's memory. The old fool had allowed himself to be drugged and robbed. At the time Catherine had believed one of the Cheney sisters to be responsible, Gabrielle most likely.

The young woman always had been too clever for her own good and it would be like Gabrielle's impertinence to mock Catherine by substituting a Bible for the *Book of Shadows*. Or perhaps there had never been any *Book of Shadows*. Perhaps it had all been a ruse concocted by the Comte de Renard to save his sister-in-law. Perhaps like so many foolish daughters of the earth before her, Catherine had merely been chasing a myth.

She had heard nothing more of the book in all these years. At least not until this morning, when Lucie Paillard had whispered her dying words in Catherine's ear.

Catherine rubbed her pounding temples. Was it possible that she had been wrong about the Cheneys, that on that long-ago night there had been another watching and waiting in the shadows, a sorceress who had outwitted them all and walked off with the prize?

Despite the heat, Catherine shivered, her blood chilled by the thought of that powerful book in the hands of some sorceress as skilled and ruthless as herself. That would make Mistress Paillard's talk of a coming revolution more than the ravings of a feverish girl. This Silver Rose might well prove a greater danger to Catherine's power than all the famine, floods, civil war, and ambitious nobles put together. But if the unknown sorceress had possessed the *Book of Shadows* all these years, why had she waited until now to make use of it? The book was said to be complex, written in an ancient tongue, not easily deciphered.

Perhaps thus far all the witch had learned from it was

how to grow poisoned roses. Or perhaps this woman didn't have the book at all. Only one thing was certain. All this useless speculation did nothing but exacerbate the pain in Catherine's head.

She had to get to the crux of this new threat and do it quickly. This Silver Rose needed to be unmasked and destroyed. But how? Any clue to the woman's identity had died with that wretched girl. Catherine might have despaired except for one thing.

This was not the first time she had heard tell of the Silver Rose.

✺✺✺

CATHERINE LONGED TO SINK down upon her bed, command her ladies-in-waiting to fetch possets and cooling cloths for her head. But she had no time to waste upon such self-indulgence. Dismissing all her attendants, she hobbled toward the magnificently carved cabinet of Italian design that she kept in her study. The small key that opened it dangled from her chatelaine.

Catherine's fingers were so swollen, her knuckles so stiff, she had difficulty working the key in the lock. Softly cursing her inability to perform such a simple task, she gritted her teeth until the lock sprang at last and the doors swung open. Upon the lower shelf resided a small chest in which Catherine kept a sheaf of private correspondence.

Pawing awkwardly through the contents, she dug until she found what she was looking for, a thin stack of dispatches sent by Simon Aristide that Catherine had bound together with a black ribbon.

The reports had not been sent to Catherine, but to her son. Years ago Henry had engaged Simon Aristide and his mercenary troop of witch-hunters to launch a crusade, Henry announcing a pious intent to rid France of all sorcery. Of course Catherine had known what Henry was really doing, using Le Balafre in an attempt to intimidate her, warn her off from meddling in affairs of state. Just another aspect of the game waged between her and her son, a private tussle for power.

A game that the king had eventually grown bored with, as he did with much else. The troop of witch-hunters had disbanded, the notorious Le Balafre falling from royal favor much to Catherine's relief.

Simon Aristide was intelligent, ruthless, and incorruptible, a dangerous combination in any man, let alone a witch-hunter. She was glad when Aristide had faded into obscurity. Little had been heard from the man until these dispatches had begun to arrive about a year ago. Reports that Henry had ignored, not even bothering to break the seal.

Catherine had read and saved them more out of curiosity than anything else. It was always good to know what one's enemy was about . . . But now, she slid off the black ribbon and perused the dispatches with new interest.

The pain in her head caused her vision to blur. She had to grind her fingertips against her eyes, holding the parchment almost at arm's length to be able to focus. Fortunately, the witch-hunter wrote in a large, bold, and blunt hand. The first report contained nothing particularly alarming, only Aristide's growing concern over a new coven.

"The initiation into this coven appears to involve a rite

of the most heinous kind, the sacrifice of newborn babes, healthy male infants . . ."

When Catherine had first read this report, she had dismissed it as the actions of a few demented women, although she had to admit, it had given her a sharp pang. Such a stupid, senseless waste, destroying a healthy boy. She compressed her lips, thinking what such a child could mean.

If her son ever managed to produce an heir, it would do much to quiet the rumblings against him, secure the future of his throne. But when Henry bedded a woman at all, it was seldom his own wife, and the act of coupling so exhausted the king, he was obliged to take to his bed for days afterward.

"What kind of Frenchman is this?" That was what many of his scornful subjects had been overheard to whisper about him. *"No proper Frenchman at all, but more a devious Italian like his mother."*

Small wonder that more and more of the Catholics were turning their hopes to the virile duc de Guise, while the Huguenots gave their support to a lustier Henry, the king of Navarre.

Catherine sighed, wondering what she had ever done to be plagued with such weak sons. She should have had nothing to worry about. She had given birth to four male children who had survived to adulthood. But she had already outlived three of them.

If Henry were to die young as well, without leaving an heir, what would become of her? Another nagging worry that Catherine shoved to the back of her mind as she perused the next few reports. Aristide's dispatches to the king grew more urgent with each writing.

". . . and I implore Your Grace to take some action in the matter and aid me in my investigations. The ranks of this coven are swelling, their power growing. These witches range about the countryside, leaving death and havoc in their wake wherever they go. What their ultimate aim is, I do not know. But I finally have a name for their leader. She calls herself the Silver Rose and waxes increasingly bolder about announcing her presence."

Catherine squinted at the rest of the lines on the page, but they contained little more than another plea for the king to turn his attention to the problem. It was the last report Aristide had sent and it was dated over six months ago.

Had Aristide finally despaired of seeking the king's assistance or had the witch-hunter given up his pursuit altogether? No, that was unlikely, Catherine thought as she carefully bundled up the dispatches, wincing at the twinges of pain in her hands. Aristide was a true hunter, shrewd and relentless.

Catherine had recognized those qualities in Le Balafre when he was a mere boy, apprenticed to the witch-hunter Vachel Le Vis. Unlike his master, Simon was not easily fooled. Catherine had made use of Le Vis in her battles with the wise women of Faire Isle. Le Vis had never suspected that the queen might also be a sorceress until it was too late, but young Simon had. More than suspected, the boy had known. And the clever, perceptive lad had grown up to become a formidable man. He had already accomplished what Catherine had begun to think no man ever could, vanquishing the wise women of Faire Isle, forcing the Lady herself into exile.

Yes, a truly dangerous man and one Catherine would as soon keep at a healthy distance. But the advent of this Silver Rose left the queen little choice. Stepping to the door of her study, she sent one of the pages to summon Ambroise Gautier, the most trustworthy and reliable member of her private guard.

"Find Simon Aristide and fetch that accursed witch-hunter to me," she commanded. Lest there be any mistakes about what she desired, she added softly,

"Alive."

Chapter Seven

SIMON HUNKERED DOWN, PULLING WEEDS AWAY FROM THE stone he'd left to mark the grave. He paused to wipe away a trickle of sweat that threatened to seep beneath his eye patch. The sun inched below the horizon as though reluctant to yield its power over the scorched land. The air was heavy and unmoving, even here at the crest of this hill in the Loire Valley. The countryside that stretched out below him should have been lush and green, but bore the scars of the drought, the meadow grass dry as straw, the leaves in the vineyard wilted.

But it was not the heat of the day that had bothered Simon so much as the brightness of it. The sun had blazed without mercy, or perhaps it only seemed that way to him because he was unused to it. He feared that he had become a creature of darkness as much as the women he hunted.

He had traveled many weary miles during the fortnight since he'd journeyed to Faire Isle to find Miri Cheney. A completely futile journey, but he didn't blame Miri for that, for refusing to help him. He could hardly have expected any different answer, given their history, yet the depth of his disappointment had surprised him.

Still, he had kept his promise, ridden away and left her in peace. No doubt she was glad to see the back of him, especially after the ruthless way he had dragged her into his arms and kissed her. What devil had possessed him? He'd been stewing over that question for days and still had no satisfactory answer.

Perhaps it was merely because he'd gone without a woman for so long or that he'd been feeling tired, lonely, frustrated. Or because the path beyond her cottage had been dark and storm-ridden, and she was all that was warmth, all that was light and gentleness. Whatever madness had seized him, it was over and done with. He'd never see Miri again. The thought brought a heaviness to his heart that was stupid. They had been parted for years. But at least there had always been the possibility that—

No, he was a damned fool. There had never been any possibilities between him and Miri. A witch-hunter and a woman bred amongst witches. He needed to forget her, figure out what the blazes he was going to do next.

But as he doggedly stripped the weeds away from the grave, never had his wits felt so dull and leaden. He couldn't seem to form any sort of coherent thought let alone a plan of action. Since his trip to Faire Isle, he had lost the trail of the Silver Rose and her agents of darkness.

Of course, all he had to do was wait and no doubt the witches would find him. He was surprised they hadn't already. Perhaps the Silver Rose still didn't know her last assassin had failed. As soon as she did, it would only be a matter of time before she sent someone else to kill him. But he couldn't summon the energy to care about watching his own back or continuing to track this she-devil.

All Simon's urgent dispatches to the king about the Silver Rose and her coven had met with no response. Miri had only half-believed him. Simon wondered why he persisted in grinding himself into the dust trying to battle this evil alone when no one else noticed or cared.

The answer to that rested at his fingertips. Simon brushed aside the dirt that had accumulated on the grave marker and traced the single word he had carved in the stone, the letters a little crooked and crude.

Luc.

Simon compressed his lips at the memory of the infant who had been the first of the Silver Rose's victims. Or at least the first that he knew of. He had found the infant not far from this spot on a frigid winter night over a year ago. At a time when the rest of the world was celebrating the memory of another male child born in a stable.

Luc had not even known that much comfort or the warmth of a mother's touch. His mother had left him exposed on a barren hillside to freeze to death. Simon had heard tell that freezing was not such a terrible way to die, that one slipped into a state of false warmth as one's limbs went numb. He wondered if it had been that way for Luc.

A hard lump formed in Simon's throat that both embarrassed and annoyed him. He'd seen so much of death and cruelty, the brutal murder of other innocents just as helpless as this babe had been. He had thought himself completely toughened, immune to any feelings of compassion.

He had no idea why he had been so moved by Luc's death or those of the other abandoned babes he'd found. But he had grieved over each of them as though they had been his own sons, the children he might have had.

The children he *should* have had if his life had unfolded like that of his grandfather and his great-grandfather before him. A good, simple existence lived out in a small village, a tidy cottage, an honest day's toil in the fields, a loving wife to cheer him, strong sons and daughters to be a comfort in his old age.

Simon felt bemused by how damned sentimental he was becoming. It was a sign of the years creeping by, he supposed, this tendency to look back, not forward. But it was not as though he had anything much to look forward to, only the dark cold of a grave, one not even marked as well as Luc's.

Simon regarded the marker he'd carved pensively, recalling what his old master Le Vis had taught him of the fate of unshriven babes like Luc. Condemned to an existence in limbo, forever denied the joys of heaven.

Simon wasn't sure how much he believed that or anything else anymore. It had been a long time since he'd set foot in a church, longer still since he'd truly prayed. He felt cursed awkward, his fingers wooden as he made the sign of the cross. As he folded his hands, he was not even certain which lost soul he was praying for, the babe's or his own. He fumbled for words that didn't come, his thoughts as heavy and earthbound as the rock that marked Luc's grave.

The dried grass whispered behind him. As he knelt, his head bowed, he felt a hand come to rest on his shoulder.

"Simon . . ." The voice was as soft as the touch, but Simon's heart slammed against his ribs.

He leapt up and spun around, seizing the wrist of the person who had crept up on his blind side. He had his knife unsheathed and started to raise it when his captive cried out.

"No, Simon. Don't!"

Simon froze, all movement, even his breath suspended as he stared in disbelief.

"It—it's me, Miri," she faltered, trying to shrink away from the blade he held aloft.

Simon expelled a long breath, slowly lowering his weapon as her words registered. Her reassurance was unnecessary once he was able to make out her form, squinting at her past the last blaze of brilliance from a dying sun.

He would have recognized Miri anywhere despite the fact that she was garbed in loose peasant breeches and tunic. Her long fall of white-blond hair was braided tightly, wound about her head. She'd had it tucked beneath a wide-brimmed felt hat that had fallen off when he'd grabbed her. Or maybe she had been carrying the hat when she had stolen up behind him so silently.

He might have believed she truly was some sort of fairy, the Lady of the Wood who could materialize at will, a spirit born on the winds of his imagination. Except that the throb of her pulse beneath his fingers felt warm and human, her soft skin definitely that of a woman, delicate flesh, blood, and bone. A woman he had never thought to see again.

He didn't realize how hard he was gripping her until she murmured, "Simon, please, you are hurting me."

He released her and sheathed his knife. Finding his voice at last, he demanded hoarsely, "Miri, what—what the devil are you doing here?"

She rubbed her reddened wrist, looking remarkably calm and dignified for a woman who'd just been threatened with a foot-long hunting blade. Instead of answering his question, she stepped past Simon to peer down at the grave marker.

"Who is Luc?"

"It is the name of an apostle."

Miri tipped her head, leveling at him one of those clear, piercing looks. "I don't think it is any apostle buried in that grave, Simon."

Simon was annoyed to feel himself flush, embarrassed that Miri should have found him here, caught him in such a foolish, vulnerable moment.

"It—it is just the grave of one of those abandoned infants I told you about," he muttered.

"Why is he buried up here alone? So far from the village?"

Simon's jaw knotted. "Because the damned priest would not let Luc be laid to rest in hallowed ground. A bastard, never baptized, and the son of a girl believed to have consorted with the devil to boot. I had no choice but to bring his body up here and—"

"*You* buried him?" Miri interrupted, her eyes wide.

Simon felt his flush deepen. "No one else would. Even his own grandparents feared to touch him. So what the hell was I supposed to do? Leave his corpse lying about for wild animals to drag off and devour?"

"No, of course not." Miri rested her hand on his sleeve. "You did right by him, Simon. The earth is his mother. No matter how cold, how cruel the world above, she would welcome Luc back into her gentle embrace."

Simon had always been disquieted by some of Miri's more pagan notions. She seemed to sense this because she said, "I am sorry. Have I offended your Catholic sensibilities?"

"No." Actually the image that Miri painted was oddly comforting, the idea that instead of shoving Luc into cold, unfeeling ground, he had returned him to a mother's arms. Certainly the earth was a better mother than the one he'd had.

Simon surprised himself by confessing, "I am not much of a Catholic anymore. I haven't attended mass in years."

"And yet you chose to name this little boy after an apostle."

"I thought it might help if he was named for one of the saints. Maybe it would gain him some sort of concession or pardon, if the laws of heaven really are that harsh." Simon shuffled his boots, feeling incredibly foolish for explaining all this. "As you can probably tell from what I call my horse, I'm not good at coming up with names."

"You did very well." She smiled at him although she continued to search his face with that look of hers he always found so uncomfortable. As though looking for something in him that Simon was damned certain wasn't there.

He found it easier to direct his gaze to the hand that still rested on his arm. He was dismayed to see that the red imprint left by his fingers had not faded. Covering her hand with his own, he massaged her wrist, experiencing a mad urge to carry it to his lips, try to kiss the bruise away. And an even more insane urge to draw her into his arms, hold her close, taste her mouth just to be certain she truly was real and not some dream born of heat and exhaustion.

He released her hand, taking a wary step back from her.

"You still haven't answered my question," he said. "What are you doing here?"

"Looking for you." Miri bent down to retrieve the hat she had lost. "You came to Faire Isle seeking help, didn't you? And now I need yours." She lowered her gaze, fingering the brim of her hat, a slight tremor in her voice as she added, "You see, I—I found a Luc of my own."

Simon inhaled sharply. He recalled too vividly his own shock when he had stumbled across those scenes of infant sacrifice, pulled back the edge of the blanket to gaze at those small wizened faces. But to think of such a horror visited upon Miri's gentle spirit. She was the kind of woman capable of absorbing another's pain with but a look and bearing the wound of it thereafter.

Forgetting the wisdom of keeping his distance, Simon closed the space between them, cupping his hands about her upper arms. "Miri . . ."

"It's all right," she said quickly, looking up at him, attempting to smile. "I mean, *he's* going to be all right . . . I hope. The babe I found was more fortunate than Luc. This one was still alive. I took him to Port Corsair to—to a kindly woman who was able to nurse him.

"Unlike you, I didn't think to give the little boy a name. I was just so—so stunned by it all." She pursed her mouth tightly for a moment before continuing. "I am sorry that I didn't entirely believe all the things you told me that night. I am not so naïve that I don't know that such ignorance exists, that there are those cruel enough to sacrifice a small, helpless babe. I just never expected to find such wickedness on my island. Not my Faire Isle."

Simon squeezed her arms gently, resisting the urge to draw her closer, cradle her against him. How often in the past had he been exasperated with Miri, frustrated by her stubborn refusal to recognize the existence of evil, especially among those she called wise women? Gazing down at her pale face, the bruised look in her eyes, he wished he could spare her this hurt, urge her to forget. But the witch-hunter in him needed her to remember, to give him all the details she could.

"Tell me what happened," he commanded. "Tell me everything."

※※※

MIRI TRUDGED down the hill beside Simon, winding her way down the rows of a small vineyard. It was the time of year when there should have been laborers busy, trimming and binding the vines. But perhaps the owner of this field had already despaired of this year's crop because the hill-side was deserted. The small farmhouse appeared equally sullen and silent in the heat. A mastiff dozing in the yard lifted its head as Simon and Miri passed, but could only summon enough energy to emit a half-hearted woof.

Miri's voice was so low Simon had to stoop to hear her as she relived that terrible moment when she'd found the abandoned child and believed him dead. She hesitated only when she revealed whose babe it was, the identity of the proud and truculent girl who had left Faire Isle, either enticed or forced to join the coven of the Silver Rose.

Perhaps Miri should have questioned the wisdom of speaking so freely, offering up Carole Moreau's name to a witch-hunter. She had promised both Marie Claire and herself that she would be cautious with Simon. Ally with him to defeat the Silver Rose, yes, but hold him at as much distance as possible.

Unfortunately, her resolve had weakened from the moment she had found him kneeling at the grave of a child only he had cared enough to name or bury. Looking so vulnerable as he had quietly grieved, fumbling to remember his prayers.

He had been harsh in his dismissal of what he had done for this unknown child, trying to behave as if it were nothing. And yet she suspected that he had also performed this same tender rite for all those other abandoned babes he'd found, although she was sure he'd fiercely deny it. God forbid anyone discover the dread Le Balafre might still possess a heart.

". . . and as soon as I made sure my cottage and animals

would be well looked after, I left Faire Isle to come in search of you," Miri concluded.

Simon had listened gravely to her recital, his hands locked behind his back. Making no interruptions, asking no questions, he allowed her to unfold her story after her own fashion. But by the end of her tale, his jaw flexed in a hard line.

"Damnation," he said. "I should never have come to Faire Isle. The Silver Rose's cursed witches must have followed me. I led them straight to your doorstep." He lashed out, stripping off withered grape leaves as he stalked down the hill.

"If you will take a moment to reflect, Simon, you know that can't be true. Before you ever arrived, Carole was already boasting about these powerful new friends of hers. The women had to have been lurking on Faire Isle for some time, enticing Carole to join them." Feeling that the poor beleaguered vines had already suffered enough damage, Miri caught Simon's arm to stop him. "Your warning was all that prevented me from touching that poisonous rose. You actually saved me."

"I am glad of that much then. Rest assured I will do my best to apprehend these evil women and see that this Moreau girl is punished along with the rest."

Dismayed, Miri drew her hand away. "No, that is the last thing I want. Carole is not like those other women. She is only frightened and confused."

"Sweet Jesu, Miri—" Simon began, but Miri cut him off, insisting, "She never meant to hurt her babe. I am sure of it."

"Then the girl has some damned peculiar notions about mothering."

"Don't you see? There are many remote and inaccessible places on Faire Isle and Carole would have known of them. But she wrapped her child tenderly in her best shawl and left him near the stream not far from my cottage. She must have guessed that that is where I go to draw water. She placed her little boy where she was certain I would find him."

"And find that cursed rose. Rather than hoping you'd rescue the babe, she might have been trying to kill you. Did you ever think of that?" he demanded.

Miri sucked in her breath, momentarily daunted. Such a dreadful thought had never occurred to her. She was quick to reject it. "Carole does not possess that kind of evil. Whatever happened, her companions were to blame. If she was the one who left the rose, they forced her or—or tricked her. I am convinced of it."

The difficulty was convincing Simon. His face hardened in that expression she so dreaded. His witch-hunter's look, she'd always called it.

"Simon, please, you have got to believe me and for once trust my instincts instead of yours."

His lips thinned in a harsh line, but as his gaze rested upon Miri, something in his visage softened. "Very well, when I track down these harpies, I will do my best to make sure this girl is judged fairly. I hope that satisfies you and you will return home. You have already taken a damnable risk, haring after me, all alone. To say nothing of the jolt you gave me, appearing out of thin air. How the devil did you manage to get here anyway?"

"I flew in on my broom."

When Simon shot her an exasperated look, she said wryly, "I traveled in the ordinary way, like everyone else. By horse." Miri gestured to her mount, grazing near where Simon had tethered Elle in the only shade to be had, a stand of poplar trees at the base of the hillside. Contrasted to Elle's sleek lines and glossy black coat, Miri's gelding appeared dull and heavy. Mud-colored with a blaze of white upon his forehead, Samson was not the handsomest or the swiftest of horses. But he had a powerful chest and hindquarters. Strong and sturdy, he possessed a remarkable degree of stamina.

Shading his gaze with his hand, Simon squinted in Samson's direction. "I don't recall that beast being stabled in your barn."

"He wasn't. I borrowed him."

Simon regarded her uneasily. "Borrowed or, er, *liberated* him from his owner?"

Miri smiled slightly, surprised that Simon would even remember her girlhood determination to free every abused animal from cruel or neglectful owners.

"I didn't *steal* Samson if that is what you are afraid of. I have finally learned to accept that the world's views on animals as property are far different from mine, and happily Samson did not require rescuing. He was loaned to me by—by a good lady, a merchant's wife from Saint-Malo. She sent three of her servants as well to act as escort until I found you."

"What escort? I don't see anyone hovering about."

"They left as soon as I overtook you. My new acquaintances are not, er, comfortable around witch-hunters."

"And yet they abandoned you to one."

"Because I bade them go." Miri lifted her chin proudly. "I am Evangeline Cheney's daughter, and unlike most women, I was taught to make my own decisions. The choice to seek you out was mine."

"And a damned poor choice it was," Simon growled. "Beyond helping this benighted Moreau girl, what did you hope to accomplish?"

Rescue Carole and . . . somehow manage to save you as well. Miri lowered her eyes, wondering where that thought had come from. If she were honest, she had to admit that it had been in the back of her mind all along. But she didn't have to admit that to Simon.

"I thought my purpose in coming should be clear to you," she said. "I have come to help you unmask the Silver Rose, put a stop to her wicked schemes."

Simon looked thunderstruck for a moment, then folded his arms across the broad barrier of his chest.

"No."

Miri blinked, dismayed by the forbidding look that settled over Simon's countenance. Up until this moment, she had believed that he had actually been glad to see her. More than glad. Now he glared like he wished her at the far ends of the earth.

"You are refusing my offer?" she faltered.

"Damned right I am. Whatever made you think I'd accept?"

"Because that is why you came to Faire Isle, isn't it? Looking for help."

"Not yours," he said bluntly.

When she flinched, he went on in a gentler tone, "Miri, it is not that I don't appreciate your offer, but I never wanted—"

"I know what you wanted," Miri interrupted sadly. "The Lady of Faire Isle. Regretfully, you will have to make do with me. If nothing else, I can at least provide an extra pair of eyes, help you to watch your back."

"Or distract me so I end up with a witch blade thrust through my heart."

"I am glad to hear that that is of concern to you. I was afraid you no longer cared whether you lived or died."

"I don't," he snapped. "But use your head, woman. If I fell, what the devil do you think would happen to you? By now you ought to realize how deadly this sorceress and her minions are. You can't get involved in this dangerous pursuit."

"But I am already involved, whether I like it or not," she said. "I may not have the power and influence Ariane once wielded among wise women, but I can help you, Simon. I possess certain . . . connections and abilities of my own. I managed to track you down, didn't I?"

"Not to belittle your accomplishment, my dear, but I have been making no effort whatsoever to conceal my whereabouts."

"That was remarkably careless of you. The Silver Rose's agents could have—" Miri shivered as comprehension dawned on her. "You wanted them to find you!"

Simon shrugged. "I lost all trace of the Silver Rose after my return from Faire Isle. Another attack is my only hope of picking up the scent again."

"No, it isn't. Do you realize the pair that took Carole from Faire Isle has been journeying in the same direction? I have been able to follow them as well as you."

Simon paled beneath his layering of beard. "Are you completely mad, Miribelle Cheney? Do you realize what could have happened to you if you had overtaken those witches on your own?"

"I was being careful, far more so than you have been." Miri paced slightly ahead of him, frowning. "Too careful, perhaps. I lost all sign of them near Tours. I believe they might have taken to traveling by river and I am sure we will have no trouble—" She gasped as Simon seized her by the shoulders and spun her about to face him.

"No! Let us get one thing straight here and now. There is no *we*. Go back to Faire Isle. This is not your battle."

"Yes it is." She tipped back her head to peer at him from beneath the brim of her hat. "Oh, Simon, how can I make you understand? I am a true daughter of the earth and the evil this woman is doing— Not only does she threaten innocent lives, she defiles all the goodness and harmony I believe in, every principle that I hold dear. It is my duty to stop her as much as it is yours."

"And how can I make *you* understand? If you were killed or even hurt— Damn it, Miri, I have enough regrets where you are concerned. Don't tempt me to make use of you again."

He thrust her away from him, giving her a small shove down the hill in the direction of her mount. "Saddle up and go find those fools who escorted you here. Go home, Miri. Before it is too late."

Miri staggered a little to regain her balance, then dug in her heels. "I am sorry, Simon, but I can't do that."

"Would you prefer that I truss you up and drag you back to Faire Isle myself?" Simon's voice was low, almost silken, but she could tell from the dark glitter in his eye that the threat was very real.

"You could do that," she replied with a stubborn lift of her chin. "You are much stronger than I. But it would be a great waste of time for both of us. You might be able to make me return home, but you'll never be able to keep me there. As soon as your back is turned, I will only have to set out again."

Simon stalked away from her, swearing under his breath just as Miri had often heard Renard do whenever he became frustrated by what he termed Ariane's obstinacy. Simon and her brother-in-law were such bitter enemies. How appalled both men would be to discover they had anything in common. The thought would have provoked a smile from Miri under other circumstances, but she rubbed her arms, feeling at a loss.

It should have occurred to her Simon might refuse her help, but his rejection hurt all the same. She had always been accounted the youngest, the weakest of the Cheney women, the little sister who needed to be sheltered and protected, safe in her world of dreams. And for so long, she was ashamed to admit, she had preferred it that way. Perhaps she still did.

She trailed after Simon where he stood near the edge of the vineyard, gazing moodily toward the valley below. A small village of white stone cottages dotted the banks of the Cher River like beads from a broken strand of pearls. The rays of the setting sun made the thatched roofs appear as though they had been spun from gold. Despite her exhaustion, worries, and fears, Miri was touched by the simple peace and beauty of the scene.

She wondered if Simon felt the same, but she doubted it. Judging from his tight-lipped expression, she suspected that all he saw were the lengthening shadows, the dangers of another night about to descend.

From the nearby grove of poplars, Elle emitted a soft whicker. She twisted her head to nuzzle Samson when he lipped playfully at her ear, the pair behaving as though they had been pastured together all their lives.

Miri smiled ruefully. "Our horses appear to be getting along far better than we are."

Simon cast a cursory glance toward the horses. "That is because they have nothing at stake, nothing like our past history."

"No, I think it is because animals are more sensible than humans. They view the world in much simpler, uncomplicated terms. I often envy them." Stepping closer to Simon, Miri said quietly, "I am sorry that you doubt my strength and courage for this enterprise."

"Damn it, Miri, I never said—"

"And I don't blame you," she rushed on, not giving him a chance to speak. "But you should know. If you won't let me come with you, I will be obliged to continue on alone."

Simon cut her a glance filled with dark impatience. "You will, will you? And if you did find the Silver Rose on your own, what the devil are you planning to do with her? Reason with her, tell her this is not how nice wise women behave? Because we both know damned well you'd never be able to shoot her or thrust a knife through her black heart."

Although she winced at his sarcasm, Miri replied with dignity, "I hope I would find the fortitude to do whatever must be done, but that is why it would be better if we joined forces. I believe I can help you find the Silver Rose, but you are much better at—at—"

"Being a cruel and cold-hearted bastard?"

Miri frowned at him. "At fighting evil, I was going to say."

"Ah, so you finally acknowledge the need for the ruthlessness of the witch-hunter."

"Just as the witch-hunter needs the lore of the wise woman," she retorted. "You'll never defeat this woman on your own either."

"I'll manage."

"You haven't succeeded thus far," Miri reminded him. "An alliance between us seems the most sensible thing, but the choice is yours. We can risk our lives together. Or alone."

Simon vented a wearied sigh and lapsed into silence, the agitation of his thoughts only betrayed by the way he flexed and unflexed his hand at his side. Miri maintained an aura of calm indifference, although her heart raced, wondering what she would do if Simon refused her offer, if she truly would have the courage to go alone. His dark eye probed hers as though testing the measure of her resolve. She forced herself to steadily meet his gaze.

At last he said, "If I was mad enough to agree to this alliance, as you call it, there would have to be certain conditions."

"Such as?"

"I will be the one in charge of our hunt, the one who has the final say in how we proceed. If I ever order you to remain behind, you'll do it, no arguments. If we ride into danger and I command you to flee, you will, no hesitations. Even if it means leaving me behind."

Miri frowned, not at all liking these terms, but realizing from Simon's grim expression that she had little choice but to accept them. She nodded. "All right. But I also have conditions."

When Simon arched his brow questioningly, she went on, "You might find my methods of tracking a little, um, unorthodox and disconcerting. You must promise not to ask questions about my ways or about any of the people I might contact en route."

"And if these people of yours are in league with the Silver Rose?"

"They won't be. You will have to trust my judgment for that."

Simon looked no more pleased with her conditions than she had been with his. He finally conceded, "Very well, damn it."

Miri held her breath, scarce able to believe she had won. "Then—then we are agreed? We continue on together?" She tentatively held out her hand. Simon gazed at it for a long time before encompassing her fingers in his strong, steady grip.

"Together." He added grimly. "And may God help us both."

Chapter Eight

THE BRASS HORSE WAS LIKE MANY OF THE HOSTELRIES situated along the Cher, a modest inn that catered mostly to the river traffic, merchants, and watermen moving goods up and down stream. But the dire events that had resulted in the infant Luc's death had left a permanent pall over the establishment run by the Paillards, the innkeepers among the first families to be devastated by the sinister designs of the Silver Rose.

Once a jovial bustling man, Gaspard Paillard's movements were lethargic as he wiped down tankards and replaced them on the cupboard shelves. When Simon entered the taproom with Miri trailing in his wake, no sign of welcome flickered in the innkeeper's dull eyes.

Paillard had been grudgingly grateful to Simon for

doing what he had lacked the courage to do himself: defy the local priest and see that his grandson was properly laid to rest instead of being burned as the spawn of a witch. But Simon was a bitter reminder of his cowardice, and Paillard would have been relieved to never clap eyes upon the witch-hunter again.

Simon would as soon have stopped elsewhere himself, but with night falling, he had only one aim—to get Miri safely bestowed within four walls.

"Monsieur Paillard . . ." It would be an insult to ask the man how he was faring. Simon contented himself with a curt nod.

"Master Witch-Hunter," the landlord replied sourly. "What ill wind brings you back to my door this time?"

"Only the need for a light repast and a night's lodgings for myself and—" Simon hesitated, trying to decide how to account for Miri.

"His cousin Louis," Miri spoke up in a husky voice that Simon feared would fool no one.

"Er—yes, Louis." Simon gave her a warning frown. He had ordered her to remain silent and let him do all the talking.

She adjusted the brim of her hat lower over her face, but she needn't have bothered. To Simon's relief, Paillard did not cast so much as an inquisitive glance in her direction. The man seemed to have lost all interest in anything beyond his own misery since the winter his only daughter Lucie had sold her soul to the devil and abandoned his grandson to freeze to death.

"I'll see what's available in the kitchen for your supper," Paillard said. "As for the room, you may take your pick. It is not as though we are swamped with custom since—since—" He paused, his throat working in a rare display of emotion.

"First room at the top of the stairs is ready and clean," he concluded gruffly.

As Simon thanked the man, he was aware of Miri regarding both of them, no doubt sensing the undercurrents. Her gaze moved on to the inn itself, the gloom-shrouded walls, the tables and chairs that would still look just as stark and empty even after the candles were lit.

Simon was quick to gather up their saddlebags and hustle her toward the stairs. A maidservant toting a jug of hot water appeared to usher them to the landing above. The young strawberry blonde was no one Simon remembered from his previous visits. Doubtless she had been engaged to replace the pair of hands lost when Lucie Paillard had vanished. The presence of the new maid suggested that the Paillards had finally accepted the fact that their daughter was never coming home.

As the chambermaid escorted Miri up the stairs, Simon prepared to follow. But a hand reached out to pluck at his sleeve.

"Monsieur Aristide?"

Simon's gut knotted as he turned to face the wraith of a woman who had melted out of the shadows. Once as pretty and youthful as her daughter, Colette Paillard looked like a lovely gown that had been worn too hard, faded from too much washing and bleaching in the sun. As much as her husband abhorred the sight of Simon, Simon dreaded encountering this woman with her tremulous mouth and tragic eyes.

He ducked his head in a curt bow. "Madame Paillard."

"Forgive me, but I was wondering if anywhere in your travels you had heard anything of—of—" She stole an anxious glance into the taproom, where her husband was serving wine to the river men. Gaspard Paillard had forbidden his daughter's name to ever be spoken beneath his roof again.

Colette sank her voice to a whisper. *"Lucie."*

"No, madame. I am sorry. I have not."

Miri and the chambermaid had already vanished up the stairs. Simon tried again to follow, but once more Madame Paillard detained him.

"But if you did learn anything—if you ever found my girl—"

Simon adjusted the weight of the saddlebags across his shoulder, his mouth tightening. Did not this pathetic creature understand what would happen to *her girl* if he did find Lucie? That he'd be obliged to see her tried and hung for witchcraft and the murder of her child?

"It—it is just the never knowing that is the worst," she quavered. "Always wondering what's become of her that keeps me awake of nights. So if you did know, if you would promise to be kind enough to come and tell me . . ."

Simon thought he would sooner have hot spikes shoved beneath his nails than be the one to inform this mother of the fate that was bound to befall her only child. But when Colette's eyes filled, he said gently, "I promise."

She blinked back her tears, made a pitiful attempt to smile before she faded back into the taproom. Simon stalked up the stairs, not for the first time cursing his profession and witches like Lucie Paillard and this damnable Silver Rose who made his work necessary. As he gained the landing, there was no sign of Miri. But the chambermaid emerged from the first door to his right.

"This way, monsieur," she said, bobbing a nervous curtsy, taking such obvious pains not to stare at Simon's eye patch, he nearly snapped at her to take a good long look. But he restrained himself. He was accustomed to the stares his scarred face attracted, and it was not this girl who disturbed him, but coming back to this cursed place. He should have tried harder to find somewhere else to safely pass the night. He had to have been mad to bring Miri to this inn, haunted with its weight of bitter memories and despair. No, he decided. When he had truly lost his wits was back there in the vineyard when he'd agreed to let Miri accompany him at all.

As soon as the maid ushered Simon into the room, the girl was quick to make her escape. The Brass Horse was not the roistering place it had once been. Even so the silence seemed deafening to Simon when the door closed, shutting him in alone with Miri. He dropped the saddlebags to the floor with a loud thud.

Someone, either the maid or Miri, had already lit the candles, fending off the twilight shadows. Most likely it had been the maid because Miri stood poised in the center of the room like a woman who had not made up her mind to stay. Her face still half obscured by the flopping brim of her battered hat, she seemed to be taking stock of their surroundings.

Not that there was much to see beyond a pair of wooden stools, a small round table, the washstand, and . . . the bed, a thick feather mattress covered by a worn counterpane, not very wide, with two pillows nestled side by side, close, intimate as any two people would be who crowded into that bed together.

After an initial protest at his decision to stop for the night, Miri had said little since crossing the threshold of the inn. But now she turned to frown at him. "You seriously expect the two of us to share this one room?"

"Well, it would look damned odd if I told the landlord that we lads required separate rooms, wouldn't it, *Louis*?" he asked caustically. "Unless you expect some sort of royal treatment because you adopted the name of kings?"

"No, I don't and I didn't call myself that because of any king." She ducked deeper beneath the brim of her hat, saying in a quieter voice. "Louis was my father's name."

Simon winced, feeling like a complete bastard. He was as edgy as she was regarding this situation, but that was no excuse. He should have remembered. Miri had spoken of her father often enough that first summer they had met, so fiercely proud to be the daughter of the bold Chevalier Louis Cheney. When they had wandered the shores of the hidden cove, how often had her gaze strayed wistfully to the channel waters, as though expecting at any moment to see the billow of sails wafting her father home.

"Sorry," Simon muttered, sagging back against the closed door. "But this is one consequence of our little pact neither one of us paused to consider, that we will be thrust intimately together for the duration of this journey, both day and night."

"We—we will manage somehow."

Simon wished he was as sure of that. After another

moment's hesitation, Miri stripped off her hat and tossed it on the bed. As she bent to retrieve her saddlebag, her tunic rode up, the fabric of her breeches drawing tight over the full curve of her derriere. Simon looked frantically around the room for something to do, anything that didn't involve staring at Miri's shapely arse.

He stalked over to the window and peered down into the yard, just able to make out the outline of the well and the stables where Samson and Elle were housed. All seemed quiet and deserted, but he ought to sit up all night watching, with a loaded pistol at the ready—

Simon checked himself with a heavy scowl, realizing he was being ridiculous. None of the Silver Rose's agents had been seen here since the night Lucie Paillard had vanished. It was unlikely they would decide to put in an appearance tonight. Never once had the witches attempted to attack him when he was at an inn with other people around.

He wasn't thinking straight and he knew why. Miri. The woman's mere presence unsettled him in more ways than he could count. He was far too aware of her moving about the chamber behind him, the splash of water as she dipped into the wash basin, cleansing away the dust of the day.

When he breathed in, it was as though her scent pervaded the room, something warm, enticingly feminine. A far too seductive aroma. He leaned out the window to clear his nostrils. A light breeze coming off the river tickled the ends of his beard. With the onset of twilight, the air had cooled, but not nearly enough, it seemed to Simon.

He should have tried harder to dissuade Miri from coming with him, he berated himself. But he knew the woman's stubborn resolve all too well. She had meant it when she had threatened to go after the Silver Rose alone.

But that had not been what had really swayed him. It had been the earnest way she had looked up at him when she had said, *"I am a true daughter of the earth, and this evil woman defiles all the goodness and harmony I believe in, every principle that I hold dear. It is my duty to stop her as much as it is yours. How can I make you understand?"*

She couldn't. Simon had never been able to fully comprehend the distinction Miri made between wise women and witches. Any dabbling with magic and the ancient lore seemed to him dangerous and forbidden. And yet Miri was so passionate about what she declared to be the true way of the daughters of the earth, she was willing to risk her life in its defense. He might not like it, might not understand it, but by God, he respected her for it.

And she was right when she said that he required her help. He'd had no success defeating the Silver Rose on his own and Miri had more abilities and connections among the community of wise women than he had ever suspected. He needed whatever knowledge and skill she possessed, needed her with him however long it took to hunt down this sorceress.

But the upcoming days and nights were going to be damned difficult if he didn't manage to draw rein on the other emotions and desires the woman roused in him. He swept one last searching glance over the stable yard before closing and fastening the shutters. When he came about, he wished that he had kept his gaze trained outside a while longer.

Miri had unpinned and unbraided her hair, the silken tresses cascading like a waterfall of moonlight about her shoulders. As she groped beneath her tunic, he caught a flash of creamy white skin. She struggled to undo the thick strip of linen she had used to bind her breasts. As it came free, she pulled the length of cloth from inside her tunic with a soft sigh of relief that whispered over him, as seductive as a caress.

With the neckline of her tunic loosened, the folds parted enough to reveal a tantalizing glimpse of the valley of her breasts, and the desire that pierced Simon was as swift and sharp as the bolt of an arrow. He knew he ought to drag his gaze away but continued to watch her as though mesmerized.

Completely oblivious to the effect she was having on him, Miri dipped a sponge in the washbasin and stroked the cool, cleansing water over her neck, her eyes closing in an expression of almost sensual delight. Droplets trickled over her delicate collarbone, past the silver chain she wore, disappearing into the soft swell of her cleavage.

Difficult? Simon gritted his teeth, feeling himself go hard. These next days and nights were going to be pure hell. As Miri toweled herself dry, she finally seemed to remember she was not alone in the room. As she came about to face him, she adjusted her neckline to a more demure position.

"We should not have come here, Simon," she said gravely. "This hostelry has an unhappy aura."

He regarded her incredulously. They were embarking on a hunt that imperiled both their lives. They were pent up in a bedchamber that seemed to him to be getting smaller by the minute and *she* was worried about the inn's blasted aura?

Miri shuddered. "It is as though some great sorrow presses down upon the very rafters."

Simon was surprised that she should have sensed that, but he supposed he shouldn't have been. Miri had always possessed a heightened sensitivity, an uncanny sympathy with her surroundings. Simon had told her nothing of the Paillards and their tragic history. He was in no humor for another argument and he feared that Miri would attempt to convince him that like the Moreau girl, Lucie Paillard was only *misguided.* Simon knew better. But at least a discussion of the shortcomings of the Brass Horse might serve to put a damper on the heat stirring in his loins.

"I admit this isn't the cheeriest place," he said. "But it's clean, comfortable, and more important, safe. And it is only for the one night."

"I still don't know why you insisted we stop at all. Samson was fresh enough to continue on and so was Elle." She plunked the towel back down on the washstand. "I thought you usually traveled under cover of darkness."

"Not with you, I don't. Look. I thought we agreed that I was to be the one in charge of this pursuit. This alliance isn't going to work if you are already questioning my decisions."

"It won't work either if you insist upon regarding me as some—some helpless woman who needs your protection," she insisted.

Simon stole a look at the silken shimmer of her hair, the soft swell of her unbound breasts that now burgeoned against the fabric of her tunic. He blew out a gusty breath.

"You *are* a woman. How the devil else do you expect me to regard you?"

"Like a brother in arms."

Simon snorted. "I am afraid that requires more imagination than I possess, despite your efforts to look like a man." He raked his gaze disapprovingly over her attire. "Do you really think this inappropriate disguise of yours deceives anyone?"

"It does frequently. People seldom trouble to look that closely. I simply pull my hat lower, deepen my voice, and lengthen my stride." Miri strutted a few steps in a remarkable imitation of a cocksure, swaggering youth. "It works, Simon."

"Until you bend over," he muttered.

"What?"

Simon squirmed, feeling he'd do better to keep the observation to himself, but the woman needed to be warned, damn it.

"When you bend over, the seat of your breeches—well, it—it hugs your—" Simon gestured uncomfortably in the general direction of her posterior. "The fabric tightens and one can see the curve of your—your arse." He broke off, annoyed to feel himself reddening.

Miri's eyes widened. She twisted her neck, peering over her shoulder as though trying to observe the phenomenon for herself. He expected her to be embarrassed, appalled, even offended. He was not prepared for her to break into a peal of delighted laughter.

"You find it amusing?" he asked stiffly.

"No, merely reassuring. For most of my girlhood, I was so flat, I despaired of ever acquiring any womanly curves worth worrying about. But I am sorry if the sight of my, um, arse distresses you. I'll take better care to remain upright in your presence. I had forgotten what a prim lot you witch-hunters are."

"I am not prim, damn it—"

"Yes you are," Miri said, her eyes dancing. "You always were. Even as a boy, you pursed your lips when you saw me roaming about Faire Isle in my baggy breeches."

"That's because it wasn't decent or respectable for a girl to dress thus."

"I come from a family of accused witches and my sister Gabrielle was once one of the most notorious courtesans in Paris. I think respectability and I parted company a long time ago. Besides, you should try traveling a long distance trussed up in a corset, clinging for dear life to a sidesaddle or riding astride with your petticoats bunched around your knees. I gave up my comfortable masculine garb once before to please you, Simon Aristide. I am not going to do it again."

"I don't recall you ever doing any such thing."

She flattened her hands on her hips in mock indignation as she accused, "I endured the torment of skirts and petticoats and you never even noticed."

But as Simon reflected back, suddenly he remembered quite well. Those had been tense and difficult days for him that first summer on Faire Isle, torn between his fondness for Miri and his loyalty to his master, Vachel Le Vis.

The Comte de Renard had succeeded in destroying most of their brotherhood of witch-hunters. The ruthless sorcerer had been fairly tearing the island apart in his efforts to finish off those few who remained. Miri had helped Simon hide in a cave just off the cove, fetching him food and wine every day. She had loaned him her own masculine clothing to replace the dark robes and cowl Master Le Vis had obliged his followers to wear.

Not only had Miri abandoned her efforts to look like a boy, she had turned up each day wearing a frock, her hair bound back in ribbons. Arrogant young cockerel that he had been, he had been aware she was completely infatuated with him. He had been fond of her, too, but from the lofty experience of his fifteen years, he had considered her mere twelve as little more than a child.

Simon grimaced. His life would be a damn sight easier these upcoming days if he could still view Miri that way, not be so painfully aware of what a desirable woman she had become.

Her lips aquiver, her eyes sparkled with mischief as she continued to tease. "I suppose if it bothers you that much, I could spare your blushes and try to purchase a gown from one of the women in this village. If you truly wish it."

Although she provoked a smile from Simon, he said, "What I wish, my dear, is that you were well out of this dangerous business. Back home on your island, completely safe."

The light of laughter in her eyes dimmed. "Completely safe," she repeated wistfully. "I have been looking for that place my entire life. I don't believe it exists, do you?"

"No, but you'd be a damned sight safer back on Faire Isle than you are here with me."

She seemed to realize he was talking about far more

than the dangers presented by the Silver Rose. She cocked her head to one side, regarding him in that curious searching way that was uniquely Miri's.

"Am I not safe in your company, Simon?" she asked. "There is something I have been wanting to ask you. About the—the way we parted on Faire Isle. That kiss . . ."

Oh, Lord. He had wondered when she might get around to reproaching him for that, had been dreading it.

"That was a mistake. I mean, I—I don't know what devil got into me," he blustered. "I am sorry. I never meant to offend you."

"You didn't. You merely startled me." Her lashes drifted down as she confessed almost shyly. "I don't believe I have ever been kissed quite so—so vigorously before. I fear I liked it more than I should have done."

Simon's breath hitched in his throat. Did the woman always have to be so infernally honest? Didn't she understand what a dangerous admission that was to make, closeted alone with a man in a bedchamber? Especially when she added fuel to the fire by unconsciously moistening her lips, rendering her mouth all too red, lush, and tempting.

"Don't worry about that kiss. Nothing like that will happen again," he said hoarsely, although he was uncertain who he was most desperately seeking to convince, her or himself. "I wasn't myself that night and I was so sure it would be the last time we met. I fully expected to be dead soon."

She glanced up at him with a quizzical smile. "You feared you were about to die and you couldn't think of anything better to do than kiss me?"

"It would seem not."

Even knowing he'd be far wiser to keep his distance, he couldn't stop himself from moving closer, skating his fingertips down the soft curve of her cheek, this woman whose life had been so strangely, so inexplicably bound up with his. A mortal maid with fairy eyes. Silvery eyes in which he could see reflections of the child who had enchanted him, the girl whose budding beauty had tugged at his heart, the woman who stirred his senses, despite all the iron-cold walls he tried to erect between them.

He had despaired of ever seeing Miri again that pearly gray evening he'd left Faire Isle and yet here she was gazing up at him, a little shy, a little wary, but with far more trust than he had any right to expect. As Simon stroked her face, she leaned into his hand, unconsciously welcoming his caress.

The realization struck him with all the force of a cudgel to the brain, the true reason he had not tried harder to dissuade her from coming with him. Not because he was afraid of what she might attempt to do on her own or because he wanted to make use of her knowledge and skills. No, he quite simply wanted . . . her. When Simon forced his hand back to his side, Miri blinked like a woman snapping awake from a dream.

"You have always been my one weakness, Miri Cheney," he murmured. His admission seemed to trouble her as much as it did him. Before she could say anything, he rushed on, "I think I had best spend the rest of this night keeping watch. From the other side of that door."

"But—but you need to get some sleep too," she said. "Of course, there is no question of us sharing the bed, but surely you could make a pallet on the floor and—"

"I think we both realize that would be a bad idea," he interrupted.

She colored, fretting the chain suspended about her neck. "Yes, perhaps you are right."

"Don't worry. I won't be that far away," he said. "There is no reason for you to be afraid."

"I am not, but . . ." she trailed off frowning.

"Of course you aren't." Simon's mouth quirked in a half-smile. "That is one of the most astonishing things about you, your lack of fear. You accused me earlier of doubting your strength and courage, but I have long thought you the bravest lady I've ever known. I can never forget that night we first met, how you were trying single-handed to fight off a score of witches to save that cat from being sacrificed."

Although Miri smiled a little at the reminder, she protested. "They weren't witches. Only a pack of stupid, ignorant girls."

"And what about that time in Paris when I behaved like such a ruthless ass? You marched through an entire troop of mercenary witch-hunters to see me. I still can't imagine why you took such a risk."

"Because I believed in you, Simon." She looked up at him, adding softly, "I still wish that I could."

"Don't. I'll only disappoint you." He deposited a brusque kiss against her forehead. "Good night, my dear. Bar the door behind me."

⚜⚜⚜

SIMON SLUMPED back in his chair, nursing a cup of wine. It was strange. He had come to regard the night as his time, comfortable with the long stretches of dark and silence that isolated him from the rest of humankind. Only him, Elle, and a pale ribbon of open road.

But tonight darkness and loneliness seemed to hem him in on all sides. Perhaps it was all those other empty chairs and tables in the deserted taproom. The Paillards had retired to their cleaning up in the kitchens, leaving Simon alone with the remains of his supper and a few candles.

Ordinarily, Simon sat with his back to the wall, but he had positioned his chair so he could keep his eye trained upon the top of the stairs. He had taken up Miri's supper tray himself awhile ago, not entering the room, simply handing it to her through the door. He assumed that Miri would be fast asleep by now and tried not to think of her soft warm body curled up in that bed, her silken hair fanning across the pillow.

At some point he was going to have to get some rest himself to prepare for tomorrow, when they would begin their dangerous search in earnest. He had resolved to stretch out in front of Miri's door, no matter what the Paillards might think of this strange behavior. Somehow he doubted either of them would notice or care if they did.

Unhitching his purse from his belt, he loosened the drawstrings and counted out enough coins to pay for the supper and lodging. He meant to settle his reckoning with the Paillards so that he and Miri could slip away unheeded at first light.

But as he laid the coins upon the table, he was aware of the other object weighting down the bottom of his purse. Something that he rarely ever allowed himself to examine except on nights that seemed lonelier or longer than the rest, a night like this one.

Delving into the bottom of his purse, he drew forth a small octagonal box he'd purchased to conceal something he'd stolen years ago. Thumbing the catch, he watched the lid spring open to reveal a lock of moon-spun hair nestled against velvet folds. Simon winced when he remembered how ruthlessly he had taken it from Miri, backing her up against the wall of the inn, hacking off the lock of hair with his knife. He'd only done it to frighten her, intimidate her into staying away from him. Far away where she wouldn't weaken him with her soft lips and searching eyes, dissuade him from what, in his youthful arrogance, he had perceived to be his manifest destiny: to conquer evil, to rid all of France of witchcraft.

That didn't explain why he had kept Miri's lock of hair all these years. As penance perhaps, a constant reminder and reproach for all the wrong he'd done her, the way he'd betrayed her trust time and again. God, she should still hate him. Why didn't she? He had never known anyone like her, with such a capacity for forgiveness, a willingness to search for the best, even in a ruthless bastard like him. It astounded him, humbled him, shamed him.

"I believed in you, Simon. I still wish that I could."

Oh, the damnable temptation, to take her in his arms and persuade her to do just that. He had glimpsed enough of longing in her face to realize it would be possible to seduce her. To slake his dark, parched soul by drinking in a little of her light, to find ease for his emptiness by burying himself deep within her welcoming warmth.

But for all she was a woman of some twenty-six years, he sensed that she was still untried, knew little of how one could be consumed by the fires of passion. He had sinned enough against Miri Cheney without teaching her that, for if he understood nothing else about her, he understood this. The woman was not capable of engaging in anything that did not involve her entire heart and soul. And neither would be safe in his cold rough hands.

Simon snapped the trinket box closed, shoving it back into his purse, resolving to end this unwise alliance between them as swiftly as possible. Track down those witches who had been on Faire Isle, force one of them to give up the identity of the Silver Rose. Then maybe if he suspended his judgment of that miserable Moreau girl and handed her over to Miri, he could persuade Miri to return to Faire Isle, leave dealing with the Silver Rose to—

Simon's thoughts were disrupted by the heavy tread of boots. He glanced up, startled to realize his musings had made him careless. He had failed to note the arrival of another wayfarer, a gentleman by the look of him, despite his travel-stained cloak, doublet, and trunk hose.

Simon studied the newcomer intently but saw nothing in the stranger to occasion alarm. The traveler glanced about the taproom as though searching for the innkeeper. When his gaze fell upon Simon, he accorded him a deep bow.

"Good evening, monsieur."

Simon responded with a curt nod and a scowl, meant to discourage any further exchange of pleasantries. Undeterred, the stranger drew closer to his table.

"Do I have the pleasure of addressing the great Le Bala-fre, master witch-hunter?" The man's voice was courteous, as soft as the curly ends of his sandy beard. But his hazel eyes were shrewd, watchful.

Simon tensed at the stranger's inquiry, although he was not particularly surprised by it. Simon was not unknown in this part of the country, often consulted by priests, magis-trates, and landowners in the district regarding matters of witchcraft. Usually it turned out to be a mere bagatelle, a waste of Simon's time, based upon the hysteria of some-one's nervous wife or the superstitious fears of the local peasants. But sometimes, especially considering the recent activities of the Silver Rose, the fear was well-founded.

More wary now, Simon hedged, "Whether or not you address Le Balafre depends."

"Upon what, monsieur?"

"Upon who it is who asks for him and why."

The man bowed again. "Captain Ambroise Gautier. An officer of her most gracious majesty Queen Catherine's royal guard, at your service, Monsieur Aristide."

Although Simon did not betray his alarm by so much as the flicker of an eyelash, he moved his hand beneath the table until it closed over the hilt of his dagger.

Royal guard, my arse, Simon thought, running his gaze over Gautier's nondescript apparel. This was one of the Dark Queen's lackeys, those private emissaries sent out on errands that usually did not bear up under public scrutiny, whether it be the delivery of clandestine correspondence, a bit of espionage, or the quiet dispatch of some enemy.

Forcing a casual shrug, Simon took a sip of his wine. "Indeed, monsieur? And what would a member of Her

Majesty's *royal guard*—" Simon laid sarcastic emphasis on the words "—want with me?"

"I bear you a message from Her Grace," Gautier said with an amiable smile. "She desires that you wait upon her as soon as may be."

"It is a damnably long way to Paris."

"Ah, but happily the queen is nearby, not ten leagues from here. In residence at Chenonceau. If we set out now, I promise you that you will be returned to this inn and still have the chance of a few hours' sleep before sunrise."

"I have had no contact with Her Majesty for years. And she would see me *tonight?* What can possibly be so urgent?"

"Her Grace does not make me her confidant, but—" Gautier leaned closer, lowering his voice. "I believe it has something to do with certain reports you have been sending to Paris."

Simon concealed his surprise, shifting uneasily in his chair. Gautier had to be referring to his reports on the Silver Rose that he'd sent to the king. For all the heed His Grace had paid, Simon might as well have been dispatching them to the bottom of the Seine. Perhaps Henry had never seen them at all. Perhaps they had been falling into other hands—the Dark Queen's. As much as Simon had wanted someone to read his reports, he would not have had it be *her.* Even he had not been desperate or mad enough to think of consulting one dangerous sorceress to fight another.

Simon flexed his fingers on his knife, heartily wishing he had not allowed himself to be caught off guard this way, that he had more time to think this situation through.

"I have had a long hard day in the saddle," he began slowly. "Tell Her Grace I shall wait upon her within the next day or two—"

"One does not keep a queen waiting, Monsieur Aristide. Especially *our* queen. My instructions were most explicit. I was to bring you to her as soon as I found you, day or night."

"And if I am not inclined to go tonight?"

Gautier's smile never dimmed, but his eyes narrowed. "Alas, I must fetch you one way or another, on your own two feet or slung unconscious over the back of a horse. I would not make this into something unpleasant, but the choice of course is yours."

Gautier lifted his gloved hand in a gesture and Simon heard the tread of boots behind him. He realized that Gautier's men had followed their captain into the taproom, were no doubt but awaiting his command. How many there were Simon could not tell. He caught a glimpse of at least two out of the corner of his eye, sensed another might be lurking on his blind side.

Tightening his grip on his knife, Simon weighed his options. If he decided to resist, he was badly outnumbered, his chances of winning slim to none. The ensuing fracas would only serve to rouse the Paillards from the kitchen, possibly put them at risk. Worse still, it might involve Miri. If she were to awaken and come rushing to his aid—

Simon cut a quick glance up toward her room. The Dark Queen had always been as much of a threat to Miri and her family as ever the Silver Rose could be. But there was no reason for this Captain Gautier to suspect that

Simon did not travel alone as usual. Not if Simon kept his head.

Holding up his hands to display that he held no weapon, he rose slowly to his feet, matching Gautier's smile with an ironic one of his own. "I am as ever at Her Grace's disposal."

Simon only hoped that would not prove true.

Chapter Nine

THE MOON PIERCED THE CLOUDS, SHEDDING A SILVERY LIGHT over the castle, causing the white stone walls to glisten like a lustrous pearl set amidst the rolling hills of the Loire Valley. No grim fortress this, but more of a fairy-tale palace with its towers and turrets, its rows of sparkling windows. It bridged the River Cher, and the dark waters flowed beneath the castle's series of graceful arches.

Chenonceau was not large when compared to other châteaus, but it was certainly reckoned among the loveliest in France. Yet as Simon crossed the courtyard, he reflected that he had had far too much experience with how evil could be hidden beneath a beautiful façade. Whether it be a castle or a silver rose.

The Château de Chenonceau owed its elegant design

not to any male architect but more to the cleverness of the three women who had owned it over the past decades: one finance minister's wife, one royal mistress, and . . . one Dark Queen.

Like many of her subjects, Simon had long suspected Catherine de Medici of being a sorceress skilled in the black arts, especially those involving poisons. Her cold smile had often challenged Simon to prove it, something he had surrendered all hope of doing. The woman was simply too careful, too cunning, and she was the queen mother of France. At one time, Catherine might have regarded Simon as a troublesome adversary, but after he had fallen out of favor at court, she appeared to have dismissed him from her thoughts. Or so he had believed until tonight . . .

Simon marched toward the torch-lit entryway, closely surrounded by his escort. Although Simon had surrendered his weapons and come quietly, Captain Gautier was watchful, taking no chances. He had hustled Simon out of the Brass Horse and straight onto the back of a waiting horse.

For all of Gautier's assurances that the queen only wished for a brief audience, Simon tensed as he passed beneath the shadow of the castle. As the entry doors slammed shut behind him, he couldn't help thinking how easily a man could be detained within these thick stone walls for an indefinite period. Or be made to disappear and never be heard from again. A cold feeling trickled down his spine, the emotion so foreign to him, it took him a moment to identify what it was.

Fear. Not for himself but for the woman he had left behind, wondering what Miri would do if he failed to return.

Waking up abandoned in a strange inn, with no idea what had become of Simon. Would she set out in search of him and risk falling into the hands of the Dark Queen herself? Would she continue alone on her quest to defeat the Silver Rose?

She had a weapon. Simon had left his sword in the room with her, not that he could imagine Miri ever using it on anyone, not even to save her own life. He could more picture the weapon being wrested away, turned against her, his own blade piercing her—

Simon ground his teeth. He was not the sort to let his mind run riot with fearful imaginings, and now was not the time to begin. Not when he needed to remain calm, think rationally. If Catherine had made up her mind to dispose of Simon after all these years, Simon reckoned he'd already be dead. Gautier was the kind of smiling bastard who would have no compunction about slitting a man's throat, apologizing while he did so. Simon had no reason to suppose that the situation was other than Gautier had described. The queen had read his reports and was disturbed by them. But Simon had been sending those reports for months. Why all of a sudden did Catherine urgently desire to question him?

Simon had to admit he was curious, and that could be a dangerous thing where the Dark Queen was concerned. The sooner he could conclude this interview and get back to Miri, the easier he would feel.

Once he had Simon securely within the castle walls, Gautier relaxed. Dismissing the other guards, the captain escorted Simon to the main stair, a wide, straight series of risers that stretched up to the landing above, the ceiling carved with the two intertwining "C"s of Catherine de

Medici. As if anyone was in danger of forgetting who was mistress here, Simon thought.

The sight of the hall stirred in Simon an unpleasant memory of the last time he had come to Chenonceau, to report to the French king the debacle of his raid on Faire Isle. He had been exhausted, weighted down by his failure to recover the *Book of Shadows,* to arrest the sorcerer Renard, to keep control over his men, to stop them from looting and burning. Riddled with guilt as well over the grief he knew he must have inflicted upon Miri.

His black mood had left Simon in little humor to find himself caught up in the wild gaiety of some court fete. A fete? No, more like an orgy, courtesans scandalously clad in venetians and nothing else draped all over the castle stair. Cooing, calling out lewd greetings to Simon, attempting to thrust their bare breasts in his face.

Simon had shrunk back, turning to the only woman present respectably garbed in silk gown and farthingale. She had sketched him a demure curtsy, fluttering her fan before her face. But when she lowered the fan, Simon had frozen in shock. Beneath the ridiculous purple wig and layers of rouge, the king of France leered up at Simon. And this was the man to whom Simon had bound himself? He had believed Henry Valois to be a young king of serious mind, upright and sincere, passionately committed to ruling over a France that would be free of all evil and corruption.

Simon had felt sick to his stomach as the king had planted a buss full on his mouth, then pretended to recoil in horror from Simon's scars. Face burning, Simon had scarce known what to do, where to look as the entire court had dissolved into laughter. And from somewhere in the shadows above, *she* had watched, the Dark Queen, her lips thinning in a smile at his discomfiture.

Simon shook his head to clear off the disturbing memory. Perhaps Miri was right. He was a bit of a prude, had been even more so in his youth. He had witnessed enough debauchery in Henry Valois's court to be far more jaded now. All the same, he was relieved to find the activity in the castle mundane tonight.

It was obvious that the queen had only recently taken up residence. Exhausted-looking servants toted chests and trunks still to be unpacked. A courier, his clothes as travel stained as Simon's, rushed past, clutching missives to be delivered.

The staircase opened onto a long hall covered with rib vaults, the candle sconces sending flickering shadows over walls of costly Flemish tapestries and many doors. As Simon and his escort reached the landing, a petite blond woman rustled forward to intercept them, the cool accents of her voice disturbingly familiar to Simon.

"Thank you, Captain Gautier. I will conduct Monsieur Aristide from here."

Gautier hesitated a moment, then bowed respectfully and departed, leaving Simon alone with Gillian Harcourt, one of Catherine's chief ladies. Ladies? There were far less kind terms some might apply to the beautiful and clever women who served the Dark Queen. Known as the Flying Squadron, they were recruited by Catherine to seduce her enemies and ferret out their secrets, to keep her powerful nobles in check by holding them in thrall.

During his days in service to Catherine's son Henry, Simon had given these notorious seductresses a wide berth . . . except for Gillian. He had always liked the woman's humor and quick wit. In fact, there had been a period of a few weeks when he had done far more than merely like her.

Simon and his former mistress regarded each other in silence for a long moment. The years had not been gentle with the courtesan. Her beauty was fading, her low-cut mauve gown revealing far too much of a bosom that was no longer firm. Lines bracketed her mouth, her face was ravaged by too many revels, too many late nights, and all the rouge she applied to her cheeks could not disguise the fact.

Like many of the queen's women, her eyes had a hard and calculating expression but something in them softened at the sight of Simon.

"Simon Aristide, it *has* been a long time," she murmured.

"Mademoiselle Harcourt." Simon accorded her an ironic bow.

Gillian drifted closer in a cloud of heavy perfume. Simon had always found it too cloying. She stroked a strand of hair back from his brow. "So you finally decided to let your hair grow back. There were some mornings, the sun glancing off that bald pate of yours was almost blinding, Monsieur Le Balafre. I would declare your appearance improved except—" Gillian wrinkled her nose. "Some clean clothing would not come amiss."

"Forgive me, milady," Simon replied dryly. "But my escort gave me little opportunity to refresh myself. Besides, it has been a long time since I have been received at court. I have grown out of the habit of waiting upon royalty."

Gillian stole a furtive look down the corridor. Two harried maids rushed by, carrying armloads of blankets and fresh linens to one of the bedchambers. Gillian waited until they passed before leaning closer to Simon and whispering, "I must admit I am surprised to see you. I thought you had enough wisdom to keep clear of the Dark Queen."

"I had little choice. Gautier took me by surprise."

"You? The great Le Balafre?" Gillian mocked. "I have never known you to be caught off guard."

Simon grimaced, remembering the way he had been mooning over Miri's lock of hair. "I was a bit, er, distracted."

"Now you truly astonish me. Even the queen says she never met a man more tenacious or single-minded. She once put a large price on your head, did you know that?"

"I have many enemies who would be happy to see my head part company with my shoulders."

"Not this head, you fool." Gillian tweaked the end of his beard and gave a throaty laugh. "This one." She slid her fingers provocatively near his crotch. "Her Majesty offered a queen's ransom in jewels to the one who could seduce you away from your mission to hunt witches."

As Gillian's fingers inched lower, Simon sucked in his breath and put her hand firmly away from him. "Then I assume you became a wealthy woman."

"Me?" Gillian snorted. "I held your interest for less than a month. That didn't even earn me a pearl necklet. Especially when the queen suspected you were only seeking a way to prove she was a witch. Of course, when you realized I would be of no help, you were done with me."

"Gillian, I am sorry—" Simon began, but she cut him off with a shake of her head.

"Don't be. I am accustomed to being used and you did it far more gently than most." A look of unexpected sadness stole through her eyes, but she was quick to rally, flashing him an overbright smile. "Despite the fact that neither of us got what we wanted, we did share a pleasant interlude, did we not?"

"Yes, we did," Simon agreed. Gillian had been a skilled and generous lover and for a time she had eased some of the emptiness of his nights. He felt a strange urge to draw her gown up over her shoulders and get her to wash the paint from her face.

"Surely you have amassed enough rewards in the queen's, er, service. Why don't you leave this life?"

Gillian's mouth thinned into a bitter line. "No one simply walks away from the Dark Queen. Remember that if you are ever tempted to sell your soul to her."

"I doubt my soul would be of any interest to Her Grace. Even if it was, I have no intention of making any deals with the devil."

"That is what we all say, my dear Simon. Come, it is unwise to keep Her Majesty waiting."

She led him briskly toward a door near the end of the hall, her perfume lingering behind her like a troubling memory. Simon fought to keep his head clear, knowing he was going to need his wits about him. He had first encountered the Dark Queen when he had been a mere lad, apprenticed to the witch-hunter, Vachel Le Vis. Master Le Vis had been fooled by the queen's matronly demeanor, but Simon had been chilled when he looked into those dark de Medici eyes.

Eyes that could mesmerize, strip a man's soul bare,

plant thoughts in his head that he should never entertain, just as she had done with Le Vis. Simon had vowed that he would never go the way of his poor master and he had resisted the queen's efforts to gain any control over him.

Perhaps he had been so successful because he had no personal ambition for her to prey upon, no one he cared about to be threatened, no point of vulnerability. Except that was no longer true. He did have a weakness and she was tucked up fast asleep, back at the Brass Horse. Simon resolutely blocked all thought of Miri from his mind. Give the Dark Queen any hint of vulnerability or fear and she would use it as a weapon against him.

Gillian ushered him into a large study with an oak coffer-style ceiling, the walls adorned with many paintings set in heavy gilt frames, portraits mixed with scenes of bucolic country life. One of the queen's ladies, an older woman, sat working on some embroidery near the hearth. Several others stood about in quiet attendance. They cast nervous glances as Simon and Gillian entered, but otherwise took no notice of him.

Near the center of the room was a writing desk littered with parchment, ink, quills, and sealing wax. The ornate chair was drawn back as though only recently vacated by its owner, the woman who had retreated to the windows at the far end of the chamber.

Her back was turned to him, but Simon had no difficulty recognizing the short, heavy figure of the Dark Queen garbed in her usual unrelenting black, her thinning silver hair drawn back beneath a bon grace cap. She rested one plump white hand against the windowpane, staring out.

Or perhaps she merely sought to escape the trio of men who trailed after her wide skirts like a pack of yipping dogs.

Their doublets and trunk hose were of good quality, but somber, not nearly fashionable enough for courtiers. The obvious leader of the group, a burly man with a florid complexion, was gesticulating fiercely. ". . . and something has got to be done, Your Grace. A regiment of the Catholic League invaded my land only last week, making off with cattle and some of my finest horses."

"And if that were not bad enough, a pack of these ruffians broke up our services," one of his thinner companions complained. "It was a miracle we were all able to escape with our lives."

"The last treaty signed by His Majesty guaranteed certain rights to those of the Reformed religion," the burly man added. "That we might worship as we chose, providing it was done quietly and that certain towns and cities would be refuges—"

"I am aware of what was in the treaty, Le Marle," the queen interrupted coldly.

Overhearing this exchange, Simon compressed his lips in surprise. Reformed religion? These men were *Huguenots* and were appealing to the Dark Queen for justice? It was surely as ludicrous as condemned men begging the executioner for mercy. Even Protestants who had been nowhere near Paris on that bloody St. Bartholomew's Day of 1572 had to be well aware that the queen was accounted responsible for the massacre of thousands of their brethren.

Le Marle continued to plead, "If Your Grace will only

present our grievances to the king. Despite all that has happened in the past, we of the Huguenot faith want to remain loyal to His Majesty. Our leader, Henry of Navarre, has nothing but good will toward his royal cousin, while the duc de Guise—

"I must speak bluntly, Your Grace. De Guise wants your son's crown for himself and he is using the Catholic League as his weapon. By attacking Huguenots, he cuts away at what little support the king of France has left among his subjects. If the duke's depredations against the Protestants go unchecked, you are going to have a bloodbath that will make all past battles in this conflict seem like mere skirmishes."

"Are you threatening me, Le Marle?" the queen demanded.

"No, merely trying to warn Your Grace. Even if the king buckles to de Guise's rising power, we Huguenots will not. There will be civil war on such scale as France has never—"

"Enough." Catherine flung up one hand in a wearied gesture. "I sympathize with your concerns, my lords, but I am very tired at present. We will continue this discussion . . . tomorrow."

"But Your Grace—"

"Tomorrow!"

The sharpness of her command caused Le Marle and his companions to beat a hasty retreat. But their frustration was evident as they stalked out of the chamber.

When the door had closed, Catherine's shoulders slumped and she vented a deep sigh. Simon wagered it was not often the Dark Queen displayed such signs of weakness. Gillian cleared her throat and stepped forward.

"Pardon, Your Majesty, but Monsieur Aristide has arrived, as you requested."

Without looking around, the queen commanded Gillian and the rest of her women to depart. One by one, the ladies curtsied and exited with Gillian bringing up the rear. She paused long enough to arch her brows as though offering Simon one last warning before shutting the door, leaving him alone with the Dark Queen.

As Catherine came slowly away from the windows, Simon moved forward to make his bow. He froze in shock as he got his first good look at his formidable adversary. The Dark Queen was advancing in years, but she had always seemed indomitable, eerily immortal. Catherine was finally starting to show her age. She looked drawn and haggard, heavy lines creasing her mouth and brow. The most startling change was in those penetrating de Medici eyes. They appeared rheumy, their dark luster dimmed.

Her voice, however, held its familiar trace of mockery. "Am I that hideous a sight, you need gawk at me, Monsieur Le Balafre?"

Simon managed to stop staring and complete his bow. "I no longer rejoice in that title, Your Grace."

"Very well, then *Monsieur Aristide*. Have you quite recovered from your shock at finding me so altered?"

"Forgive me, Your Grace, I was merely surprised. You look . . . tired, that is all."

"Gallantry from a witch-hunter? How unexpected. But there is no need for you to mince words with me. I look like a complete harridan. Growing old is the very devil."

"But the alternative is even worse."

Catherine gave a throaty chuckle. "Gallantry and a

sense of humor? Apparently, I am not the only one who has changed, although you are still as elusive as ever. I have had my agents scouring the countryside for you."

"I was not aware Your Grace was looking for me."

"Or you would have made yourself even scarcer, hmm?" She extended her hand to him and commanded. "My eyesight is not what it once was. Come closer. You need not be afraid of me."

"I am not." Simon took her hand and saluted it perfunctorily.

"What? Not one shiver of apprehension as you passed through my castle gate?" she taunted. "The thought never occurred to you how easily you could be made to vanish within these walls?"

Simon barely managed to conceal his start. Perhaps those eyes of hers had not dimmed as much as he thought. He needed to remain on his guard.

"It occurred to me. It simply did not concern me overmuch," Simon lied. He had a fleeting thought of Miri, suppressed it. "My death would be of little consequence to anyone."

"You underrate yourself. There are witches across France who would rejoice to hear you were no more. As for myself, when I die, I expect the revels in Paris to last at least a week."

The queen's mouth twisted wryly. "Well, they must all perforce delay their celebrations a while longer. I have no intentions of obliging them anytime soon. Nor that you should either. Our relations have not exactly been . . . cordial in the past, but I am hoping that will change now that we have something in common."

"Such as?"

"The same enemy. This Silver Rose is beginning to prove quite a nuisance, is she not?"

"So Your Grace knows something of this creature?" Simon probed cautiously.

"I have been aware of her for some time, thanks to all these earnest and lengthy dispatches you have been sending to my son."

Catherine hobbled past him, her movements appearing stiff and painful. She winced as she bent to pick up one of the papers strewn across the top of the desk. Simon recognized his own handwriting.

"His Grace is too preoccupied at present to have time to spare for much of anything, even the state of his own king—" Catherine checked herself. Simon knew the queen was often angered by her son's erratic behavior, but she seldom allowed her vexation to show, at least not in public. Pursing her lips for a moment, she continued, "I, however, have read your reports with considerable concern."

"A concern that has taken a long time to manifest itself, if Your Grace will pardon my saying so," Simon pointed out. "I have been sending those reports for over a year."

"I saw little to interest me at first, just some wild tales about a witch's coven. Frankly, Monsieur Aristide, I thought you had finally run as mad as your late master, Le Vis."

"And what has happened to make you change your mind?"

"*This.*" The queen reached for a small chest at the corner of the desk. Simon had assumed it must contain writing materials, quill and ink. But when Catherine flicked open the lid and gingerly pulled back a fold of linen fabric, she revealed the withered remnants of a flower. Although the petals no longer glittered, there was no mistaking the flower's strange ashen hue.

"A silver rose," Simon murmured.

"I thought the cursed thing would never wither and die. Ironic, isn't it? That the poison that extended the life of this flower and gave it such exceptional beauty should be so fatal to whoever touches it."

"How did Your Grace come by this?"

"It was given to me by one of the Silver Rose's coven, apparently as a small token of the sorceress's esteem. Fortunately, the rose came into the hands of a guard instead of mine. Well, fortunately for me, not him."

Tearing his gaze from the box, Simon directed a startled look at the Dark Queen. "Are you telling me that this witch actually—actually—"

"Had the impertinence to try to assassinate *me*? Yes." Despite her dry tone, Simon sensed the queen was badly shaken by the attempt on her life. He was a little shaken by it himself. He had accounted the Silver Rose as a threat, but even he had not fully appreciated how dangerous she was until now.

"My God," he muttered. "If this creature would dare attack Your Grace then—then—"

"Then she would dare anything," Catherine finished his thought as she closed the lid of the chest. "You stopped sending in your reports some time ago."

"No one was taking any heed of them."

"Well, now *I* am. So tell me. Are you any nearer to discovering who this witch is, what she wants?

"The identity of the Silver Rose still eludes me. As to what she wants—" Simon shrugged. "Sometimes it seems as if her only aim is to spread as much evil, fear, and misery as possible."

"Now you are talking like a witch-hunter," Catherine scoffed. "You rarely find anyone who does evil for evil's sake alone. Even madmen have reason for what they do, at least in their own mind. I need you to find out what this Silver Rose's true aims are, put an end to her schemes and her as well. From now on, you will send your reports directly to me."

Simon was taken aback by this cool demand. He rubbed the ends of his beard, trying to find some tactful way of refusing. Unfortunately, he could think of none.

"Forgive me, Your Grace," he said bluntly. "But I was not aware that I worked for you."

"Forgive *me,* my dear Le Balafre," she returned silkily. "But I was not aware that you were succeeding on your own."

"True. And in light of that, I wonder that Your Grace would even desire my services."

"Because you are the only one who even detected the existence of this sorceress. You are a clever, perceptive man, and together we can defeat this Silver Rose. I can supply you with funds, men, arms, anything you need."

"No," Simon snapped. When a tiny crease appeared between the queen's brows, he sought to ameliorate his tone. "I appreciate Your Grace's offer but—"

"You would sooner accept help from the devil," she interrupted with a dry laugh. Rustling closer, she touched his hand lightly. "Believe me, I understand. I know that in the past you harbored certain . . . suspicions of me, imagining I might even be a witch myself.

"An absurd notion that I fear may have been encouraged by my own son when Henry engaged you to rid all France of sorcery. But that was a time when relations between the king and I were . . . a little strained, although it was nothing serious. Merely a boy seeking to rebel against the influence of his mother. But Henry has long since realized how much he needs me, as do you, Monsieur Aristide."

"All the same, Your Grace, I prefer to continue working alone." Simon tried to inch away from her, but her grip tightened on his wrist.

She stared up him, trying to fix him with her gaze. But her eyes watered and she was obliged to give over the attempt. She turned away from him, muttering under her breath as she applied her handkerchief to her eyes.

As she turned to face him again, she had recovered her steely composure. "The problem with you working alone is that you have no official status. You have taken up this investigation entirely on your own, with no authority from the king or any parliament. Acting as prosecutor, judge, and executioner when you find one of these witches."

"I have only killed when I had to," Simon said. "In self-defense."

"Oh, I am sure of that." The queen cast him a thin smile. "Still, it is the sort of questionable behavior that could even get a witch-hunter detained somewhere—oh, for instance in a castle dungeon until the matter was cleared up."

"Is Your Grace threatening to have me arrested?" Simon asked.

"No, merely pointing out to you the awkwardness of your situation. Now, you would be entirely safe from any sort of prosecution if I were to give you my royal commission to pursue your inquiries unimpeded. An offer you would be most unwise to refuse."

An offer? More like a pistol being held to his head. Simon paced toward the windows, trying to buy himself time to think. It was unbelievable that only that morning he had felt so isolated and alone in his quest to defeat the Silver Rose. Now he was barraged with more help than he could have imagined and none of it the kind he had wanted. On the one side, there was Miri, gentle, earnest, and forgiving as an angel, harboring some notion that the women of this coven might yet be saved, turned back to the light. And on the other, there was Catherine, a very devil for intrigue and dark dealings, who would have no problem slaughtering anyone whom she perceived as a threat.

It was like being caught between heaven and hell. Each woman determined to make use of him after her own fashion, each doing a fine job of forcing him into alliance. Whoever said females were the weaker sex? Simon thought wryly.

But with Catherine, Simon had no other choice, not if he entertained any hope of riding away from this castle tonight. And loath as he was to admit it, a document granting him official authority might prove useful when the time came to arrest the Silver Rose and her coven.

"Very well. I accept," he said, then added grudgingly, "Thank you."

The queen smiled as though she knew how hard wrung those words were. She eased herself stiffly behind the desk and reached for a piece of blank parchment. As she dipped her quill in the ink, she said, "Now about the troop of men I propose to assign—"

"I want no men," Simon interrupted.

Pausing with her quill suspended over the paper, the queen frowned up at him. "If this coven is growing as large as you fear, you will find yourself badly outnumbered. What do you propose to do when you corner this witch? Simply command her to surrender?"

"No, I have always intended to seek help from the church or ask one of the local seigneurs to lend me some of the men from his land."

"This matter is far too important to be left in the hands of priests or a pack of peasants. I will assign Captain Gautier and his guard—"

"No!" Simon said more forcibly. "I learned to my cost years ago how difficult it is to control mercenaries like Gautier. Soldiers more concerned with fattening their purse than dispensing justice, slaughtering, looting, burning, consuming the innocent along with the guilty."

Catherine pursed her lips. "Very well. We shall leave this matter of soldiers alone for the present, until you actually find this sorceress."

Bending closely over the parchment, she squinted as she proceeded to write out the document. Simon watched in disgruntled silence as the quill scratched across the page. The queen finished with surprising swiftness, despite the number of times she had to stop to painfully flex her fingers. As she sanded the ink dry, she said, "I would recommend you begin your inquiries at the Brass Horse Inn. I

assume that is why you are there, because of Lucie Paillard. You made reference to the girl in one of your reports."

"Yes, but that was over a year ago. And her parents
know nothing," Simon added hastily, lest the Dark Queen be
tempted to order the Paillards' arrest. The unfortunate couple had already suffered enough on account of their daughter. "I have thoroughly examined the innkeeper and his wife
myself. They are completely ignorant of their daughter's
whereabouts, have not even heard from her in over a year."

"Unfortunately, I have."

"What?" Simon asked sharply.

The Dark Queen heated some red wax and dripped
some onto the bottom of the document near her signature.
Scarce able to curb his impatience, Simon waited for her to
continue, but he had a cold feeling in the pit of his stomach, a premonition of what Catherine was about to say.

"Lucie Paillard was the one sent to poison me with the
rose. She appeared in the crowd outside Notre Dame, dis-
guised as a street vendor. She would have escaped the
same way, had I not the presence of mind to have her detained."

"And where is she now?"

"She was my guest at the Bastille for a while, but the
warder's entertainment of her was a little too rigorous. The
girl died while being questioned by de Varney's men."

No one died from merely being questioned, Simon was
tempted to retort. Although he had never resorted to such
methods himself, he could well imagine what the warder's
questions had involved, the rack, the boot, whips, thumb
screws. Simon had despised Lucie Paillard for the callous

way she had abandoned her babe, allowed Luc to freeze to death on that barren hillside. But to be slowly, brutally tortured to death . . . Did anyone deserve such a fate?

Once Simon might have believed so, or convinced himself that he did. Now all he could think of was Colette Paillard with her trembling mouth and sad eyes. He wondered where he'd ever find the courage to tell that frail woman what had become of her only child.

"So did de Varney gain any information by this—this *questioning*?" Simon asked caustically.

Catherine affixed her royal seal to the bottom of the document. She hesitated before answering, "The girl did provide one clue. Right before she died, she said that the Silver Rose has possession of . . . the *Book of Shadows.*"

Simon's breath stilled. "The *Book of Shadows*? How is that possible?"

"You tell me. You were the one who let that book vanish the night of the fire at the inn." Catherine lowered her lashes. "Or so I have heard rumored. Then you ransacked Faire Isle in search of it."

"That is because I believed the Comte de Renard had taken it."

"Obviously, you were wrong. I strongly suggest you search both your memory and any records you made of that day. Figure out who else was there at the inn, had the opportunity to steal the book, and you may well unmask our clever Silver Rose." Catherine slowly rolled up the document. "The *Book of Shadows* is said to be a grimoire full of the most deadly spells ever conceived, but written in an ancient language, not easy to decipher. This sorceress has already learned to brew a powerful poison. If she is able to unlock any more of the book's secrets, I need hardly tell you the kind of danger we all will face."

"No, Your Grace," Simon murmured. Alarmed as he was at the thought of the *Book of Shadows* being in the Silver Rose's possession, other equally disturbing thoughts raced through his mind. For a woman who insisted she was not a witch, the queen knew a damnable lot about both the *Book of Shadows* and what had transpired at the Charters Inn that night.

Simon had always been afraid the Dark Queen might read his thoughts. He had never expected to find himself in the position of reading hers.

"Damnation," he thought. *"She wants that book for herself."*

Now, not only did he have the Silver Rose to defeat, he was going to have to thwart the Dark Queen as well. For a man who had already found himself on shaky ground, Simon felt as though he had suddenly sunk up to his waist in quicksand.

As Catherine bound the document neatly with a thin black ribbon, she said, "As soon as you discover who the Silver Rose is and where she is hiding, report to me. Do nothing until I give the word. This arrest must be handled properly. I want both the sorceress and that book brought straight to me. I—I will not rest easy until I see that dangerous text destroyed for myself."

"Of course, Your Grace," Simon said, thinking that he'd consign the *Book of Shadows* to hell before he ever surrendered it to the Dark Queen, even if he had to convey it there himself.

Catherine held the rolled commission out to him. "Keep

in close contact, Monsieur Aristide. I should not like to have to send Captain Gautier looking for you again. I have many worries and difficulties weighing down upon me. If you succeed in ridding me of this one, I shall be eternally grateful. You may name your reward, ask any favor you like."

Simon merely arched one brow at the offer. As he accepted the document from her hand, he could not refrain from reminding her. "You once made similar promises to my late master. The cold dark of a grave was his only reward for serving you."

"That was none of my doing, but the Comte de Renard's. Alas, I fear acquiring such deadly enemies is a hazard of the witch-hunter's profession." The queen smiled blandly up at him. "I trust you are better at guarding your back."

"Oh, I will be, Your Grace," Simon said, baring his teeth in a smile of his own. "I promise you."

※※※

IT WAS NEARLY MIDNIGHT by the time the queen's ladies helped her ready for bed. Sensing Catherine's dark mood, the women spoke in hushed voices instead of their usual chatter. Catherine scarce noticed them, her energy focused on subduing the weakness of her own body as she eased painfully into her nightdress.

She ached and throbbed in every joint, the journey to Chenonceau having taxed her to the limits of her endurance. In her youth she had been a skilled and intrepid horsewoman. But those days were long gone. Hampered by her age and weight, she now had to suffer being jarred along on a litter for days on end.

If the journey itself had not battered her enough, she had been further drained by the meeting with Le Marle and his friends. *Huguenots,* Catherine thought with a grimace. Such a dour, serious, and persistent thorn in her side.

The St. Bartholomew's Day massacre had been a nightmarish debacle, going beyond even what she had intended. Inflamed by her, the Catholics of Paris had gone on a rampage of riot and murder that had lasted for days and left Catherine with much blood on her hands and piles of bodies stacked along the banks of the Seine.

Her reputation further blackened and that of France as well, at least Catherine had congratulated herself that she had stemmed the rising power of the Protestants. But the Reformed religion had continued to spread like the plague. Once it was contained in the southwest corner of France, mostly within the borders of Navarre, but now there seemed to be enclaves of Huguenots everywhere.

As far as Catherine was concerned, men might worship however they pleased as long as they did it quietly and made no trouble for her. But unfortunately these Protestants provided the perfect excuse for enemies to meddle with her kingdom under the excuse of religious zeal. The pope, the king of Spain, and worst of all the duc de Guise.

The duke was demanding the king meet him to cede all control of the military to the Catholic League and to outlaw the Reformed religion completely. God rot the arrogant and ambitious man, Catherine thought bitterly. So many times she had been tempted to take care of de Guise after her own fashion. A little morsel of something slipped into his wine cup or the tip of a poisoned arrow lodged in his back. She was only restrained by the realization that if the duke met his death in any mysterious or violent manner, it would be laid at her door. He was so beloved in Paris, the entire city would rise up in revolution. Both she and her son would have to flee for their lives.

No, Catherine reflected sourly, the meeting would have to take place. Most likely her weak-willed son would retreat to his hermitage and leave Catherine to deal with the duke and she had nothing to bargain with, no weapons unless . . .

Unless she could gain possession of the *Book of Shadows*. It was a slim and desperate hope, but the only one left to her. Catherine was confident she could unlock the ancient book's dark secrets if only she could get her hands on it. Then what unlimited power could be hers, what freedom from fear, the threats of de Guise, even the ravages of time on her own body.

She'd had some of her own agents searching ever since the incident in Paris, but her best hope of finding the Silver Rose, of recovering the *Book,* rested with that clever witch-hunter. But she trusted Aristide no further than he did her. She feared he would destroy the book the moment he found it. That was why she had commanded Captain Gautier to shadow the witch-hunter, keep close watch without Aristide being aware of his presence.

"Your Grace?"

A soft voice recalled Catherine from her troubled thoughts. She found Gillian Harcourt at her side. Catherine's eyes were so bad tonight, the woman's face was little more than a blur as she presented the tray with the queen's nightly posset.

The brew was of Catherine's own concoction, designed to take the edge off of her pain and allow her a little sleep. Quite often, it did neither. As Catherine sipped from the silver chalice, wincing at the posset's taste, she reflected glumly that she had always been better at concocting poisons than she was at the healing arts.

Not like the Lady of Faire Isle. Catherine was surprised to feel a pang at the thought of Ariane. Enemies, they had been, but at least Catherine had always been able to depend on Ariane to be forthright and honest, her motives pure. And that was a rare quality in anyone.

Sometimes Catherine feared she had set the entire world out of balance when she had allowed the Lady of Faire Isle to be driven into exile. A great sin for any wise woman, one that had left Catherine cursed and that was why nothing had gone right for her ever since.

Draining the rest of the posset, she shivered and gave herself a brisk shake. Lord, what a superstitious fool she was becoming in her old age. As she returned the cup to the tray, Catherine was annoyed when her hand trembled.

Gillian reached out to steady the cup before it tumbled to the carpet. "Your Grace is very fatigued this evening," she murmured solicitously. "Your meeting with the witch-hunter must have been very trying."

Catherine merely grunted.

"I don't know what service Your Grace requires of him, but Simon Aristide can be a very difficult man. I would be happy to—to help you with him."

"How? By seducing him?" Catherine gave a contemptuous laugh. "My dear Gillian, you weren't able to keep the man in your bed when your looks were at their peak. Considering the extent of your charms these days, you'd be lucky to hold his attention for five minutes up against the stable wall."

The queen turned away, trudging wearily toward her bed. Otherwise even she could not have failed to note the courtesan's blistering look of hatred and resentment.

GILLIAN GROPED her way across the palace grounds, stealing a nervous glance over her shoulder. As near as she could tell, her stealthy journey through the gardens had gone unnoticed, her dark cloak helping her to blend with the night, the hood pulled far forward to conceal her blond hair and the pale oval of her face.

But she didn't know why she was so anxious, Gillian reflected bitterly. Sometimes she thought she could march brazenly out the main entry instead of slipping out the kitchen door and none of the guards would remark upon it. Strange how as a woman grew older and her beauty faded, she became all but invisible.

Besides, it was not the guards who worried her. She could fob them off with some tale of a secret assignation, stealing out to meet a lover. But should the queen ever become aware of these nocturnal wanderings of hers—

Gillian stifled a squeak of terror as she blundered into something solid and the Dark Queen herself loomed before her. Pressing her hand to her thumping heart, she gazed up at the statue bathed in moonlight. An eerie and unusual likeness of the queen, it depicted her with snakes entwined about her skirts and arms.

Gillian shivered. Her Majesty had always possessed a strange sense of humor. Who else but the Dark Queen would have herself immortalized in such a macabre fashion like some—some God-cursed Medusa? The statue's eyes regarded her with a blank stony stare. A little fogged like the queen's eyes herself often were these days.

But unlike some of the queen's other ladies, Gillian was not inclined to discount her mistress's faculties. She had lived under the power of the de Medici gaze for too many years. As a young girl, she had been mesmerized by those dark piercing eyes, lured into the queen's service with the promise of more excitement and riches than she would ever know as some man's wife.

Gillian had had her share of both, but any funds or jewels she had ever amassed had slipped through her prodigal fingers. There had never seemed any reason to be saving, not when her life at court was a constant whirl of diversion, intrigue, and the flattery of dashing men.

But each morning when she looked in her mirror, she despaired as she found another wrinkle despite all the creams and ointments she applied. Her compliments and admirers grew less and less, as did the value the queen set upon her services. Once she had depended upon Gillian to charm some of the most powerful men in France. But the last lover the queen had commanded her to take had been a mere clerk, a servant in the duc de Guise's household. Gillian had endured the man's pudgy groping fingers and garlicky breath for nothing. The clerk had imparted little information of any value regarding the duke's activities. The queen had unfairly blamed Gillian for that.

But still Gillian knew that the queen would never let her go, not until she had used up all that remained of Gillian's youth and beauty. Not until she became some dried-up old prune fit for nothing except to sit and stitch upon fine gowns intended for the queen's younger, more vibrant ladies. No, she would never be free of the Dark Queen until those stony eyes were closed forever . . .

"Psst. Gillian!"

A voice hissed out of the shadows, startling her. Gillian caught a flicker of light from a grove of trees near the hidden grotto. She hastened in that direction to find a slender figure garbed in doublet and trunk hose. From a distance, the person might have been mistaken for a young page, but up close the lantern's light revealed a sylph of a girl, so thin that if she turned sideways, she looked likely to vanish entirely.

Brown curls tumbled about a long narrow face, her right cheek, portions of her neck, and her hands marred by scars. Nanette Scoville, once employed in the castle kitchens, had been badly scalded when a pot of boiling water had overturned.

As Gillian approached, Nanette held up the lantern to guide her steps.

"Lower that light," Gillian whispered fiercely. "Do you want to be seen?"

The girl did so at once. "You're late," she complained.

"It was not easy for me to get away. I thought the queen would never retire."

Nanette looped one arm around Gillian's neck to embrace her warmly. As she did so, the girl gave a huge sniff. Gillian stiffened and drew back, eying her warily.

"Are you ill?"

"It's nothing. Only too much standing about in the night air." The girl wiped her nose on the back of her sleeve. "Never mind about me. What news have you for the Silver Rose?"

The back of Gillian's neck prickled with unease. Even though they stood alone in the garden, far from any prying eyes and ears, she wished Nanette would be more discreet, not utter that name aloud.

Speaking as low as she could, she said, "I have good news, I hope. The time and place for the meeting with the duc de Guise has been set. Next month in Paris, at the Louvre."

"And they will all be there, the duke, the Dark Queen, and the king of France?" Nanette asked eagerly.

"All of them."

"Oho!" Nanette chortled. "Our lady will be pleased."

"I fear she will not be pleased by my other tidings." Gillian hesitated before confessing, "Simon Aristide was summoned to attend the queen tonight."

"What!" Nanette squawked.

Gillian clapped a hand to the girl's mouth, stealing an anxious look around them. But the garden was silent except for a faint breeze that rustled the bushes and trees, the distant cry of a nightjar.

Nanette pried her fingers away. Although she appeared much distressed, she managed to speak in a quieter tone.

"That witch-hunter is supposed to be dead. Agatha Ferrers was especially charged with the mission. She set out after him weeks ago."

"Obviously Agatha failed. I assure you Aristide is very much alive. As for Agatha, I leave it to you to determine what must have happened to her."

Nanette shuddered and crossed herself. "Poor soul." The girl immediately brightened. "But we should not grieve for her. The Silver Rose will resurrect her when the time comes."

"Er—yes." Gillian wrapped her arms tightly about herself and shifted her feet. She was never entirely comfortable when Nanette talked like this, her eyes agleam with an almost fanatical enthusiasm.

The girl cocked her head to one side like an inquisitive sparrow. "Oh, Gillian," she said sadly. "You don't believe?"

"I am not sure," Gillian hedged. "I want to. But the promises that you tell me this sorceress makes seem so incredible. Spells that will restore youth and beauty, bring one back from the dead. Even the Dark Queen is unable to do that."

"The queen is as nothing compared to the Silver Rose. She can perform miracles. I have seen her do it myself. Only the other day, the child of one of the women at our camp, a little girl no more than two, fell into the pond and drowned. The Silver Rose kissed her, breathed life back into her. I saw it myself."

"Truly?" Gillian faltered.

Nanette nodded vigorously. "That is why you must continue to have faith."

"It would be easier if I was ever permitted to meet her, at least to know who she is."

"That will come in time," Nanette soothed. "The lady is very cautious about who she trusts. I have been telling her all about you, how clever you are, how you were the only one who was kind to me when I ended up with child and was driven from this castle in disgrace."

She tossed her head, preening a little. "Of course I was immediately allowed into the inner circle because I offered the ultimate proof of loyalty, the sacrifice of my babe."

"I can hardly offer any such proof as that," Gillian remarked bitterly. Over the years, the Dark Queen's potions had helped Gillian rid herself of a number of unwanted infants. The last abortion over two years ago had been a particularly bloody and painful one. Gillian had thought she would die. The midwife who attended her told her how lucky she was. Her womb was damaged beyond repair. She would never conceive another child.

Gillian supposed she should have been grateful. And yet those evenings she sat alone, neglected and forgotten while the other ladies attended some court revel, Gillian found herself thinking of all those small lives that were lost to her, imagining how old this child or that one might be, if she had permitted it to live.

"Was it hard for you, Nanette?" she asked softly. "To leave your little boy to die?"

"It wasn't a little boy to me. It wasn't a babe, it wasn't anything but a devil, a curse forced into my womb when I was raped by that drunken guard." Nanette's face contorted and she looked as though she was about to cry. Her nose dripped again and she rubbed it fiercely.

"Forget about all that," she sniffed. "Just tell me why that witch-hunter was here tonight. What would the Dark Queen want with the likes of him?"

"I am not entirely sure. I had to listen outside the door and it was difficult to hear everything. But I believe she means to help him in his hunt for the Silver Rose."

"*Scelerat!*" Nanette exclaimed and spat.

Gillian leaped back. "Nanette! That is disgusting."

"No, disgusting is a witch using the services of a witch-hunter."

"This is not the first time the queen has done so. She will use anyone who can serve her ends." Gillian expelled a frustrated sigh. "The queen is so beleaguered trying to thwart the ambitions of the duc de Guise, she would not even have noticed the Silver Rose if that Paillard girl had not tried to kill her. It was a stupid thing to do."

"Our lady deplored Lucie's actions as much as you do. The girl simply got overzealous and acted on her own." Nanette shrugged. "She paid the price for her folly."

"As we all may well do," Gillian fretted. "Stirring up the Dark Queen is like—like prodding a sleeping tigress, and then if you pair her with Simon Aristide—"

"You worry too much. As soon as I report this back to the lady, I assure you the witch-hunter will be eliminated. Do you have any idea where he is at the moment?"

Gillian hesitated, assailed by a sudden memory. During their brief liaison, she had always had difficulty persuading Simon to spend the entire night with her. But she could remember how pleasant it had felt to wake up with his strong arms about her. For such a ruthless man, he could be so amazingly gentle.

She sighed, shaking off the recollection. If their positions were reversed and Simon saw her as a threat, she doubted he'd have any hesitation at all about seeing her struck down. There was nothing personal in any of this. One did what one must. Simon would understand that as well as anyone.

"Aristide is . . . is staying at the Brass Horse Inn."

"Lucie's old home?" Nanette laughed. "That's perfect. If the witch-hunter is destroyed there, it will be a fitting tribute to her memory."

"Knowing Simon, I doubt he'll remain in one place for long."

"We'll find him and finish him wherever he is. There will be no mistakes this time, I promise you. So stop worrying." Nanette gave her arm a hard squeeze and beamed up at her with that glazed look on her face. "Our day is fast coming, Gillian. When none of us need walk in fear of any man, nothing but power and glory for the Silver Rose and all her devotees."

"Yes." Gillian tried to smile, stifle the feeling she might merely be trading bondage to one witch for another. But it hardly mattered if she was. She had gone too far to turn back now.

Chapter Ten

THE MORNING SUN FILTERED PAST THE SHUTTERS, PAINTING stripes of warmth across the bed. Miri stirred and rolled over, half-expecting Necromancer to clamber atop her chest and assault her face with the rough lap of his tongue. But as she forced her eyes open and focused on the room's bare stone walls, she groaned, remembering where she was.

She could have used the comfort of her cat's warm purring presence. From the moment she had crossed the threshold of the Brass Horse Inn, she had found it a bleak place and would be glad to be gone from here, no matter what dangers lay on the road ahead.

Easing back the covers, she struggled to a sitting position and stretched, feeling a little stiff. The bed had been comfortable enough, but she had passed an uneasy night.

Thankfully she had not been beset by one of her strange dreams. No harrowing nightmares about palaces overrun with salamanders and monstrous-sized chess pieces, the shattered white knight left broken and bleeding.

But she had had a difficult time dozing off, far too conscious of the man just outside her door. She wondered how Simon had fared last night, stretched out on the floor, across the room's threshold. She felt guilty he had been obliged to do that and resolved not to allow such a thing again. After all, she had been the one to insist upon accompanying him, overriding all his objections. She ought to bear her share of the difficulties and inconveniences of the situation. And yet, perhaps Simon had been wise to put the barrier of the door between them, far wiser than she.

She had seen the longing in his gaze, had been fully alive to the danger of it, the more so because she had felt her own pulse quicken in response. That tender kiss he had pressed upon her brow last night had affected her as deeply as his fiery parting embrace at the cottage, although in a far different fashion.

She had been raised in an atmosphere of love that had easily found expression in physical demonstrations of affection, warm hugs, busses on the cheek. Despite the kinship she felt with Necromancer, the other creatures of her forest home, she had not realized how starved she'd been for human contact until Simon had erupted back into her life.

But her craving for intimacy went even deeper with him, becoming something more primal. Simon's hungry gaze, the mere caress of his fingers down her cheek had been enough to arouse womanly urges she had allowed to remain dormant inside of her for so long. The ache for a man's touch, the warmth of his mouth on hers, the hot, hard feel of his hands exploring her most intimate places as he tumbled her onto the bed.

Although Miri's face warmed at the thought, she wasn't ashamed of the feeling. Simon was a strong, healthy male. She was a female still in the prime of her childbearing years. Pen two such creatures up together and the urge to mate was natural. As a true daughter of the earth, she knew this.

But as her gaze fell upon the locket she had left resting atop her folded breeches, Miri wondered why she had never experienced any such *natural* urges with Martin. A troubling question and one she did not feel up to examining too closely. At least not this early in the day.

She stumbled out of bed and set about the task of performing her morning toilette and getting dressed. She had slept only in her shirt and the dawn air was cool against her bare legs. There was some fresh water left in the ewer and she splashed it over her face, washing the sleep from her eyes. Tucking the locket down inside her shirt, Miri struggled into the rest of her discarded clothes. She started to braid her hair when a knock sounded.

Miri tiptoed over to the door. Before she had a chance to call out, Simon's voice echoed through the panel. "Miri, open up. It's me."

She made haste to unlatch the door and swung it open, catching her breath at the sight of him. He looked haggard, as though he hadn't slept all night, his face pale beneath his beard. But there was something else about his face, the grim set to his mouth, the darkness clouding his gaze that filled her with foreboding.

"Simon, what's happened?" she asked anxiously as he stalked into the room, closing the door. "What's wrong?"

༺༺༺

MIRI SANK DOWN on the edge of the bed as Simon finished relating the events of the previous night, the details of his meeting with the woman who had been a figure of nightmare to Miri ever since her childhood.

Catherine de Medici, the Dark Queen. Miri shivered, rubbing her arms. Although Catherine had been her family's longtime adversary, she had only ever come into close contact with the queen once, that fateful August Miri had gone to stay with Gabrielle in Paris.

She had accompanied her sister to a tournament held on the lawns of the Louvre, the courtly display of arms nothing but an elaborate façade, masking Catherine's plot to dispose of Captain Nicolas Remy, the man who had eventually become Gabrielle's husband.

The queen's attempt on Remy's life was but one more incident in the havoc that Catherine had wrought in Miri's family over the years. Although she had once claimed friendship with Evangeline Cheney, the queen had employed one of her seductive courtesans to seduce Louis Cheney, breaking his wife's heart. And it had been Catherine who had first set the witch-hunters upon Faire Isle, seeking to recover the incriminating pair of gloves she had used to murder the Huguenot queen, Jeanne of Navarre. Lovely but deadly apparel that had nearly succeeded in killing Gabrielle as well.

But the worst thing that Catherine had done was something Miri had only witnessed in her dreams. She had been tormented by nightmares of St. Bartholomew's Day long before the massacre had ever happened, visions of the Dark Queen uncorking her miasma, using her dark arts to incite an entire city to hatred and a lust for blood.

Three years later when Miri had finally seen Catherine in the flesh, she had been expecting someone far more sinister, not a plump, matronly looking woman. There was no denying the queen had a dark aura, eyes that were far too piercing, but Miri had found something pathetic about Catherine as well. The queen was possessed of strength, intelligence, and extraordinary perception, gifts that could have been put to better use than a life wasted in bitterness and a lust for power.

But Miri's pity for the woman did not blind her to how dangerous Catherine could be. She raised troubled eyes to Simon.

"My God. Why—why didn't you wake me when those men came to fetch you?"

Simon was availing himself of the last of the water in the ewer in an effort to wash the grit and weariness from his face. "What? And have you dragged off to face the Dark Queen as well? Especially when I had no idea what the she-devil was after."

Miri shoved to her feet, saying with a thread of impatience, "I thought we had settled this matter of our partnership last night. You have got to stop protecting me!"

As he reached for the sword he had left propped in the corner, she demanded, "That is what you were doing, isn't it? The reason you went alone to meet with Catherine."

Simon paused in girding on his sword to glance at her with a slight frown. "Yes, why else?"

"I—I don't know." Miri searched his face, tried to dismiss the dark suspicion that nagged at her, but it refused to be quelled. "It is just that you worked for the Dark Queen once before."

"That was Master Le Vis's choice, never mine." Simon buckled his belt with a sharp tug. "Believe me, I would just as soon steer clear of Madame Catherine as you would."

"I'd like to believe that, Simon. But you have not exactly been forthcoming with me. I sensed as soon as we entered this inn that there was something amiss here and yet you chose to tell me nothing of Lucie Paillard's tragic history."

"There didn't seem to be any point," Simon began impatiently, only to check himself with a heavy sigh. "I am sorry. You are right. I should have told you. I don't know why I didn't. I guess I am just too accustomed to being alone, keeping my own counsel."

He stalked over to her, gripping her by the shoulders. "Miri, I promise you I am not engaged in any plot with the Dark Queen. If that were the case, I would not have told you anything about my meeting with her, would I?"

"No. No, you wouldn't have." Miri conceded.

"I completely deplore having anything to do with Catherine de Medici, but I had little choice but to agree to her involvement. And she might prove of some use. The Silver Rose is her enemy as well. She wants to see the woman's evil activities brought to an end as much as we do."

"No, I fear what the queen wants most is to gain possession of that *Book of Shadows*."

"And I mean to do my best to make sure that doesn't happen." Simon squeezed her shoulders gently. "Miri, I realize how hard it has been for you to place any faith in me again, but I swear to you that I'll find a way to thwart both of these witches, the Dark Queen and the Silver Rose."

Miri nodded, even managed a slight smile, but she insisted, "*We* will find a way. All I ask is that the next time you are summoned to any mysterious meeting, you remember I have a stake in this, too. Since you have told me what happened to Lucie, I am more afraid for Carole than ever. I can't speak for Lucie, but I can tell you that Carole is only a desperate, unhappy girl. How is this sorceress able to do this, lure such—such normal young women away from their homes, bewitch them into committing such fearsome acts?"

"I don't know," Simon replied. "Lucie's case was a bit different from what you have told me of the Moreau girl. She was much doted upon by her parents, even after she got herself with child by some young man she refused to name. Gaspard Paillard offered a considerable dowry to get her a husband, an older man, an earnest and respectable miller who was willing to marry her despite everything, but Lucie would have none of it. It was then that her father lost all patience and threatened to keep her locked in her room until she came to her senses, but her mother, Colette—"

Simon broke off at the mention of the woman's name, his mouth thinning as though at some unhappy recollection.

"Simon, what it is?" Miri asked.

"Nothing. I just remembered something I have to do before we leave here. You finish getting ready while I—"

He grimaced. "While I keep a promise I never should have made."

✢✢✢

MIRI FINISHED doing up her hair, tucking the braids beneath the concealment of her hat. Simon had instructed her to wait for him in the room while he set about the difficult task of informing the Paillards their only child was dead. But Miri found herself unable to do so.

As soon as she stepped out into the hall, she was assailed by the sound of a woman wailing, the voice full of such shrill anguish, it pierced straight through Miri's heart. She hastened down the stairs, only to freeze on the threshold of the taproom.

Madame Paillard doubled over, clutching her stomach as though she had sustained a mortal blow, her face streaked with tears. Her husband made no move to go to her aid. Hunched into one of the chairs, Monsieur Paillard sat and stared at nothing, a hollow expression on his face. It was Simon who attempted to place a comforting hand on the woman's shoulder.

Madame Paillard turned on him with a feral cry. She dealt Simon such a ringing slap across his cheek, it caused Miri to wince. The woman fell upon him, pounding him with her fists, raining blows and curses.

"Damn you! Damn you to hell."

Miri pressed her hand to her mouth, expecting him to pin the woman's arms, thrust her away from him. He was so much stronger, he could easily have done so. Instead, he stoically accepted the abuse as Madame Paillard sobbed and railed. "Why d-didn't you do s-something? You—you are a witch-hunter. You're supposed to protect us from evil. If you had s-stopped those terrible women from ever coming here, l-luring my girl away, she would never have— never have—Lucie! Lucie!"

Her arms grew slack, her rage dissolving into incoherent sobs. As she collapsed against Simon, his arms came around her, awkward at first, then more tenderly. He cradled her head against his shoulder, mumbling something incoherent, his face a dark mirror of the woman's pain.

Miri hesitated, awkward and unnoticed in the doorway. She wanted to help, but feared any clumsy interference on her part would only make the situation worse. Before she could decide, Monsieur Paillard roused himself. He bellowed for the maidservant, who crept timidly from the kitchen. Hauling his wife away from Simon, he thrust her in the direction of the girl, bidding her look after her mistress. As the maid helped the weeping woman into the kitchen, a terrible silence descended.

"Monsieur Paillard," Simon began hoarsely. "I am sorry. I wish I could have—"

But the innkeeper waved Simon off with a dispirited gesture. "You have now done all you can, Master Witch-Hunter. Just—just go, I pray you. And never return."

As Monsieur Paillard vanished into the kitchen, Simon stood with his head bowed. Miri felt strangely like an intruder, an outsider to these tragic events in which she had played no part.

She approached Simon tentatively. He looked up as the floorboard creaked beneath her boots, his expression so bleak, Miri ached for him. The imprint of Madame Paillard's hand had faded, but Miri knew somehow that Simon was going to feel the impact of that blow for a long time to come.

Miri gently touched his cheek where the woman had struck him. "Simon—"

But he caught her hand, putting it away from him, something closing down in his gaze, shutting her out.

"Come. Let's just gather up our things and get on the road," he said. "It's going to be another damnably hot day."

※※※

MIRI GUIDED HER HORSE down the rough track that snaked along the river, the morning sun shimmering across the sluggish waters. Since Miri believed that the three women they pursued had taken to traveling by boat, Simon had deemed it best they begin their inquiries along the Cher.

The waterway showed signs of activity, a pair of grizzled old men fishing off the opposite bank, a raft laden with some merchant's goods being poled upriver. It appeared to be tough going owing to the low level of the river, the men aboard cursing when they became mired on a sandbank. The Cher, like everywhere else in the valley, was experiencing the effects of the drought. Adjusting the brim of her hat, Miri could see where the waterline had fallen along the muddy banks, revealing pale white roots and tangled reeds that were usually submerged.

It was as though the river had been wounded by the sun, all its most tender secret places left mercilessly exposed. Not unlike the man who rode at Miri's side. Simon had said little since leaving the Brass Horse Inn, his expression forbidding any discussion of that unpleasant scene back in the taproom.

Miri could well guess the dark thoughts that consumed him and at last she could keep silent no longer. Nudging Samson closer to Elle, she said, "Simon, Madame Paillard was distraught with grief. Otherwise I am sure she would never have blamed you—"

"Why not?" Simon interrupted harshly. "I *am* to blame. I am supposed to protect families like the Paillards from sorcery. It's the only good reason I have ever had for being a witch-hunter."

"But you have been trying your best to stop the Silver Rose. You are only one man and you have been acting entirely alone. You can't possibly believe that you are responsible for protecting all of France from evil."

But Miri was dismayed to realize that he did. His mouth was compressed in a bitter line of self-blame, his face tormented with regrets. Simon cast a haunted glance over his shoulder as though even now he wished he could return to the Brass Horse Inn and somehow make things right for the Paillards, turn back time itself.

"Christ, I should have never told Colette Paillard anything, no matter what I promised," he muttered. "I softened the account of Lucie's death as best I could, but her mother would have been better off not knowing what happened to the girl."

"No, she wouldn't," Miri said sadly. "My father was missing for years. You cannot imagine the pain of having someone you love just vanish that way, the torment, the uncertainty. I didn't learn of his death until last autumn. It grieved me deeply that he was never coming home, but it was also a relief to finally know the truth."

"I am sorry about your father, Miri. Very likely you are right. It is better to know and yet the grave is a damned cold and final place. I realized that the day I had to bury my father, my mother, and my younger sister."

He sounded flinty and hard. If she had not become so accustomed to the cadence of his voice, Miri would never have caught the thread of grief beneath it. She remembered a long time ago Simon telling her about his family, who had perished during a plague along with the rest of his village, a plague that he believed had been caused by a witch.

She reached out to touch Simon's arm. "You seem so self-contained, so independent, sometimes I forget you ever had a home, a family. You have never told me much about them."

"That is because I have done my best to forget."

"It can hurt to remember, but memories can also be a great comfort, sometimes all that one has left." She added gently, "If we allow ourselves to forget the people we loved, they truly are lost to us."

Simon shrugged off her touch. "Miri, I realize that you are only trying to be kind," he said curtly. "But there are some aspects of my life I'd prefer that you left alone. Let's just get on with this search, shall we?"

He spurred Elle onward into a faster pace, obliging Miri to do the same to keep up with him. She didn't look hurt by his rejection of her comfort, merely sad. He knew he'd acted like a surly brute ever since they'd left the inn, but she kept probing places inside him that were too raw, even for her gentle touch.

Lack of sleep and a heavy dose of guilt weren't doing much for his disposition either, guilt over far more than the way that he had failed the Paillards. As Miri cantered alongside him, Simon avoided looking at her, but that didn't stop his conscience from hammering away at him.

He had meant to be completely honest about his meeting with the Dark Queen, but he had ended up suppressing one significant fact, all mention of the document Catherine had given him, authorizing him to take any measure necessary to hunt down and destroy the Silver Rose's coven.

He didn't know why he had failed to show Miri the decree. Perhaps because she had already been shaken by his meeting with the queen, wary of Catherine's involvement. He was afraid Miri might demand he tear up the document and Simon knew he'd never be able to do that. Not when such a royal authorization might prove useful.

Is that what you are really afraid of? A voice inside him jeered. *That she'd want the document destroyed? Or is it more that you fear how she'd react if she knew you had it, meant to use it? That she'd shrink from you, her eyes once more full of mistrust and doubt.*

Lord, what a blasted fool he was, Simon thought in self-disgust. He'd warned Miri himself of the dangers of believing in him and yet he liked that soft, confiding way she often looked at him. More than liked it. He had begun to need that look from her and that scared all hell out of him. He had to find some way to conclude her role in this dangerous venture, send her back to Faire Isle and out of his life. Before she chipped away any further at the armor in which he had encased his heart all these years. And before he did something to hurt her again . . .

As the morning wore on, he paused to question anyone they came across who lived by or traveled upon the river, barge workers, merchants, fisher folk, and ferrymen. But it was difficult, gleaning any information. Simon had long ago discovered that men could be as wary as women when it came to being questioned by a witch-hunter.

Even those who might have been inclined to help shrugged their shoulders in regret. Times were hard. There were so many desperate people abroad these days, looking for work, begging for bread. Who could be expected to notice or remember three more such vagabonds, no matter how earnestly Miri tried to provide a description of the Moreau girl?

By midday they were both hot and discouraged as they cantered into the village of Longpre. Here, Miri insisted that she would do the questioning. She hesitated before admitting that she knew someone who might prove helpful, a chandler's wife. But like Miri's friend from Saint-Malo, this woman was very leery of witch-hunters, so it would be best if Miri went to consult her alone.

Simon had no difficulty interpreting the meaning of this. The chandler's wife was one of those Miri called wise women, versed in arts and practices Simon had been taught to consider forbidden. He didn't much like the idea of letting Miri out of his sight, but he had promised to allow her the freedom of consulting her own people without his interference. The witch-hunter in him found it a difficult promise to keep, the urge to assess this sorceress for himself very strong. But considering he had already broken his vow to be completely honest with Miri, it behooved him to keep this part of their agreement.

While Miri vanished into the shop, Simon positioned himself on rising ground just outside the village, where he could keep the chandler's shop and the lane leading to it well in view. He loosened the girths on the horses' saddles, permitting Elle and Samson to find what tender shoots of grass they could on this sere hillside. Later, when Miri returned and the horses had cooled down enough, he would lead them to the river to drink.

As the horses grazed nearby, Simon leaned up against a sprawling elm, fighting the exhaustion that threatened to overwhelm him. The village spread out below him, Longpre like so many other hamlets along the Cher, tucked between the river and the sprawling farmlands and vineyards beyond.

As the bell in the church tower chimed out the angelus, Simon could see workers pausing in the fields for their noontime meal. These were common lands that they tilled for their own sustenance and to pay their tithes to the local seigneur, just as Simon's own father had done.

His father . . . Simon felt the familiar stab of pain, sought to thrust all thought of the man aside. But Miri's words haunted him.

"If we allow ourselves to forget the people we loved, then they truly are lost to us."

Simon raked his hand down over his face, for the first time in years allowing the images to come. Like blowing the dust off a book that had remained closed for a long time, the pages at first seemed aged and brittle, then became achingly crisper and clearer. In his mind's eye, he could see the whitewashed cottage where he had been born, small but meticulously kept by both of his parents from the vegetable patch to the tiles of the roof. The front door had always been a little low. Simon's father had often banged his head when entering the cottage, and muttered some fierce exclamation, but never a curse.

Javier Aristide would never have sworn in front of his wife and children. In fact, Simon could scarce ever remember him uttering a cross word. A gentle, big-hearted man, his face had been permanently leathered from tilling the fields, his nails cracked, his palms callused from a lifetime of labor. Unlike many of the men from their village, he had been temperate in his habits, both with regard to drink and spending his hard-won coin. Except for that September when Simon had turned eleven and Javier had been standing the entire village to quaffs of wine.

"A toast to my son, Simon," he had called out. "He becomes a man today with a great future before him. No backbreaking labor in the fields for my boy. Tomorrow he leaves to take up his position in household of the Seigneur de Lacey."

"Papa," Simon had murmured, torn between basking in his father's pride and embarrassment. "I will only be a stable hand, mucking out stalls, spreading straw."

"Ah, only a stable boy today. But with your way with horses, it won't be long before you are a groom. And then who knows? Perhaps one day the seigneur's Master of the Horse."

And before Simon could prevent him, his father, usually

the shyest and most retiring of men, had leaped onto one of the tables, demanding that everyone drink to his son's health.

Simon rested his head back against the trunk of the tree, surprised he could actually smile at the memory. It was harder to think of his mother that day, Belda Aristide's eyes red-rimmed from trying not to cry as she pounded the wad of dough, kneading it with unwonted energy.

"Maman," Simon had protested, looking at the array of provender she had assembled to stuff into his pack. "The kitchen at the château is enormous. They have plenty of food there. I shan't starve."

His mother sniffed. "Don't tell me about his lordship's kitchens, Simon Aristide. I know the woman in charge of the baking. A clumsy, careless wench. Her bread will never be as light and crusty as mine."

"Of course not, Maman," Simon had soothed. "But even though I will be living above the stables, I will be able to steal home for a visit sometimes. The château is scarce three miles from here, an easy walk across the fields."

Belda had attempted to smile, smearing a smudge of flour across her cheek as she mopped her eyes. Simon's little sister, who had been anxiously listening to the exchange, crept closer to tug at his sleeve.

"Simon?"

He had hunkered down to her level, "What is it, petite poule?"

Lorene pouted at his teasing name for her, grumbling as she always did. "I am not a little chicken. I just wanted to know if you will ever be able to take me to the château. I want to see my lord's stables and all the grand horses you will be taking care of."

Simon rocked back on his heels, pretending to eye her askance. "I don't know. These are mighty big horses with very big teeth. They might gobble up a little chick like you."

She poked him in the shoulder with her small fist. "Horses don't eat chickens, you great fool. And even if my lord's horses were very ferocious, I wouldn't be afraid. Not with you there." She flashed him a gap-toothed grin. "I know you would always protect me, brother."

Except that he hadn't protected her, Simon thought bitterly. Not his mother or his father either. Caught up in the excitement of living above the stables at the château, looking after sleek hunters so different from Javier's swaybacked plow horse, Simon had seldom spared a thought for home. By the time he had managed to return for a visit, it was already far too late . . .

He swallowed hard, thrusting the memories aside as he saw Miri making her way up the hill. There was a spring to her step that suggested her errand had been successful, that at long last they had stumbled across some useful information.

She was a little out of breath by the time she reached him. Removing her hat, she tossed it down and wiped a trickle of sweat from her brow. The tendrils escaping from her braid looked a bit damp from the heat, but she beamed at Simon, displaying a small basket. "An offering from Madame Brisac," she said, drawing back the cover to reveal some grapes, a crusty loaf of bread, and a creamy white hunk of brie.

Simon had little interest in the food, although he'd scarce eaten anything since yesterday. Shattering the last of Madame Paillard's hope had left him with little appetite.

But as Miri settled on the grass beneath the tree, he sat down to join her.

"I am assuming since you look like the cat that got into the cream, you learned something. What did this wise woman tell you?"

Miri paused in the act of dividing up the bread to blink at him, then her mouth widened in such a dazzling smile that Simon demanded, "What?"

"Nothing." Miri fought to subdue her grin, but her lips quivered, dimpling her cheek. "It is only you used the term wise woman instead of witch. There may be hope for you yet, Simon Aristide."

"I wouldn't count on that. Now are you going to tell me what the woman said or not?"

Miri handed him a hunk of the bread and cheese, unable to suppress a shiver of excitement. "Oh, Simon, they were seen passing through this village several days ago. From what Madame Brisac told me, it has to be Carole and those two witches."

"Ah. For once you are willing to say witch instead of wise woman," Simon was unable to refrain from teasing. "Maybe there is hope for you as well, Miribelle Cheney."

Miri crinkled her nose, pulling a face at him. She paused to nibble at her own portion of the cheese before continuing, "Madame said there were three of them, one a very tall and hefty blonde who went by the name of Ursula. The other woman was short and dark, with sharp elfin features. That sounds very much like the way old Sebastian described the women who took Carole. And these two did have a young sandy-haired girl with them."

Miri's bright expression dimmed. "Madame said that

the girl looked pale and sickly. And so unhappy. She was often on the verge of tears, but didn't dare cry or the big one, Ursula, would cuff her about the head."

Simon leaned forward to curl his fingers about Miri's wrist. "Don't worry. We'll find the girl, rescue her." It was a rash promise to make, but Simon thought he'd have done or said anything to ease the troubled furrow from Miri's brow. "It would seem that you were right about the girl not going willingly. You may feel entirely free to say 'I told you so.'"

Miri shook her head, but she appeared grateful for his reassurance. The hopeful light flickered back into her eyes. "It seems that they are no longer traveling by river. They acquired a pair of pack mules from somewhere."

"Stolen most likely," Simon said after swallowing another mouthful of bread and cheese.

"The villagers certainly seemed to suspect as much. Madame Brisac said the three women were taken to be *gitanes* and not encouraged to linger."

"That would fit. That is how the members of this coven frequently travel about the countryside, in the guise of gypsies. I suspect that is how Lucie Paillard became involved with them. The girl was said to be very fond of consulting *gitans* to have her fortune told." Simon dusted crumbs from his hands, accepting the cluster of grapes Miri offered him. "So does Madame Brisac have any idea which way they went when they left the village?"

Miri had to finish chewing before she was able to reply, "Madame believes that they took the road that heads north toward Paris."

Was that the witches' final destination? If it had not

been for Miri, Simon would have been tempted to trail the women, see if they would finally lead him to the Silver Rose herself. But Miri would be far too concerned about Carole Moreau to hold back and it was his own hope that once Carole was rescued, he might be able to persuade Miri to return to Faire Isle.

As soon as they finished their repast, Simon was ready to set out again. He thought Miri would be just as eager, but when he tried to rise, she leaped to her feet, pressing her hand on his shoulder to stay him.

"No, Simon. Rest awhile."

"But those witches have a considerable start. If they are traveling by mule, that's in our favor. We should be able to overtake them if we keep pressing on. The horses are rested—"

"But you are not," she insisted. "You look almost gray with fatigue and I noticed earlier you were practically nodding off in the saddle."

"I do that sometimes when I have had little sleep," Simon admitted as he shrugged off Miri's hand, struggling to his feet. "Elle is used to it. She just slows her gait when she feels my hand start to slack on the reins."

"But she cannot catch you if you tumble off. You make her very nervous."

"Oh, I suppose she told you that," Simon drawled.

"Yes, she did," Miri replied somberly.

He eyed her askance, realizing she was not jesting. From the first that he had known Miri, she had insisted she had this extraordinary ability to communicate with animals, a claim that had always rendered Simon uneasy.

She bumped up her chin, frowning. "Don't look at me

that way, Simon Aristide. As though you think I am either mad or possessed. Elle speaks to you, too. You told me that she has frequently warned you of danger."

"Yes, but that's different," Simon said. "I can tell that from the way she whinnies or shies back or—or tosses her head."

"She speaks to you in dozens of different ways, just as all animals are capable of doing. I am simply able to hear and understand them better than most humans can. And I happen to know you are a great source of concern to Elle. She doesn't think you look after yourself properly."

Simon shifted his gaze from Miri to his horse and was disconcerted when Elle lifted her head and pricked her ears as though she knew they were discussing her.

"But I can't just doze off out here in the open, in the middle of the day, leaving you unprotected—"

Miri pressed her fingertips to his mouth to silence his protest. "Yes you can. We are safe enough here. You said the Rose's coven has never attacked during the day and you won't be much of a protector if you collapse in a heap. You asked me earlier to trust you. But you have to learn to do some trusting yourself. Lie down for a while and close your eyes," she coaxed. "Depend upon me to look out for you."

She didn't know what a difficult thing she was asking. It had been so long since he had ever depended upon any-one but himself. But she was right. He was dead on his feet. He would be of little use to her if his vigilance was im-paired.

"All right," he consented grudgingly. "But you are not to let me sleep more than five minutes, do you hear?"

Miri only gave him a serene smile. She led the horses down the hill to water them as Simon stretched out under the tree. By the time she returned, he was fast asleep, one arm pillowed beneath his head.

Miri eased down beside him, taking great care not to wake him. He looked so worn down, as though even in sleep he could not entirely escape a lifetime of cares and regrets. She was unable to resist stroking a tangle of hair back from his face. Her fingertips brushed up against his eye patch and she was tempted to remove it, but she feared Simon would find that another intrusion. He didn't like exposing his wounds, either those of the flesh or those buried deeper in his heart.

She had known him for a good portion of her life, from the boy she had been infatuated with to the man she had believed she'd hated. Simon Aristide, the infamous Le Balafre, master witch-hunter, the bane of Faire Isle. But these past two days she had glimpsed another side of him as well, the man who had chastely kissed her good night and gallantly placed the barrier of a door between them. The same man who had risked going alone to confront a dangerous enemy to keep Miri safe, the one who had cradled Colette Paillard in his arms, trying to absorb her pain. Simon Aristide . . . the protector.

"Who are you really, Simon?" Miri whispered. "I warn you, this time I mean to find out, no matter how fiercely you try to guard your heart."

But for now she was content to watch over him while he slept.

※※※

SIMON STUMBLED *through the village, the lanes empty and silent, rakes and plows abandoned in the fields, cottage doors boarded over.*

"Maman? Papa? Lorene?" he called frantically. But there was no answer, only the eerie moan of the wind, the thunder of his heart. It was as though he was the only one left alive in the entire world.

Except for the old woman on the village green, her straggly gray hair blowing in the wind as she tossed something down the well, muttering curses.

"You there! Stop!" Simon shouted. "What are you doing?"

The hag straightened from bending over the well and grinned, revealing the blackened stumps of her teeth. As Simon darted forward to seize her, the witch rose into the air with a cackling laugh.

He ducked down as she flew at him, her nails extended like claws. But as she swooped past him, he was horrified to realize he was not her target. She flew toward a child picking daisies in the meadow. Her dark head bent earnestly over her task, she did not see the hag bearing down upon her.

"Lorene!" Simon screamed his little sister's name but his voice was torn away by the wind. He started to run, legs pumping, but he knew he'd never get there in time. Lorene looked up at last, screamed in terror as the witch descended.

"Lorene!" Simon came awake gasping, sitting bolt upright. He squinted against the bright flood of sunlight, his mind still fogged from his dream. He felt disoriented, unable to place where he was until he became aware that a woman hovered over him, her face set beneath a silken blond crown of braids, her eyes gentle with concern.

"Simon, are—are you all right?" Miri asked.

He blew out a gusty breath, and dragged his hand down his face, trying to clear off the last vestiges of sleep. "Yes. It was only—only—"

"A bad dream," she filled in. She paused, then asked softly. "Who is Lorene?"

Simon grimaced, mortified to realize he must have been muttering in the throes of his sleep, whimpering like some frightened child.

"No one," he started to snap, but for once the denial stuck in his throat. He stared down at his hands dangling between his knees. "She is . . . she *was* my sister."

Miri reached out, took hold of one of his hands, the gesture soft and encouraging. Her eyes were full of questions, but she didn't press him, just waited. But Simon felt he had already taken enough painful journeys into his past for one day. Lord! He hadn't had that particular nightmare for years. That's what came of letting himself remember.

"Look. I'm fine. It was nothing but a stupid dream." He carried her hand brusquely to his lips, then released it. "I am sorry if I alarmed you. Damned embarrassing way for a man to behave."

"No, don't be embarrassed. Everyone has bad dreams." Her lashes swept down as she confessed, "I—I sometimes do myself."

"Yes, my dear, but I am a witch-hunter. I am supposed to be the stuff of nightmares, not cringe from them myself." He attempted to smile, lighten the mood as he struggled to his feet.

He extended his hand to her. She retrieved the hat she had discarded, then allowed him to pull her up. Simon frowned when he saw how far the sun had journeyed across the sky.

"Miri, I told you not to let me sleep so long."

"You were tired. You needed the rest."

"But you must have been bored to distraction just sitting there watching me snore."

She fingered the brim of her hat and shook her head, smiling softly. "No, actually I found it good to steal a moment of peace. Despite the drought, this valley is still a lovely place and after all the darkness we have been facing, it was comforting to watch people going about normal, everyday sorts of tasks."

Simon swept a glance down the hill and understood what she meant. The village of Longpre seemed as far removed from danger and evil as any place could get. Simon knew from hard experience how quickly that could change, how such serenity could be shattered in the time it took to draw breath. But still there was something reassuring about the sight of two small boys racing a little black dog down the lane, a plump housewife hanging out her wash to dry, some lusty lads jumping off a raft, splashing noisily about in the river.

Some lusty *naked* lads.

Simon cleared his throat and stepped quickly to one side, trying to shield Miri from the sight. She smiled when she perceived what he was doing, looking amused by the gesture.

"It's all right, Simon. I have been watching those young men cooling themselves off in the river for some time now.

With great envy, I might add," she said, fanning herself with her hat. "A swim would be tremendously refreshing."

"But Miri, those men are—are—"

"Naked?" She shrugged. "I don't think there is anything shameful about the human body. We are as God made us. And those young men are fine, strapping examples of His creation. Although not quite as fine as you."

"But you have never seen me naked." He added uneasily, "Er—have you?"

Her lashes swept down demurely. "Not completely. But there was that time when I hid you on Faire Isle. I brought you those clothes to change into so you could get out of your witch-hunter's robes. When you retreated into the bushes to change, I tried to peek."

"Miribelle Cheney!"

Her smile was completely unrepentant. "I couldn't help myself. I was curious. It was Gabrielle's fault. She kept telling me that the reason witch-hunters hate women so is because their man parts were all shriveled."

"I don't hate women and there is nothing wrong with my—my male parts," Simon spluttered indignantly.

"I will have to take your word for that. I wasn't able to see enough to tell." Her eyes danced with mischief. "But what I did see of you was quite lovely."

Although Simon was annoyed to feel his cheeks fire, he couldn't help laughing. "I never had any idea you were such a little devil."

"You were too busy imagining I was a witch."

"No, I never thought that about you." His smile softened into something more tender as he touched her cheek. "Not once."

She smiled back at him, her eyes as silvery as the river, her lips soft and moist. It would be so easy to slide his hand behind the nape of her neck, draw her closer, so easy to taste the sweetness of those inviting red lips . . . so easy to love her.

The last thought shook Simon to the core. He hastily dropped his hand back to his side. "We had better be going and make the most of what daylight we have left. With any luck we might be able to overtake those witches by late tomorrow."

He trudged toward the horses, finding it easier to concentrate on tightening Elle's girth than to examine too closely the effect that Miri had upon him. The desire—God, how he wished it was only desire she roused in him. Lust, passion, those things he could understand and deal with. It was the deeper emotions she evoked that alarmed him.

She had followed him over to the horses, but instead of readying Samson to depart, she lingered by Simon.

"Simon . . ." She touched his sleeve.

When he risked a glance at her, he saw she was looking subdued, the shadows back in her eyes. He supposed it was his mention of the witches that had done that, reminded her.

She looked up at him gravely. "When we do overtake these women, you—you will remember your promise, won't you? You do accept that Carole is innocent and that she is not to be harmed?"

"Yes," he replied.

"And the others?"

Simon couldn't bring himself to reply, but the taut set of his mouth must have been answer enough.

Miri shivered. "But what if some of the other members

of this coven are like Carole and they were tricked or—or coerced?"

Simon fetched a heavy sigh. "Miri, I will try to see that these women are judged fairly and with as much compassion as possible. Except for one." His lips thinned.

"There will be no mercy for the Silver Rose."

Chapter Eleven

LIGHT FADED FROM ANOTHER SWELTERING DAY IN THE CITY of Paris, the shades of evening offering little relief from the heat. Another day of blistering sun and no rain had rendered the city a strange blend of lethargy and tension, especially in the poorer quarters of the city. Along the rue de Morte, another fight had broken out near one of the taverns, fists flying, knives flashing. It was far too hot for such an incident to draw the usual crowd of jeering onlookers, even the pickpockets too listless to take advantage of the distraction a brawl offered to their trade.

The three women who made their way down the narrow street gave the tavern a wide berth. Ursula Gruen, who led the way, was tall and big-boned, with straw-colored hair. She made a striking contrast to Odile Parmentier, dark and petite, with a sharp little face, almost elfin features.

Ever since they had entered Paris, the pair had been engaged in a low-voiced argument, occasionally pausing to glance back at the unhappy girl who trailed in their wake.

"We ought to get rid of her now while there is still time," Ursula grumbled. "Stupid worthless blubbering little chit. You made a mistake recruiting her and you just won't admit it, Odile."

"Oh, for mercy's sake, the girl is very young. Give her a chance," Odile whispered back. "Let the Silver Rose decide her fate."

Carole Moreau trudged along behind the two women, fully aware that she was the subject of this fierce conversation. But she was so consumed by her own misery, she was beyond caring. Exhausted and hungry, her throat was parched, her legs aching from fatigue. The leather of her shoes had worn so thin, she had raised an ugly blister on her heel and her filthy shirt and gown were soaked with sweat, clinging to her thin frame. Her right cheek was bruised and swollen from the last blow she had received from Ursula's ham-like fist. Odile had cautioned Carole upon more than one occasion.

"You don't want to provoke Ursula. She has a vile temper. She murdered her own husband, you know. Bashed in his skull with the fire iron. That is the reason she had to flee her village and why she became a follower of the Silver Rose, to avoid doing the hempen jig."

"T—the hempen jig?" Carole had faltered.

"The gallows. Death by hanging, you little fool." Her head bent to one side, her arm upraised, Odile had mimed

*someone dangling from a rope, her feet tapping out a fre-
netic little dance.*

Although she had shuddered at Odile's warning, Carole had always had difficulty minding her tongue. She had
earned her latest blow from Ursula by daring to complain
of the woman's treatment of the stolen mules. After the
poor things had been ridden to the point of collapse, Ursula had insisted they get rid of the mules before they were
caught with them. She had turned them loose, leaving the
creatures to fend for themselves in a thicket of trees.

The heat had made Ursula even more surly than usual.
When Carole had tried to object to this cruelty, Ursula had
struck her to the ground, snarling that they were close to
their destination. The mules were no longer necessary, but
at least they had served some useful purpose, which she
was sure was more than would ever be said for Carole.

That brief altercation had taken place just outside of
Paris. Since then, Carole had maintained a glum silence,
reflecting that for once Ursula was right about something.
Carole was no longer of use or value to anyone. The last
time she had caught a glimpse of her own reflection, she
had been shocked and disgusted by what she had seen, a
pale, thin, waif of a girl clad in dirty, ragged clothes, her
hair matted and filthy.

She had never had much to call her own, but at least
she had taken pains to present a clean and tidy appearance.
She had faults aplenty, but being a slattern had never been
one of them. She could be too quick-tempered and sharp
with her tongue and, as her mother had tried to instruct
her, she needed to rein in some of her stubborn pride. She
had lied to her aunt and uncle when she had sneaked out

for her trysts with Raoul, but other than that, she had always been a basically honest girl and never asked anyone for so much as a crust of bread.

But since meeting up with Ursula and Odile, she had been reduced to the lowest kind of vagabond. She had become a beggar, a thief, and perhaps a murderess as well. Her little boy . . .

A lump rose in Carole's throat and she worked hard to swallow. She had always hated to cry in front of anyone, but since leaving Faire Isle she constantly found herself on the verge of tears, a dangerous weakness around Ursula, who had no patience for any display of sentiment. The slightest sniffle could earn Carole another kick or cuff to the head. Even Odile would frown, looking mighty disappointed in her, unable to understand why Carole was so unhappy. Carole had been offered the great privilege of serving the Silver Rose. She had a glorious future before her.

But Carole felt as though she had left her future, her entire life back on Faire Isle, when she had been obliged to abandon her babe by the stream near Miri Cheney's cottage. She had been so sure she would hate the alien thing that had grown inside her all these months, turning her life into one long misery.

What she had never expected was the rush of feeling that came over her at her first sight of the babe. He was so small, so helpless, and . . . so utterly perfect with his diminutive fingers and toes.

"Don't look at him and whatever you do, don't name him," Odile had advised.

But Carole's heart had already christened him, Jean

Baptiste, after her much-loved grandfather. Gathering the babe closer in her arms, Carole had stammered out her thanks to Odile and Ursula for helping her through the ordeal of childbirth, but she had changed her mind. She no longer had any interest in joining the coven of the Silver Rose.

It was then that she had first seen the ugly side of Ursula Gruen. It was too late for second thoughts, Ursula had growled. They had trusted Carole, taken her into their confidence. She knew too much about the Rose to be simply allowed to turn away. Their pact had been sealed with blood. It could not be broken. Carole must join the Silver Rose or die. And the child must be sacrificed.

Carole had clung to the babe, pleading. She would go with Ursula and Odile as promised, but there was no reason her babe had to die. Jean Baptiste could be left with her aunt and uncle. They had always promised to care for her child if it was a boy.

But her pleas had fallen upon a heart of stone. Ursula had pried the babe from her arms. As Jean began to wail, Carole had been obliged to release her grip, fearing he'd be hurt in the struggle. Weakened as she was from the ordeal of childbirth, all Carole could do was cry as Ursula tore the infant away from her.

Odile had leaned over the bed to soothe her, urgently whispering in her ear. "For mercy's sake, come to your senses or Ursula will dash the child's brains out right in front of you, then kill you as well."

Carole had smothered her sob, trying desperately to think of something to do or say that might save her child. How she wished she had never stumbled across Odile and

Ursula on the beach that day, never heard all of Odile's enticing stories about the Silver Rose, how the sorceress was the champion of all women who were abused by their lovers, their husbands, their families, and all the rest of the harsh, unfeeling world. Join her and Carole would never know fear or want, never have to suffer scorn and cruelty or feel so helpless ever again.

What a fool she had been to listen, to believe their wild tales. Why had she been so angry and pigheaded that day when Miri Cheney had been kind, offering to help—

Mademoiselle Cheney. At the thought of the Lady of the Wood with her soft but compelling silvery-blue eyes, an inexplicable feeling of calm had descended over Carole, a glimmer of hope, perhaps the only one for her petit Jean. She had swallowed her tears, apologizing for her moment of weakness.

It had been hard, but she had pretended to be revolted by the babe, declaring she knew the place he should be abandoned, on the rocks by the river deep in the wood. No one lived anywhere near there. The site was perfectly isolated, she had insisted, the lie tripping off her tongue.

Her courage had almost failed her when the moment had come to abandon Jean, but she had gulped back her tears and laid him carefully near the stream, wrapped in her best shawl. She had tried not to think how fragile he looked, how dark and threatening the forest loomed around them. Instead she had prayed that all the love her grand-mère had woven into that shawl would somehow protect her little boy, keep him safe until Miri Cheney found him.

She thought she had Ursula and Odile completely fooled. Ursula in particular with her mean squinty eyes was not all that bright. Carole didn't realize how badly she had underestimated the woman until they were in the dinghy rowing away from Faire Isle, when Ursula had informed her with a malicious grin of the other gift she had left for the Lady of the Wood, that poisonous silver rose.

Very likely, by now both Mademoiselle Miri and Jean were dead. Carole's eyes burned and she winked fiercely to hold back her tears. No. She could not allow herself to believe that. If she didn't think it, it wouldn't be true.

She prayed that the angels in heaven would somehow look out for her son and the Lady of the Wood, protect them. Carole's lip quivered. Perhaps the Almighty would not listen to the prayers of a girl as evil as she. She prayed instead to the soul of her gentle grand-père, begging him to intervene with God on behalf of his namesake. That Jean Baptiste might be permitted to live, grow tall and strong, become a good man, have a good life.

That was the only thought that had kept Carole going all these weeks, that and the idea she might somehow escape, make her way back to Faire Isle. But in the beginning part of the journey, she had felt so weak from giving birth and Ursula had kept such close watch over her.

The big woman had relaxed some of her vigilance since they had passed through the gates of Paris. She and Odile were so deep in conversation, Ursula did not appear to notice that Carole had lagged behind. This might be Carole's last, her only chance to flee before they reached the lair of the Silver Rose. She slowed her steps even more. Neither of her companions looked back.

But as Carole darted a glance around her, her heart quailed at the prospect of trying to lose herself in this maze of dirty, narrow streets, amidst a sea of so many rough-looking strangers with cold, indifferent eyes. What hope would she have of survival with no money, nothing more than the ragged clothes on her back? Even on Faire Isle she had heard too many grim tales of the kind of thing that might befall a young girl on her own, swallowed up by a city like Paris.

She could be ravished, compelled to work in a brothel or—or forced into a life of other crime. She could even end up doing the hempen jig herself. But could any of those fates be worse than what might await her if she was delivered into the hands of this Silver Rose and found wanting?

Her pulse racing with uncertainty, Carole froze. Her hesitation proved costly, for Ursula noticed her lagging behind. The woman glared at her, hands on hips.

"Keep up, you worthless little bitch, and don't even think of trying to run off. If I have to come after you, you'll be damned sorry."

Carole had no doubt she would be. Even if she was rash enough to make a run for it, she'd never get far, not with her blistered foot, and tired, aching legs. It was hopeless. She was trapped, completely trapped, had been from the moment she had first set foot off Faire Isle.

All she could do was stumble after Ursula like a whipped cur. She avoided a kick from the woman's thick boot by crouching closer to Odile. The petite dark-haired woman risked giving her an encouraging smile. "Don't worry, Carole. We are almost there. Look."

Carole lifted dull eyes in the direction Odile pointed, toward a large house looming behind a high stone wall at the end of the street. The manor was an incongruous sight set next to the tenements and squalor of the surrounding area, like a relic of other days before prosperity had taken itself off to some more promising quarter of the city.

Silhouetted against the fading light of day, the rambling stone house with its pepperpot turrets appeared dark and decayed. But as Carole drew nearer, limping to keep up with her two companions, she saw that someone had been making efforts at repairs. Sections of the wall surrounding the property appeared recently mortared, less grime-ridden than older portions of the stonework.

Carole ventured a peek past the iron grille. Evening shadows enveloped the courtyard beyond, but she was still able to make out a garden of roses. No deadly unnatural silver things, but lush, living blossoms, a profusion of both red and white. Their sweet aroma wafted to Carole, a pleasant contrast to the stench of the streets.

Despite the heat and drought, it was obvious someone had managed to keep this garden well tended, each rose lovingly watered by hand. The sight filled Carole with confusion. She had been so numbed with misery during her journey, she had scarce allowed herself to think about her final destination, to imagine the sort of place a sorceress might dwell.

If she had, she would have been more likely to conjure up images of a cottage set deep in some dark, sinister wood, or the ruins of a castle perched high upon some rocky, inaccessible cliff. She would never have expected to find the formidable Silver Rose dwelling in a place so ordinary as the old house with its pretty garden.

Carole blinked, experiencing a stirring of renewed hope. Perhaps all the wretchedness she had endured so far, including being forced to abandon Jean Baptiste, was more owing to the cruelty of Ursula than the Silver Rose.

If this sorceress was the champion of desperate women that Odile claimed that she was, perhaps Carole could appeal for mercy from the Rose herself, explain that she had made a mistake, that she just wasn't suited to become a witch. She could swear upon her mother's grave that she would never tell anything she had learned about the Silver Rose. The sorceress could even cut out Carole's tongue if she wished to ensure her silence. Carole trembled at the thought of such a ghastly thing, but she was willing to brave any pain, accept any punishment. If only she could be allowed to go home . . .

✳✳✳

THE CANDLE BURNED LOW in the sconce, casting a feeble glow over the rough stone walls of the gatehouse where Carole was interred, awaiting her audience with the Silver Rose. The prospective meeting filled her with both hope and dread, but no matter what was about to happen to her, she longed to have it over.

She slumped down on a stool, anxiously watching the candle, knowing that when it guttered out, she was going to be left in darkness. The only windows in the gatehouse were high apertures, too narrow to let in more than the merest sliver of moonlight. The lack of ventilation rendered the chamber hot and airless and Carole felt sweat trickle down her spine.

Despite the closeness of the room and her mounting anxiety, many of Carole's other discomforts had been relieved.

After they had been admitted to the grounds of the manor house, Ursula and Odile had disappeared in the direction of the house. Carole had been consigned to the care of a girl named Yolette, who had guided her toward the gatehouse.

Carole had been given food, wine, and water to bathe and refresh herself. Although Yolette had been reserved and silent, refusing to answer any of Carole's anxious questions about the Silver Rose, she had at least treated Carole with far more consideration than her traveling companions ever had. She had applied a poultice to Carole's sore foot, and furnished her with a frock to wear, the garment a little coarse, but clean.

Carole had been somewhat heartened by this. If she was being treated this kindly, that must be a good sign. Unless she was merely being prepared for some sort of hellish sacrifice. A terrifying notion and Carole sought to repress it. As dour as the girl was, Carole had wanted to beg Yolette to remain and bear her company until she was summoned. But before Carole could swallow her pride to do so, the girl had gathered up Carole's filthy clothes. Carole would be fetched soon, Yolette said.

It was the longest sentence the girl had spoken and she did so as she exited the gatehouse, locking Carole in. How long ago that had been, Carole had no idea. She had nothing to do to pass the time except worry and fret and watch the candle burn lower and lower.

Her nerves were strained to the snapping point when she finally heard the chink of the key in the lock. The door creaked open and this time it was Odile who entered, carrying a lantern. There was no sign of Ursula, much to Carole's relief.

Odile was likewise scrubbed and wearing fresh garb. As Carole struggled to her feet, Odile rustled closer.

"Come, my dear. It is time." She beamed, taking Carole by the hand. But as she felt the tremor in Carole's fingers, her smile dimmed.

"Oh, child, you really are going to have to gain more command of yourself than you have shown thus far. Then everything will be all right, I promise you." Odile leaned closer, saying in a conspiratorial voice. "Ursula is in a great deal of trouble. The Lady is not at all pleased with her.

"When we came to Faire Isle, we were only sent there to uncover the truth of all these rumors our Lady had heard about one of the Cheney women returning to Faire Isle. To see who the witch was, assess her powers, and then report back. Ursula completely exceeded her authority when she left that rose to kill the Lady of the Wood."

Odile's cheeks puffed as she blew out her breath in a gusty sigh. "But I know Ursula Gruen too well. She will try to deflect the Lady's anger by turning it on me. She is already back there in the hall complaining that I have jeopardized the safety of the Silver Rose by recruiting someone who is unworthy.

"That is why you have got to pluck up, my dear." Odile gave Carole's fingers a tight squeeze. "If you make your curtsy to the Lady all weak and weepy, you are going to make me look very bad."

Carole tugged her hand free, saying resentfully. "I have been given plenty of cause to weep, so what exactly would you have me do, Odile?"

"Why, behave more like the tough little thing you were

when I first met you. Cursing your lover, your family, and all those stupid prim island women. Whatever happened to that spirited girl?"

She died when she was forced to abandon her babe, Carole wanted to retort, but she knew it would be useless. Odile might be a great deal kinder, but she was no better able to comprehend Carole's feelings than the brutish Ursula.

"Oh, Carole." Odile ruefully shook her head. "I realize you have been obliged to do things that must have seemed harsh to you. That is because as yet you do not fully understand the Silver Rose and her purposes. Everything will be so much clearer to you when you are admitted into the inner circle.

"But first you must survive your audience with the Lady. I don't want to frighten you, but Ursula is insisting you are too weak to be admitted to our court, that you ought to be sewn up in a sack and cast into the Seine like a useless kitten. It's up to you to prove her wrong.

"Our Lady admires women who are tough and strong." Odile gave her a coaxing smile. "You just hold your head high, behave like the warrior maiden I saw on Faire Isle, and the Lady will take no heed of Ursula. All right?"

Carole nodded uneasily. "I'll try."

"Good girl." Odile patted her cheek. "Come along then. It is never wise to keep the Lady waiting."

Holding the lantern aloft, Odile led the way out of the gatehouse. Carole squared her shoulders and followed Odile across the darkened courtyard, trying to screw her features into a fierce expression.

But her courage flagged as they entered the house, her heart thudding uncontrollably at the thought that within moments, she would at last find herself in the presence of the formidable Silver Rose.

She trailed Odile into a great hall that was lit by an iron candelabrum suspended by an iron chain from one of the rafters. The light from the candles played over a sea of faces, all of them women. A dozen or more by Carole's dazed reckoning, some appearing not much older than herself, others more in their middling years like Odile. Plump, thin, dark, fair, the women were all alike in one thing, their rapt expressions, their air of suppressed excitement, as though waiting for something important to happen.

The hall was silent except for the rasp of one voice emanating from the front of the room. Craning her neck, Carole saw a throne-like chair mounted beneath a silken canopy, but it was empty. Two figures occupied the dais near the chair. One was Ursula, the huge woman on her knees, cowering before a tall thin female garbed in a gown of unrelenting black, the skirts stiffened by a farthingale.

"The Lady," Odile whispered in Carole's ear, but Odile had no need to tell her that. From her first sight of the woman, Carole had little doubt that she was at last in the presence of the Silver Rose.

Never had Carole ever seen anyone who so much fit her notion of a sorceress. A mass of silver-streaked black hair flowed back in a widow's peak from an exotic face with high slanting cheekbones and a slim straight nose. The lady's complexion was so ice-white as to appear completely bloodless, her dark eyes cold, her mouth a cruel red slash. One thin hand curled like a talon around a long wooden staff she carried, the other toying with a strange five-sided medallion she wore suspended about her slender neck.

As Carole took in these details, her heart plummeted, any hope that she might find compassion from the Silver Rose completely dashed.

Her head bowed, Ursula Gruen groveled before the sorceress. "Milady, I—I know you regard the Cheney women as enemies, that they have done you grave injury. It was hard to glean information about the Lady of the Wood. She—she is so reclusive, but I was sure you would want her destroyed. To—to have your revenge, I thought—"

"You *thought*?" the sorceress interrupted scornfully. "The Silver Rose does not require any of her followers to think, only obey. My vengeance is none of your concern, Ursula Gruen. I will deal with the Cheneys in my own way and in my own time. All that is expected of you is that you will do as you are told. Is that too much to ask?"

"N-no, milady. But I was not the only one who disobeyed," Ursula whined. "Odile was no better."

Carole heard Odile suck in her breath at the mention of her name.

"Instead of carrying out our mission, she was more concerned about recruiting some puling girl. Revealing the existence of our coven to someone completely not to be trusted—"

"Damn her!" Odile muttered. "I knew she'd try to turn me into the scapegoat." She surged forward, pushing her way past the other women. Scrambling up onto the dais, she prostrated herself beside Ursula, kneeling before the sorceress.

"Your pardon, milady. But what Ursula is saying is simply not true. I have achieved high enough rank in our order. I have the right to initiate new members if I find any that I feel might prove worthy—"

"Which this miserable little wretch is not." Ursula glowered at Odile. "Any fool could tell that."

"But she did what was required of her," Odile argued. "She sacrificed the male infant she bore."

"Not willingly," Ursula shot back. "If that treacherous little bitch had had her way—"

"Silence. Both of you!" the sorceress commanded icily, striking her staff against the wooden floor. Ursula and Odile subsided immediately, cringing back.

"I will judge the girl for myself," the sorceress said. "Where is she?"

"Over there," someone called out, pointing to where Carole cowered at the back of the room.

Carole shrank down even farther as all heads turned toward her, a myriad of eyes trained upon her, curious, critical, assessing.

"Come forward and present yourself, girl," the sorceress commanded.

Carole seemed to have frozen, unable to move of her own volition. Someone gave her a shove and she staggered forward, the crowd of women falling back to make way for her. Carole felt her cheeks burn under the weight of all those staring eyes. As she approached the dais, she tried to remember all that Odile had told her. Head high, chin up. Be brave, tough, fierce.

But her mind had gone numb with fear, her heart thudding in her chest. Her legs trembled so badly they threatened to give way beneath her as she mounted the dais. Ursula and Odile had risen, drawing back out of the way. Ursula's mouth curled in an ugly sneer, Odile offering Carole a look that was part encouragement, part plea.

"The wretch is here, milady," Ursula announced as though the Silver Rose could not see that for herself.

The sorceress held out one dead-white hand. "Come closer, child."

When Carole hesitated, Ursula was only too pleased to give her a push until she stood quivering, only a foot away from that cold countenance. She bit down on her lip, uncertain what she should do. Curtsy? Kneel as Ursula and Odile had done?

"What is your name, girl?" the sorceress demanded.

"C-carole Moreau." Her voice came out in a frightened squeak.

"Say *milady*," Odile instructed her in a loud whisper.

"M-milady."

The sorceress crooked both hands about her staff. "And so, Carole Moreau? You wish to become a follower of the Silver Rose?"

This was the moment to tell the sorceress no, to make her plea to be allowed to go free, to return to Faire Isle. But as Carole looked into those flat, empty eyes, her tongue went dry, cleaving to the roof of her mouth.

She gulped and was horrified to hear herself whisper meekly, "Y-yes, milady."

"And are you worthy of such an honor?"

"I don't know," Carole replied miserably.

"Give me your hand."

It seemed like such an innocuous command. Carole could not have said why she found herself terrified to obey it. She extended her fingers timidly. An expectant hush seemed to fall over the entire assemblage as the sorceress groped the air, seeking Carole's hand. Carole blinked, stunned by a sudden realization.

The witch was blind. But Carole's shock at that discovery was as nothing compared to the jolt that went through her when the sorceress's hand closed over hers, her touch so cold. She ran her fingers over Carole's palm, scoring her lightly with her nails.

Carole shivered at the disturbing feeling that swept over her, as though she was being pricked by needles, the freezing sensation shooting like a current through her wrist, up her arm, across her chest, probing her heart with fingers of ice. It was as though every memory, every secret, every emotion she'd ever experienced in the span of her fifteen years was being drained from her.

She wanted to wrench her hand free, but even though the witch's fingers felt thin, almost brittle, it was as though she were caught in the grasp of an iron manacle. By the time the sorceress released her, Carole trembled from head to toe. She drew her hand close to her breast, trying to massage some warmth back into her chilled fingers.

The sorceress murmured, "I do sense some qualities in you that might prove useful, Carole Moreau. Anger, resentment, hatred. But you are also imbued with a degree of weakness, useless sentiment as well. I am not sure . . ." she trailed off with a deep frown.

Carole's breath hitched in her throat, aware that her life hung in the balance of those last four words.

Ursula all but crowed in triumph. "Ah, milady, it is exactly as I tried to warn you. The girl is not worthy. She should be disposed of and Odile punished for—"

But Odile interrupted swiftly, "If milady is not sure, why not let the Silver Rose herself decide the girl's fate?"

The suggestion was immediately taken up and seconded by other voices in the hall. "Yes! Yes, let our Silver Rose decide."

Carole blinked in confusion. She had thought this terrifying woman who loomed before her *was* the Silver Rose. The witch pursed her lips as though annoyed by the enthusiastic chorus that swelled louder by the minute. Then she shrugged. "Very well. Our queen is young and untried, but it will be good for her to gain experience in making these decisions."

Tapping with the end of her staff, using it to guide her, the witch moved past Carole until she stood at the edge of the dais. Facing the throng, she called for silence. When quiet had once more fallen over the assemblage, the sorceress intoned, "The time has come when you the privileged few will be permitted to pay homage to the Silver Rose."

She barked out commands to two of the women, bidding them go escort their queen. As the two vanished up a pair of broad stairs, the entire hall hummed with renewed excitement. Momentarily forgotten, Carole glanced about her in bewilderment, still reeling from her mistake. She turned her questioning gaze toward Odile, but the woman's face was as rapt as that of every other woman present, all eyes now focused expectantly upon the stairs.

The escort appeared first. Each woman bearing a glow-

ing candle, they solemnly lit the way for the mysterious figure behind them in the shadows.

The black-haired woman touched her medallion, then
rapped her staff once more. "On your knees, all of you.
Make your obeisance and all hail Megaera. Our Silver Rose,
our future queen."

"Hail Megaera." The assembled women intoned, everyone sinking reverently to their knees.

Ursula and Odile did likewise, Ursula not giving Carole
a chance to obey of her own volition. She yanked Carole
down so hard, she crashed to her knees. But Carole scarce
felt the pain, a new surge of fear swelling through her.
Dear God, if this alarming blind witch was not the Silver
Rose, then how much more terrible the true sorceress must
be. She scarce dared look up as the procession approached.
The hall had fallen so silent, she heard the rustle of a gown,
a light footfall as the Silver Rose mounted the dais.

Curiosity finally getting the better of her fear, Carole
risked a peek upward. The sorceress had settled upon her
throne, small slight fingers gripping the arms of the gilt-
trimmed chair.

Carole's wondering gaze roved over a diminutive figure
clad in royal purple robes embroidered with silver roses. A
golden circlet crowned thick brown tresses that fell to the
sorceress's waist, her pale oval of a face dominated by large
green eyes, that at once seemed strangely older and younger
than Carole's. Carole's mouth fell open, her mind reeling
from her second shock of the evening.

The formidable sorceress, the dread Silver Rose . . .
was only a little girl.

Chapter Twelve

A JAGGED STREAK OF LIGHTNING CUT ACROSS THE SKY, thunder rumbling in the distance. Simon lingered in the doorway of the old barn, hoping they might be in for a deluge at long last. The oncoming storm had caused the light to fade early, enough that Simon had felt the need to break their journey. He and Miri were tired from another day of tracking the Moreau girl and her two companions.

Their search had yielded nothing but frustration during the days since they had left the village of Longpre. They had gleaned but vague reports of their quarry. An elderly gamekeeper might have seen three such women passing across his master's lands. A farmwife was certain she had seen the trio, but she was so frazzled between tending her flock of chickens and brood of unruly children, she could not be pressed to remember when.

If they didn't manage to overtake the Moreau girl and her companions before they were swallowed up by the maze of streets and teeming populace that was Paris, Simon despaired of ever finding them. That is, if Paris was even where they were headed. As Simon massaged the back of his aching neck, he was assailed by the feeling of failure that had weighed him down all these months.

Only it was worse now because he felt as though he was failing *her*. He had promised Miri he would find Carole Moreau, make sure the girl was safe, but they might be better off pursuing the one clue the Dark Queen had given him regarding the day the *Book of Shadows* had gone missing.

Search both your memory and any records you made. Figure out who else was there at the Charters Inn, had opportunity to steal the book, and you may well unmask our clever Silver Rose.

But the passage of ten years was too long to call to mind all the details of a particular day, even one as eventful as that. Simon had been so obsessed with his plan to entrap the Comte de Renard, he had taken little heed of anything else. He had kept journals of those years of his life, but they were locked away in the trunk he had placed in storage.

Stopping to consult the journals would mean abandoning their pursuit of the witches and the Moreau girl, a decision that would distress Miri. And she had been so remarkably patient these past days, never once complaining about the heat, the grueling hours in the saddle, the long silences of a man accustomed to keeping his thoughts to himself. She had not even groused about the prospect of spending the night in this old barn.

Simon had an uneasy feeling they were being followed in the last village they had passed through, the inexplicable instinct that had insured his survival upon many occasions. He would have felt foolish trying to explain this instinct to anyone else. Another person might have scoffed, thought him behaving irrationally, but Miri was so fey herself, she had nodded in complete understanding, accepting his decision to abandon the main road. He had led them through a thicket of trees and across fields to the Maitlands' farm.

The Maitlands were a quiet, reserved couple, indebted to Simon for a service he had once rendered them. Simon hated to trade upon that. The Maitlands had suffered enough trouble. Simon didn't want to bring any more down upon them, but with another night falling and the prospect of a storm, his first concern had been Miri, getting her sheltered someplace safe.

Since the Maitlands' burgeoning family filled their cottage to overflowing, the barn was the only accommodation Monsieur Maitland could offer Monsieur Aristide and his young companion, the farmer had stated regretfully. But that had suited Simon, the better for him and Miri to remain close to the horses and to shield the secret of her gender. The Maitlands were good people, but rigid in their notions of propriety. They would be scandalized to realize that Simon's traveling companion was actually a woman in disguise.

Another flare of heat lightning streaked across the sky, lighting up the cottage and the low stone fence that surrounded it. All was quiet there, Monsieur Maitland and his

family retired for the night. But a pair of fierce-looking
mastiffs kept guard by the gate, ready to set up a flurry of
barking at the least sign of any intruder.

Satisfied that all appeared secure, he retreated into the
barn. Although the storm had not yielded more than a few
drops of rain, the air had cooled enough so at least the inside of the structure was not stifling.

The barn was well kept, but small. Simon had stepped
outside to offer Miri a little privacy while she bathed with
the water he'd drawn from the farm's well. Not wanting to
catch her at any awkward moment, he called out, "Miri?"

"Over here," her voice echoed. A lantern suspended
from a peg on one of the posts spilled a soft glow over the
structure's interior. A dairy cow chewed a wisp of straw, regarding Simon with wide, placid eyes. The Maitlands' plow
horse was asleep, as was Miri's stolid gelding.

Simon found Miri in the last stall with Elle. Her hair unbound and falling loose about her shoulders, Miri was plait-
ing the mare's black mane, using bits of her own ribbon to
fasten the braids. Both the woman and the mare were such
pictures of contentment, Simon felt some of his tension
ease. But he strode toward the stall with a mock growl.

"Woman, what the blazes are you doing to my horse?"

"Braiding her mane. It's keeping her mind off the thunder and—" Miri's compressed her lips as she concentrated
on finishing off the plait she was weaving. ". . . and I
thought at least one of us should be lovely."

"I am a witch-hunter. I am supposed to strike terror
into the hearts of malefactors. Did it ever occur to you that
I might look a trifle foolish riding a beribboned horse?"

Miri flashed him an unrepentant smile. "Heaven forfend that we meddle with your fearsome reputation, Monsieur Le Balafre. I will strive to undo the braiding before we leave in the morning, although Elle might object. She likes her new finery."

The mare snorted, Elle tossing her head almost as if she were preening, causing Simon to give a reluctant smile. He leaned up against the neighboring stall, watching as Miri continued her ministrations. Elle was often edgy at the prospect of a storm, but she seemed oblivious to the distant rumbles of thunder.

It didn't surprise him to see Elle calm beneath Miri's touch. She had always had that extraordinary effect upon any creature that walked upon four legs. And one that walked upon two as well, Simon admitted wryly.

Just being in Miri's presence was enough to make him feel the cares and frustrations of the day roll off his shoulders. Her skin was flushed with a rosy glow, the pale ripples of her hair shimmering down her back.

"You are quite mistaken," he murmured. "Elle is not the only one who is lovely."

Although her color heightened at his compliment, Miri only laughed and gave a deprecating shake of her head. She leaned closer to Elle, nuzzling the mare's nose, crooning a low sweet song that melted through his very bones. The words were in some strange tongue he could not understand, but Elle responded with a soft whicker.

It should have unnerved him, this eerie ability of Miri's to commune with animals, but Simon found himself growing accustomed to her strange gift, even awed.

"So what secrets are you ladies sharing now?" he asked in a half-teasing tone to conceal his fascination.

"Nothing of import. Just some girlish gossip."

"About me no doubt. I suppose Elle is complaining to you about what a surly, inconsiderate bastard I am."

Miri laughed. "No, I would never hear anything like that. At least not from Elle." Miri's eyes softened as she added, "Your horse adores you, Simon. She would willingly die for you."

"Poor foolish lady," Simon said, but he entered the stall, patting Elle's neck.

The mare gave him a coy nudge with her nose. He massaged his fingertips over the one particular spot between her eyes that caused the mare to toss her head with bliss. His face relaxed into a fond smile until he realized Miri had drawn back, watching him. Fearsome witch-hunters weren't supposed to go all soft and sentimental over their horses. Although he continued to caress Elle, he cleared his throat and said gruffly, "I am sorry I could not find us any better accommodation for tonight than this barn. I should have—"

"Good Lord, Simon." Miri cut him off with a silvery laugh. "Have you entirely forgotten who you are talking to? When I was a child, I would have happily slept with my pony every night if my mother had allowed it. As far as I am concerned, barns are the closest place to heaven on earth."

"Especially in the evening," Simon said. "When the animals are settling for the night, that feeling of well-earned rest at the end of a hard day. Of complete peace, journey's end. Even if it is only an illusion."

Miri nodded in agreement. "I love the night sounds, the hoot of an owl in the rafters, the rustling of the straw, and the stamp of hooves in the stalls."

"The soft snorts and the whickers—"

"And the sweet scent of fresh hay."

"The smell of warm horse mingled with the leather—" Simon checked himself, a little embarrassed by his outburst of enthusiasm.

Miri subsided as well, smiling shyly up at him. His gaze locked with hers in a moment of complete understanding, a feeling of deep accord that seemed to bind them closer together.

Simon felt his heart trip with that awareness of her he often found himself fighting. The lantern light spilled over her, the glow reflected in her eyes, the golden sheen of her hair. She looked so soft and accessible, her linen shirt clinging to her womanly curves, revealing intriguing hints of her unbound breasts.

Simon's body stirred with a hunger to draw her close, hold her hard against him, and breathe in her warm feminine scent. He was quick to turn away. He did a fair job of managing the desires Miri aroused in him during the day when his thoughts were occupied with the hunt, all his senses focused on detecting any approaching danger.

But when they were alone, these quieter moments threatened to be his undoing, fraught with the danger Miri might tempt him beyond all reason and burrow her way under his skin, even deeper into his heart.

Although Miri had done a fine job currying Elle, Simon snatched up a brush and focused his attention upon stroking the mare's glossy back. A low mew sounded as a calico-colored barn cat brushed past Miri's skirts.

Scooping the creature up in her arms, she asked, "So who are these Maitlands? Are they friends of yours?"

"Witch-hunters don't have friends, Miri."

His answer disturbed her. As she scratched the cat beneath its chin, she frowned. "I had the impression Monsieur and Madame Maitland were very pleased to offer you shelter for the night."

"Only because they felt obliged. I was able to render them a trifling service last autumn."

"Oh?"

Simon would as soon not have discussed the incident, but he might have known Miri would not let the matter drop that easily. Not that she ever hammered him with questions or demanded answers. She merely waited, regarding him expectantly.

He sighed and continued brushing Elle. "Someone vandalized the local church, splashing pig's blood over the altar. The Maitland family was suspected and a drunken mob of men from the village headed out here to exact retribution. I, er, managed to convince the good people they were wrong and persuaded them to return home."

"How on earth were you able to do that?"

"I intercepted the mob by drawing my sword, rearing Elle up out of the darkness on the road ahead of them." Simon's mouth thinned with satisfaction at the memory of all those cowering torch-lit faces, the wide eyes, the mouths gone slack with fear. "Elle and I can conjure up quite a spectacle of terror when we try. You ought to see how she can snap, toss her mane, and roll her eyes, her hooves striking the air like a dark, avenging demon horse, springing straight from the jaws of hell.

"At least, when she is not all beribboned and braided," Simon added dryly.

Miri moved closer to the stall. As Elle snuffled curiously at the cat in her arms, the feline took umbrage. Scrambling out of Miri's grasp, it climbed along the top of the stall, and then leapt down, streaking out of the barn. Miri scarce noticed as she gaped at Simon.

"This is what you call rendering the Maitlands a *trifling* service? Those evil men could have set fire to their cottage, burned them alive, and you along with them."

Simon shrugged. "The mob was comprised of the ordinary kind of laborers one might find in any village. But, yes, the situation could have turned damned ugly. Even simple men can wax dangerous when their courage is fueled with too much wine, bad temper, and outrage. The entire village was angered and shocked by the defilement of the church."

"Why would anyone suspect the Maitlands of doing such a thing? I only met them briefly and even I can tell what kind, gentle people they are."

"But they are also known to be advocates of the Reformed religion."

"And—and *you* knew that when you defended them?" Miri faltered.

Simon understood her astonishment. The summer he had first met Miri, he had been trying to help his old master, Le Vis, hunt down and destroy the Huguenot captain, Nicolas Remy.

As he moved toward the front of the stall, brushing Elle's withers, he said, "I defended the Maitlands because I knew they were not responsible for the vandalism at the church. It was more random mischief caused by some member of the Silver Rose's coven. Or maybe it wasn't so random.

"Those harpies delight in causing misery or stirring up trouble in the villages they pass through, setting people at each other's throats, especially Huguenots and Catholics. I actually discovered one of them had carved the crude semblance of a rose in the altar. When I showed that to the priest the next day and tempers were calmer, I managed to convince everyone the damage to the church was the work of witches and that the Maitlands were innocent."

"*Innocent?*" Miri bit her lip and then went on hesitantly. "Forgive me, Simon, but—but that's not a term I ever expected to hear fall from your lips. Not when applied to a Huguenot. Didn't Vachel Le Vis teach you to hate all members of the Reformed religion, regard them as heretics?"

"He tried." Simon paused in currying Elle, troubled as he often was by the memory of those long-ago days when he had been Le Vis's apprentice, wanting to please the man who had saved his life and yet disturbed by so many of Le Vis's teachings.

Coming out of the stall, Simon absently ran his fingers over the bristles of the brush. "He said as a good Christian and true Catholic, I should despise all heretics, condemn them to burn in hell. He made me feel so confused, I spent hours praying over it." Simon gave a mirthless laugh.

"Believe it or not, I did actually still pray in those days. I wanted to be a good Christian as Master Le Vis preached, but his tenets were so different from the gentle doctrine I had learned from my father.

"He was astonishingly more tolerant than most of the folk in our village, perhaps because he had some experience of the wider world. He oft told me how my grandfather had been to the wars in Spain and how his life was saved by a very kind and skilled Moorish physician. And once when my father traveled to a fair in another village, he himself was set upon by brigands and rescued by a Jewish merchant.

"Jews and Moors . . . Master Le Vis would have condemned them all, along with the Huguenots, no matter how brave or kind. But my father was always wont to say if there are so many roads to a city like Paris, just think how many more there must be to heaven. We don't need to all follow the exact same path to get there in the end."

Simon suddenly had a vivid image of Javier Aristide sitting by the hearth as he had imparted his simple wisdom, the big man's work-roughened hands busy with his whittling. His father's hands had seldom been idle, always fashioning something, a new leg for a broken stool, a wooden bowl for his mother, or some whimsical carved animal for Lorene. For the first time in years, the memory was more poignant than painful.

He didn't realize he had allowed his thoughts to drift off until Elle nudged him with her nose, coaxing him to continue his brushing. Miri was gazing up at him, with a soft light in her eyes he wished he deserved.

"Don't look at me that way, Miri Cheney," he warned.

"What way is that?" she asked.

"Like you think that I am in any way like my father. I am not. I helped the Maitlands simply because—because it suited me to do so. I can hardly hope to prosecute the Silver Rose if others are blamed for her crimes. I am no hero."

"I doubt the Maitlands would agree. When I think of what could have happened to them—" Miri shuddered. "These religious conflicts are terrible enough without anyone deliberately sowing more discord. If that is what this Silver Rose is trying to do, then the woman truly is a monster. When will all this senseless cruelty between Huguenots and Catholics ever end? I—I worry so much about Gabrielle and her family."

"I wish I could tell you that you have no cause," Simon replied somberly. "But from what I overheard that night at Chenonceau, the war is only going to get worse. If the Dark Queen is not able to check the ambitions of the duc de Guise, he will gain complete control of the royal army and march on Navarre, try to crush the Huguenots once and for all. You might want to warn your sister."

"I am sure Remy is fully aware of the danger and will make sure his family is protected, but I will send word to them at first opportunity—" Miri broke off, her face suffusing with a telltale flush. Ducking her head, she stammered, "That—that is, I would warn Gabrielle if I knew where she was. Which—which I don't."

What a poor liar she was. But in a world full of people far too gifted at dissembling, Simon found Miri's transparent honesty one of her most endearing traits.

"You might try dispatching a message to their farm in Pau," he suggested.

When Miri's head snapped up, her eyes widening with consternation, he added, "I have known for a long time where Gabrielle and her Huguenot captain fled, but I had no interest in pursuing them. It was the Lady of Faire Isle and her sorcerer husband who eluded my hunt."

"Now that you know Renard doesn't have the *Book of Shadows,* you no longer have any reason for searching for him, do you?" she asked.

"With or without the *Book,* the Comte is still alarmingly well versed in black magic."

"Renard would never use his knowledge for any ill purpose, Simon." Miri said, her face upturned to his, her lovely eyes anxious and pleading. "You must believe me."

He wished that he could. He regretted ever mentioning Renard. Like casting a pebble into the serene surface of a pond, it threatened to disturb the newfound harmony between them. Simon had known few times of peace in his life, especially with Miri, and it was all the more precious to him for that. He compressed his lips and found himself making a concession that he'd thought he never would.

"Should I ever cross paths with Renard again, I—I will do my best to turn away and leave him be. For your sake."

"He's a good man, Simon. I would rather you did it for his."

"Ah, now you ask entirely too much of me. He is the grandson of the notorious Melusine, the witch who passed so many of her dark skills onto others, including the hag who destroyed my village."

"You cannot blame Renard for that. That would be the same as if—as if I blamed you for being raised by a witch-hunter."

"Le Vis didn't raise me," Simon snapped. "But he did save my life."

He tensed as he always did when he was obliged to defend Le Vis. He had struggled in vain before to justify to Miri what he often had trouble justifying to himself, why he had spent so many years in service to a madman.

"You think Le Vis a monster and he gave you reason. There were times when his fits of madness came upon

him that I, myself—" Simon broke off, checking the dark
memory. "But there were other times when he could be the
most patient of teachers. He taught me Latin and Greek,
how to read, write, and cipher, skills such as a mere peasant boy could never have hoped to acquire.

"But beyond the education, I owed the man my very
survival. I—I don't know what that blasted hag threw down
the well that night, but a plague struck of such virulence, it
spread throughout our village and the surrounding lands,
including the estate where I worked in the stables. As word
carried, we were cut off by the rest of the world. The closest anyone would come was a nearby hill where food was
left, food that few had the strength to eat as everyone I
knew died off one by one."

Simon swallowed hard as he stumbled back into the
darkest part of his past, a place that he seldom revisited.
"In my own family, my father was the first to go, then my
mother. Lorene was the last, so out of her mind with fever
and pain, she didn't even know me anymore, but I held her
in my arms until the end."

Elle lipped at his sleeve, tugging to gain his attention,
rubbing her head against his sleeve. He patted her absently
and moved away, sagging back against the opposite wall as
he concluded his tale.

"I was so weak myself by that time it took me the better part of a day to dig her grave and she—she was such a
wee slip of a girl. After I finished burying my sister, I just
collapsed into a ditch alongside the road. For some unknown reason, I was spared the ravages of the plague."

Miri had heard him out in silence, only her eyes speaking of her sorrow. But she drew closer, gently touching his

hand. "That is the way it happens sometimes, Simon. My mother, who was unusually gifted in treating plague victims, often remarked upon the wonder of it, how some people seemed completely immune. Even with all of her knowledge of ancient medicine, she never understood it. Maman only thanked God that it was so."

"I don't know whether my being spared was the work of God or the devil. All I know is that I lay there by the roadside waiting to die and that was where Le Vis found me. No one else was willing to venture near a place cursed by a witch. He was the only one who dared to come."

"My mother would have dared, and believe it or not, so would Renard." Miri pressed his hand. "I am glad Le Vis saved you, Simon. I am grateful to the man for that much, but oh, how I wish you had been found by anyone else but him."

"Believe me, my dear, so do I," Simon replied bleakly. It was the first time he had ever admitted that to anyone, even himself. But these past few days with Miri, he had found himself examining parts of his life he had kept locked away for years. It was those fey eyes of hers, reaching deep inside of him, shining light into the darkest corners of his heart whether he was willing to let it happen or no.

She seemed to sense how hard this was for him, when he had shared as much as he was able. When he fell silent, she didn't press him for more details. Moving closer, she brushed back a tangle of hair from his brow, stroked her fingertips over his forehead in the same calm quiet way she had soothed his mare's fear of thunder.

But there was little to be done for a man when the storms were all in his own soul, Simon thought. He should have eased away from her, but there was so much comfort, so much warmth in her caress and he'd felt cold and isolated from the rest of the world for so damned long.

She ran her hand through his hair, the ends still damp from his own efforts to wash away the sweat and dust of the road. He grimaced, scarce able to imagine what a gargoyle he must appear, between his scarred face, unkempt beard, and tangled black hair. When her fingers snagged on a knot, she patiently worked it free.

After the grim discussion they had been having, Simon tried to lighten the mood by teasing her. "I hope you aren't getting any ideas about prettifying me the way you did Elle. It would be well beyond your power, my dear."

"I have no intentions of trying to tame you, Monsieur Aristide. Although I do wish I could persuade you to get rid of this." When Miri tugged at the string that secured his eye patch to remove it, he stiffened, catching her wrist to stop her.

"No."

"But, Simon, it can't be comfortable for you to wear that thing all the time. Your skin needs to—to breathe and it is not as though I haven't seen your wound before. You showed me that time in Paris, remember?"

"Only because I was trying to intimidate you, make you feel guilty."

"It worked. Quite well, I might add." She tried to laugh, but it was a soft, sad sound. Her lashes lowered to conceal the unhappy look in her eyes, just one more shadow he had put there.

He gentled his grip, taking her hand in his. "I really was a complete bastard to you, wasn't I? Whatever I said to you back then, it was my own bitterness and nasty temper talking. You never did anything to me to feel guilty about."

"I was the one who interfered in your duel, the reason Renard's sword broke through your guard."

"But I was the one who challenged him. When a man draws a sword, he'd better be prepared to accept the consequences of his actions. You very likely saved my life that day. Renard was a far better swordsman. He might have killed me if you had not tried to stop the duel."

"Or you him. He was weakened from the ordeal of his imprisonment in the Bastille. That day is one of the worst memories of my life. I—I have never dealt well with anger or violence. It makes me sick to the soul and—and being forced to watch you and Renard go at each other like that, not wanting either of you to be hurt. You cannot imagine what that was like for me."

He could not have. At least not then. He had just been informed that his master was dead, cruelly cut down by the Comte de Renard. Le Vis, the man who had become everything to Simon, his only family, his protector, his teacher. Simon had felt as alone as he'd been after his village had been destroyed, lost, frightened, and angry. Needing to channel his rage and terror against someone, he chose the sorcerer Renard, whom Simon already blamed for trying to turn Miri against him.

But he had managed that well enough on his own, Simon reflected. Caught up in the dark turmoil of his own anguish, he had given little thought to Miri, the pain he would inflict upon her by fighting someone she cared about, forcing her to take sides, tearing her heart in two.

He squeezed her hand. "Miri, I am sorry. I will never put you through anything like that again. I swear it."

It was a damned rash promise to make, as rash as drawing her closer. But he could not seem to think beyond the need to banish the hurtful memory, drive that bruised look from her eyes. He did what he'd ached to do for days, wrapped his arms about her and held her close. She resisted for only a moment before melting against him, burrowing her face against his shoulder.

They clutched each other, the only sounds the cozy rustlings of the other creatures in the barn, another faint rumble of thunder from the darkness beyond. It struck Simon that it had been like this with Miri ever since he'd known her, a few quiet stolen moments before the next storm broke over their heads.

This could only be but one more of those moments, he thought sadly. And he held her all the tighter for that. She finally stirred, raising her head. When she reached up with trembling fingers to ease away his eye patch, this time he didn't stop her.

It was difficult not to turn that half of his face to the shadows, avoid her earnest regard. It had been a long time since he'd inspected himself in the mirror, but when he had been a foolish boy, mourning the loss of his looks more than the loss of his eye, he had bitterly studied his own reflection, memorizing the shape of his scar. The ugly pucker of raised flesh that sealed his right eye closed.

He had learned to use that deformity to savage effect over the years, to intimidate, to terrify, to repulse. None of which he wanted to do to Miri. Nor did he wish to arouse her pity. He flinched when she gently touched his scarred eyelid.

"I need to make you some of my special salve for this," she murmured.

"I'm a little past any hope of healing, don't you think?"

"You have made it worse than it has to be, chafing your skin by wearing that patch too much. I want you to leave it off—at least when we are alone together."

"All right," he agreed, trying to sound indifferent. Vanity. It was only stupid vanity and Le Vis had always accused him of having far too much of it. It was one of the few things his late master had been right about.

His breath hitched in his chest as she leaned closer and brushed her mouth against his cheek, then his eyelid, then his brow. When he felt a warm splash of moisture against his face, he groaned.

"Ah, Miri, don't do that. Don't cry. You've already wasted far too many tears on me and I was never worth a single one of them."

He eased her back and caught her face between his hands, pressing his mouth to her eyes, her cheeks. Only wanting to kiss her tears away. He would have sworn that he meant to do no more than that, except one droplet cascaded over the corner of her mouth and he captured it without thinking. His lips settled over hers, the salt of her tears mingling with the sweetness of her mouth.

He made a half-hearted effort to retreat from temptation, but she buried her fingers in his hair, holding him captive and surrendering in the same breath, her lips parting, an invitation he had not the strength to resist. He kissed her, tenderly at first, then by degrees deeper, his tongue exploring the warm hollows of her mouth. Miri responded eagerly, straining toward him.

He cupped her breast through the linen of her shirt, feeling her warmth, the thud of her heart, which seemed to have quickened in time with his. His body hardened with need of her, the urge to sweep her up into his arms and carry her—

Carry her where? To lay her down on the rough planks of the barn floor like some marauding soldier seeking a brief toss with a milkmaid? There was no bed, no bower in which to make love to her. No soft safe place for them to be together. There never had been, never would be.

He dragged his mouth from hers with a low groan, although he still found himself unable to release her. He wrapped his arms about her waist, resting his brow against hers, their breaths mingling in ragged sighs. When she caressed his neck, her hand trailing down the opened vee of his shirt, his pulse jumped at the soft feel of her fingers against his bare skin. He captured her hand, trapping her fingers over his racing heart.

"Oh, God, Miri. This—this is not wise," he said.

"I know," she whispered. "But why does it feel so right?"

"I have no idea. I have never understood this madness between us."

"Madness?" she repeated sadly. "Yes, I—I suppose it is."

She drew away from him and he reluctantly let her go.

"I—I am sorry," she said, her cheeks aflame. "I don't know what came over me. I—I am so ashamed."

"Don't be. It's more my fault than yours. I promised you I would never kiss you again."

Miri sighed. "In case you hadn't noticed, Simon, I was also kissing you." She ran her fingers up and down the silver braid of her necklace, something that she often did when she appeared worried or troubled. For the first time he noticed the chain was attached to an elaborately engraved locket.

"What is that? Some sort of amulet to ward off demons? It doesn't appear to work," he jested, desperate to ease the tension between them.

Miri looked stricken with guilt as she replied, "It is a gift from a friend. You met him that time you were quartered at the Charters Inn, although I doubt you'd remember. His name is Martin le Loup."

Simon grimaced. He remembered all too well the handsome rangy youth who had trailed after Miri like an adoring wolf cub.

"Ah, yes, that street thief from Paris. I had no idea you were still acquainted with him."

"I—I should have mentioned him sooner. I don't know why I didn't. It is just with so much else happening and remembering how much you disliked him—"

Simon gave a dry bark of laughter. "As I recall, the loathing was mutual. The boy always glared at me like he wanted to cut off my head and parade it around on a pike."

"Martin would want to cut off more than that if he knew what just happened between us. He would think me the worst sort of trollop, which I suppose I am."

"You are nothing of the kind and I'd hack out the tongue of any man who said so." Simon tucked his fingers beneath her chin, forcing her to look up at him.

"Miri, you've done nothing wrong. We merely shared a few heated kisses. A man and a woman thrust together day and night in such strange circumstances, both of us feeling a little tense, a little raw. It's not surprising we got a bit carried away. It happens, but we stopped before it went too far. It was just a foolish moment of weakness, nothing that your Wolf ever need hear about, all right?"

Rather than comforting her, his words seemed to make her even sadder. But she nodded, attempted to smile. Gesturing toward her locket, he asked, "May I see that?"

Miri displayed it to him reluctantly, a large silver oval engraved with a wolf baying at the moon. He opened the catch and sought to ignore the irritating inscription. *Yours until time ends.* Instead he focused on the exquisite timepiece and whistled softly.

"An expensive trinket. Er—pardon me for asking, but are you sure your thief didn't steal this?"

"Of course he didn't," Miri said indignantly. "Whatever he may have been in his youth, Martin is no longer a thief. He has risen greatly in the service of the king of Navarre and has become quite the gentleman. He cuts quite a dash among all the ladies at court."

Simon had little doubt of that. Even when le Loup had been no more than a common thief, he had had an annoying tendency to swagger and he was probably still as handsome as ever. *Damn him.* He felt a stab of something that was ridiculously like jealousy and did his best to suppress it.

"Despite his gallantries to the other ladies, he obviously is still quite devoted to you," Simon remarked.

"The man is a hopeless romantic, treating me as though I was this unattainable goddess, calling me his Lady of the Moon, ever striving to perform bold deeds in my honor, to win my heart." Miri smiled ruefully. "Sometimes I wish he would not try quite so hard, that he would remember that—that—"

"That you are a woman with very earthbound needs?"

She glanced up at him, clearly surprised by his perception. Although she nodded in agreement, she said quickly, "Not that I am complaining. He truly does love me and he has been my most devoted friend for years, always making me laugh, lifting my spirits whenever I am sad."

But do you love him? Simon wanted to demand and didn't, partly because he dreaded her answer and partly because it was none of his concern. But he couldn't seem to stop himself from asking, "So why haven't you married him? Do your sisters not approve?"

"Oh, yes, Gabrielle in particular has urged me to marry him for a long time. Both she and Ariane love Martin."

As much as they despise me, Simon thought, the contrast between himself and le Loup vivid and painful. On the one hand, a dashing, handsome courtier, who had remained loyally at Miri's side all these years. And on the other a scarred and wearied witch-hunter, haunted by more memories and regrets than he could count, the bane of her family, the man who had hurt her time and again.

Not that it mattered. He had never had any hope of winning Miri for himself. He had never even realized how badly he wanted her . . . until now.

He snapped the locket closed and let it fall back against her, saying in a tone of forced cheerfulness. "I daresay your sisters are right. When we have concluded this infernal hunt for the Rose, you ought to settle down with your Monsieur Wolf. He'll be able to give you a grand home, a family of your own."

All the things I never could.

"After all the grief you have endured, you deserve to be happy, my dear," he added softly.

And what about you, Simon? What do you deserve? Miri wanted to ask, but he was already striding away from her, muttering something about taking one last look around the farmyard to be sure all was secure. She ran her tongue over her lips, tasting the passion of his kiss, still feeling the heat of his arms around her.

As he vanished through the barn door, she shivered, feeling suddenly cold and bereft. She cupped Martin's locket in her hand, staring unhappily down at it.

Marry him. That was what her sisters and Marie Claire had said, what Miri had even told herself she would do. And now even Simon was saying it. But as she tucked the locket back inside her gown, Miri knew she never would and after all this time, she finally understood why.

She was hopelessly in love with Simon Aristide.

⁕⁕⁕

MIRI LAY FLAT ON HER BACK, the blanket that Madame Maitland had provided shielding her from the rough bed of straw she had fashioned for herself in the loft of the barn. She was exhausted, but sleep eluded her, consumed by her own troubled thoughts and awareness of the man who slumbered but yards away from her.

She had had a difficult time convincing Simon to bed down for the night instead of maintaining vigil outside. The dogs would alert them at any hint of trouble, she had argued, and what if the storm broke after all? He would get soaked, spend a miserable night keeping watch or catching a few winks on the hard ground, be completely exhausted tomorrow, and all for no good reason.

He had yielded in the end, much to her surprise. Perhaps he had simply been too tired to argue, although he'd had to have been as aware as she was that for once he was unable to put a door between them as he did at every inn.

But Simon didn't need the barrier of a door. As they had settled in for the night, he had been silent and withdrawn, building a wall between them where there was none. He was infernally good at that.

She rolled onto her side and could make out the outline of his form, barely visible by what little moonlight penetrated the cover of clouds and filtered through the open window of the loft. Simon Aristide, the man she had always loved, no matter how hard she'd fought to deny it.

She had loved him ever since she'd been a naïve young girl, smitten by the handsome boy she'd met on a windswept cliff one midnight, his dark curls and eyes as lustrous as the night, his smile rife with a devastating charm.

But what she felt for Simon now ran so much deeper than the infatuation of her girlhood when she had been entranced by his physical beauty. She saw his flaws all too clearly. Not the superficial ones on his face, but the scars that were ingrained deeper on his heart. The pain, the tormented memories that caused him to retreat into himself, hold the world at a distance.

She realized he was capable of being quite ruthless if he felt he was justified. He could be hard and suspicious, and had no use for anything that hinted of magic. And he was as inflexible and obstinate as ever when it came to Renard. Loving Simon would be a betrayal, not only of Martin's devotion to her all these years, but of her own family as well.

Even knowing that that was true, seeing the harsh reality of the situation, realizing all these things didn't help. She yearned even now to reach out to Simon, touch him, caress him, and seek the warmth of his lips in the darkness. She had to hug herself tightly to curb the impulse.

He had traveled such a long, hard road since that summer he had stormed onto Faire Isle, an angry and embittered young man. No matter how much he disclaimed, he had put himself at great risk to save the Maitlands. And not out of any self-interest as he insisted, but out of that same concern and compassion that had led him to comfort Madame Paillard, to grieve and pray over the grave of an abandoned babe. It was a testament to his character that he had survived horrors that would have broken most men, the destruction of his village, and the loss of his family.

He obviously harbored regrets about his apprenticeship to Le Vis, the fanatic who had transformed Simon into Le Balafre, the remorseless witch-hunter and loner. Only with his horse did Simon ever relax completely, showering Elle with an unreserved affection he seemed unable to show anyone else. Miri could understand that. It was so much safer to love a horse, a dog, or a cat . . . the companionship of the simpler creatures of the earth offered uncomplicated, total acceptance, affection, and trust. Simon's existence was even lonelier and more isolated than Miri's had been this past six months when she had returned to Faire Isle, hoping for a peace and happiness that were no longer there.

Simon seemed to have given up hoping for anything

years ago. Even if Miri were to completely forget all that she owed to Martin and her family, and offer her heart to Simon, she knew he would reject her. He'd learned to fear the very mention of love, regard it as a weakness. The wisest, most sensible thing for her to do was learn to conquer her own feelings.

That was something that she suspected was going to be far easier said than done. She sighed. As she shifted restlessly on her makeshift bed, she heard Simon stir. Although she could not see his face, she realized he was as wakeful as she was. Had he sensed her watching him, this man so alive to the darkness? He startled her when his voice suddenly rumbled.

"The storm seems to have passed over."

"Yes," Miri agreed sadly as she stared upward through the open window. The last trace of clouds had vanished, the moon shining hard and bright.

"Another day with no rain. Poor mother earth," she mourned.

"Le Vis would have said the drought is a sign of the wrath of God, that the French people are being cursed to hell for their sins."

"And he would have been wrong. God is not that cruel, Simon. He would never destroy what he so lovingly created. I think he strives to refashion even the worst of souls into something finer. I don't really believe in hell."

"I do. Although I don't think it is any lake of burning fire and brimstone as Le Vis claimed."

Miri wished she could make out his features. But even with the moonlight streaming in, she saw no more than the shadow of his beard-roughened face, his head propped on his arm as he rested on his back, gazing up at the window.

"What do you think hell is like, then?" she asked softly.

"Cold. Dark. And when you reach out into the void to touch someone, there is no one there."

The emptiness in his voice tugged at her heart. All her resolves about the wisdom of holding herself at a distance were forgotten. She scooted closer, groping until she found his hand. Although he tensed, he didn't draw away, his fingers entwining with hers. After a long moment, he spoke again, more hesitantly.

"My father would have agreed with you . . . about the drought. I remember something he said to me the year much of the village's crops were destroyed by an overabundance of rain. He told me there is no fathoming the ways of nature. One can only try to live in harmony with the earth, rejoice in the days of bounty, put something by to get you through the seasons of want, and have faith in God to see you through."

"Live in harmony with the earth," Miri murmured. "That is exactly what my mother taught me."

"You would have understood my father. He—he would have gotten on well with you."

"I am sure I would have liked him, too. Tell me more about him," she coaxed, gently massaging his fingers.

She feared he would refuse. It was hard to get Simon to talk about his family, but perhaps he found it easier lost in the shadows, only their hands connecting. He spoke slowly at first, then warmed as he described for her life in his small village, until she could see it so clearly, from the winding lane to the well-tended cottage.

Javier Aristide with his work-roughened hands, imparting his gentle wisdom, teaching Simon all he knew of animal husbandry. His mother, fiercely reigning over her kitchen, keeping both her cottage and her family in tidy domestic order, but always free with a gentle caress, a beaming smile. And his little sister Lorene, trailing adoringly after Simon, running to him first every time she skinned her knee or had any small treasure she'd found to display.

Although Miri was certain he was unaware of it, Simon revealed to her the kind of boy he had been as well, kind, openhearted, quick to laugh and to tease. She caught glimpses of the gentleness she had seen when she had first met him, even after he'd fallen under Le Vis's influence, traces that still remained in the man who grasped her hand in the darkness.

Miri found herself talking about her own mother, the wondrous Lady of Faire Isle who had taught her the magic of brewing herbs, how to apply Maman's healing skills with people to the simpler creatures of the earth. Her bold, handsome father who had taken her on so many journeys into the rich realms of imagination, hunting for unicorns in the woods. And her sisters, solemn and gentle Ariane, who had become like a second mother to her. Impulsive, teasing Gabrielle, with whom Miri had so often quarreled, but whom she had known she could always count on to be her fiercest protector.

As she held Simon's hand, she suddenly realized how dangerous this was, this sharing of memories only deepening her feelings for him, forging bonds stronger than mere desire. And yet she was filled with a peace she had not known for a long time.

Her eyelids grew heavier and heavier. She fell asleep, her hand still linked with his. But it was a peace that didn't last as she was drawn into the dark world of her dreams . . .

The salamanders were crawling up the palace walls. Miri avoided them as she hammered against the castle door, frantically seeking admittance. As she paused to catch her breath, she heard voices that seemed to float from somewhere far away, across the green expanse of lawn.

Miri stumbled in that direction, racing along garden paths that sloped down toward a sparkling river. The path ahead was barred with statues. No, not statues, she realized, her heart thudding. But the familiar menacing figures of the chess pieces towering above her.

Only there was something strange about them, something more disturbing. Miri froze as she saw there was no white queen, only two dark ones and the hapless white knight was trapped between them.

The pawns rumbled to attack as they had done before. Miri tried to call out a warning, but her voice came out in a hoarse croak. One pawn moved forward, smaller than the rest, not wielding a mace or a club, but a book. As the pawn cracked the volume open, it exuded a sinister green mist that enveloped the white knight.

He breathed it in and tumbled to the ground, helpless as the other pawns attacked, smashing him. Miri rushed to his aid, but as always, she was too late. The stone shell had fallen away, revealing a man, broken and bleeding.

When Miri stroked his hair back, her fingers came away dark and sticky. But this time, she could see his face all too clearly, blood streaming in a dark river over his scarred cheek.

"Simon," she moaned.

"Miri!"

She felt strong hands seize her by shoulders. Although she struggled desperately to free herself, both the hands and the voice were insistent, dragging her clear of the dark webs of her dream.

"Miri, wake up!"

As her eyes fluttered open, she gasped, uncertain where she was until she saw the shadow of the man hovering over her.

"S-simon." Her nightmare was still so strong, so vivid in her mind, she bolted upright and ran her fingers frantically over his brow, his cheeks, and his beard. Finding no trace of blood, no gaping wound, she snapped fully awake with a sob of relief.

Simon caught hold of her trembling fingers, squeezing them gently. "Miri, what's wrong? Were you having a nightmare?"

"Yes," she whispered.

"Come here, then." He drew her into his arms, cradling her head against his shoulder. Stroking her hair, he murmured, "Shh. You're awake now and I'm here. It was nothing, only a bad dream."

Miri snuggled against him, soothed by his caress, the rough timbre of his voice. But the tears still coursed down her cheeks as she choked, "No, you—you don't understand. I—I've had nightmares like this ever since I was a little girl. Strange dreams that spin out over and over again until—until they come true."

His hand stilled in her hair. "You mean like a—a prophecy?"

"Y-yes."

Miri could sense his frown and knew that the witch-hunter in him would be leery of anything that hinted of visions or the forbidden art of divining the future. But he resumed stroking her hair, his voice gentle as he said, "All right. Tell me about this one."

She drew in her breath with a shuddery sigh and described her dream in halting sentences, the palace crawling with lizards, gigantic chess pieces, the shattered white knight.

"And then—then I realized it wasn't a chessman at all, but you. And you were broken and bleeding," she concluded in a whisper.

Simon was silent for a long time, as though he did not know quite how to respond. He finally patted her shoulder and said, "Very well. I promise I'll steer clear of salamanders and never play chess again."

Although his voice was solemn, Miri could tell he was humoring her, doing his best to banish her fears. She could well understand how completely mad this must all sound to him, but she was filled with frustration all the same.

Thumping her hand against his chest, she drew back, straining to peer up at him through the darkness. "This is not a jest, Simon. You have got to take me seriously. I know it seems incredible, a jumbled lunacy, but my dreams are never clear at first. The things that happen are—are masks, symbols of events I never understand until it is too late."

Her lips quivered. "And my nightmares never fail in coming true. The worst one I ever had was years ago. I—I kept dreaming about the massacre on St. Bartholomew's Day. All those slaughtered innocents. I can't even begin to tell how dreadful it was."

"You don't have to," Simon said. "I was there in Paris with my master, remember?"

Miri remembered, but it was something she'd always dreaded to think about, wondering what terrible things Simon might have done that night under Le Vis's orders. She stared at him, wishing she could see his face.

"Then you went out with Le Vis that night to—to—"

"No."

Simon's reply was brusque, but it flooded her with relief. She melted back in his arms as he continued, "Master Le Vis could tell I was not up to the task of—of—administering God's judgment upon the heretics, as he called it. He forbade me to leave the house, but even tunneled deep in the cellars, I could still hear the screams of—of the women and children.

"May God forgive me, Miri, I did nothing to help them. It was like there was a madness abroad that night, some foul contagion that infected me. I have never felt such fear, but—but such anger and hatred as well."

"That was the Dark Queen's doing," she sought to reassure him. "She released a miasma into the air."

"What?"

"It's a potion of the most dangerous kind. When you breathe it in, it clouds your reason, heightens all of your darker feelings."

"Is such a thing truly possible? It would be comforting to believe that witchery was responsible for the horrors of that night, but there is a violence in men that requires little encouraging. I—I felt almost insane with pent-up fury. I actually had my knife gripped in my hand ready to rush out into the street and—and—I had to struggle so hard to fight my black impulses. I flung the knife away and sank to my knees, retching my guts out. I was every bit as weak as Master Le Vis accused me of being."

"No, you weren't!" Miri reached up to stroke his cheek. "Full-grown men are unable to resist the power of a miasma and yet you did and you were only a confused boy of fifteen. Do you realize how remarkable—"

Miri broke off, struck by a chilling realization. "Simon, I—I think I know what my dream means. Or at least some of it. The two Dark Queens. They are the Silver Rose and Catherine and you are somehow going to be caught between them. And one of them will release something— a miasma, perhaps—to harm you."

"Well, if, according to you, I survived it once before—"

"But—but this time I am so afraid you won't."

"I hope you are wrong, but even if you aren't . . . Miri, I can't turn back from hunting the Silver Rose just because you've had a bad dream."

"I know that," she replied, clinging to him. "Oh, Simon, I am beginning to despair that we will ever defeat these witches." She swallowed, finally giving voice to the fear she had been fending off for days. "We—we have lost all trace of Carole and those evil women who took her, haven't we?"

Simon sighed, brushing his lips against the top of her head. "I am afraid so," he said gently. "That is why I have been thinking that we need to take another approach, hunt for clues somewhere else. But to do that, I need to—to take you home."

"No! I told you before. I'll not return to Faire Isle."

"I didn't mean your home, Miri." He hesitated and then astonished her when he added gruffly, "I am talking about mine."

Chapter Thirteen

THE SILVER ROSE TRUDGED UP THE STAIRS TO HER BED-chamber, dismissing her attendants with a wearied wave of one small hand. The circlet she wore threatened to slip over her ears again and she shoved it back impatiently. Her frail shoulders were weighted down by the mantle, the thick velvet garment stifling in the summer heat. Her gown, soaked through with perspiration, clung to her thin frame.

Megaera felt exhausted after another audience with the throng of women who assembled daily in the hall of the old house. To gape at her in awe, to make obeisance before her throne, to eagerly seek her favor. Her court, as Maman persisted in calling them.

No, not *Maman,* Meg reminded herself. She was to refer to Cassandra Lascelles as the Lady, just as everyone else did.

Maman became quite vexed with her when she forgot. Meg fingered the five-sided medallion suspended about her neck with a tiny shiver. If there was one thing the girl had learned from an early age, it was that it was unwise to vex her mother.

She stole inside her bedchamber and closed the door, leaning up against it with a tiny sigh, relieved to shut out all her worshipful followers, even if it was only for a brief time. To be free of all those begging hands reaching out to her, those hopeful eyes, those expectant faces that nibbled away at her like a swarm of hungry mice. Barraging her ears with their pleas.

"Great queen, please restore my youth . . . heal my crippled leg . . . lay a curse upon the man who stole my innocence."

Or the pleas Meg dreaded most of all . . . *"Oh, most powerful Silver Rose, I lost my sister . . . my mother . . . my daughter. Can you not bring her back to life as you did petite Lysette that day she fell into the pond and drowned?"*

Meg wanted to shriek at everyone. Lysette only *nearly* drowned. The little girl only seemed to stop breathing. She wasn't really dead or Meg would never have been able to revive her with the Kiss of Life, a healing magic she had learned from her old nurse.

But Maman had sternly forbidden Meg to speak of that.

"Let them think you brought the child back from the dead. It will only enhance your reputation as a great sorceress."

"But—but it's a lie," Meg had stammered. *"I don't have such power."*

*"You could have, you foolish child. If you would learn
to apply yourself."*

Meg was uncertain what frightened her more. The
prospect that she would never be able to keep all the dark
promises she was forced to make. Or that someday she
might . . .

She tugged at the clasp fastening her mantle and
breathed a sigh of relief when the heavy folds tumbled
from her shoulders. She wanted to kick the much-hated
garment into a heap, but she knew she would be roundly
scolded for not taking better care of her "robe of state."

Grudgingly she picked up the mantle and hung it from
a peg mounted on the wall. Next she stripped off the silver
crown. Her fingers inched toward the medallion suspended
about her neck. The braided chain chafed her skin near her
collarbone, her perspiration stinging the raw streak of red.

Meg wanted to remove the medallion, but knew she
didn't dare. She quailed, thinking what the dire consequences might be if she even tried. No, she most definitely
did not dare.

Unhappily, she peered at herself in the small looking
glass fixed above her ewer and basin. With the crown and
mantle removed, the Silver Rose vanished, leaving only
Meg. That thought was the only satisfaction her reflection
gave her. She studied her sharp, angular features, her lank
brown hair, and wrinkled her nose in distaste before turning away.

Feeling tired and dragged out by the heat, she kicked
off her shoes and flung herself down upon the massive bed
that dominated the room. Carved of heavy oak and hung

with blue damask embroidered with silver roses, it was a bed fit for a queen, or so her mother said.

Meg hated the bed even more than she did her mantle and her crown. It was not so bad napping here in the middle of the afternoon, but when she was alone at night, in the dark, she often felt as though the great bed would swallow her up like some giant maw the moment she closed her eyes.

It was an infantile fancy for a girl of nine years, Meg knew, but she could not help herself. Her heart pounding with fear, she would clutch her pillow tight to her chest and indulge in a few quiet tears where there were none to see and chide her for her weakness.

She would weep and think wistfully of their English days before she and Maman had sailed back to France. Three years ago, but Meg could remember so clearly the little cottage by the sea in Dover and her nurse who had taken care of her from her earliest hours. A plump genial wise woman by the name of Prudence Waters, but to Meg, she had never been anything but her beloved Nourice.

Meg had never been afraid of the dark then, not tucked up in her small cot with Nourice's arms about her, lulled to sleep by the whisper of the sea. Nourice had always called her little Meggie, something that infuriated Maman.

"Her name is Megaera," her mother would rage. All the Englishwoman had done was shrug. Nourice had been one of the few people who had never seemed afraid of Cassandra.

But she should have been, Meg thought as she stared up at the carved ceiling of her bed. A lump formed in her throat as she recalled the spring day when her mother's friend Finette had taken her for a walk down the beach to gather shells. Meg had raced ahead, eager to return to the cottage and show Nourice the starfish that she had found.

But there had been no beaming woman awaiting her, to exclaim with delight over Meg's small cache of treasures, to comb the salt and sand from her hair, to wash her hands and face and set her down to her supper. Nourice was nowhere to be found, not in the kitchen, not in the garden, and her mother's only explanation was, *"You are too old to have a nurse any longer, Megaera. She has taught you all she could. I have sent Mistress Waters away, back to her family."*

Meg had been forbidden to cry or ask any further questions. She hadn't really wanted to, something about the cruel set of her mother's mouth frightening her. She had swallowed her grief, learned to accept the fact that Nourice had vanished from her life. Just like Cerberus, the remarkable old dog who had for so long been Maman's eyes.

Holding up one hand, Meg examined the pale scar on the back of her arm where Cerberus had bitten her that summer she'd turned five. It had been a sweltering day like this one and Meg was sure Cerberus had never meant to do it. The poor old mastiff had been miserable with the heat like everyone else and had not wanted to be petted by the sweaty hands of a little girl.

But Maman had collared the dog. She and Finette had marched him off down the beach. Some hours later they had returned without Cerberus and Maman had said curtly, *"I got rid of him."*

"But why, Maman?" Meg had asked, astonished and

dismayed. Her mother had loved that dog more than anyone or anything in the world. Especially Meg.

Cassandra had replied coldly, *"Because of you. Nothing must threaten my Silver Rose."*

Not my daughter or my only child, but the Silver Rose, Meg reflected sadly. The legend upon which Maman had pinned all her dreams, so much that she had even been willing to sacrifice her beloved Cerberus. But she had resented Meg for it. Even as young as she had been, Meg had been able to sense that.

Meg shivered, thinking how much she had wanted to warn the new girl whom she had permitted to join their coven. That night when Carole Moreau had knelt cowering before her, awaiting her verdict, Meg had looked deep into the girl's eyes.

Meg was good at the old wise woman magic of reading the eyes. Nourice had taught her well and Meg had a natural gift for it, although she didn't often like to use her ability. Stare too deep into someone's eyes and one might stumble over dark thoughts or secrets one didn't want to know.

But as she had studied Carole, Meg had realized at once that Carole was different from the other angry, embittered women in the great hall. Carole was sad, confused, and afraid, so much like Meg herself, she had felt an immediate kinship with the older girl. Carole just wanted to go home, back to Faire Isle, and Meg wished she could have let her. But Maman would never allow that. The only way to help the girl, keep her safe, was to declare her fit to become a member of their order.

But as Carole had paid homage, kissing her hand, Meg had longed to lean forward and whisper in her ear. *"You must be careful. Never anger or displease my mother. She will make you disappear."*

Sometimes Meg wondered if that was what had happened to her father. She had never met him, never even known a child was supposed to have a father until the day she had seen the little fisher boy on the beach, his papa teaching him to mend nets.

Meg had marched straight home and wanted to know where her papa was, a question she had oft repeated. When she was in a more mellow humor, Cassandra Lascelles would spin tales about Meg's father being a mercenary, a man who sailed the world plying his fearsome trade, such a fierce warrior, so savage he was known as the Scourge.

At other moments, the dark times Meg called them, when Maman had had too much whiskey, she would growl at Meg and tell her she was the spawn of the devil. Meg found both answers equally daunting and after a time, she had given up asking, learning to weave her dreams instead.

Her father had really been a king, she had decided. A handsome man, tall and brave with raven hair and twinkling eyes who had laughed, lifted her up into the air and danced her about, calling her his petite princess. Meg had been stolen out of her cradle in the palace and spirited away.

But her father was out there somewhere searching for her. One day he would ride up on a great white horse and swoop Meg off to his kingdom by the sea. There was only one problem with her fantasies and that was when she pictured herself perched on the saddle before this magnificent man . . . an ugly little troll of a girl. So in her dreams she transformed herself as well, into a fairy princess with golden curls and eyes of blue.

None of this could ever be true. She was old enough to realize that, but she didn't care. She had long ago discovered living in a castle in the air with a papa who adored you was much better than the real world with a house full of bitter women with alarming expectations and a mother who despised you for being weak.

Soothed by her imaginings, Meg curled on her side, burrowed her nose deeper into the pillow, and fell asleep. She was awakened all too soon by a rough hand shaking her shoulder.

"Megaera! Wake up, you lazy child."

Meg's eyes fluttered open. The sunlight had disappeared, her bedchamber enshrouded in shadows. She squinted through the gathering gloom, peering up at the woman who had awakened her. She didn't have to see her properly to know who it was. She recognized the shrill voice and sour smell of Finette all too well.

Wriggling away from Finette's grip, Meg yawned and knuckled the sleep from her eyes.

"What the devil do you think you are doing, girl?" Finette scolded. "Lolling about in bed in the middle of the day."

"I don't know," Meg muttered. Besides Cassandra Lascelles, Finette was the only woman in the coven who dared to speak to Meg harshly and with so little respect. Perhaps because Finette was Cassandra's oldest and most trusted servant. That is, as much as Maman trusted anyone.

Meg had never liked the woman. Unlike her kind soft Nourice, Finette was all hard angles from her sharp face and sly eyes to her flat bosom and bony hips. And no matter how fine a gown she wore, Finette looked like a slattern because she never washed. Her skin encrusted with layers of grime, her stringy hair matted and filthy, she reeked of a pungent combination of sweat, dirt, and urine.

Standing over Meg with her elbows propped akimbo, Finette sneered. "So does your royal highness have any idea what time it is?"

Resisting the impulse to hold her nose, Meg scooted to the other side of the bed. She glanced toward the window and was dismayed to see the sun had nearly set. She had no idea that she had slept that long.

"Oh, no," she moaned.

"*Oh, no,*" Finette mocked. "The Lady has been waiting for you forever. You should have been at your studies hours ago."

Meg cringed inwardly at the mention of her mother, but she didn't want to give Finette any satisfaction by showing it. Scrambling off the bed, Meg hastened to find her shoes while Finette harangued her.

"You are such a selfish little brat. Do you realize how many women have risked their lives, given up everything to follow you? They are all counting on you to decipher the *Book of Shadows* and master those spells."

Meg ducked her head, letting her hair fall forward to mask her expression of fear and loathing. She despised that book, wished she could hurl it into the fire, but it was a thing of such evil, she wondered if it would even burn.

Long ago, Nourice had taught Meg the rudiments of reading mysterious symbols and runes, crowing with delight at Meg's rapid progress.

"What a wonder you are, my little poppet. To have learned so quickly and at your young age. I have known full-grown women who have never been able to master the ancient language, but you have a gift for it. I vow you will even surpass your old nurse one day. I am so proud of you, dearie."

At the time, Meg had flushed with delight at Nourice's praise, but now the memory saddened her. Nourice would no longer be proud of her, not if she knew how Meg had used the skills she'd been taught.

She *was* good at puzzling out the old symbols, even though the *Book of Shadows* was very hard to read. But the more she managed to decipher of those enigmatic pages, the more terrified she became. Even the most innocent of spells came out wrong. The powder to preserve the life of the roses turned them to deadly poison. The magic needle that could rush healing medicine into a person's veins became a terrible weapon. At least, in her mother's hands.

Sometimes Meg worried that it wasn't the book that was bad, but Cassandra. But that was far too dreadful a thought for a girl to entertain about her mother. Meg quashed it as she finished putting on her shoes.

Finette loomed over her, tapping her foot. "So what spell are you going to try to translate today?"

"I don't know. Whatever Maman—I mean, the Lady, tells me," Meg replied sullenly.

"Just remember I was the one who acquired the *Book,* stealing it out from under the noses of both that witch-hunter and the Dark Queen," Finette bragged. "And at no little risk to myself. I—"

"Yes, yes," Meg interrupted with a long-suffering sigh. She had heard the story of how Finette had tricked the Dark Queen's spy and snatched the book at least a million times. So had everyone else.

She gasped when Finette's hand clamped down hard, pinching her arm.

"You just remember what's due to me, that's all. I have been waiting far longer than all of those other wenches to be rewarded for my services. I want you to find me a potion that will make me lovely and desirable."

Meg pulled a face. There was not a spell in the world powerful enough to do that. She was tempted to suggest there was one magic Finette might try. It was called hot water and perfumed soap. But Meg was wise enough to keep the thought to herself. Yanking away from Finette, she marched out of the bedchamber, making a dignified exit with her small chin thrust into the air.

◊◊◊◊

THE CHAMBER OCCUPIED BY Cassandra Lascelles was situated at the highest point of the house. Those summoned to attend upon the Lady often approached the chamber with dread, including her own daughter. Even during the brightest part of the day, the north tower seemed gloomy and sinister, a place of shadows and secrets.

Her palms slick with sweat, Meg hovered at the top of the winding stair. She wondered how angry Maman would be because of her tardiness. She prayed that her mother had not been drinking. Cassandra's temper was much worse when the demons crept out of the whiskey bottle and invaded her heart.

Meg clutched her medallion and gulped, the amulet feeling like a noose, just waiting to tighten. But she was only making matters worse by delaying. Dusk had crept over the landing, rendering it pitch-black, but she could see light emanating beneath the crack of her mother's door.

Meg drew in a deep breath and knocked. "M-maman . . . I mean, milady?"

There was no response. Perhaps she had been so timid, her mother had not heard her, although that seemed unlikely. Even though Maman could not see, her other senses were extremely sharp, especially her hearing.

Meg risked another knock, a little louder. When the silence stretched out, her pulse skipped a beat. Sometimes when Maman drank too much whiskey, she made herself so sick she fell down or slipped into an alarming deep sleep from which Meg could not rouse her.

Fear for her mother superceding her other apprehensions, Meg turned the knob and cracked open the door enough to peek inside. The furnishings of the tower room were sparse, a narrow bed, a chair, a table, the cupboard where Maman kept her dried herbs necessary to brew potions, and the small locked chest that contained the dreaded *Book*. None of Maman's things must ever be touched or moved lest she trip or be unable to find what she wanted. Meg had learned long ago that that was the way to make Cassandra really angry.

"Milady?" She dared to open the door a little farther until she spied her mother near the chamber's empty hearth. Meg froze, choking back a dismayed cry at the sight that met her eyes, far worse than Cassandra Lascelles plying her bottle or tapping her walking staff in a temper.

Maman was at her conjuring again . . .

Cassandra bent over a copper bowl positioned in the center of the table, muttering some incantation under her breath. A brace of black candles burned with a white-hot flame, casting an eerie halo over the Lady's gaunt features. She shook back her thick mane of silver-streaked dark hair as she waved her hand over the basin.

Her mother was a formidable woman, but she waxed even more alarming as she swayed, sinking deeper into her trance. She seemed to grow taller, stronger, her shadow stretching up the wall. Her eyes, usually so dark, still burned with an inner fire as she focused on the cauldron. Maman was only blind in the land of the living. When she parted the veil into the netherworld beyond, Cassandra could *see*.

Meg shrank back, trembling. How often had Nourice warned Meg against necromancy, the forbidden practice of summoning the dead.

"It is magic of the blackest kind, my pet. Not only is it wrong to disturb the peace of departed souls, no matter how much we love and miss them, necromancy can be very dangerous. Any time one disturbs the realms of the dead, one risks setting loose evil and vengeful spirits seeking a portal back into our world."

As her mother muttered over the copper vessel, Meg wanted to rush into the chamber and stop her. Clutch at her skirts and beg, "Ah, don't, Maman. Please don't."

Not only would Maman never heed her pleas, she might force Meg to participate. Maman had tried on several occasions before to teach her the conjuring, all to no avail.

"You clearly have no gift for necromancy," her mother had complained when Meg had failed. *"You are too stupid to be taught."*

Meg knew she wasn't. She had simply not wanted to learn the dark art.

As a terrible mist began to rise out of the bowl, Meg crouched down, wanting to look away, to close the door. But she continued to watch with a kind of horrified fascination as her mother intoned in a louder voice.

"Nostradamus! Hear me, master. I summon your spirit from the realms of the dead. Come to me. I would speak with you about the future."

The water in the bowl threatened to boil over, emitting a furious hiss of steam. A deep voice rumbled from the depths of the vessel, sending a cold chill through Meg.

"What now, witch? Why do you again disturb my peace with your endless demands about the time to come? I have answered your questions over and over again. What more can I tell you?"

Meg shivered. She had been told that Michel de Nostradamus had been a learned doctor and seer when he had still walked the earth, advising and helping many people. His spirit was usually furious whenever Maman summoned him, although this time the ghost sounded more wearied than enraged.

It was Maman who was angry as she railed, "What can you tell me? How about the truth for once instead of all your endless falsehoods and evasions?"

"What falsehoods? When have I ever lied to you?"

"You told me that one day there would be a revolution in France, that kings would be swept from the throne.

You predicted there would come a time when women would no longer be subservient to men *and* you foretold that Megaera is destined for greatness."

Meg flinched at the mention of her name. It was frightening to hear yourself discussed with a ghost even when Nostradamus agreed with her mother.

"The child you call Megaera is fated to become a powerful woman. All these things I have foretold will come to pass."

"When? I see little sign of any of it coming true, although I have done my best to make it happen. I am hardly any nearer to placing my daughter on the French throne than I was years ago. You—you have deceived me."

"You deceived yourself, witch," the sepulchral voice replied. *"I never said anything about Megaera ruling France. It is you who have taken all these separate events I spoke of and woven them into a cloth of your own mad design."*

"Because you tricked me. You led me to believe!" Cassandra clenched her fists, grinding her teeth. "I want no more of your evasions and vague prophecies. Tell me once and for all. What did you mean when you said my daughter will possess great power? Will she become queen or will she not?"

"Megaera's fate rests with . . ."

The voice faded to a whisper. Meg's heart thumped anxiously. Who? Who did her fate rest with? She pressed her face to the crack in the door, straining to hear.

Maman leaned closer over the bowl. "No! Master. Don't you dare fade away until you assure me—"

She stared into the cloudy water with a heavy scowl.

"Who—who is that lurking there? Who comes? I summoned Master Nostradamus, not you. Go back. Back, I say and—"

Cassandra broke off, recoiling from the bowl with an alarmed cry. "Mother, is that you? No, no!" She waved her hands frantically as though fending off a blow.

"Serpent's tooth. Treacherous witch." A woman's angry voice rang out, so shrill it pierced through Meg, made her want to clap her hands over her ears.

"You betrayed me and your sisters—"

"No. No, I didn't," Cassandra shrieked, stumbling back from the table. "Leave me alone."

The mist whirled, assuming a darker, more menacing cast. To Meg's horror, she thought she saw a skeletal hand rise up out of the haze, clawing at her mother. As Cassandra screamed, Meg covered her eyes, too terrified to look.

She heard a thud and then a loud clatter and realized Cassandra must have lashed out, knocking the bowl from the table. A dread silence descended, the only sound Cassandra's ragged breathing. Or was it her own?

When Meg finally dared peek, nothing remained of the mist except a lingering wisp of smoke. The bowl was overturned, water spattered over the floor. Her mother hunkered down by the table, her eyes dimmed as tears cascaded down her cheeks.

Meg bit down on her lip, her chest feeling squeezed tight. She had only ever seen her formidable mother cry once before, the night Cerberus had vanished. Her mother had sat twisting the dog's lead in her hands, weeping as though her heart would break. Meg had rushed to fling her arms about Cassandra, trying to apologize through her own sobs, to say how sorry she was for making Maman obliged to get rid of the dog. She had only wanted to comfort her mother, but Cassandra had shoved her savagely away with a hate-filled scowl.

Which is what her mother would do if Meg dared approach her now. Cassandra regarded tears as a weakness, and Meg sensed that she did not like appearing weak in front of anyone, especially Meg. Any attempt to console Maman would only make her despise Meg more than she already did.

Meg lingered in the doorway, distressed by her mother's tears, not knowing what to do. As she shifted from foot to foot, she lost her balance and stumbled against the door, causing it to creak.

Cassandra froze, her head snapping up immediately. She dashed the tears from her cheeks, demanding, "Who is that? Who is there?"

Meg swallowed, her tongue cleaving to the roof of her mouth. It was pure folly not to answer. Her mother would know she was there. She always did because of the matching medallions they wore, the amulets forging a dark and inescapable bond between them, allowing Cassandra to sense Meg's whereabouts until recently . . .

These past few months, Meg had learned how to render herself invisible. All she had to do was imagine there was a magic trunk deep inside her heart, then picture herself climbing into it, pulling down the lid, and hiding. Maman could not find her there, not even with her dark inner eye.

But this time Meg was not quick enough to react. Cassandra clutched her medallion, the tentacles of her mind reaching out, and Meg betrayed herself with the quickening of her breath, the speeding up of her heart. Panicked, she searched for her magic trunk. But it was too late. Her mother snapped, "Megaera! I know you are out there. What have I told you before about lurking and spying? Get in here."

Quivering, Meg pushed against the door until it opened enough to let her slip into the room. Clutching the table leg, Cassandra dragged herself to her feet. She pointed imperiously to the space directly in front of her.

"Come here. Right now."

Meg slunk forward, nearly slipping in the puddle of water by the overturned bowl. The copper vessel scraped against the floor as she bent to retrieve it.

"What's that sound? What are you doing?" her mother snarled.

"I—I'm just picking up your bowl, tidying up . . ."

"Am I raising you to be a queen or a scullery maid? Leave that to Finette."

"Yes, madame." Meg meekly placed the bowl on the table. She crept closer until she was within range of her mother's hands. Her mother gripped her shoulders, placing Meg directly in front of her. She could feel the chill of her mother's fingers through the fabric of her gown.

"What have you been doing all afternoon?" Cassandra asked. Before Meg could frame an answer, her mother rapped out, "Have you been spending more time with that Moreau girl?"

"N-no."

"Finette tells me that ever since that girl was permitted to join our coven, you have showed a special interest in her."

Meg swallowed. She liked Carole. The older girl was the closest thing to a friend she had found since her arrival in Paris. But Maman would not like to hear that.

"Mademoiselle Moreau is—is a little shy," Meg said. "I have just been trying to make her feel welcome."

"*Welcome?* The girl is not a guest in this house. She is here to serve our cause, to further the glory of the Silver Rose and the new age of power for wise women. Your interests, Megaera."

No, those are your interests, Maman, not mine. Meg was quick to suppress her thoughts. Maman could not read eyes, but she could still divine thoughts, drawing out secrets and memories with her touch.

She felt relieved when Cassandra released her icy grip, although Meg knew she didn't dare move an inch from where her mother had placed her. She sought to deflect her mother's displeasure by complaining about Finette.

"Finette is—is such a sneak, milady. I—I am supposed to be her queen too, but she is very rude to me. And she is always carrying tales—"

"Silence! It's Finette's duty to report to me when you forget yourself. If you want Finette to respect you as a queen, then you must act like one, stop behaving in such a familiar manner with your subjects. I hear you even gave Carole Moreau permission to call you Meg."

Meg stared down at the floor as she mumbled. "I—I like it better than Megaera. My name is so odd."

"Megaera was a goddess, one of the avenging furies in Greek myth. But what is the point in giving you such a magnificent name if you are going to behave like a commoner?"

"I—I don't know, Maman. I—I mean milady. I—I will try to do better, I promise."

"You always promise." Her mother expelled an exasperated breath. "Why do I never seem able to make you understand, Megaera? From the moment of your birth, nay even before, you have been singled out for greatness. It was predicted that I would conceive a daughter who would be very powerful.

"But it will not be power given to you by any man, but taken through a revolution of wise women. I have told you the legends, child. There was once a time when the daughters of the earth were not the slaves of men, when they could practice their magic without fear and not be burned for sorcery. Nostradamus has seen a time in the future when the daughters of the earth will resume their rightful place, only I cannot force the old fool to tell me when."

Cassandra spread her hands in an impatient gesture. "I have no intention of waiting for decades to pass, until I am dead and gone. These changes are going to happen in my lifetime. The daughters of the earth will topple thrones and strip all men of their power, beginning here in France. You are the one fated to lead us to this new age of glory, Megaera. A queen among queens, the most powerful sorceress the world has ever known."

Meg cringed as she peered up at her mother. She hated when Maman talked this way, getting flushed, her features contorting. She looked and sounded a bit mad and Nourice had thought so, too.

Meg frowned, a memory niggling at her, something she had all but forgotten, the quarrel she had overheard between her mother and Nourice the night before Prudence Waters had disappeared.

"*Sweet heaven, Cassandra,*" *Nourice exclaimed.* "*Bad enough you have been practicing necromancy, but all this talk of prophecy, revolution, putting Meggie on the French throne. It is completely mad. You can't really believe all this nonsense.*"

"*I assure you that I do,*" *Cassandra replied coldly.* "*And you can either support me in my plans for my daughter or get out.*"

Nourice rarely ever looked stern, but she had scowled at Cassandra. "*And leave that poor child to be swept up in your insane ambitions? I think not and what's more, if you persist in pursuing this dangerous lunacy, I will have to send word to the Lady of Faire Isle.*"

"*The Lady of Faire Isle,*" *Cassandra scoffed.* "*She is no one now that she has been banished from her island, forced into exile.*"

"*You are quite wrong. Ariane Cheney still commands enough respect among decent wise woman to be able to stop you. As for Meggie, I will remove her from your care, take her where you'll never find her . . .*"

Meg scrunched up her forehead in her efforts to remember. Had her gentle Nourice really threatened Maman or did Meg merely imagine the entire quarrel? All she was truly certain of was that the next day Nourice had vanished and Maman had forced Meg to start wearing the medallion.

"Megaera!"

Her mother's harsh voice shook Meg out of her reverie. "Are you paying heed to me?"

"Yes, milady."

"Then be so good as to make some response. Here I am telling you about your great future, about how hard I have worked on your behalf. Because of me you now have a considerable following of other wise women ready to kill and die for you. Yet I hear no mark of your gratitude."

"T-thank you, milady. But—but . . ."

"But what?"

Meg hung her head, knowing she would do better to hold her tongue. How could she explain to Maman she didn't want anyone killing or dying for her? How much it hurt her, like a huge fist crushing her heart, knowing all these evil things her followers were doing in her name.

She said in a small voice, "I guess there is so much I don't understand. Especially about all those helpless babes, those little boys. Why do they have to die?"

Her mother pursed her lips. "How many times do I have to explain that as well? Male children are of no use to the coven. I realize abandoning them seems cruel to you, but the same thing has been done to helpless infant girls for centuries."

"But how does that make it fair to treat little boys the same way?" Meg argued. "It—it just makes two bad things instead of one. And if this is what must be done to make me queen, I don't want to be."

Meg realized at once that she had gone too far. Cassandra's hand tightened on the medallion so hard, her knuckles turned white. Meg could feel her mother's rage pulse through her own amulet, like a hot searing knife piercing Meg's heart.

She clutched her chest and cried out, sinking to her knees, almost dizzy from the pain. "Maman! P-please don't."

"Never let me hear you say anything like that again," Cassandra grated.

"I won't, Maman. Milady! Please . . . please stop," Meg sobbed, tears streaming down her cheeks.

Cassandra released her medallion, letting it dangle back around her neck. Meg's pain eased as though the knife was being inched from her heart. She cowered at her mother's feet, weak and trembling.

Cassandra bent down, reaching out until her hand came to rest atop Meg's head. Her wrath spent, she looked suddenly drained and exhausted.

"Oh, child, why do you force me to punish you this way?"

She dragged Meg up and into her arms, holding her so tight Meg could hardly breathe. But she was so hungry for any scrap of affection from her mother, she sniffed back her tears and endured the bruising embrace without protest.

Cassandra edged back until she struck the chair. She sank down into it and did something that shocked Meg, something she could not ever remember her mother doing before. She drew Meg onto her lap and held her close.

Meg scarce knew how to respond. Cautiously, she rested her head against her mother's shoulder. Cassandra trailed her fingers over Meg's face until she found her tears and wiped them brusquely away.

"Megaera, you have had so little experience of the harshness of life. That is my fault. I have protected you far too much in ways that I was never sheltered as a child. Did you know that I grew up here in this very same house?"

"N-no."

"I did, but unlike you, I did not sleep in any lovely bed-chamber like a pampered princess. I spent most of my years here confined to the hidden room below the house."

Meg lifted her head to gape at her mother. When they had first moved to the house, Maman had shown her the secret passage behind the aumbry in the great hall. Should the coven ever be surprised by witch-hunters or the Dark Queen's soldiers, Meg was to flee down those stone steps and hide, but she shuddered at the prospect. The chamber below was dark and cold like a dungeon, infested with spi-ders and the occasional rat.

"You lived in that awful hidden room? But why, Maman?"

For once her mother did not rebuke her for failing to call her milady. Cassandra's face was clouded with memo-ries and judging by the crease in her brow, they were not pleasant ones.

"I had to hide from the witch-hunters. They raided this house, capturing my mother and my three sisters. Do you know what witch-hunters do to sorceresses?"

"Yes," Meg quavered. Finette delighted in telling her lurid stories of the fate of captured witches and always right before bedtime so that Meg's dreams were haunted with dungeons, women screaming in pain as their arms were racked from their sockets, their thumbs crushed, their fingernails ripped out.

"Sorceresses are tortured until they confess and give up the names of their friends. Then they are all burned at the stake." Meg shivered. "Alive."

"That is right, and out of all the women in my family, only I escaped such a dire fate."

Meg pondered this, thinking of her mother's most recent séance, which had somehow gone wrong. How pale and frightened Maman had looked when that other spirit had appeared, the one Cassandra had called . . . *Mother.*

Had that shrill voice and clawlike hand belonged to Meg's own grandmother, a woman she had rarely heard of until now? If that was true, why was her grand-mère so angry and accusing, as though she somehow blamed Cassandra for her terrible fate?

Cassandra was not inclined to discuss her past or answer any questions about the family Meg had never known. But seated upon her mother's knee with Cassandra absently stroking her hair, Meg was emboldened to ask. "What were my grandmother and aunts like?"

Cassandra frowned as though taken aback by the unexpected question. Then she shrugged. "They were sorceresses, although not as skilled as me. I was the best of all of us, even without my eyesight."

Meg recalled troubling whispers she heard amongst her followers, rumors regarding her mother's blindness. She ventured timidly, "Maman, I—I have heard some of the women say that—that my grandmother made a pact with the devil. She traded your eyes so that you could have the gift of necromancy."

"A foolish tale," Cassandra said, much to Meg's relief.

Playing idly with a strand of Meg's hair, she continued, "But your grandmother *was* responsible for the loss of my eyes. All because she loved my father, the bishop, more than she did me."

"My grandfather was a bishop? But isn't that a holy man? I didn't think they were supposed to have wives."

Cassandra's lip curled in an ugly sneer. "My mother wasn't his wife and my father was far from holy. My mother, my sisters, and I were his eminence's shameful secret. Although he gave us this fine house, he had to skulk here to visit us, which he did infrequently. But whenever he deigned to come, the entire world stopped for my mother. She was consumed with pleasing him. So much so, the night that I was sick with scarlet fever, she neglected me for his bed. That is how I came to lose my eyesight and I never forgave my mother for that."

Meg squirmed, uncomfortable with these confidences, only able to understand part of what Cassandra was telling her. But she could feel her mother's bitterness and pain. Impulsively she hugged Cassandra, wishing things could have been different for her mother, for herself as well.

How much more pleasant it would have been to return to Paris if, instead of this house full of demanding half-mad women, she had been greeted by her grandparents. Not some cold bishop and a witch, but gentle, affectionate *married* grandparents who would hug her and call her Meggie, welcoming her to their house.

And her father would be there, too. Not a king perhaps, but still handsome and charming. He would be terribly in love with Maman and then maybe she would forget about conquering France and be happy just to—

"Stop it!" Meg winced as her mother's nails dug into her shoulder.

"Damn it, girl. I know what you are doing. I can read you like an open book."

Meg cringed. Caught up in her daydream, she had forgotten her mother's ability to discern her thoughts through touch. Cassandra gave her a hard shake.

"I hate this habit of yours. This penchant you have for losing yourself in pretty dreams to escape the real world."

You do the same thing, Maman. Only you use a bottle of whiskey.

The resentful thought popped into Meg's head before she could suppress it. Cassandra sucked in her breath with a furious hiss. She dealt Meg a ringing slap that caused her eyes to water. She shoved Meg off her lap. Meg tumbled down, her hip hitting the floor with a jarring thud.

She sat up slowly, rubbing her throbbing cheek and blinking back fresh tears. She felt a stab of some emotion so foreign, it took her a moment to understand what it was. Anger.

But the emotion fled before her usual fear as Cassandra sprang to her feet. Meg's hand flew to the medallion suspended about her neck. She held her breath and braced herself to be punished.

Although Cassandra's lips thinned, she made no move to reach for her own amulet. "Enough of this nonsense," she declared. "It is time you were about fulfilling your duty to me and the rest of your courtiers."

Cassandra fumbled with the belt that held her chatelaine and produced a heavy iron key. "Here. Go fetch the *Book of Shadows.*"

Meg picked herself up off the floor. She accepted the key from her mother with shaking fingers and went to unlock the small chest beside her mother's bed. It contained only two objects. A heavy signet ring bearing the letter *C* and a book no bigger than Nourice's bible had been.

The dread *Book of Shadows* looked so harmless, an old volume with yellowing brittle pages bound together by a worn leather cover. But as soon as Meg lifted it into her hands, it was as though the *Book* took on an eerie life of its own. She could feel the pulse of its dark lore in some strange way that repelled and called to her.

Meg carried the *Book* over to the table and laid it down, nervously wiping her hands on her gown. Cassandra had retrieved her walking staff. Using it to test the path before her, she made her way to Meg's side.

"What do you want me to work on today, Maman?" Meg asked bleakly. "The spell to restore your eyes?"

"If you were any kind of daughter at all, you would have already mastered that," Cassandra replied scornfully.

Meg held herself very still, seeking not to betray her secret by the slightest whisper of breath. She had mastered the spell some time ago, but for Maman to have her sight restored, another person would have to surrender theirs. Cassandra would have no qualms about sacrificing someone else, but Meg quailed at the thought. Perhaps her mother would not be so angry or bitter if she could see, but the cost was still too high.

How she longed to beg Cassandra, *"Maman, let's get rid of this awful book, forget all these mad plans and schemes before something really bad happens. Let's go back and live in our pretty little cottage in Dover. I would take good*

*care of you. I swear I would. I would be your eyes just like
Cerberus was."*

But to give voice to such a plea would only elicit more
of her mother's wrath, so Meg swallowed her words. She
was getting better at concealing things from Cassandra, a
growing power that both thrilled and frightened her.

"Forget about the spell to restore my eyes for now,"
Cassandra said. She startled Meg by suddenly demanding,
"Do you know what a miasma is?"

"Y-es," Meg replied nervously. "Nourice explained it to
me when I overheard some stories about the Dark Queen.
She said a miasma is a poisonous mist that—that makes
people go mad, want to hurt each other, and only someone
as wicked as Queen Catherine would ever think of using
such black magic. Only a miasma is so dangerous and can
get so far out of a sorceress's control, even the Dark Queen
no longer meddles with it."

"Mistress Waters told you all that, did she?" Cassandra
murmured with a frown. "The woman was a great fool and
I believe I forbade you to ever mention her to me again."

Cassandra ran her fingers over the table until she found
the *Book of Shadows.* She thumped her hand down on the
cover. "This book is said to contain all the most powerful
spells known to the daughters of the earth. There has to be
a miasma in there somewhere. I want you to find it, translate it for me."

Meg stared at her mother in consternation. This was
by far the worst thing Cassandra had ever told her to do.
"B-but why, Maman? What use would you have for such a
terrible magic?"

"Our revolution moves too slowly. I intend to hasten

events, but that is all you need to know at the moment. Just do as I bid you."

Meg gripped her hands tightly together. She couldn't . . . she *wouldn't,* but she did not dare to refuse her mother outright. Desperately seeking some way to avoid the alarming task, she hedged, "Even if the book has such a spell, it—it will be very difficult and it is already so late. Could we not go down to supper and then tomorrow—"

"There will be no supper for you or breakfast either. You will remain locked in here until you find a way for me to brew a miasma, stronger and more potent than anything the Dark Queen could conceive. Do you understand me, child?"

Meg's mouth thinned into a mutinous line. Her mother could hardly keep her shut up in the tower until she starved to death, could she? But as she studied the grim determination in Cassandra's face, she was not so sure.

"Yes, milady," she whispered.

Gripping her walking staff, Cassandra made her way to the door. She paused on the threshold, long enough to warn. "I don't want to have to punish you again. So don't fail me, Megaera."

"Yes, milady," Meg repeated. She slumped down at the table, staring at the book, her chin sinking despondently on her hands. Only after the door had closed and she was sure her mother was out of earshot did she dare to add rebelliously:

"But my name is Meg."

Chapter Fourteen

SIMON REINED ELLE IN AFTER A HARD GALLOP, SLOWING
her to a walk as they left the main road and headed down
the lane leading through the woods. Little more than a narrow track, the path was often impassable in the winter or
after a heavy rain, wagon wheels tending to stick in the
mud.

The drought had rendered the path dry, the grooves left
by the farm carts hard and baked deep into the earth. But
at least the trees offered some shade from another afternoon of blistering sun.

Elle was sweating a bit, but her recent run had done little to tax her endurance or her speed. Simon had had to
hold the mare back to keep her from racing full out or Miri
would never have been able to keep pace. Although Sam-

son possessed more stamina than Elle, the stolid gelding would have been left in the dust had Simon given Elle her head, a fact that had worried Simon.

When they had saddled up in the Maitlands' barn that morning, he had urged Miri to trade mounts with him. Elle might be skittish with anyone else, but she would have allowed Miri to ride her. Miri however had adamantly refused.

"No," she had insisted. *"It will make Elle unhappy and jealous to see you astride another horse. Even if I try to explain it to her, she'll still think she displeased you, be afraid she did something wrong."*

But the mare's hurt feelings had not concerned Simon so much as Miri's safety. Should they be overtaken by any danger on the road, he had wanted to make sure Miri could get away, especially considering his concern that they were being followed. Not long after they had left the Maitlands', Simon had realized his apprehensions of the night before were justified.

They *were* being followed, by a trio of mounted riders, barely visible on the road behind them, sometimes disappearing for miles at a stretch and then reappearing. The trio seemed to have vanished when he and Miri had paused to rest in the last village. But once they had taken to the road again, Simon spied the familiar silhouettes behind them, never gaining, but never falling back either, so persistent that he was left in little doubt they were being pursued.

The trio were not agents of the Silver Rose, that much was certain. It was broad daylight and the riders were men. Growing weary of this game of cat and mouse, Simon had given Miri the signal and they had taken off at a swift gallop. Simon was familiar enough with this part of the country that they were able to lead their pursuers on a difficult chase, over hills, through fields, across a narrow stream, finally striking out on this worn path through the woods.

Urging Miri to go ahead of him as they rode deeper into the trees, Simon fell back. Slewing round in the saddle, he glanced behind him. All was quiet except for the clopping of Elle and Samson's hooves, the faint rustle of a breeze through the branches, and the racket of a determined woodpecker hammering away at one of the trees.

Simon saw nothing but the undisturbed stretch of shaded path. They had managed to outstrip their pursuers for the moment, but he didn't congratulate himself too heartily. He suspected the persons trailing him and Miri had no real wish to overtake them. Simon had finally glimpsed enough of the first rider to guess his identity and if he was right, their pursuers likely knew where Simon was headed. These woods marked the boundary of the modest holdings Simon had received as a gift from the king.

Miri slowed Samson until Simon caught up to her. The path was barely wide enough to let them ride abreast and her knee brushed against his. Peering worriedly at him from beneath the brim of her hat, she asked. "Do you think we have lost them?"

"For now, but it scarce matters. If those men are who I think they are, they know where I live. The Dark Queen is quite familiar with the property her son gave me."

"So you believe those men work for Catherine?"

"I thought I recognized Ambroise Gautier in the lead.

It would make sense for the Dark Queen to have me watched. I should have expected as much." Simon added wryly, "Her Majesty is not the most trusting soul."

Miri patted Samson's steaming neck. "What are we going to do, Simon? If we do manage to find the Silver Rose's hiding place, we will lead Catherine's agents straight to her and the *Book of Shadows*."

"Don't worry. I'll figure out some way to shake Gautier off before that happens. Come on. We're almost there. My place is only about a mile farther past this wood."

Simon nudged his horse onward and Miri did likewise, the pair of them falling silent as they continued on through the trees. Matters had been a little awkward between them ever since they had awakened from a night spent in each other's arms, as warm and familiar as though they had become lovers. Miri had blushed, drawing away from him and he had been as tongue-tied as a raw boy after he had just tupped his first maid. He would have found it easier if they had made love instead of what they had done. There had been something too intimate about sharing those whispers in the dark, confessions, memories, and emotions he usually kept shoved down deep inside him. It was a devil of a lot easier to strip the body naked than it was the soul.

And yet, he didn't feel as exposed and vulnerable as he would have expected this morning, although he was damned tired. He hadn't gotten much rest. After he had comforted Miri over her nightmare and coaxed her back to sleep, he had lain awake for a long time.

The soft warmth of her body pressed so close to his had been a kind of exquisite torture, rousing him to a state of painful erection. He'd had to fight hard to check his desire, keep his hands from roving where they shouldn't. Beyond his physical ache for Miri, he had savored the feel of her head snuggled so trustingly against his shoulder, the light rise and fall of her breath. He had strained to keep awake, not wanting to let a single sweet moment escape him, because he knew he'd never hold her like that again.

But there was no sense tormenting himself by desiring a woman he could never have. If he had ever been in any doubt about that, he had the sight of that locket dangling around Miri's neck to remind him.

As Simon and Miri cleared the line of trees, the path continued through an open field, winding toward the house nestled atop the gentle rise of a hill. Simon had designed the place himself, a modest two-story structure of gray stone, its one extravagance the diamond-paned windows that reflected the afternoon sun.

Simon had not been near the place for over a year. But as they drew nearer, Elle's ears pricked forward. Sighting the pasture where she had frolicked as a filly, the mare pulled eagerly at the bit.

"Whoa, easy, girl," Simon said, firmly but gently reining her in.

He squinted into the sun as he surveyed his property. The house was flanked by a series of well-kept outbuildings, the stables, a hen coop, a laundry house, the granary, a shed for the plow. The wheat had been harvested, whatever poor crop had survived the drought. But the orchard looked like it was thriving and the water in the duck pond was not too low.

Simon became aware of Miri beside him, straining upward in the stirrups as she craned her neck, glancing curiously about her. His decision to bring her to his lands had seemed so simple and logical last night. The farm was where he had left his journals, the diaries that might provide the vital clue they needed to the Silver Rose's identity. But he felt oddly self-conscious, as though he was offering up yet one more private part of himself for her inspection.

"So . . . so this is your home?" she asked wonderingly.

Simon had never thought of the farm that way, had never called the place *home*, at least not until he had spoken of it to Miri.

"My home," he repeated slowly, as though the word was foreign to his tongue. "Yes, I suppose it is."

Miri shoved back her hat, her eyes so round with frank astonishment, Simon didn't know whether to be amused or take umbrage.

"What the blazes did you expect? That I lived in some dank dungeon surrounded by my torture implements?"

"I didn't think you *lived* anywhere. You spoke of trying to settle somewhere that first night, but I got the impression you had abandoned the attempt. You said you didn't feel as though you belonged here."

"I don't, but I need somewhere to stow my documents, clothes, and books. I am getting too damned old to only live on what I can carry in my saddlebags. But I haven't come here since the Silver Rose started sending her assassins after me. I don't want to put any of the people here in danger. I wouldn't have risked it now except for the need to consult my journals. I have a very capable steward who keeps things running smoothly, making my presence here unnecessary."

His explanation caused that familiar crease to appear between Miri's eyes. As they proceeded at a slow walk down the lane, her head shifted from side to side. Simon attempted to imagine how the farm must look to her. She couldn't be all that impressed, not a woman who had been raised in a fine manor house amidst the beauty of Faire Isle with its deep forests and breathtaking coastlines.

His farm was certainly nothing compared to what she might expect when she married Martin le Loup. According to Miri, her dashing Wolf held a place of high favor with the king of Navarre. Not some half-mad, perverted monarch like the French king Simon had reluctantly served.

Henry of Navarre was reputed to be shrewd and courageous, with a lusty zest for life, not unlike le Loup himself. He and Miri would probably have a grand set of apartments at the royal palace. Maybe le Loup would even acquire an estate of his own, far more impressive than Simon's modest acreage. Not that it mattered, Simon told himself. It is not as though he was setting himself up as le Loup's rival.

All the same he watched Miri, anxiously awaiting her reaction.

"The land stretches from those woods we rode through, all the way to those upper fields and beyond." Simon made a sweeping gesture with his hand. "Over that next rise is a small village and some of the cottagers from there help with the wheat harvesting and apple picking in the fall. The meadow borders a brook and the part of the woods where the goats can roam free to forage. There is also a small herd of sheep, a few pigs, and . . ."

Simon trailed off, grimacing as he realized he was once

again talking too much. He had acquired a lamentable habit of doing that around Miri.

"And, er, well, there it is," he concluded, letting his hand fall back to the reins. "Just a small farm. Nothing much."

Miri faced him, adjusting her weight in the saddle.

"Simon, it's perfect," she said, her smile seeming to blossom inside of him. He had to check the impulse to grin back at her, an even stronger urge to lean forward and kiss those tempting lips.

How was it possible for a woman to look so enticing with wisps of hair escaping from her braids, her face shaded by that battered hat, her willowy body clad in a shapeless tunic and breeches? But she did, her lovely face possessing a natural glow, the azure of the sky reflected in her silvery-blue eyes.

Simon tried to imagine Miri in a palace, amidst all the artificiality of court life, attired in corsets, farthingales, costly silk gowns, and jewels, her moon-spun hair confined beneath a fashionable bon grace cap. Tried to picture it and couldn't. It was like imagining some wild woodland fairy captured and trapped beneath a glass jar until her wings drooped and her glow dimmed.

He could far more easily envision her here on this farm, roaming the fields or splashing through the brook, her hair tumbled loose about her shoulders as she wandered out into the meadow, her eyes lighting with laughter as she scooped up a newborn lamb and it nibbled at her chin.

A foolish and futile vision. Just because the differences between them seemed to have blurred over these past few days, that didn't mean anything had changed. Those differences would resurface sharply enough if Miri's family got wind of her being in his company and sent someone after her. Or when he apprehended the Silver Rose and her coven and was obliged to see them tried for witchcraft.

He'd do his best to keep his promise and see the Moreau girl handed safely over to Miri. He had no doubt Miri would not linger long after that. No matter how much she deplored the Silver Rose's activities, Miri's tender heart would never be able to endure the trials, the executions.

She'd take Carole and return to Faire Isle. He'd never see Miri again and that was as it should be, the better for both of them. They had no future, their past shadowed with painful memories and far too many regrets. Beyond that, there was only the present. Although Simon was beset by a hollow feeling of loss, he shook it off, determined not to waste a moment of the pleasure he saw on her face as she looked over his farm.

As they rode toward the stable yard, he pointed out to her the vegetable and herb garden beyond the house. Although Miri nodded, her gaze was more on Simon. Just when she felt she had begun to know the man, he surprised her yet again.

When he had spoken hesitantly about bringing her to his home, she didn't know what she had expected. Some indifferent lodgings he had leased above a shop or inn, perhaps, nothing like this prosperous, sprawling farm.

He had given her the impression of being a lonely drifter, no real place to call his own. Although he had kept this farm, he insisted he didn't feel as if he belonged here. But it was only Le Balafre, the witch-hunter with his sinister eye patch, unrelenting black garb, and restless gaze, who did not belong in this serene setting. Simon Aristide *could,* Miri thought, if only he would give himself half a chance.

When an elderly groom and a stable hand emerged to take charge of the horses, Miri saw no apprehension of Simon on the men's faces. They were wary and respectful as they greeted Simon, welcomed him home. Any distance Miri sensed came more from Simon as he dismounted. Not that he was curt or unfriendly as he returned the men's greetings, merely stiff and reserved, his invisible wall in place.

A wall that did nothing to deter the young man who had been at work in the garden. He dropped his hoe with a loud whoop when he spied Simon, loping across the stable yard with a black-and-white dog at his heels. The boy was large and ungainly, with a bristle of pale blond hair, a round flushed face, and jug-like ears. His long arms and massive hands flailed wildly as he bounded toward Simon, calling out joyously. "Master Simon! Master Simon! You've come back."

He hurtled at Simon at such a speed, he appeared about to bowl him over. But the young man skidded to a halt at the last minute. He flung his arms about Simon in a rib-cracking hug while the dog raced about them in frantic circles barking.

Miri dismounted, surrendering Samson to the stable hand, scarce noticing what she did as she watched the astonishing scene unfold. She half-expected Simon to rebuke the boy or thrust him away. Although Simon appeared considerably embarrassed with Miri and the grooms looking on, he patted the burly young man's shoulder awkwardly.

"Er—yes, I am glad to see you too, Yves. But I need to breathe."

The boy released Simon, beaming. When the dog crouched back, flattening its ears, barking and emitting a low growl, Yves rebuked it sternly.

"Here now, Beau! Quiet! What's the matter with you? It's our Master Simon. You remember him. Mind your manners and greet him proper."

The dog cocked its head, emitting another low woof. But Simon did exactly what Miri would have done herself, hunkered down and held out his hand to be sniffed, making no sudden movement as Beau crept forward. In another instant, the dog was wagging his tail as Simon scratched him behind the ears.

"That's better," Yves approved. "Beau is just being extra vigilant, just like you told us all to be, Master Simon. In case any of those witches should—" He broke off as he suddenly took note of Miri.

The stable hands had cast Miri questioning but polite glances. Yves regarded her with undisguised curiosity, his eyes orbs of deep blue. As Miri gazed into their depths, she saw a gentle simple soul, one of those destined to remain a child forever despite his massive size and rawboned limbs.

"Who is this, Master Simon?" Yves demanded.

Simon glanced up from petting the dog to cast Miri a half-smile. "A friend of mine. Miri, this is Yves Pascale, my steward's son."

Miri smiled gently at Yves, but when she held out her

hand and tried to greet him, the boy blushed and shied back. He raced off in the direction of the house, bellowing at the top of his lungs, "Maman! Maman!"

As the dog tore off after Yves, Simon rose to his feet, brushing off his hands.

"I am sorry," Miri said. "I didn't mean to frighten him."

"You didn't. Yves is just rather shy, that's all, and— a little slow in his wits." Simon hastened to add, "But he's a hard worker and good with all the animals. He can grasp most tasks if you explain what he is to do carefully. All the other hands on the farm are very patient and understanding with him."

And if they weren't, Miri strongly suspected they would have Simon to answer to. A protective note had crept into his voice when speaking of the boy.

"Yves is obviously very fond of you," Miri observed.

"The poor boy doesn't know any better." Simon shrugged, as always trying to deprecate any good opinion of himself.

Before Miri could attempt to argue with him, Yves burst back out of the house, tugging a diminutive woman by the hand.

"Hurry Maman," Yves urged. "Master Simon has come home and he's brought a friend with him. Hurry!"

"I am hurrying," his mother protested with a laugh. She was as tiny as he was tall, garbed in a plain gown and apron, her snowy waves of hair tucked beneath a modest linen cap.

Her face lit up at the sight of Simon. Although she did not embrace him as Yves had done, she rushed forward to take his hand.

"Master Simon!" she exclaimed. "Welcome home. You have been gone so long this time. We were all very worried. What a relief to have you back unharmed."

"Er—yes, thank you, madame," Simon replied gravely.

"But far too thin," the petite woman scolded. "How are you to fight that dreadful Silver Rose if you don't take proper care—"

"Maman," Yves interrupted, tugging at his mother's sleeve. He pointed at Miri. "Look, there is master's friend. Her name is Miri." He added in a loud whisper. "She's a girl even though she dresses like a boy."

Miri drew back shyly as Madame Pascale's attention turned in her direction.

"Miri, this is Madame Esmee Pascale," Simon said. "She acts as my steward."

Miri had assumed the woman worked in Simon's house in some capacity, but his *steward*? A position of great trust and responsibility that few would consider a woman fit to hold.

She could not conceal her surprise as she gaped at Madame Pascale. The woman stared steadily back. She barely came to Miri's shoulder, her face fine boned and as wrinkled as a dried apple, but her eyes were bright blue like her son's, shrewd and penetrating.

As their eyes met, Miri experienced a jolt of recognition, each woman seeing the other for what she was—a daughter of the earth. Miri stripped off her hat. Simon had already revealed her secret when he had slipped and called her Miri in front of Yves, but it wouldn't have mattered anyway. There would have been no deceiving another wise woman like Madame Pascale.

"Madame Pascale, this is Miribelle Cheney," Simon began. "She—"

"I know who she is," Esmee Pascale interrupted, sinking into a deep curtsy. "She is the sister of the Lady of Faire Isle."

"No," Simon astonished Miri by saying. He added with a quiet smile. "Well, yes, she is Ariane's sister. But Miri is better known as the Lady of the Wood."

❦❦❦

ESMEE FLITTED ABOUT the kitchen, reminding Miri of an industrious hummingbird as she set the household into motion, sending off one young maid to air the bedchambers, another to fetch more water from the brook, and urged the kitchen boy to run home.

". . . and tell your Maman to send us both your sisters. We are going to need the extra help since Monsieur Aristide is here and he has brought a guest."

Seated out of the way at the broad kitchen table, Miri wondered if the man who deemed himself unnecessary to this place had any idea of the flurry of excitement his arrival had caused. Simon had allowed himself to be dragged off by Yves to inspect a cow due to calve at any moment. Miri would willingly have accompanied them, but Simon insisted that she refresh herself after their hard morning's ride. He had consigned Miri to the care of Esmee Pascale, who had seemed so eager to wait upon her, Miri had been unable to refuse.

Besides, she was more than a little curious about both

Simon's house and the wise woman who dared to dwell beneath the roof of a witch-hunter. If Simon had any idea what Esmee was, he had given little sign of it and thus far Miri had had little chance of conversation with the woman.

While Esmee handed out her orders, Miri waited quietly, taking stock of her surroundings. Simon's house was a modest one, constructed with a simplicity she found pleasing. There was no ostentatious great hall, the main floor given over to an enormous kitchen that served as both cooking and dining area. It boasted a hearth large enough for a man to walk into, shelves laden with every cooking implement imaginable, kettles and cauldrons, skimmers, spoons, scoops, spits and skewers, colanders, mortars, pestles, and graters. Besides a massive table with its bench and stools, there was a well-stocked spice cupboard and a rack for drying herbs suspended from the ceiling.

Handing a pile of fresh linens to the young maid, Esmee shooed the girl upstairs and then bustled over to Miri, bearing a steaming mug of some fragrant liquid.

"I am sorry to keep you waiting and that we are so ill prepared to receive you, milady. But Master Simon comes here so seldom, alas, and we have never entertained such an exalted guest."

"I am very far from being exalted," Miri protested, peering ruefully down at her travel-stained clothing. "Nor am I titled milady."

"Master Simon says that you are and that is good enough for me."

Miri only smiled and shook her head. She had been

embarrassed and astonished when Simon had introduced her as the Lady of the Wood, but touched as well. For so long he had repudiated who and what she was, but when he had presented her to Madame Pascale, he had almost sounded proud of Miri.

Drawing nearer, Esmee pressed the mug into her hands. "Please favor me by trying some of my herbal tea. I realize it would be a much more welcome brew on a cold winter's day, but the tea is very restorative after a long hard journey."

Esmee did not need to tell her that. Miri held the mug beneath her nose and inhaled, breathing in the familiar aroma that spoke to her poignantly of home and Ariane. Her older sister had taught Miri to concoct a similar brew but her tea had never tasted as good to her as Ariane's.

As she took a sip from her cup, Miri realized that Madame Pascale's did. She gave a grateful sigh. "Thank you—" she began, but she was interrupted by the maid calling down the stairs, wanting to know which bedchamber Miri was to have.

"She is to be placed in the master's room, Marguerite," Esmee shouted back.

Miri choked in the act of taking another sip of tea. She had been so overwhelmed with other impressions upon arriving at the farm, she had given little thought to the conclusions Esmee might draw about her traveling alone with Simon.

She blushed and stammered, "Oh, no, madame, I—I realize how improper it must seem—but I assure you that Simon and I do not—" Recollecting how she had just spent the previous night in the man's arms, Miri's face flamed even hotter. "I don't want you to think—"

"I don't think anything, milady. Don't fret yourself over the matter of the bedchamber. Master Simon never uses it, but the room is the finest in the house and he would want you to have it." Esmee pulled a wry face. "Whenever the man sleeps at all, he tends to nod off in that little coffin of a room that serves as his study."

Reassured, Miri sought to recover from her embarrassment as Esmee fetched her some fresh bread and honey.

"Just a little something to tide you over. I promise there will be a very fine supper." Esmee sighed. "Not that Master Simon will notice. The man never takes much heed of what he eats and from the look of you, I daresay you will not be any better. But I vow I will find something to tempt your appetite."

Miri would have been more than content with just the bread and honey, but not wanting to disappoint Esmee, she declared that after so many days on the road, she was looking forward to a fine meal. As Esmee settled upon the bench opposite her, Miri struggled to combat the bashfulness that often overtook her in the presence of someone new who did not possess fur, a tail, or paws.

"Your tea is as excellent as your very fine kitchen, madame," she said.

"Thank you, but it is not my kitchen, although Master Aristide insists that I treat the place as my own. But the design is entirely owing to him." Esmee mopped a trace of perspiration from her brow. "When I first met the dread Le Balafre, I would have expected him to be far more adept at stocking a torture chamber than a kitchen. I believe when he furbished this place, his head was filled with memories of his mother, and he fashioned the sort of place that would have been her dream."

"Simon told *you* about his mother?" Miri exclaimed.

"No . . . not directly." As Esmee colored guiltily, lowering her eyes, Miri's earlier suspicions about the woman were confirmed.

"Then I was right when I guessed you are a wise woman. You—you can read eyes."

"A bit," Esmee confessed sheepishly. "As did the generations of women in my family before me."

"So does Simon know that—that—"

"That he has offered shelter to one of our kind? He could hardly help knowing, considering he is the one who saved me from being tortured and burned at the stake. I daresay that astonishes you."

"No." Miri took another swallow of her tea. "At one time it might have, but not so much anymore, considering what I have learned about Simon Aristide these past few days."

"Good." Esmee's small shoulders appeared to relax with a great amount of relief. "I wanted to explain that to you straight off. I could tell you sensed what I was and I worried you might find it so wrong and strange for any wise woman to be employed by a witch-hunter."

"No more strange than myself," Miri said. "Although I am not employed by Simon, I have joined forces with him to—to—"

"To hunt down the Silver Rose."

"So you know about that as well?"

Esmee nodded gravely. "Master Simon usually never refers to his other occupation here, but he felt obliged to warn us about the Silver Rose lest any of those dreadful witches turn up at the farm. I wish I could have done something to help him, but I confess anything to do with black magic scares me spitless. But I am glad he has you at his side now. How very brave of you, my dear."

"Not at all. There was simply no one else." Embarrassed by the older woman's admiration, Miri made haste to change the subject. "Do you mind telling me how Simon came to rescue you?"

"No, but it is hardly an interesting tale or a new one." Esmee spread a generous dollop of honey on a slab of bread and thrust it toward Miri, urging her to eat. Miri took a few bites to please her, waiting impatiently for Esmee to commence her tale.

She finally did so with a reluctant sigh. "I was once married to a prosperous vintner and merchant. Marcellus and I had many babes, but the only one who ever survived infancy was Yves. But he is a gentle and loving son and we considered ourselves quite blessed, our life a happy and prosperous one."

Esmee's face clouded over. "That is, until the spring my husband was caught in a rainstorm and took a chill. It was one of those inexplicable tragedies. A man so hale and hearty one day and the next stricken with fever, his lungs so congested with pneumonia, none of my ancient remedies could save him. He—he died on a soft May morning when the roses were just beginning to bud."

Her eyes misted and she blinked fiercely. "My husband had no other living relatives except for a nephew, his sister's son. Marcellus was scarce cold in his grave when Robert swooped in, assuming that my husband could not have left his valuable property to a mere woman and that 'idiot boy,' as he called my sweet Yves.

"Yves may—may not be the cleverest lad, but he is not an idiot. That is a far better description of Robert, the sniveling bastard." Esmee broke off, her cheeks going pink. "Um—I am sorry, milady."

"Don't apologize. From what I saw of Yves, he possesses something rarer and more valuable than cleverness. He is rich in the gifts of the heart. I have never met this Robert, but I would be inclined to call him a bastard myself."

Esmee smiled gratefully at her, an oddly endearing gap-toothed grin. She drew in a deep breath and continued, "Robert was prepared to *generously* allow me and Yves to remain in one of the cottages on the estate while he took over the vineyard and countinghouse. Imagine his outrage when he found that my husband had been wise enough to leave a will, clearly naming myself and Yves as his heirs.

"Robert could have contested the will in the courts and he might well have won, but that would have been costly and time-consuming. He found a swifter and surer means to get his hands on the property. I was known throughout our community as a skilled midwife, well versed in many of the ancient herbal medicines. I had often butted heads with the local physician over some of his ignorant remedies, so it was an easy matter for Robert to—to—"

"To have you charged with witchcraft," Miri finished grimly.

"I need hardly explain to you, my dear, that it is the risk all wise women run for displaying any unusual abilities. No real proof is ever required, the suspicion alone enough to get a woman convicted. When I heard that the dread Le Balafre had arrived to assist in my interrogation, I completely despaired. Not so much for myself, but for my poor Yves, wondering what would become of him when I was gone.

"My courage entirely failed me when I was dragged before Le Balafre. As I looked up into that scarred face, I trembled, scarce daring to stare into that single dark, unrelenting eye, expecting to find a devil lurking there."

Esmee smiled, shaking her head in remembered wonder. "What I found was a man of reason and extraordinary perception. Monsieur Aristide saw through my nephew's plot at once. But Robert had so much support from the local authorities, not even Le Balafre could bring a halt to the proceedings. The best he could do was to spirit me and Yves away.

"I lost all my property, my entire estate except for a few belongings I managed to snatch up before Yves and I fled. After arranging our escape, Simon brought us here to live and that is where we have been ever since, Yves helping out on the farm where he is able and me employed as Monsieur Aristide's chatelaine, although it pleases him to honor me with the title of steward."

"A position of great trust for a woman," Miri said.

"A position of great trust for *anyone*. I share the responsibilities with old Jacques, who manages the stable and the livestock. He once worked as head groom for one of the larger inns in Paris until he was deemed too old and turned off. Monsieur Aristide is a great one for offering people a second chance."

"Everyone but himself," Miri reflected softly.

"Ah, so you have noticed that about the man, have you?"

"Oh yes, and whenever you ask him why he helps anyone, he shrugs off the question, pretending it was in his interest to do so."

"I know. He actually tried to convince me that I had done *him* a favor. That rescuing me helped him to make atonement for past sins." The woman cast an uneasy glance at Miri. "From what I could read in his eyes, he was thinking of you, the destruction he wrought upon Faire Isle."

Miri rested her chin upon her hands, her brow furrowed as she considered Esmee's remark. "That might also explain why he let my friend Marie Claire escape, if Simon feels the need to make reparation," she mused, more to herself than Esmee. "Simon very likely believes himself that that is what he is doing."

Esmee eyed her curiously. "But you don't?"

"I don't think his motives are that simple." Miri traced her finger around the rim of her cup, struggling as she had been doing for days. To sort through all the contradictions that were Simon Aristide, make some sense of the man.

She said hesitantly, "I think Simon's actions have as much to do with the boy he once was before his family and village were destroyed. Before that monster Le Vis sought to remake Simon into the infamous Le Balafre, a mold so against Simon's nature, it nearly destroyed him."

Miri spread her hands in a helpless gesture as she sought the words to explain. "Simon is a man whose life has been shattered more than once and it is as though he has been left with all these broken pieces of himself and he is desperately trying to fit them back together."

"A task he must accomplish for himself, but the love and understanding of the right woman would help." Esmee flustered Miri by arching one eyebrow at her suggestively.

"Oh no, madame," she stammered. "Whatever you are thinking, that woman isn't me."

"Isn't it? Your eyes tell me differently, my dear."

Miri's cheeks warmed. "No matter what I might feel for Simon, that we should ever be together is impossible. Not after some of the things he has done, especially the raid on Faire Isle. I—I might be able to forgive him for that, but my family never could."

"Most women are governed by their families, their marriages arranged. But wise women have often been more fortunate in that regard, able to follow their own hearts, particularly the ladies of Faire Isle."

"That might be true for my sisters, but it cannot be for me. There is far too much bad blood between Simon and my family, especially my brother-in-law, Renard. Although Simon has sworn to me that he will never draw sword upon Renard again and I am sure Ariane could make Renard—"

Miri paused, considering the possibilities. Perhaps if her family learned how Simon had saved Esmee and protected the Maitlands, they might—

Miri checked her wistful imaginings with a sad shake of her head.

"No, it is quite hopeless," she said to remind herself of that as much as Esmee. "Simon considers Renard an evil sorcerer, and Renard loathes witch-hunters. And even if I could persuade Ariane that Simon has changed, Gabrielle would never believe it. As much as my family loves me, I don't think any of them could ever learn to—to be fond of Simon or accept him."

"Families don't always have to dote upon one another, child. If they don't stick forks into each other at the supper table, sometimes that is all one can ask." Esmee reached across the table to give Miri's hand a gentle squeeze. "My own parents were not fond of Marcellus either, but they came round in the end. I am sure your sisters love you enough, they could do the same."

Miri smiled sadly. "Even if that were true, there is a greater obstacle between me and Simon and that is the man himself. He shies away from any kind of tenderness. How could I offer my heart to a man who considers his affection for me a weakness?"

"It is up to you to teach him otherwise." Esmee rose briskly to her feet. "We should begin by getting you cleaned up and into some more womanly attire. None of my clothes will fit you, but I am sure we can find you a gown amongst one of the women—"

"No, madame, please, I couldn't—"

"You can and will," Esmee said firmly. The old lady added with a slightly wicked twinkle in her eyes. "I am sure that masculine garb of yours is mighty comfortable, but you are not going to get anywhere with Master Simon until you shed your breeches."

✻✻✻

SEVERAL HOURS LATER Miri wandered across the stable yard, the skirt of the light wool gown swirling about her ankles. It was a little small for her, lacing tightly across her bosom, but it was dyed the softest hue of blue, as though she had draped herself in a piece of sky.

Miri nervously smoothed her fingers down the folds, thinking she should never have accepted the loan of the gown, fearing that she was only encouraging Esmee Pascale's matchmaking urges. But now that her identity was known, she could hardly continue to strut around in masculine garb, Miri reasoned. For propriety's sake, that was the only reason she had capitulated, Miri tried to tell herself.

That didn't explain this foolish fluttery sensation inside her, the same one she'd experienced as a young girl when she had donned her best frock, determined to make Simon take notice of her, stop seeing her as a child. Feeling absurdly self-conscious, she raised her hand to check the ribbon that held back her unbraided hair, spilling loose down her back. As she did so, her fingers brushed against her neck, making her guiltily aware of what was missing.

Martin's locket. She had removed it when she had bathed and forgotten to—. No, if she was honest, she had to admit that she had deliberately left the locket on the small table near the ewer and basin. No matter what else happened, she knew she was going to have to return it to him and she dreaded the pain she must cause her dear friend.

As Miri crossed the yard, she was startled when Yves suddenly came bursting out of the stables, looking distraught. The boy stumbled to a halt when he spied her and Miri expected him to turn shy as he'd done before.

But he bolted up to her, tugging at her hand. "Oh, Wood's Lady. You must come at once. Master Simon needs you. There is no one else. Jacques had to go herd the sheep in and one of the lambs has gone missing so he had to take Bertrand to help and there's only me left—"

"Yves, please." Miri gently pressed her hands to his lips to stop the frantic rush of words. "Just tell me what is wrong. Has—has something happened to Simon?"

"No!" The boy looked ready to burst into tears. "It's Melda. She's having her calf and it's all gone wrong."

Miri rushed into the barn to find Simon already there. Stripped to the waist, he lay in the straw beside a brown spotted cow, clearly in a state of distress. Flecked with blood and dirt, his arm buried deep inside the cow, he grimaced as her contractions tightened on his arm. But he looked considerably relieved at the sight of Miri.

"Simon. What's wrong?"

He grunted. "The calf is not presenting right. Its head is turned clear around and there is barely any room at all. It's set now to come out legs first."

He didn't have to explain to her what that meant. If the calf came out legs first, the cow's pelvis could be crushed. Both mother and calf could be lost.

"I am trying to get a rope around the calf, so I can turn the head."

Miri nodded. She didn't think twice, unlacing the bodice of her gown and slipping it off her shoulders, stripping down to her chemise despite Yves's wide-eyed stare. She crouched down beside Simon.

"Here, let me do that. My arm is smaller."

"And more likely to get crushed." Simon winced as another contraction hit, the cow's pelvis tightening on his arm. "I can do this. I—I just need you to hold the end of the rope and pull when I tell you."

Miri knelt beside him, wiping the sweat from Simon's face as he tried to inch his arm deeper inside the straining cow. Yves hovered nearby, wringing his large hands as the moments crawled by. Miri watched Simon's efforts anxiously, but she had little hope. Even with all her skills with animals, she knew that calves in this position were usually born dead. It would be a miracle if they did not lose the mother too.

Simon clenched his teeth and pushed with everything he had. His grim expression lightened a little as he panted, "All right. I—I think I have the noose secure around the calf. If you pull on the rope, I am going to push the calf and the head should come round."

Miri did as he bade her, seizing hold of the end of the rope, maintaining a steady tension. Simon's face quickened with excitement. "Miri, I think the head is turning. Keep pulling."

Simon withdrew his arm to help her, the pair of them working in unison until the calf emerged, first the head, the rest of it following swiftly. Yves fairly danced in his delight, but his face crumpled as the little animal lay motionless on the stable floor.

"Oh, M-master Simon. It's dead."

"No," Miri said, refusing to give up. She cleared the

calf's mouth and blew down its throat. Following her lead, Simon applied pressure on the ribs. The calf gasped, jerking its leg.

They both fell back, exhausted, laughing with relief, Yves joining in. Simon grasped the calf and lifted it toward its mother. The cow wearily raised its head, snuffling her babe. All exhaustion forgotten, she licked her calf. The little creature stretched its neck and tried to wobble to its feet.

Miri had witnessed this miracle many times before and it never failed to move her. But she had never had anyone to share her feelings with until now. As her gaze met Simon's, she saw this was one magic he understood as well as she. He reached out to grasp her hand, the silent communication that passed between them deeper than any words.

*

MIRI LEANED into the stall, scratching the calf's forehead as it looked up at her with great velvet brown eyes. Yves had raced off excitedly to inform his mother of the farm's newest arrival, leaving Miri and Simon to clean up.

They had done so with quiet efficiency, mucking out the stall, laying down fresh straw. It was strange, Miri thought. It almost felt as though she and Simon had been working together this way all their lives.

Scrubbed clean herself, she had donned her dress, but had been reluctant to lace up the tight bodice, restricting her movements again. She smiled when the calf attempted to nibble at her undone laces. As she drew back to rescue her bodice strings, she glanced toward the tack room where Simon was washing himself with the bucket of water Yves had fetched.

Now that the crisis was over, Miri had leisure to study what she had only fleetingly noted before, the broad expanse of Simon's chest, the tensile strength in those bare arms and shoulders. She had once found the boy's physique beautiful, but the man was utterly magnificent.

An involuntary sigh of appreciation escaped her. When Simon turned to glance her way, she lowered her gaze, a little embarrassed to be caught ogling. But she entered the tack room to fetch him a towel.

After he thanked her, one of those awkward silences threatened to descend. Miri leaned up against the tack room door, trying not to stare as Simon rubbed the linen briskly over his hair-roughened chest.

"That was an amazing thing you did just now, turning that calf. Wherever did you learn how to do that?"

"Back in my village." He added wryly, "I wasn't born a witch-hunter, Miri."

"I know that. I am glad you are finally starting to remember it."

He said nothing, wincing a little as he worked the towel down his arm.

"You are likely going to have some hideous bruises," Miri murmured.

"It was worth it," Simon said with a soft smile, glancing toward where the calf was nursing.

Miri reached out and ran her hand gently along the bare warm skin of his arm. Simon tensed at her touch, but as his gaze met hers, Miri felt the pulse of desire between them. She reluctantly drew her hand away, turning her attention to the stables inside.

"This is a grand building, large and airy, but there are so many empty stalls."

"At one time, I thought of breeding horses."

"Why didn't you?"

"I don't know. I was never here enough, especially after the attacks of the Silver Rose started."

"But after she is defeated, you could come back here, Simon. Settle down and—"

He cut her off with a shake of his head. "I told you. I tried that before. It didn't work."

"Because you claim you don't belong here and yet I wonder if you've really tried. From what Madame Pascale tells me, you are good at giving everyone else second chances. Why not Simon Aristide?"

He looped the towel about his neck, the damp ends of his unruly dark hair tangling about his face as he cast her a wary glance. "Ah, so now you have been discussing me with my steward as well as my horse. I didn't think Madame Pascale was as fond of gossiping as Elle."

"Esmee only told me what you never would, how you saved her life, and don't try to pretend that it was to your advantage do so. I never heard tell how any witch-hunter profited by letting a condemned witch go."

"Esmee is not a witch any more than you are." Simon frowned. "I can only tell you what I told her. That helping her was in the nature of atonement for past sins and I committed enough of them, don't you agree? Not that anything I ever do will be enough to put right what happened on Faire Isle, what I did to you."

Miri gazed up at him softly. "I find it enough that you are even trying to do so. Most men would just go on making excuses, repeating the same mistake over and over again."

"There is no guarantee that I won't." Simon turned away from her, bracing his hands on the table. "That is the fear that makes it so hard for me to settle down here and forget the past. It's a good life here and I—I admit that I love this place, at least during the day when I am occupied with tilling the soil or looking after the livestock."

Simon's face clouded, a haunted look stealing over his face. "But at night, it's a different story. I have too much time to think and there is no escaping what I am, what I've done, and I am still just as alone."

"It doesn't have to be that way, Simon. There are people willing to forget your past even if you cannot, willing to—to love you if only you would let them."

And one of them was standing right in front of him, although Miri did not dare say as much. She tugged at his arm until he came round to face her. Trembling at her own boldness, she flattened her palms against his chest. She ran her fingers up the rugged planes, the mat of dark hair a delicious contrast to the silk-sheathed steel of his muscles.

She raised her gaze to his, allowing her heart to shine through her eyes, to tell him all that she couldn't say. Simon stared at her, his breath stilling at the realization of what she was offering him, all that he couldn't take.

"Miri . . ."

But she silenced him with her lips, her mouth far too sweet and enticing as it whispered over his. He fought his inevitable response, the hardening of his shaft. Gripping her shoulders, he tried to put her gently away from him, but her lips parted, her tongue teasing the breach of his lips.

With a low groan, he found himself hauling her closer instead of thrusting her away. Crushing her to him, his mouth hungrily devoured hers, his body nigh desperate with the need of her he had so long suppressed.

He drew his head back with a gasp, feeling his reason, any decent impulse he had toward this woman reduced to a thread.

"Miri," he rasped, his voice a ragged plea. "Don't do this to me. You know how hard it is for me to resist you."

"Then stop trying," she whispered, wrapping her arms about his neck, pressing so close he was aware of the thunder of her heart, the warm soft feel of her breasts beneath her half-open bodice.

Her mouth claimed his again and he felt the remaining thread snap. He kissed her fiercely, burying his hands in her hair. But his passion was abruptly checked when he heard voices, the sound of Yves returning to the barn, no doubt with his mother in tow.

Simon drew hastily away from Miri, each regarding the other in dismay. Her face flushed, she bore the unmistakable look of a woman who had just been thoroughly kissed and he feared his own face must be equally revealing.

Gathering up his scattered wits, he stepped out of the tack room, determined to shield her from any embarrassment.

Yves entered the barn, announcing cheerfully, "Come right this way, monsieur. She's in here."

Monsieur? Simon tensed. He had warned the boy before about being wary of any strangers who came by the place, although the man who followed Yves into the barn did not look threatening.

The tall handsome man was garbed in a lined cloak and feathered hat, his apparel elegant despite the fact he'd obviously been doing some hard traveling. Any menace there was came from the steely glint in the man's eyes.

As their gazes met, Simon experienced a jolt of recognition. He knew who the man was even before Miri crept out of the tack room. Her face went pale with shock as she cried out, "Martin!"

Chapter Fifteen

ARTIN LE LOUP STRODE HALFWAY DOWN THE STABLES, coming to an abrupt halt as Simon intercepted him, the two men regarding each other with an ages-old antagonism, although it was more wariness on Simon's part as he studied his adversary.

He saw little trace of the swaggering boy he remembered from that long-ago summer. Martin le Loup seemed to have grown another inch or two, his shoulders had filled out, his lean face sporting a trim beard and mustache. He was as damnably handsome as Miri had led Simon to believe, but there was none of the softness of the courtier about him, despite his fancy doublet and trunk hose. As he flipped back his cloak, his hand coming to rest on the hilt of his sword, there was an edge of danger about the man, angry emotion flashing in his narrowed green eyes, hurt mingled with accusation.

Simon's gaze flickered toward where he had left his own sword, propped near Melda's stall, where he had shed his shirt and jerkin. But he restrained himself as he caught sight of Miri's face. She looked sick with apprehension, but she approached Wolf, attempting to smile.

"M-martin, this is a great surprise."

"Evidently," he said, raking his gaze over Miri's unlaced bodice in a way that brought the blood to her cheeks. She fumbled with the laces, looking so miserably guilty Simon wanted to box Wolf's ears. He stepped protectively in front of Miri, a gesture that caused Wolf to scowl.

The only one unaware of the mounting tension was Yves, who bounded forward, prattling happily, "Isn't this the best day ever? First Master Simon returns bringing with him the Lady of the Wood, then Melda had her calf, and now Milady Miri's friend has come to call. Is he not the finest fellow you ever saw?" Yves beamed admiringly at Wolf. "Just look what a splendid cap he has . . ."

Yves trailed off, his gaze moving uneasily between Wolf and Simon as he began to sense something amiss. "Master Simon, did I do something wrong? I forgot the rule about strangers, didn't I? But—but Monsieur le Loup said he was Miri's friend."

"He is," Miri hastened to reassure the boy. "You did nothing wrong."

"Then why is Master Simon looking so angry at me?"

"I am not angry at you, lad." Despite his own tension, Simon managed to speak to Yves in gentle tones. "Don't worry. Everything is all right."

"I regret to differ with you, Monsieur Le Balafre," Wolf replied, baring his teeth. "But I am finding this situation far from all right."

"Martin, please." Miri tried to intercept him, but he swept her aside, stepping menacingly closer to Simon.

"There has been a reckoning due between us for a long time, Master Witch-Hunter, and you have just increased your debt. Bad enough all the hurt you inflicted upon Miri in the past, but now you have the effrontery to lure her away from Faire Isle, place her in danger by demanding she help you hunt this sorceress."

"Martin, that is not the way it was," Miri interrupted, but Wolf continued furiously.

"By God, if you have also tampered with my lady's innocence, impugned her honor, I will—"

"The only one impugning her honor is you, you fool," Simon growled. "I realize how all this must look. But I would advise you to get command of yourself and think twice before you speak again."

Wolf tugged the fastening of his cape, sweeping it off and casting it aside. His hat swiftly followed. "I am a man of few words, monsieur. I prefer action."

"Really? My memory of you is that you could never keep your mouth shut for more than two seconds at a time."

Wolf's eyes flashed. Simon's retort had done nothing to ease the situation. But he found the man's flair for drama damned annoying. He would have liked nothing better than to seize Wolf by the scruff of his fancy doublet and propel him out of the stable. But Simon was fair enough to admit Wolf had some cause for his fury. He knew how he would have felt if he had found Miri in the arms of a much-hated enemy, so he struggled to keep his temper in check.

As Wolf began to draw his sword from its scabbard, Miri seized hold of his arm. "No, Martin, stop! Surely you can see Simon is not even armed."

"That's easily remedied." Shaking Miri off, Wolf stalked over to where Simon had left his sword propped. Snatching it up, he tossed it to Simon, scabbard, belt, and all.

Simon caught it reflexively, but he made no move to buckle it on. Yves shrank back against the side of the stall, whimpering, not understanding what was going on, but frightened by the sight of the sword. Simon could also hear Elle. Sensing the danger to him, the mare gave a shrill whinny, stamping in her stall. But Simon's gaze focused on Miri's face. She had gone white, agonized with memories of another place and time when she had watched two men she cared about try to kill each other, something Simon had promised he would never put her through again.

"Please don't," she whispered, but her plea was directed at him as though he alone had the power to stop this from going any further. And she was likely right. Le Loup looked beyond the reach of reason.

"Don't worry, my dear," Simon assured her. "I have no intention of fighting him." Simon tossed the sword down. It landed on the straw-strewn floor with a dull thud.

Wolf's lip curled in a furious sneer as he demanded, "What is the matter, witch-hunter? Oh, I forgot. You prefer your opponents to be defenseless women and even then you like to have an army at your back."

Wolf's verbal thrust found its mark. Simon gritted his teeth, determined not to be goaded.

"Martin, be quiet," Miri said fiercely, but Wolf ignored her.

"Miri may have forgotten all the havoc you and your men wrought on Faire Isle, but I haven't. A bunch of scurvy cowards terrorizing poor old ladies and young girls. Is that all you are fit for? Are you too afraid to stand up against another man?"

Simon fixed Wolf with a steely glare. "No, I merely have too much sense to engage in a pointless duel that will only cause Miri more pain. If you knew anything about her at all, you would realize how much this is distressing her. To say nothing of the fact you are frightening Yves and upsetting my horse. So either calm down or get the hell out of my stable."

"Fine. Let's take this outside."

Simon folded his arms across his chest. "We're not taking it anywhere. I told you. I don't fight any man without a good reason."

"Reason? You want a reason?" Wolf snarled. "Try this."

His fist shot out with such lightning swiftness, Simon had no chance to duck. The blow cracked into his face, sending him reeling back, his jaw exploding with pain. Miri cried out in protest, but before she could react, Yves grabbed Martin's arm.

"No. You must not hurt Master Simon," he wailed.

Wolf shoved the boy ruthlessly away. Yves stumbled and fell against one of the stalls. Simon's tautly reined temper snapped. With a savage oath, he hurled himself at le Loup and slammed him back against the stable wall.

Wolf fought back, aiming another blow at Simon's face. He dodged, the fist grazing his ear. Simon hammered a series of hard blows in the man's gut. Wolf doubled over, sinking to his knees.

Drawing back his fist, Simon barely managed to check his next blow when Miri dove in between them. The sight of her stricken face as she bent over Wolf penetrated the red haze of Simon's anger.

He stepped back, panting just as Jacques and the other young stable hand, Bertrand, burst into the stable, drawn by the noise. Old Jacques took in the situation at a glance. Both he and Bertrand seized hold of the still-winded le Loup, over Miri's protest. Bertrand in particular looked ready to take up where Simon had left off.

Simon straightened, his breath coming quick and hard. He tasted blood on his lip as he surveyed the chaos of the stable. Yves was crouched down, crying, his hands flung over his head. Elle reared and plunged in her stall, in danger of hurting herself in her desperate efforts to get to Simon. Even the stolid Samson snorted and stamped, and the new calf was bawling plaintively.

As his men prepared to drag Wolf out and "teach him a proper lesson," Simon intervened. "No, let him go."

Looking uncertain, Jacques and Bertrand slackened their grip. Wolf shook himself free, straightening, attempting to recover some of his dignity. Simon strode over to Yves, wrapping his arm bracingly about the boy, while Jacques and Bertrand hastened to calm Elle and the other animals.

Simon caught Yves's chin in his hand, gently forcing the trembling boy to look at him.

"It's all over, lad," Simon soothed. "You see now? All over. Now come and help me convince Elle of that."

Teary-eyed, the boy sniffed and nodded.

Miri's agonized gaze darted between Wolf and Simon. She stepped toward Simon, faltering, "Oh, Simon, I am so sorry—"

Simon waved her brusquely away. "Never mind about that." He glared at Wolf. "Just get him the devil out of here."

He didn't wait to see that his command was obeyed, his attention fully claimed by the task of restoring peace to his stables. Not until he was able to get both Yves and Elle to stop trembling did he glance back and see that Wolf and Miri were gone.

He regretted having snapped at Miri that way. He didn't want her thinking she was in any way to blame for this. If he and Wolf had both kept their heads, the situation need never have turned so ugly, although the devil knows he had tried.

He rubbed his hand gingerly over his swelling jaw, worrying about Miri being alone with Wolf when he was in such a cursed temper. Not that he feared Wolf would hurt her, at least not physically. But to Miri, harsh words were as bad as a blow.

Turning Yves over to Jacques's gruff but kind care, Simon shrugged back into his shirt and leather jerkin. He strode toward the entrance of the stables, cautiously looking about for Miri, not wanting to set off another confrontation with her hotheaded swain.

He spied the couple over by the pond, silhouetted against the last fiery gold rays of the setting sun, Wolf's horse tethered nearby. Simon relaxed, a little relieved. Although Wolf had Miri clasped by the shoulders, he appeared to be pleading with her as well as scolding, no doubt trying to convince her to mount up behind him and ride off immediately, reminding her how much he loved her and what a bastard Simon was. Miri shook her head, her chin tipped to that stubborn angle Simon knew all too well, but she made no move to draw away from Wolf either.

It was all Simon could do not to charge out there. As he watched the two of them together, he felt as though a demon of jealousy was gnawing at his heart. He now had some idea what Wolf had gone through when he had discovered Miri and Simon together.

There was one difference. Simon had no right to be jealous because Miri didn't belong to him, not like she belonged to this handsome man who had been her devoted friend for years, whose pursuit of her was both welcomed and sanctioned by her family.

For a few fleeting moments back there in the stable, Simon had allowed himself to stray into a fool's paradise of remembered dreams and forgotten hopes. When he had held Miri in his arms and kissed her, and she'd looked up at him with a hunger that matched his own, he'd scarce dared to believe what he'd seen shining in her face, all the love that she had offered him. And God help him, he had almost been mad enough to take it.

If Wolf had not arrived when he had—Simon vented a sigh filled with bitterness and regret. No, it was just as well Wolf had come, reminding both him and Miri of what they were in danger of forgetting. This farm, peaceful as it seemed, was no enchanted island, insulated from the rest of the world. There was no escaping his past here or anywhere else, which is something he had known all along.

He'd managed to keep his promise to Miri, avert any sort of tragic outcome this time. But neither her friends nor her family would willingly surrender her to a bastard like him and after all he'd done, why should they? The next time someone came after her, matters might not reach such a bloodless resolution. If it was the sorcerer, Renard—

Simon clenched his jaw, not even wanting to think about that. It was far better if Miri left with Wolf right now. This sweet interlude they had shared would come to an abrupt end, far sooner than Simon had expected. He had thought they would have more time . . .

But time for what? To make their inevitable parting more painful? As Simon watched Miri with Wolf, their intimacy was obvious despite their quarrel. Simon didn't know how it could hurt any worse than this.

⚜

MARTIN CLASPED Miri by the shoulders, his green eyes roiling with anger, hurt, and outrage. "Damn it, Miri. What were you thinking of, going off with that treacherous miscreant? How could you do this to me, to your family? And what the devil did you mean by apologizing to that bastard?"

Torn between her own anger and guilt, Miri glowered at him. "Someone needed to do it and it was obvious you weren't going to. At least you should have told Yves you were sorry. How could you manhandle him that way? Despite his great size, couldn't you tell what a gentle soul he is, little more than a child?"

Martin flushed, looking ashamed and uncomfortable. "I realize that now and I am sorry. I never meant to—" He released her, flinging up his hands in a frustrated gesture. "Damnation! When did I become the villain of this piece?"

"When you came swaggering onto Simon's land, ranting and raving like—like some performer overacting in a bad farce."

"*Overacting*," Martin repeated in strangled tones. "Mon dieu, woman! Do you have any idea what I have been through these past weeks, tracking you the length and breadth of France, pushing myself to the brink of exhaustion, mad with worrying about you in the clutches of that witch-hunter. When Marie told me—"

"I can't believe she did that," Miri interrupted. "She promised me faithfully she would tell no one."

"What did you expect the poor woman to do after you took off on some demented mission to battle an evil sorceress and seeking out the help of that snake in the grass? When I arrived on Faire Isle, she was practically hysterical."

Miri cast him an impatient glance. "Marie has never been hysterical a day in her life and well you know it, Martin. I am sorry if I have worried her. Marie, at least, understood why I had to go. I had no other choice."

"Yes you did." Martin struck his fist against his chest. "You could have sent for me."

"Even if I'd had time to do that, where in God's name would I have found you? When I lived in Pau with my sister, I scarce knew where you were half the time. You were always off on some quest or another mad adventure for the king of Navarre."

"Mad adventure? You dare to speak to me of mad adventures?" Martin demanded, furiously wagging his finger in her face. When she struck his hand aside, he paced off a few steps, flinging up his arms and crying, "This—this is unbelievable. We are having a lovers' quarrel and we have never even truly been lovers. All this time I have adored you, respected you so much I have scarce dared to kiss the hem of your gown. Then I arrive here and find you with Aristide half naked and your laces all undone."

"We had just delivered a calf, Martin!"

"Oh, is that what they call it out here in the country? We had a far different term for it on the streets of Paris."

Miri flushed hotly. "My virtue is still intact if that is what's worrying you."

"What worries me is that that bastard had his hands all over you, seducing you—"

"He wasn't seducing me. I was seducing him. I love him." The words came out more bluntly than she had ever intended. She added in a quieter tone, "I always have."

Martin paled, but he shook his head in the familiar denial. "N-no, you don't. You are just confused, that's all. He has always been able to do that to you, damn the man. He might well be some God-cursed sorcerer himself the way he has bewitched you. But you can't possibly be in love with him, not after all the terrible things he has done to your family, the way he has betrayed you time and again."

"Simon has changed—"

"The devil he has. Once a villain, always a villain."

Martin folded his arms across his chest, but beneath his anger, Miri could see the full depth of the wound she had dealt him.

She rested her hand gently on his shoulder, her eyes burning with tears of regret. "The only villain here is me. You have every right to be angry and upset with me. I— I never meant to hurt you, but I did betray you."

Martin gave her a stricken glance. "You said nothing happened back there in the stables. That he didn't . . . you didn't . . . you are still a maid."

"I am not talking about tonight. The day I betrayed you was when I let you fasten that locket around my neck, permitted you to hope—"

"Don't say that, Miri." He stopped, his breath hitching. He brushed her hair back from her throat. "My locket . . . you—you are not wearing it."

Miri found it hard to meet his wounded gaze. "No, but I have it safe. I meant to give it back to you the next time we met."

"I won't take it," he said fiercely. He swallowed thickly, attempting to smile. "What, my Lady of the Moon? After stealing my heart, do you mean to try to rob me of all my hopes and dreams as well?"

"My dearest friend." Miri laid her hand alongside his cheek. "I should have known years ago that I could never be what you want me to be. But I was so lonely, so unhappy, and I needed your friendship so much, but that's no excuse. I should never have allowed you to hope for more than that. I have done you the greatest wrong."

"Never!" he insisted, capturing her hand, planting a kiss on her palm. "This is not the best time for us to be discussing this. We are both tired and distressed, saying what we don't mean.

"You were right about me always being off on some wild adventure. But—but I'll change, become more settled, I swear it. I am sure the king esteems me enough to offer me a position in his household and we could take up residence in the palace. Or a fine house in Nerac."

"Oh, Martin!" Miri groaned. He still refused to heed anything she was telling him.

He rushed on, "We don't have to decide anything right now. The important thing is to get you away from this wretched place."

Taking hold of her wrist, he tugged her toward his horse as though he intended to swoop her up and ride off with her in typical impulsive Martin fashion. It would never occur to the man that she left her own horse and belongings behind until they were several miles down the road. He didn't even notice her trying to protest or pull free of his grip.

"It's not that far to Paris. We could be there before morning. There is a banker I need to consult anyway, about some funds that are going to be secretly diverted to Navarre. Then I'll be free to make arrangements for our journey back to Pau."

Miri dug in her heels. "I have no intention of going anywhere. Have you forgotten why I joined forces with Simon in the first place? There is still the matter of the Silver Rose to be settled."

"Let the witch-hunter deal with the evil sorceress. That's his duty, isn't it? And maybe if we are lucky, they'll finish each other off."

"Martin!" Miri wrenched her hand free. "It's my duty as well. Have you forgotten who I am?"

"You are the lady I adore, my best and brightest reason for living."

Miri vented an impatient sigh. "I also happen to be a daughter of the earth and one of the Cheney sisters of Faire Isle. In Ariane's absence, it is my responsibility to find this Silver Rose and prevent her from doing any more harm."

"All right. All right. I'll take care of the witch after I send you home."

"Do you ever listen to anything I say?" Miri demanded indignantly. "You are not sending me anywhere. You are the one who need not become involved in this. You should continue on to Paris and take care of your business for the king—"

"And leave you here alone with a man I don't like and don't trust? A man who has displayed to me that he has a disturbing penchant for—for delivering cows? I don't think so, my sweet."

They glared at each other, their eyes locked in a contest of wills, but for once Martin appeared to recognize the full measure of her resolve.

"Fine!" He rolled his eyes, flinging up his hands in a dramatic gesture of surrender. "If you want to hunt witches, we'll hunt witches."

His mouth twisted ruefully. "I don't suppose I can persuade you that we can manage the business ourselves and dispense with the services of Monsieur Cyclops."

Miri frowned, drawing in a sharp breath, but he flung up one hand to forestall her.

"Never mind. It was just a suggestion. A completely

sensible and delightful one, I thought, but I can tell you are not as enamored of the idea as I am."

She squeezed his hand and said earnestly, "My dear friend, you are a very clever and brave man, one of the bravest I have ever known. But I doubt Simon will ever agree to you joining us. Not after that scene in the stables. And frankly I could not bear it myself, having you two constantly at daggers drawn."

"It would not be like that, I swear to you. If he can restrain himself, I certainly can," Martin protested with a look of injured innocence. "You know me, Miri. I obey your slightest wish. If my Lady of the Moon commands me thus, I will treat that miserable deceitful varlet as though he were my brother. We'll be just like—like Cain and Abel."

※※※

MIRI TRUDGED back to the stable, rubbing her brow. Her head throbbed from her efforts to persuade Martin it would be best for him to leave. She had forgotten how hardheaded her friend could be. He had insisted that whether Simon gave him permission to remain or not, Wolf was staying, even if he had to erect a tent on the doorstep.

He was perfectly capable of carrying out such a threat and Miri's stomach knotted at the prospect of another confrontation between the two men. Although Simon had behaved with a forbearance that had astonished her, Miri quailed at the prospect of his patience being put to the test again.

She stole inside the stables to find it much quieter than

when she had left. Yves and the grooms were gone, leaving only Simon. He was in the stall with Elle, bending down to check the mare's forelegs. Fearing that the mare had injured herself when she had thrashed about in her stall, Miri rushed toward them, exclaiming, "Simon, what is it? Is Elle hurt?"

Although Simon tensed at her approach, he didn't so much as glance up at her. Finishing his inspection of Elle's other leg, he said curtly, "No, she appears to be fine."

"And Yves?"

"He's all right. I sent him off to his mother."

"And—and you?"

"I'm fine as well."

As Simon slowly straightened, Miri thought he looked anything but fine. She hadn't expected him to be pleased about Martin's arrival. She had even anticipated he might still be angry. She would have preferred that to the way he did look, closed off and distant. His lip was split and swollen where Martin had hit him, but when Miri tried to examine his injury, he shied away from her.

"You need to let me put some salve on that."

"I can tend to it myself."

"I am sure you can, but—" Miri faltered, dismayed by his forbidding expression. Considering the way she had been locked in his embrace before Martin had arrived, the contrast in Simon's manner was painful. Elle was far more welcoming, blowing out a soft breath and nudging Miri with her head.

As Miri stroked the mare's velvety nose, she said, "Simon, I am so sorry for what happened. I—I had no idea

Martin would turn up here, behaving so badly. I can't tell you how grateful I am to you for not accepting his challenge."

"I told you I'd never put you in such a painful position again," he said tersely. "After all the times I've lied to you, it was high time I kept at least one of my promises, don't you think?"

"All the same, I realize how hard it must have been for you to keep your temper when Martin was being so provoking. It meant more to me than I can possibly tell you." She moistened her lips nervously and continued, "I daresay Martin would apologize to you too, if—if he wasn't so blasted proud and stubborn. He would like to—to—"

"Rescue you from my clutches? That's what I expected, that he's come to fetch you back home, but it's getting too late for you to set out now. The morning will be soon enough. I can contrive to tolerate your betrothed for that long."

Simon stepped out of the stall and strode off as though the matter were settled. Momentarily stunned, Miri hastened after him. "I am not betrothed to Martin and I have no intention of being. If I was, do you think I would ever have kissed and caressed you that way? What sort of woman do you think I am?"

"A very inexperienced one when it comes to passion. I should have stopped you before we got caught up in the heat of the moment. You were confused—"

To his surprise, Miri's eyes flashed with anger. "The next man who tells me how confused I am is going to get his ears boxed. I know what my own heart tells me, Simon."

"What it is telling you is wrong. We shared a few

heated kisses, that was all. It's just as well that le Loup arrived to take you away—"

"I am not going *anywhere* until we have defeated the Silver Rose and I am sick to death of being told what I should do, what I am supposed to feel." Miri spun on her heel, storming toward the stable door. She paused to fling back at him over her shoulder. "Oh, and don't be alarmed, Simon. I won't throw myself at you again. Nor do I have any intention of marrying Martin. All men are more trouble than they are worth. When all this is over, I am going home to my cat."

※※※

THE HOUR WAS LATE, the moon had risen. Miri sat on the wooden bench at the edge of the pond, her skirts hiked up to reveal her shapely legs as she dangled her feet in the water, her hair shimmering down her back.

Simon watched from a stand of trees. He should have insisted she return to the house. It was damned reckless for her to be out alone at night, even on his land. But he understood what had caused her to do so. She was hurt by his rejection and troubled by the tension between him and le Loup. It had driven Miri out here to the water and the soft night breezes to recover her sense of harmony.

Le Loup was a romantic idiot, but Simon could see why he called her the Lady of the Moon. There was something ethereal about Miri, but there was also a passion and strength in her that the other man entirely failed to recognize.

"Perhaps you'd like to train that hot gaze of yours elsewhere, witch-hunter. Before you lose your other eye."

Simon started at the silken voice hissing at him. He whirled around to find Wolf behind him, his fingers clenched on the hilt of his sword.

"Mon dieu, would I love to run you through right here and now."

"So why don't you?" Simon demanded.

Wolf glowered in frustration, allowing his hand to fall back to his side. "Because I'm afraid she'd never forgive me if I did."

"Beyond the pale of Miri's forgiveness is a desolate, cold place. You'd be wise to avoid it. Believe me, I know," Simon replied wearily. "I didn't follow her out here tonight with any lust-filled purpose in mind. It's not safe for her to be out here alone."

"Looking after Miri is my job, not yours. I am the one who has been her most ardent and devoted adorer for years."

"Instead of looking after her, maybe you should try really looking *at* her for a change," Simon said. "She is not some goddess, some Lady of the Moon to be worshipped from afar. She is only a woman, albeit a most remarkable one, with a woman's needs—"

"I hardly need the likes of you telling me anything about my lady," Wolf snarled.

"No? Do you really think she'll be happy imprisoned in some palace apartments, shut off from the open fields and woods?"

"She'd be a damned sight happier with me than she would with you on this wretched farm. At least she'd still have her family. You tore her life apart on Faire Isle once. Would you now seek to separate her from her sisters forever? I may not be worthy of my lovely Lady of the Moon, but you certainly are not."

"Don't you think I already know that?" Simon asked dully. Pivoting on his heel, he strode away, saying, "Watch out for her. Make sure she gets safely back to the house."

As Martin watched his enemy vanish into the darkness, he frowned. This was hardly the tame response he had expected from the ruthless Aristide. For a moment, it had actually sounded as though the bastard did care about Miri.

But Aristide had always been a good liar, abusing Miri's trust and innocence, betraying her. Except that the witch-hunter wasn't the only one, Martin thought uneasily. The sin lay heavy on his soul, no matter how hard he tried to forget it, shove it back onto the darkest, deepest shelf of his conscience.

His love for Miri had scarce been days old that night ten years ago in Paris, the night that he had let himself be lured into the bed of a witch . . .

Chapter Sixteen

MEGAERA HUDDLED IN THE CENTER OF HER MASSIVE BED, her body curled up tight as though warding off a blow. Exhausted from her labors with the *Book of Shadows,* she slept deeply, unaware of the silent figure of her mother hovering over her.

Cassandra groped until she found the coverlet, tucking it over her daughter's frail shoulders with a rare gentleness. Megaera stirred restively on her pillow as Cassandra brushed her cold fingers over the child's cheek. Even in her sleep, Megaera sought to draw away from her.

Her daughter had been doing far too much of that lately. Cassandra touched her medallion and brooded. She had once been able to divine Megaera's every thought. Now she was no longer so sure. Her daughter seemed to be growing more secretive every day, as though her life was becoming a separate entity from her mother's, and the thought maddened Cass.

As far as Cass was concerned, their best days had been when Megaera was still tucked within her womb, their hearts beating as one, sharing breath, sharing blood, Megaera entirely dependent upon Cass for her very existence. She had felt so close to her daughter when Megaera had been no more than a flutter of movement, a chrysalis of all Cass's ambitions and dreams, so full of promise. There had been no frustration, no disappointment, and no apprehensions of failure then. And none of Megaera's sullen withdrawal, her marked preference for other people like that Waters woman and now this wretched Moreau girl. None of Megaera offering her trust to strangers, the love that was her mother's due. Cass feared that the only hold she had over her child rested in the medallion suspended over Megaera's heart.

Cass's own heart twisted with the pain of rejection she seldom allowed herself to feel. If you carried a child in your womb, went through the agonies of labor, devoted your life to the girl, working and scheming every waking moment to make that child great, then surely that child ought to love you . . . even if no one else did.

Cass swallowed hard, telling herself fiercely it didn't matter.

"Love me or hate me, you are mine, my Silver Rose. And you always will be," she whispered, running her fingers lightly over Megaera's face.

Megaera whimpered in her sleep, rolling onto her side away from Cass. She clenched her jaw and withdrew her hand. But she congratulated herself that in their latest battle of wills, she had emerged the victor.

She had forced Megaera to translate the instructions for the miasma, write them out on a sheet of parchment. The paper was even now folded and tucked within the bodice of Cass's gown. Tired and hungry, Megaera had finally surrendered the translation this morning.

"You are sure you have gotten the miasma right?" Cass had demanded. *"Found me the powerful potion I have needed?"*

"Yes, Maman—I mean, milady," the child had replied in that grudging tone that made Cass want to slap her. *"But the one described in the* Book *is not exactly a potion. It will be more like a powder or dust."*

"I don't care what form the miasma takes. Only one thing matters to me. Will it be as powerful as the Dark Queen's?"

"It will be worse than hers. The Book *said no one can fight this one. It will drive anyone mad, make anyone who breathes the dust angry and full of hate, wanting to kill and destroy, even themselves. The only protection from the miasma is a special ointment that you rub under your nose. I wrote down the instructions for that, too."*

Cass had caught Megaera's face in her hand, uncertain whether to believe her or not. She had pinched the girl's chin, seeking to divine her thoughts, but Megaera had— Cass frowned. Megaera had not precisely blocked access to her mind, but her thoughts had eluded Cass, racing out of reach as though they were engaged in some frustrating game of hide and seek.

Cass would have been tempted to clutch her medallion, teach her daughter another painful lesson about defiance, but the document Megaera had penned seemed to speak for itself. Cass could not read the words, but as her fingers closed over the parchment, she felt as though she could sense its power as well as the splotches of Megaera's remorseful tears.

Cass's mouth thinned. If there was one thing about her daughter that she deplored more than any other, it was Megaera's tenderheartedness, her unwillingness to embrace the dark measures necessary to put her on the French throne.

Cass blamed Prudence Waters for her daughter's weakness. She had heartily regretted that she had ever engaged that old woman to act as Megaera's nurse, but it was not as though she had had much choice. Mistress Waters had been one of the few wise women skilled enough to instruct Megaera in the art of deciphering the ancient runes.

If the Englishwoman had confined her lessons to that, all would have been well. Instead, she had sought to fill Megaera's head with nonsense about the true calling of a daughter of the earth, to spread compassion, peace, and healing, to eschew the more valuable darker arts. Cass supposed that she should have paid more heed to what was going on during Megaera's early years. But she had never been one to go all soft and sentimental over children as other women did.

Infants were singularly uninteresting creatures, able to do nothing but squall and soil themselves. Small children were not much better. Megaera's chirping little voice had often given Cass a headache. By the time she realized what a bad influence Megaera's beloved Nourice was, it had almost been too late. At the same time, Prudence Waters had learned about the *Book of Shadows* and Cass's true plans for her daughter.

The woman had actually dared to threaten Cass, declaring she would remove Megaera from Cass's care. She could only suppose that Mistress Waters had discounted Cass's ability to defend what was hers, reckoning her helpless simply because she was blind, a serious mistake on her part.

Cass wondered idly if the old woman's body had ever been found. Not that it mattered. There would hardly be enough left of the Englishwoman to identify.

As for the unfortunate softening influence Mistress Waters had had on Megaera, Cass had hoped that her daughter would outgrow that in time, but to her savage disappointment, the girl had not. Cass had begun to fear that Megaera's weaknesses were more inherent, the result of bad blood, her daughter's flaws not a legacy of Mistress Waters's but the girl's unknown father.

Employing her staff, Cass made her way carefully over to the bedchamber window. The casement had been left cracked open, no hint of a breeze stirring. A hot summer night, the air still and stifling. So different from that night a decade ago when the sky had boomed with thunder and crackled with lightning, a dark wind howling outside the inn where Cass had waited.

As the storm had raged outside, she had known it was the perfect night to conceive a girl child, destined to become a great sorceress, a leader among wise women, a conqueror who would make the likes of Alexander the Great and Genghis Khan seem mere puling boys. A perfect night and Cass had chosen the perfect man to sire her babe. Nicolas Remy, the Huguenot captain who had won such renown for his ruthlessness and fierce skills as a warrior he was known as the Scourge. The Scourge's fire and steel united with her dark power would produce a girl child who would be strong and invincible.

The only hitch to her plan was that Remy was the beloved of Gabrielle Cheney, a woman whom Cass had once considered her only friend. But Gabrielle had owed her a favor and it had seemed such a small thing to ask. She had only wanted use of the Scourge for one night. It still outraged her that Gabrielle had been selfish enough to refuse.

But Cass had been prepared for the possibility of Gabrielle's ingratitude. She had tricked Gabrielle into giving Remy the medallion that would allow Cass to gain control over him. She had never expected that Gabrielle would be able to trick her as well—

Cass gripped the windowsill, her heart burning with anger and resentment as she remembered how she had waited for Gabrielle to send Remy to her. She had been tense, edgy, knowing that her entire future depended upon this one night.

The waiting had been especially difficult because she had recently resolved to conquer what had always been her greatest weakness, a fondness for strong spirits. Although she felt shaky, she had managed to subdue her demon, determined to keep her head clear on this, the most important night of her life.

And then *he* had entered her chamber, identifying himself as a waiter bringing her refreshments she had never ordered. She had ordered him to be gone, but he had persisted. Such a clever rogue, with his silky voice, tempting her with the glass of whiskey and she had been so desperate for a drink. Just one to steady her nerves.

But one had led to another and then another, until she had felt her strength disappearing into a bottle as it had done so many times before. Her hazy mind had registered the fact that her future was in danger of slipping away from her. Nostradamus had been most specific in his prediction for once. Her wondrous child must be conceived this night or never and Remy still had not arrived.

Frantic, befuddled with drink, Cass had done the only thing she could. She had used the special perfume she had concocted to seduce the nameless villain who had invaded her bedchamber. Even after all these years, she had no idea who he had been. All she recalled was his honeyed voice and a remark he had made, referring to himself as a lone wolf.

She had been so preoccupied with her ambitions for her daughter, her desire for vengeance had had to wait, a luxury she could not afford at present. But someday, somehow, she would hunt them down, make them pay for tampering with her dreams, Gabrielle and her Scourge. And as for the *lone wolf,* she would make him suffer mortal agonies such as no man had ever endured. He would crawl at her feet, begging to die before she was through—

A soft rap at the bedchamber door disrupted her bitter thoughts. Before she could answer, the door creaked and someone entered. She did not need to inquire who it was. She was all too familiar with the pungent aroma of her servant.

Finette crept over to where Cass lingered by the window. "Mistress," she said in a low voice. "A messenger has arrived. There is word from our spy in the Queen's household."

"I'll receive her up in my tower," Cassandra replied. She produced the parchment from her bodice. "After you have escorted me there, I want you to single out two of our order who are most skilled at brewing potions. Odile and Yolette, I think. Set them to work on the miasma and the protective ointment at once."

Finette eagerly took the paper from her hands. "Do you think Megaera has really managed to translate the miasma correctly? Can we trust the child?"

"Of course we can. She is my own daughter. She does what I tell her," Cassandra snapped, unwilling to admit even to Finette what she feared, that her control over Megaera was weakening.

※※※

THE DOOR TO THE TOWER ROOM creaked open. Cass heard the rustle of skirts and a familiar sniff as Nanette entered the room.

"All hail milady, revered mother of our Silver Rose." The girl prepared to eagerly salute Cassandra's hand, but she pulled away impatiently.

"Yes, never mind all these formalities. Just tell me what I need to hear."

"There is great news, milady. The meeting you have hoped for is slated to take place. The king of France, the

Dark Queen, and the duc de Guise will all be assembled at the Louvre a few days hence. We can strike them all at once."

Cass frowned. That did not give them much time to brew and test the miasma.

"But there is a problem."

Cassandra gripped her staff tightly. She did not want to hear about any more problems. "What the devil now?"

"It's the witch-hunter. Le Balafre is still alive and worse than that, he is now working with the Dark Queen to bring you down."

Cassandra sagged back against the wall, feeling momentarily overwhelmed.

"So Agatha Ferrers failed. That man has more lives than a cat. How hard can it be? Can no one rid me of this devil?"

"I could," Nanette volunteered. "I even know where he is. The alliance between the witch-hunter and the Dark Queen is not an easy one. She has had him followed. Gillian has reported to me they have trailed the witch-hunter back to his home."

"He has a home?" Cass snapped. "Why did no one discover this before?"

"Because he is very clever, milady. But he has gone back there and it is not far from here."

"I want someone sent after him and no mistakes this time. We need to send our best people and perhaps a change of tactics. Whoever goes must be prepared to be bold and resourceful, willing to lay down their lives and trust in the Silver Rose to resurrect them."

"Let me go, milady," Nanette pleaded. "I beg you to bestow this great honor upon me."

Cassandra wished the girl's size matched her fanatical enthusiasm. "You may go, but we will also need a woman of great strength. Ursula would be the best choice. She will be thirsting for the man's blood when she hears about Agatha Ferrers. The woman was her cousin."

"Ursula thirsts for any man's blood." Nanette giggled. "It is her favorite quaff."

Cassandra drummed her fingers upon the windowsill. The idea came to her slowly, causing her lips to curl in a thin smile. "We shall send one other. A new recruit named Carole Moreau."

"Your pardon, milady," Nanette said. "But do you think it wise to send someone untried on so important a mission?"

"Ah, but Mademoiselle Moreau has risen high in the favor of our Silver Rose."

Far too high, Cass reflected grimly. This would be a great opportunity to test the Moreau girl's loyalty. And if she should fall in battle, dying heroically in the service of the Silver Rose, so much the better. A few quiet words in Ursula's ear should be enough to arrange it.

Chapter Seventeen

BREAKFAST WAS A TENSE MEAL, MIRI PUSHING AROUND her food on her dish, feeling caught between the two men at the table. Martin was slouched down in an idle posture, making a hearty meal, but Simon seemed as little inclined for his breakfast as she. He maintained a morose silence. He wasn't so cold and distant this morning, but there was a wearied sadness about him.

Madame Pascale had served them, but had gone off to tend to her morning chores, leaving the three of them alone. Miri sought to relieve the tension by speaking with forced cheerfulness.

"We shall have some relief from the drought at last."

"How can you be so sure of that, my love?" Martin drawled.

"The frogs told me when I was down by the pond last night."

Martin almost choked. He gave her a warning scowl, his message clear. Be careful what you say in front of the witch-hunter.

But Simon clearly astounded him, by agreeing. "I heard them as well."

Martin scowled as though the two of them were in collusion to mock him.

"Frogs croaking is a sure sign of coming rain. You have never heard of such a thing before?" Simon asked.

Martin shrugged. "In Paris, if one wants to know it's going to rain, one just sticks one's head out the window."

Silence descended again. Simon gave over all pretense of eating, shoving his plate away from him. Despite all of his steadfast efforts to avoid Miri's eyes, his gaze locked with hers and she thought that she saw a frustrated longing that matched her own.

When she had sat alone by the pond, she had sensed Simon watching her through the darkness and had hoped that he might come to her so they could mend the rift between them. She wondered if he would have done so but for Martin. She felt ashamed of herself for wishing her dear, devoted friend hundreds of miles away.

Sighing, she made another effort to break the silence. "It was so lovely and peaceful down by the pond last night. I believe I am regaining my ability to connect with nature that I thought I had lost on Faire Isle."

"Mon Dieu, Miri. Never tell me you have been caressing trees again," Martin teased.

Surprisingly, Simon came to her defense. "When I was

young, I used to do something similar. By stretching myself out on the ground, I thought I could feel the pulse of the earth. I haven't been able to do that for years."

"Maybe you just haven't tried hard enough. Go a little deeper, like six feet under, Monsieur Cyclops."

"Martin!" Miri rebuked him.

Simon winced at the insult. He got to his feet. "It is of no consequence. I have been called worse. If you will excuse me, I have work to do."

He strode from the room, heading up the stairs. Miri frowned at Martin. "I realize you don't like Simon. But you are here enjoying his hospitality."

"It was only a jest. I make them often."

"But I have never known you to be cruel before."

"I have never been this jealous before."

When she said nothing, he added. "That was your cue, Miri. Your next line should be, my darling Martin, you have no reason to be jealous."

"This is not a performance, Martin."

"If it were, it would be more a farce than a tragedy," Martin groused. "Ever since I have arrived here, not only have I had to hear you defend the man, his people are going out of their way to point out to me Aristide's virtues. What a great, kind man their master is, so fair and just, generous to the poor, protector of widows and orphans, the savior of beleaguered cows. He appears to have gone from the evil Le Balafre to Saint Simon in a single breath. It is enough to make a man dizzy."

Miri gave a wearied sigh. "I wish I could make you understand about Simon. You have no idea what he has endured. What his life has been like."

"And what of mine, Miri? Though I don't go moaning about it, my youth was no day at the fair either. A bastard child, abandoned by my mother, not the least idea who my father is. Growing up in the streets of Paris, learning to survive by thieving and stealing purses. At least he had a family for eleven years."

"That's true, but you had the good fortune to cross paths with Nicolas Remy. My brother-in-law is a good and noble man. Simon was rescued by a lunatic, a half-mad witch-hunter. That he survived at all is a testament to his character."

Martin slunk farther down in his chair, looking disgruntled. "Fine, if this is what you admire in a man, I am sure I could—could learn to deliver cows."

Miri laughed in spite of herself at the idea of Wolf, with his penchant for fine doublets and shirts with lace cuffs, lying in the mud and blood of the barn.

"I could," he insisted in an injured tone. "I have been thinking some things over. You feel that I never listen or really know who you are. I do. It's just that having been so poor and risen so far in the world, it is natural I would want to give the lady I adore fine gowns and jewels and a grand home. But if you want me to live in a cottage out in the woods on Faire Isle, I would do that in a heartbeat."

"Oh, Martin." She reached across the table to press his hand. "You would be bored and miserable within a fortnight."

"No, I wouldn't," he insisted. "Not if I was with you."

Miri only smiled sadly and shook her head. She knew this man far better than he did himself.

"The thing I regret most about what has happened between us is the day I took off that locket; I fear that I lost my friend."

He smiled tenderly at her, carrying her hand lightly to his lips. "No, he is still here. Whatever happens, Miri, I promise you this. You have my friendship always."

ᕼᕼᕼ

AS SIMON RETREATED into the fastness of his bedchamber, Miri's soft laughter at something le Loup had said carried up the stairs. The man had an abundance of charm, the ability to make people around him smile and laugh instead of shrink back in fear. Traits Simon himself had once possessed.

Despite the animosity he had aroused upon his arrival, Martin had already done a great deal to mollify Simon's people. Coaxing smiles out of Madame Pascale, even getting crusty old Jacques to laugh. He'd taken great pains to make amends to Yves, and not out of some desire to impress Miri or to manipulate the boy. For all the man's grand gestures, there was a genuine kindness in his overtures to Yves. Simon might have liked the man for that, if not for the way Martin looked at Miri, calling her his love, all those honeyed phrases tripping from his tongue, the things Simon could never say.

Simon looked in the mirror above the washstand, desperately seeking some trace of the handsome, carefree boy he had once been. All that was reflected back to him was the weary, embittered visage of a man whose face was as scarred as his soul.

This room more than any other in the house whispered

to Simon of dreams he had never acknowledged until now, hopes he had fashioned into the very walls when he had built this place.

The chamber and the bed were far too big for a solitary man; they cried out for the presence of a woman, a wife to hold fast in his arms on a cold winter's night, the window seat a good place for her to stitch and dream, the large diamond-paned windows framing the sky for her, a view of the trees, the birds, and the animals in the yard.

The place at the foot of the bed would have been perfect for a cradle . . . except it was already occupied by the bitter reminders of his past, the trunk he seldom liked to open. All the diaries and records of his witch-hunts, journals that he had kept meticulously when he had been arrogant enough to believe his work was of paramount importance. He had stopped keeping the journals years ago, when he had started wanting to forget, not remember, the trials he had borne witness to.

Those diaries were full of the vituperative writings of a bitter and angry man. A man he was ashamed to have been, feared he might become again. The trunk was a Pandora's box of all the evils in the world, of which he had been one. But now the box also might contain the answers that he sought, so he had no choice but to open it.

He lifted the lid and began sifting through years of dark memories, cases that he had tried. He wondered how many other mistakes he had made besides Faire Isle.

Many of the records of his earlier days had been lost in the fire at the Charters Inn. He had later tried to painstakingly re-create them with only his memory to rely upon. He sifted through the various journals until he found the one dealing with that last day at the Charters Inn. He flipped it open and it made painful reading because his thoughts that day had not been consumed with justice. They had been dark, full of bitterness, vengeance against Renard, anger with Miri for making him feel weak, hesitant about betraying her trust, trying to justify it to himself.

That time in Paris, he had been busily interviewing dozens of people, offering coin to anyone who would come forward with tales of those practicing witchcraft. He flattered himself at the time how much fairer and more just his approach was. Unlike his master, he did not torture anyone for information. He used more subtle weapons, clever questioning, intimidation, bribery.

He had learned to his cost that there were people willing to sell out their own mother for a sou. One notable example of that had been the woman who had betrayed Gabrielle Cheney.

Cassandra Lascelles. She had claimed to be Gabrielle's friend, but for whatever angry reason, she was the one who had told Simon how to find the evidence necessary to arrest Gabrielle. She had been in possession of the Dark Queen's ring and those damning medallions, which had disappeared along with the *Book of Shadows.*

He still didn't know to what extent Miri's sister had been guilty of witchery or just mere foolishness. He hadn't really cared. Her arrest had merely been a ploy to lure the Comte de Renard into a trap.

He had meant to investigate the Lascelles woman more fully at the time. It wasn't the first time she had betrayed her own kind to witch-hunters. According to records left by his old master Le Vis, Cassandra had sought to save her own skin by naming her mother and sisters as witches. Ordinary betrayal would not have been enough to have saved her. But the girl's youth and blindness had moved Le Vis to a rare display of mercy. After the raid on her home, Cassandra had disappeared for years, only resurfacing that summer when she had laid information against Gabrielle.

But Simon didn't see how she could have been the one to steal the *Book of Shadows* amidst the chaos of the fire. Not only was the woman blind, Simon was certain she had been nowhere near the inn that day.

He had conducted no interviews, turning away all those eager to turn in their neighbors for a handful of coin. Besides his own men and the Cheneys, there was only one other person mentioned in his notes. A persistent, scrawny, filthy wench clamoring for admittance outside the kitchens. According to Simon's records, her name was Finette and she had whined something about coming to claim a reward on behalf of her mistress, who had furnished Simon with information the week before.

The week before . . . about the same time Simon had arrested Gabrielle. He scowled. Was it possible this Finette was the witch who had made off with the *Book of Shadows,* and the mistress she served was Cassandra Lascelles? Could the Lascelles woman truly be the infamous Silver Rose?

As Simon pored over the journal, seeking further clues, he became aware of something drumming against the window. A sound he had not heard for so long, it took him a moment to register what it was.

Rain . . . and not those few pitiful drops that had teased France all summer with the prospect of relief. After all those false storms, the thunder and lightning that had yielded nothing but flash and noise, the skies had opened up at last, showering a healing rain down upon the parched earth. A genuine blessed downpour.

Simon rushed eagerly to the window, feeling his heart lift at the sight and he wasn't the only one. Miri had raced out of the kitchen into the rain, heedless of the fact that she was getting soaked. True daughter of the earth that she was, she raised her arms, embracing the rain, twirling about in a joyous dance that brought a smile to Simon's lips.

Wolf was apparently watching her from the safety of the doorway. Miri ran back to the house laughing and caught him by the hands, dragging him out. Simon half-expected the man to rush back inside like a scalded cat, but Martin laughed. The two of them locked hands, capering about in a wild dance.

Simon watched them, wishing he still possessed that kind of lightness of heart, was capable of such abandon. But instead he felt himself tense, his neck prickling with the uncanny sensation something was wrong.

He fast realized what it was. Elle. She had been left out in the paddock and she was behaving in skittish fashion, shying back, tossing her head. Storms upset her, but there was no thunder or lightning. If she wanted to escape the deluge all she had to do was trot through the side door back into the barn. No, whatever was upsetting her, it wasn't the rain.

Simon pressed his face closer to the glass, attempting to peer through the driving rain. He was barely able to make them out. At first they seemed like mere shadows, but there could be no shadows where there was no sun. It was three figures creeping stealthily closer and even from this distance Simon was able to discern they were women.

No, not women, his instinct warned him. *Witches.*

Simon snatched up his sword and ran, tearing down the stairs. As he burst out into the yard, he brushed back his hair and the rain from his eye. Wolf had Miri in his arms, swinging her around, still unaware of the danger.

Simon ran, his boots splashing through the puddles. He roared out a warning. Wolf snapped alert as the first figure charged. He shoved Miri out of the way, starting to draw his sword, but he made a fatal error.

He hesitated when he saw his opponent was a woman, the chivalrous impulse so typical of the romantic fool, Simon thought. Not until the huge woman brandished a knife did Wolf react. He caught her arm, but she whipped her head down, cracking her skull into Wolf's jaw.

Wolf reeled back and slipped in the mud. Coming down hard, he was momentarily dazed and defenseless. The giantess bared her teeth and raised her knife to finish him off. Simon leaped over Wolf, deflecting the blow with his sword just in time.

The woman came at Simon with a savage snarl. He slashed out, cutting her down. He didn't wait to see her fall, barely registering her shriek of pain. He spun about to deal with the other two witches.

One had flung herself at Miri, wrapping her arms about her waist, threatening to drag her down. As Simon rushed to her aid, the third witch came at him. Through the rain he caught a blurred glimpse of a small dark woman with wild eyes, her hand clutching a familiar deadly weapon, the witch blade.

She circled Simon, trying to find an opening to lunge at him. But the next instant a dark shadow loomed over both of them. Elle had leaped the paddock fence and reared up out of the rain, her dark wet mane whipping back, her hooves striking the air.

The witch stumbled back with a terrified cry. Her hands flailed in a desperate attempt to ward the horse off. Elle knocked the witch down, her hooves pounding down again and again.

By the time Simon caught Elle's reins and managed to draw her off, the witch lay dead, her blood mingling with the rain and mud of the yard. Elle was blowing and trembling with fear and rage. Simon stroked and murmured, seeking to calm the mare while he looked frantically for Miri. But Wolf had recovered his footing and rushed to her aid, dragging the other witch away from her.

By this time Jacques and one of the other hands had come running. Simon consigned Elle to the old groom and hastened to Miri. The young witch nearly broke free of Wolf's grip in her desperate efforts to get at Miri.

But when Simon raised his weapon, Miri caught his arm, "No, Simon, please don't. It's Carole."

The girl had sagged down in a heap at Martin's feet, A soaked, bedraggled creature, she looked more like a cowering child than a witch. She desperately tried to call out to Miri, stammer words that wouldn't come from her terrified lips.

But Miri had frozen, her stricken gaze elsewhere. She went white at the sight of the two dead women in the yard. Simon hurried to block her view, gathering her hard against him, stroking her wet hair. The fire in his veins that had sent him roaring into battle went out, leaving him cold and trembling with fear of what could have happened to her.

Miri sagged weakly against him for a moment, then began to struggle anew as though still straining to see.

"No, my dear, don't look," Simon said hoarsely. "I am sorry for what I had to do, but there was no choice. Those witches."

"No, it's not the witches," Miri choked. "Simon, look. Elle—"

He couldn't understand what she was talking about until he glanced back and saw Jacques crouched down by Elle, examining her chest. Had she sustained some injury?

Simon rushed toward him, demanding, "What is it?"

Jacques turned toward him wordlessly, holding out the object that he had pulled from Elle's chest. The witch blade, its plunger depressed.

"No," Simon rasped. He ran his hand desperately over her shoulders and chest as though he could somehow stay the poison from its slow but inexorable course through her veins.

He staggered back a step, raking back his wet hair and clutching his head, feeling as though his mind was exploding with grief and rage. Whipping about, he stormed back toward the only surviving witch. She was clinging to Miri, but Simon dragged her away. Seizing her by the throat, he shook her like a rag doll.

"Damn you! God damn all of you witches to hell. You tell me right now before I break your neck. What devil sent you? Who is the Silver Rose?"

The girl gasped, her teeth chattering with fear. "No, I c-can't."

Simon gave her another savage shake. "Is it Cassandra Lascelles? Tell me right now or—"

Both Miri and Wolf seized his arms, prying the girl away. Wolf leaped in between them, shoving Simon back.

"Stop it. Can't you see you're scaring her half to death? You'll get nothing from her this way."

Simon snarled and thrust Wolf aside. But the girl had swooned, sinking down into a dead faint. Miri managed to catch her, keep her from hitting the ground as Wolf sprang forward to help.

Simon staggered back, panting, his anger giving way to despair as he returned to Elle.

"Master, shall I—" old Jacques started to ask, the old man's eyes welling with sympathy.

Simon took the reins from him, shaking his head. "No, she is my lady. It is me that she has always trusted to—"

He broke off, unable to continue. Elle's head had already begun to droop, but her sad dark eyes regarded Simon with that same devotion and trust she had always shown. Drawing in a ragged breath, he seized her by the reins and led her out of the rain, back into the stables.

Taking her home one last time.

Chapter Eighteen

THE RAIN DRUMMED AGAINST THE STABLE ROOF, THE SOUND that had been so welcome only hours before now bleak and melancholy as Miri and Simon labored over Elle. Her damp gown clinging to her back, Miri applied a poultice to the puncture wound in an effort to draw out as much of the poison as she could. But it wasn't working. The wound was raw and angry looking, the mare's glossy coat soaked with sweat.

Simon worked desperately, sponging her with warm water, trying to cool her down. Elle hung her head listlessly, far different from her usual jaunty manner. She attempted to rally, straining toward him when Simon rubbed down her neck.

He caressed her favorite place between her eyes, murmuring hoarsely, "There now, my beauty. I'm right here. Don't be afraid. I won't let anything—"

He broke off with a bitter laugh, mocking his own words. "Not let anything hurt her. Christ, I've already done that. I'm no better at keeping my promises to Elle than I am to anyone else."

"Simon—" Miri straightened, tried to rest her hand comfortingly on his arm, but he shook her off. He looked almost wild, his hair a dark wet tangle, his face white beneath its layer of beard. He had stripped off his soaked eye patch and his scarred eye stood out in sharp relief, giving him the appearance of some battered warrior who had fought his way through a storm.

But his hand was gentle as he massaged his fingertips between Elle's eyes. "I should have had that damned fence built higher. I—I knew she could jump the blasted thing. She's been able to ever since she was a filly, but I never worried about it, because she never roamed off like other horses will. She—she just always made her way up to the house, looking for me."

"It would not have mattered how high you built the fence, Simon. She would have just broken it down, hurt herself trying to get to you."

"At least she would have never gotten between me and that God-cursed witch. Why did you have to do that, Elle? Why?" Simon rasped.

Elle's dark eye flickered. Despite her own misery and confusion, the mare lipped gently at Simon's hand, not fully understanding his distress, but as ever seeking to comfort him. For once Simon made no effort to conceal his emotions, resting his brow against Elle's, his shoulders bowed in despair.

Her eyes burning, Miri ached for both of them, the magnificent and innocent creature who had done nothing to deserve this pain, and the man who had kept himself isolated for so long, never daring to love anything save this one horse. Life had handed Simon Aristide enough disillusionment and painful loss. Miri could not allow him to be dealt one more.

She blinked fiercely. It would avail neither Simon nor Elle for her to give way to useless tears. She needed to remain calm, to think. As Simon resumed sponging Elle, Miri ran her hand along Elle's lower jaw until she found the mare's pulse. She pressed her finger to the artery, counting. Elle's pulse raced at a rate well above what was normal for a horse at rest. The mare's flanks rose and fell rapidly, making it painfully obvious her breathing was becoming more labored. Miri frantically sorted through her mind for other remedies she had employed for everything from colic to grass sickness.

Resting his hands upon Elle's glistening back, Simon cast Miri an agonized glance. "This is hopeless, Miri. I don't know why I even allowed you to persuade me to try these useless remedies. I knew from the minute I saw Jacques pull that damned witch blade out of her that Elle was done for."

"No, she isn't, Simon. We can't give up. We've got to—"

"Got to do what?" he interrupted harshly. "There's nothing else to be done, Miri. All we are going to do is prolong her suffering. I have seen the effects of the witch blade's poison before. I know how it will progress."

"Then describe it to me."

"Just as it is with Elle. I had a slim hope it might be different for a horse. She's so much larger, stronger than a man, that maybe somehow she could weather—" He broke off, shaking his head in despair. "But the poison is progressing just the same as I've seen before. First the sweats, the listlessness and the fever, the labored breathing. And it will only get worse, moving on to hideous muscle spasms, convulsions, delirium that can last for days, the pain so bad I've seen full-grown men go mad, scream themselves hoarse."

Simon clamped his lips in a tight line, his throat working. "My lady has—has served me faithfully, trusted me far too long for me to allow it to end for her that way. I won't let her suffer."

"Neither will I," Miri cried. "But I refuse to give up so easily. You have to at least give me the chance to fight this poison."

"How the devil are you going to do that? What do you know of poisons?"

"Only what I learned from Renard."

Miri saw Simon tense immediately at the name as she'd feared he would. She thrust up her chin and continued doggedly, "Thanks to his grandmother, Renard was well versed in poisons, but he put his knowledge to good use developing antidotes and he taught me—"

"I don't care what he taught you. If you think I will let Elle be further tormented with that sorcerer's dark magic—"

"How can it be dark magic if it can save her?" Miri protested. "And I am going to need the use of that witch blade as well."

Simon's face suffused with outrage. He came out of the stall, hands on hips as he squared off with her. "Damnation, woman. I can't even believe you'd suggest such a thing. Bad enough she endured being stabbed once, but you propose to use that hellish weapon to—"

"It's not a hellish weapon or a witch blade," Miri said fiercely. "It's only a syringe and I can use it to speed the antidote into Elle's veins."

Simon gave an incredulous snort. "You expect me to believe you can use the same device that is killing her to save her?"

"Yes!" Miri stepped toward him, resting her hands on the unyielding expanse of his chest. "Oh, Simon, I know that Le Vis taught you to revile and fear anything to do with the ancient knowledge, all that he considered dark magic. But you've seen for yourself how the same thing can be used for good or evil depending upon who wields it. The same axe that could be used to cut off a man's head can also be employed to chop wood and build a fire, keep his family from freezing. The thing that you call a witch blade is no different. Do you think I would ever use it for any evil purpose?"

"Of course not. But—" He stared down at her, frowning, the first flicker of uncertainty appearing in his stern gaze. "Even if I did agree to let you try this—this antidote of Renard's, where would you brew up such a thing? It is not as though I have any witch's storeroom on my lands."

Miri bit down on her lip, hesitant to tell him, but having no choice. "Actually you do. Esmee has a stillroom tucked in the back of your laundry house."

"What!" Simon's mouth fell open, his expression a

mingling of astonishment and betrayal. "After I saved that woman from being condemned for witchcraft, brought her here, she's been practicing sorcery under my very nose?"

"Not sorcery, Simon, only the kind of magic and healing ways that wise women have preserved for centuries, despite the ignorant superstition and cruelty of men like your late master. Esmee has been using the ancient knowledge to keep your people here well, your very lands thriving. Did you not notice how your orchards and your vegetable gardens have survived when so much of the rest of the country is blighted by drought?"

"Yes, but I thought—" He raked his hand back through his hair. "Hell, I don't know what I thought. But whatever sort of—of white magic Esmee might have practiced is one thing. The kind of sorcery Renard embraced is a different matter."

"This isn't about Renard. This is about me. I beg you to trust me as you never have before. At least give me a chance to save Elle."

He glanced over to Elle, clearly torn between hope and the mistrust that Le Vis had bred in him for years. His gaze came back to rest on Miri's face, something softening in his eye as he yielded. "All right. What do you want me to do?"

"Stay with Elle. Keep sponging her down, talk to her, keep her from getting agitated and shifting about too much." Miri looked up at him earnestly. "And promise me you'll do nothing desperate until I return."

Simon nodded reluctantly. "And if this antidote of yours doesn't work, if her suffering becomes too great?"

"Then I'll let you do what must be done." Miri pressed his hand, adding softly, "And help you to say good-bye."

MARTIN CREPT THROUGH the empty kitchen, his head still throbbing from the blow he had taken from the witch. No man liked a good fight better than he did. If there was one flaw that Miri possessed, and Martin was far from willing to concede his Lady of the Moon had any . . . But if Miri did have one failing, it was her marked aversion to any form of confrontation, always wanting everything settled by peaceful means.

And sometimes that just wasn't possible. There was nothing like a bit of mayhem to get a man's blood pumping through his veins. But the exhilaration of a duel or a bout of fisticuffs with another man was one thing. There was something unnerving when one's attacker was a crazed giant of a woman. Martin preferred his ladies soft and feminine, stitching up a fancy embroidered handkerchief to bestow upon an ardent admirer, daintily wielding scissors to snip the thread, not a knife to slit his throat.

He was mortified that he had been caught so off guard. If not for Simon Aristide, it would be his blood soaking into the muddy yard and likely Miri's as well. Now he was in Aristide's debt, not a situation Martin relished.

Not only did his debt to the witch-hunter weigh heavily upon him, he was haunted by something Aristide had said when he had roared at Carole Moreau.

"Who is the Silver Rose? Is she Cassandra Lascelles?"

Cass Lascelles. Martin shivered from more than his wet clothes. There was a name he'd done his best to forget, could have happily gone his entire life without hearing again.

Both sorceress and madwoman, she'd had some crazed scheme to seduce Nicolas Remy, force him to sire her witch child. Remy, the man who had been everything to Martin, friend, brother, mentor, and captain. Martin would have done anything for his hero and that night, when Martin had gone to the Cheval Noir in Remy's stead, he had inadvertently . . .

Despite his wet clothes, Martin felt a bead of sweat trickle down his back as he remembered being locked in that stifling hot inn chamber with the witch, trying to render her drunk enough to steal the evil amulet with which she had threatened his captain's life. Martin had never anticipated the witch's dark charms might be turned upon him instead.

The witch groped until her hand struck up against his chest, pawing at him. When Martin had realized the direction her thoughts were taking, the hairs prickled along the back of his neck.

"Are you fer-ferocious?" her drunken voice had slurred. "You said somethin' before about being tough, sinewy?"

Martin gulped, edging away from her. "I have a tendency to boast far too much."

"You feel hard 'nough to me to father a fierce babe."

"I'm more of a lone wolf. I'm not really the fatherly sort."

"Who cares 'bout that? As long as you're the f—ing sort."

Before he could stop her, the witch's hand caught him between the legs and his shaft stirred in inevitable response. The strange heady essence of her perfume assaulted his nostrils, fogging his brain. Even as some dim corner of

his mind struggled to resist, the honeyed poison of her lips
destroyed what remained of his reason. With a fierce growl,
he fell upon her, ripping away the bodice of her gown—

Martin shuddered, blocking the rest of what had happened that night from his mind. Sickened, shamed by the lust the witch had aroused in him, Martin had done his best to forget.

Cassandra Lascelles had vanished not long after. The witch had not been seen or heard from in years. What the devil made Aristide think Cassandra was mixed up in this affair of the Silver Rose? Whatever had aroused the witch-hunter's suspicions, Martin hoped the man was wrong, but if there was any chance that witch had turned up back in France, any danger Martin might cross paths with her, he needed to know and know now.

But he could hardly question Aristide. Not only would the witch-hunter be disinclined to answer any questions posed by Martin, the man was too torn up over his horse at the moment to think of anything else. Despite his dislike of Aristide, even Martin had been moved to feel a pang of sympathy for him.

Not that he completely understood the intense bond between the man and his horse. Martin was fond enough of his current mount. The big gray stallion was the kind of horse Martin liked, swift with a bit of a dash about him. But it was only a means of getting him from one place to another.

When all was said and done, Martin's preferred mode of transportation was still his own two feet. As a boy in Paris, he'd had little to do with horses other than trying to keep out of their way, cursing whatever oaf had nearly ridden him down or splashed him with mud in the streets. He'd stolen many things during his days as a street thief, but horses were not among them. They were simply too damn big to hide. Any ease in the saddle he had eventually acquired, he owed to Nicolas Remy and Miri.

Martin had not much expertise in the care of animals, but even he could tell Aristide's mare hadn't looked good. But if anyone could save the creature, it was Miri. Ordinarily Martin's instinct would have been to remain close to Miri's side, but there was nothing he could do to help the situation. Although his every jealous impulse made him not want to leave her in the company of that witch-hunter.

Damn it. He scowled. He was finding it hard to keep calling Aristide that—not since the bastard had had the impertinence to save his life. After so many years it was hard to let go of the suspicion, the anger, and the jealousy Simon aroused in him. But Martin had other thoughts to preoccupy him, the tormenting possibility that Cassandra Lascelles had resurfaced, and there was only one person besides Simon who could put his fears to rest.

But first . . . Martin scowled down at his wet and muddy clothing. He had best spruce himself up a bit because he had a young lady to charm.

※※※

CAROLE MOREAU WAS TUCKED UP in Madame Pascale's bedchamber behind the kitchen. Madame Pascale had disappeared with Miri in the direction of the laundry house, both women deep in consultation about some medicine they planned to brew for the horse. They seemed likely to be gone for some time.

Martin crept quietly to the door of the bedchamber. He felt more himself now, attired in a clean doublet and venetians, his hair combed and fastened back into a queue. If it hadn't still been raining, he would have been tempted to filch a few flowers from Madame Pascale's garden.

He knocked softly, half dreading to find Mademoiselle Moreau asleep. He knew Madame Pascale had taken a posset in to the girl earlier. But apparently even the old woman's herbal remedy had not been enough to soothe the girl's fear and distress.

A wan voice bade him enter. Martin cracked the door open and peeked inside. The girl lay tucked up in Madame Pascale's bed, and although it was not a large one, Carole still looked small and childlike, her freckles standing out on her pale face.

She might have been a fetching little thing under other circumstances. But deep shadows pooled beneath her blue eyes, her expression so forlorn, it stirred all of Martin's chivalrous impulses.

Her eyes widened at the sight of him. Obviously she had been expecting Madame Pascale. With a soft gasp, she sat bolt upright, dragging the coverlet protectively up to her chin.

"Please, mademoiselle. Don't be alarmed," Martin hastened to assured her, summoning up his gentlest smile. "I only wanted to see how you are faring."

Huge tears welled up in Carole's eyes. "Then you are n-not angry with me, monsieur?"

"Why would I be angry with you?"

"B-because I tried to help kill you."

Martin waved his hand dismissively. "Ah, think nothing of that, child. I frequently inspire murderous urges in my fellow human beings, although not usually, I must confess, among the fairer sex."

To his horror, two large tears escaped to trickle down Carole's cheeks. "No, no, ma petite, I beg you. Don't cry."

If there was one thing Martin could not endure, it was the sight of any lady in tears, especially such a sad little damsel as this one. He drew out a fine cambric handkerchief and presented it to her.

Carole took the cloth and dabbed her eyes. "Thank you. I hate to cry in front of people, but I seem to be doing that far too much these days."

"Completely understandable after all you have been through."

"Then you don't hate me for being with those evil women? I d-didn't want to come, truly I didn't." She sniffed. "W-well, maybe I did a little bit. I th-thought I might find a chance to escape, but f-first I wanted to be brave enough to help get rid of the witch-hunter. F-for Meggie's sake, you understand."

Martin didn't understand at all, but he nodded encouragingly.

"When we entered the yard, it—it was raining. And we couldn't tell. We mistook you for the witch-hunter."

"Mon Dieu!" Martin had taken many blows to his pride lately, but to be mistaken for a witch-hunter! It was entirely too much to be borne.

He drew himself up indignantly, exclaiming. "Mademoiselle, you cut me to the quick. Do I look to you like I am that sort of devil?"

"No. At least not now that I can see you more clearly." Her lashes drifted down as she cast him a gaze of purely feminine appreciation.

"Then I shall contrive to forgive you," Martin said. "How could I do otherwise with such an enchanting young lady? I now see where your son has acquired his own charming looks."

She sat up in bed eagerly, color filtering back into her cheeks. "You have seen my little Jean Baptiste?"

"Bien sûr, Mademoiselle. When I went to Faire Isle looking for Miri."

"How did he look? How did he seem? Is he faring well?"

"How can he not be? He is like a prince surrounded by a court of adoring women. He is receiving the best of care from all of your friends on Faire Isle."

Her face clouded over. "I have no friends, m'sieur."

"Most certainly you do. Mademoiselle Miri for one." He bowed. "And Martin le Loup for another."

She tilted her head, regarding him shyly. "That is you, monsieur?"

"Most certainly, ma petite." Martin carried the girl's hand lightly to his lips. She actually dimpled with the hint of a smile, but she became grave the next instant, curling her fingers around his.

"May I ask you something, Monsieur le Loup?"

"Martin," he said.

"Martin," she repeated, smiling again. "What—what became of my two companions? Are they—are they really dead?"

"I'm afraid so. I believe they've laid them out in one of the sheds out back until some sort of burial can be arranged."

She slipped her hand out of his, her fingers curling in the coverlet, her lashes downcast. "You may think me very wicked, monsieur, but I am not sorry that they are dead. Ursula, the big one, she was a mean brute of a woman and Nanette—she wasn't so bad, but she was quite mad. She was frightening."

"I don't think you are wicked at all, mademoiselle. What little I saw of those two witches was enough to chill my blood, but I suppose they are nothing compared to the Silver Rose."

The girl stiffened, tensing at his mention of the sorceress. He went on, speaking in his softest, most persuasive voice. "I don't want to alarm you, mademoiselle, but eventually the sorceress is going to find out that you've failed in your mission, and she's bound to send someone else."

Carole shivered. "Yes, she probably will."

"However, if you could just tell me who she is, where I might find her . . ."

"I don't—I don't know exactly where, monsieur. We were living in some old house in Paris and I never heard the woman's name. I just know that she was always spoken of as the Lady."

"Can you describe her?"

The girl's brow furrowed. "She looked exactly like what you would think a dread sorceress would look like. She had long thick black hair with silver streaks. Her skin was dead white. And her touch . . . her fingers were so cold when she touched you, you almost felt as though she was draining every thought, every memory that you ever had."

Martin swallowed. Could there be two such women who matched such a description?

"And her eyes . . . they were so dark. Empty."

"Because she's blind?"

Carole looked up at him in surprise. "How did you know that, monsieur?"

Martin's heart sank at the confirmation of all of his fears. "I believe that I may have crossed paths with this woman . . . this Silver Rose before."

Carole squirmed as he said this. She looked down at her hands a long time before she said, "The Lady is the evil one. She's the one who runs the coven and she's the one behind all these evil deeds. But she's not the Silver Rose. That's—that's Meggie."

"Meggie?" Martin asked in confusion.

"She's not evil." Carole looked up at him earnestly. "Meggie is not evil at all. Far from it. But she has the misfortune to be this terrible witch's daughter."

"Her daughter? This witch has a child?" Martin felt all the blood draining from his face. "How old is this girl?"

"Meggie is nine, going on ten."

Martin moistened his lips. "And—and the child's father?"

"No one knows who that might be, monsieur. But the Lady is so cruel she is always telling Meggie she was fathered by the devil."

His mind reeling from the shock of what he had just

heard, Martin had to walk over to the window to hide his countenance from Carole. The child sired by the devil? He would like to believe that himself. But he was afraid there was a far different, far worse explanation.

The Silver Rose was Cassandra Lascelles's daughter, but he was terrified that she was also his.

✷✷✷

THE SHADOWS LENGTHENED along the stalls where Miri and Simon kept anxious watch over Elle, waiting for some change. No longer able to stand, Elle lay on her side in the stall, her head stretched out toward Simon, her lids half closed, her chest heaving as she panted.

When Miri had administered the antidote, Simon had soothed Elle's fears as best he could, but he'd averted his own face, unable to watch as Miri had thrust the syringe into Elle's neck, delivering what she'd hoped would be the lifesaving antidote. But now, all they could do was wait, hope, and pray.

Elle had seemed so sensitive to noise, they had cleared the stable of all other creatures. It had been a little more difficult to keep Jacques and Yves away. But the boy was far better off back at the house with his mother. The day's incidents had been very unsettling to him, and Elle needed as much peace and quiet as they could give her.

As Simon stroked Elle's nose, he said to Miri, "Do you realize it was only a matter of chance that Elle ever came to be my horse? There was a merchant who wished to purchase her for his daughter to ride. Elle would have had a fine life, pampered in a fancy stable, only ever taken out on occasion for light rides, but I got there first that day. I offered the horse breeder a great deal more money for her." He caressed the horse's nose. "Elle would have been so much better off."

"No she wouldn't," Miri said. "She would have been just another possession to that girl, a new bauble, nothing of what Elle means to you. Elle loves you, Simon. It's you that she wants to be with. She'd rather be with you for a short while, for whatever time she has, than live for years in the finest—"

Miri broke off, not entirely sure who she was speaking about, herself or the horse. She reached down to stroke Elle's neck, sending her thoughts to the mare.

Please, Elle. You can do this. Fight your way back.

The horse's hazed thoughts came back to her. *So tired . . . tired . . .*

No. You can do it. Fight your way back. You can't die. Please. You've got to stay for him. He needs you.

Watching her, Simon clenched his hands tightly together, muttering, "I should never have agreed to this. It isn't working. Miri, we're torturing her for nothing."

Miri was beginning to despair herself, but she realized the success of this was much more important than just saving Elle's life. Simon had been so convinced that magic was evil, poisoned by Le Vis's teachings. Miri felt that she wasn't just battling for Elle, but for the very soul of Simon Aristide.

Stroking the horse once more, she tried to infuse the mare with both her thoughts and her will. *Elle, please, you've got to try. He needs you. You have no idea how much.*

Was it her imagination, or did the horse's eye flicker and then open, the dark depths startling liquid and clear? Elle struggled to raise her head, a little awkwardly at first. Simon held his breath. The horse emitted a soft whicker, then slowly she rolled, getting her feet under her. A little shaky at first, she clambered to her feet.

Kneeling, Miri pressed her hands to her mouth, unable to speak as she watched Simon get to his feet as well, his expression stunned, awed, full of wonder. In the next instant, he flung his arms about the horse's neck, tears coursing down his cheek. He caressed her, gazing mistily down at Miri, fiercely trying to bank his emotion.

"Thank you," he said hoarsely.

※※※

MIRI LINGERED in the barn, giving Jacques final instructions about keeping watch over Elle tonight. The horse seemed to be getting stronger by the moment and Miri had no apprehensions now, but just in case, she left instructions for Jacques to come and find her should Elle show any signs of relapse. Then she left the stables to go in search of Simon.

As soon as he had been sure that Elle was going to be fine, he had disappeared. Now that the crisis was over, she feared that maybe his attentions had returned to Carole, to questioning her. Miri believed that his anger was spent, but she was determined to place a shield between him and the frightened girl if necessary.

But when she emerged from the stables, she was surprised to see Simon sitting on the wooden bench at the edge of the pond, watching the last of the daylight spread fingers of light across the shimmering water.

She approached him tentatively, feeling that he had come here for the same reason she had last night, that this was Simon's way of restoring his harmony, too. The man may not want to believe it, but they did have so much in common.

But as she approached, he did not look as though he was finding any peace. He was staring down at the syringe that had both brought great harm to Elle and saved her life.

At Miri's approach he looked up, placing the implement carefully to one side. He glanced up at her anxiously. "Is Elle still doing all right?"

"She's doing just fine. As a matter of fact, the whole incident seems to have left her starving. I believe that she is trying to charm old Jacques out of an extra measure of oats."

Simon gave her a smile. "She's good at that."

Miri settled beside him on the bench. She reached up to brush back a tangle of hair from his brow. "At the moment, I am more concerned about how Elle's master is doing."

He grimaced. "Not very well. I've been trying to sort through some things, trying to make sense of . . . well, I guess my entire life, for that matter. Long ago, when Le Vis came into my village and he rescued me, I wasn't exactly grateful. I really wanted to die. I wished I was dead. I couldn't understand why I alone out of my whole family and my entire village, had been the only one spared. Le Vis told me that the reason I had survived was to fight against evil. The kind that had destroyed my family, so that others might not suffer the same fate. For so many years, that's the belief that has sustained me, governed my life. But I'm not sure of that anymore, Miri. I'm no longer sure of anything I've ever done, anything I've ever thought I understood. I almost feel like my entire life has been nothing but one long mistake."

"Oh, Simon." Miri curled her hand around his.

"I, better than anyone, realized what Le Vis was. But I was always so determined that I would never lose myself in his madness. That I would not become like him. But when I think of some of the ways I've behaved, when I went after that poor girl, and I look down at myself, at my reflection . . ." Simon's gaze turned down to his image shimmering in the water below. "It's Le Vis's reflection that I see staring back at me."

Miri clasped his hand tighter between hers. "That's not what I see, Simon. That's not what I've ever seen. When I've looked at you, I've seen a good man, despite all your wounds and your hurts. A good man struggling to survive. Trying to find his way back to the light."

Although he responded by entwining his fingers with hers, he continued to stare bleakly into the pond. "For so many years I truly have been blind in my bitterness against the Comte de Renard, so convinced he was a sorcerer, but now I know I owe Elle's life to his knowledge."

Simon swallowed. "I think this anger that I've harbored against him from the very beginning was just a product of my own guilt. I keep remembering when he charged in with his sword to attack the brethren of our order of witch-hunters. That day, Le Vis was planning to put you through the ordeal of the trial by water. I should have been grateful to Renard for saving you. Maybe the reason I was angry was because he was the one who saved you and it should have been me."

"Oh, Simon, you were no more than a boy at the time, as confused and frightened as I was."

Simon only shook his head darkly. "Even that time later in Paris when I attacked Renard, when I came to seek vengeance against him for killing Le Vis—"

"It wasn't him. For so long, I tried to tell you that. It was the Dark Queen's doing. At the time of your master's death, Renard was a prisoner at the Bastille."

Simon nodded bleakly. "I should have believed you. But it was so much easier to blame him for doing what I wanted to do myself." He vented a heavy sigh. "I never finished telling you the rest of the story about St. Bartholomew's Eve.

"I was half out of my mind with rage, my knife clutched in my hand. But—but it wasn't the Huguenots I wanted to destroy. It was Le Vis I wanted to kill . . . the man who had saved my life. I came so close to rushing after him and—"

Simon raked his hand through his hair, his gaze full of anguish. "I felt so torn and confused, Miri, so broken inside. That is why time and again I have tried to drive you away from me."

"But you have been slowly mending. It was not any madman like Le Vis who risked his life to save the Maitlands or rescued Madame Pascale and Yves. Or sought to protect and spare me time and again. Your spirit has been struggling to resist the darkness, but you are so tired, Simon." Miri gently stroked his hair back from his tormented face. "Let me love you. Let me help you."

Although he pressed a fervent kiss against her palm, he said, "I can't, Miri. I am so afraid. You have been the one good, the one constant thing in my life. If I were to infect you with my darkness . . ."

"You won't," she cried. "I can be strong enough for the both of us, more than I ever knew myself before. All you have to do is open your arms and let me in."

Simon stared at her for a long moment, his dark eye roiling with the battle between his fears and his longings. The longing won, and he slowly opened his arms. As Miri fell into them, he crushed her to him. Miri buried her fingers in his hair, hungrily seeking his lips.

Lost in the passion of their embrace, neither of them noticed the solitary man silhouetted in the doorway of the stables. As Miri surrendered herself to Aristide's embrace, Martin le Loup watched all his dreams turn to dust.

His heart quietly breaking, he crept inside the stables to fetch his horse.

Chapter Nineteen

THE RECENT RAIN HAD LEFT THE STREETS SLICK AND muddy, but it had done much to cool the air and tempers of the city. The relief from the heat was cause for celebration. The sounds of laughter and carousing could still be heard spilling from some of the taverns even at this late hour. But along the rue de Morte where Martin le Loup crept, all was dark and silent.

Under other circumstances, he might have been tempted to join in the revelry. As hard as his life had often been, the struggle to survive in the streets, he had always loved the great city of Paris and the noise, the bustle, the teeming humanity, the towering houses, the thrum of life that had made his own veins quicken with excitement. But swallowed up by the dark, he felt cowed by the sinister shape of the house looming ahead of him.

The Maison d'Esprit.

In his youth, like so many others in the city, he had crept past, making the sign of the cross. Even then, the house had had an evil reputation as a place where witches had once dwelled, the curse ready to fall upon anyone who entered there. And in those days, Martin had had a great dread of anything dealing with the supernatural.

He could see that the house was in better condition than it had been then. The windows were repaired, the breaks in the wall mortared over, but to him the place still held a sinister brooding aspect, carrying him back to the night so long ago when he had first stood outside here with his Captain Remy, warning the man that this was a place best avoided. A warning he now wished they'd all taken heed of. Especially Gabrielle Cheney. Then they would have known nothing of Cassandra Lascelles. She would have played no part in their lives.

Peering through the iron gates, Martin thought the house still looked like a place of ghosts, curses, and secrets. And now one of those secrets might very well be his, if Carole Moreau had been telling the truth. He still hoped somehow to find out that the girl had been hysterical or was wildly mistaken about this Silver Rose only being a little girl, the witch's child. And very possibly his. One night. One time. That's all Martin had lain with the woman. Surely that wouldn't have been enough. But he knew better.

Carole had described this child to him as being remarkable, almost an angel, but the things that she had told him about this Meg chilled him; that she had actually brought a child back from the dead, that she had eyes that seemed like they could reach right inside of you and touch your heart. Mon Dieu, that sounded far more like a witch to Martin than any angel.

As he leaned outside the gate staring in, he knew he'd never rest until he knew the truth. Perhaps he had been rash to take off from the farm that way, only leaving word with the boy, Yves, but he hoped that he would somehow make it back there before morning. In any case, he thought bitterly, reflecting on his last sight of Miri, locked in Aristide's embrace, he wondered if she would even notice he was gone.

Perhaps it was just as well they were preoccupied. He wasn't eager for either Aristide or Miri to learn his shameful secret. Martin had never told anyone about the night he had been seduced by a witch. His very flesh had felt tainted by the contact with the woman. He remembered kneeling on the pavement retching his guts out afterward, feeling as though he was somehow cursed, tainted for all time.

If it did turn out to be true, may God help him; he wondered how Miri would react to finding out that *he* was the father of this Silver Rose, this devil child. It might even be enough that she might turn away from him. But she already seemed lost to him, and entertaining such bleak thoughts when he was alone in the dark, contemplating doing something as dangerous as setting out to spy on a witches' coven, did nothing to bolster his courage.

He told himself the most prudent and sensible thing to do was to return to the inn where he had stabled his horse, see if he could find some of his old cronies from his street thief days and perhaps approach the house by the light of day. Even then, Martin thought, what was he going to do? Just march boldly up to the door, knock, and say, "Excuse me, any chance that a dreaded witch lives here that I might have gotten pregnant ten years ago?" No, his only course was to go over that wall himself. And as for being prudent and sensible? Martin shrugged. Well, he hadn't been particularly prudent in any time during the past twenty-eight years of his life. Why start now?

Taking one more nervous glance at the house before his courage failed him, he edged close to the stone wall. The surface was rough enough that he was able to get foot- and toeholds, and he scrambled over quickly. He had changed his brighter garb for a doublet of black velvet and trousers that helped him blend in better with the night. As he landed in the garden, he tensed, looking about him for any sign that anyone might have spied him coming over. He remembered that at one time the witch had kept a fearsome dog, but from what young Carole Moreau had told him, there had been no dog, just a houseful of witches. But the grounds seemed quiet.

Where there had once been weeds and moss-blanketed fountains, he now saw well-tended beds of roses. There was something all the more disturbing about the contrast of all that innocent beauty and the brooding house that towered above him. The place looked entirely dark. He crouched down a moment, uncertain what to do next, when he heard sounds that seemed to come from the back of the house. Creeping carefully through the shrubbery, he made his way around to where he could see light spilling through the windows.

One of them had been left open a crack, to draw in the breeze that the recent rain had brought. Crouching down, Martin made his way there stealthily, so that he was just able to peer into the window. He found himself looking into the kitchen of the great house.

It was lit by candlelight and at least three of the witches were there. He could only see one clearly, a small, dark, elfin-looking woman. There was another, scrawnier one whose back was turned to him. These two were pouring out glasses of wine and gleefully engaging in some sort of toast. A third also stood nearby, holding a cup of wine, but she looked strangely out of place with her beautiful silk gown with her farthingale. A petite blonde, she wore one of those court masks that women used to shield their complexions. Strange that she seemed reluctant to remove it even indoors, continuing to shield her identity.

The other two witches paused in their toasting to peer into some cauldron that simmered over the hearth, and Martin sniffed, crinkling his nose. Whatever they were brewing, he was damned sure it wasn't any stew. A rather foul, pungent odor emanated from the pot, drifting out the window.

The smaller of the two, the elfin one, said, "Do you think it's supposed to look like that?"

The scrawny wench with the dirty hair said, "How would I know? It's not like I've ever brewed up a miasma before."

Martin stiffened. Miasma. He had heard that disturbing term before. It was the potent magic that the Dark Queen had supposedly loosed on Paris to induce the terrible madness of the St. Bartholomew's Day massacre. Mon Dieu, were these wretched witches plotting another such bloodbath?

The scrawny wench reached in with a poker. "It seems to be hardening against the pot. That can't be right."

"According to the Silver Rose, that's what it's supposed to do," the elfin one replied. "After it hardens, then we can grind it into a powder. It will become a dust and then when it's breathed in—"

"The Dark Queen will run mad." The scrawny witch giggled. She sounded more than a little drunk. "She'll destroy the duc de Guise."

"Then the citizens of Paris will turn on her and her son, and that will be the end of the House of Valois," the elfin one cried. "Oh, I wish I might be the one chosen to deliver the miasma to the queen."

"The Lady will not entrust such an important task to anyone. She means to do it herself. However, as her long-time servant and friend, she will allow *me* to accompany her," the scrawny one boasted. She raised her glass. "Here's to the coming of revolution!"

"And the rise of our Silver Rose."

The two clicked their glasses together and then they turned to the third one.

"Mademoiselle Harcourt, why do you not join us in our rejoicing?"

The woman smiled wanly, but she didn't offer to clink her glass against theirs. Instead she took a quiet sip. "I won't be able to rejoice or feel easy until the deed is actually done."

For the first time, the scrawny creature turned around

and Martin got a good look at her face. Memory stirred in him and his heart sank. He knew the woman. What was her name? Francine? Fabrianna? No. Finette. That was it. She had been Cassandra Lascelles's maid all those years ago. Martin had gotten one of his friends to seduce and distract her so that Martin had been able to steal into the chamber where Cassandra had waited for Remy.

He shrank back a little, knowing that where Finette was, her mistress would not be far behind. But he'd come too far, and he had to find out what these damned witches were up to and he needed to find out about the Silver Rose. Could the little girl actually be in on this horrible plotting?

As Gillian Harcourt sipped her wine, refusing to join in the other two's gleeful celebration, Finette gave a sniff. "Humph. Looks like milady of the court is above our company, Odile."

Gillian retorted, "No. Milady has just learned to be really cautious. I'm the one who's been in servitude to the Dark Queen all these years. I know much more about how dangerous she is than the rest of you do."

"Oh, yes. Poor thing," Finette sneered. "What a terrible life she's had, living all pampered in the palace and seducing all those handsome men at the Dark Queen's command." Finette lasciviously licked her lips.

But the one who had been referred to as Odile looked more sympathetic. "I can't think that it would be all that pleasant a life."

Gillian shrugged her shoulders. "It was, sometimes. But, yes, I've always been very much at the Dark Queen's disposal. I had to seduce whoever she commanded me to."

Finette scowled. "I even heard tell that you were the mistress of that witch-hunter for a while."

What? Martin tensed.

"Yes. For a time. But that is why I am also nervous about Simon Aristide. You can't discount him either."

"Oh, I assure you," Odile smiled, "he is being taken care of this time. The Lady sent Ursula and Nanette after him, and Ursula might not be good at some things but she is great at killing."

"I hope you are right," Gillian said, "because I haven't slept easy since I realized that Simon Aristide and the Dark Queen are working together. The Dark Queen gave him complete authority to do whatever he pleases. Which means if he discovers where we are, we would all be at his mercy. And I can tell you now that the man has none."

Martin's breath hitched in sharply. He had to clap his hand over his mouth to smother his outraged oath. So Simon was in league with the Dark Queen after all. He'd almost started to listen to Miri after the man had saved his life. He'd begun to change his mind about Aristide, but once more, as usual, the bastard was betraying Miri's trust and she was going to be hurt by him. And in more ways than one.

If this woman was telling the truth, and she had been Aristide's mistress . . . Martin took a step back from the window, torn between wanting to uncover the truth about the Silver Rose and wanting to get back to Miri. He had left her alone with that bastard Aristide. But before he could decide what to do a twig snapped behind him. He whirled around, but it was too late. He found himself facing the point of a drawn sword wielded by a small, fierce-looking woman. The tip rested at his throat.

"Don't move," the creature hissed fiercely, "or I'll run this straight through your throat, splattering your blood everywhere, all over the windows."

Another voice echoed out of the darkness. "And that will make me mighty unhappy since I was the one who had to wash them the other day."

Martin raised his hands, saying, "Forgive me. I wouldn't want to put any of you ladies to great inconvenience. I realize my appearance here must occasion some alarm." His gaze darted between the two as he spoke, trying to judge his chances of whipping away from them and getting to his own blade, but before he could react, a third appeared and seized hold of his arms.

He could hardly make out their forms in the darkness except for the fanatical, almost ratlike gleam of their eyes. But he could tell they were all armed to the teeth with swords and knives. Why couldn't the woman have still been guarded by a dog? He would have much preferred a dog to these half-mad creatures.

He tried to summon up a charming smile. "Ladies, I realize how bad this must look, but I assure you I have merely—I was looking for the house of Pierre Tournelles. I believe I must have the wrong place."

The one who had accosted him first flashed her teeth in a gleaming smile. "Well, as long as you are here, monsieur, you might as well come inside and join the party."

Martin's arrival brought the revelry in the kitchen to an abrupt end. He found himself thrust into a chair, his hands

tied behind his back, his feet bound together. Silently cursing his own stupidity, he hoped that word never got out that
Martin le Loup, one of Navarre's cleverest agents, had allowed himself to be captured by a pack of women. Though,
if he didn't keep his wits about him, he thought, neither
word nor anything else about him would ever be heard
from again.

He noted that the court beauty, the witch-hunter's erst-
while mistress, had nervously taken her leave as soon as he
had been dragged inside. Besides the one fierce guard who
had first attacked him, the only two who were left were the
elfin woman who was called Odile and Finette, Cassandra
Lascelles's maid, who had never had a pleasant odor. It was
worse now that she was reeking of whiskey. She paraded
around Martin, trailing her dirty fingers over his face.

"So, we have captured a spy. What do you suppose we
should do with him?"

"Cut out his eyes," the guard offered.

"Or perhaps we should lop off his ballocks," Odile
suggested.

Martin did his best not to cringe. "Ladies, I fear I am
attached to both those parts of my body. I'd hoped that we
could be a little more reasonable about this. That you might
have a little mercy." He sighed. "I've been having a pretty
rotten day. Well, if you want to know the truth, the entire
week hasn't been that great. Actually, come to think of it,
the whole year has been pretty miserable."

Finette gave a shrill laugh. "Not as miserable as things
are going to get for you, monsieur."

The sour-faced little guard suggested, "I think maybe
it's his tongue that ought to be cut out."

To Martin's dismay, Finette straddled his lap, saying, as she stroked back his hair. "Oh, I think that would be a waste of a fine tongue and a fine pair of ballocks. Perhaps I will take him for my plaything."

Martin leaned back in the chair as far as he could, shuddering, thinking he would rather part with both his tongue and his ballocks before that ever happened. "Ladies, please, I assure you, this has all been a mistake . . ."

"And you are the one who made it." The icy voice seemed to come out of nowhere, chilling Martin's blood. Finette scrambled off his lap. Sucking in his breath, Martin braced himself, turning toward the figure silhouetted in the doorway, her white hands clasped on her walking stick.

His heart almost stopped at the sight of Cassandra Lascelles. Her thin face was still framed by that heavy mass of ebony hair, although there were now streaks of silver in it. And there were still the same dead eyes, the same cruel mouth, though she had aged considerably in ten years, and that terrible seductive beauty that she'd once had was gone, leaving in its wake only the cruelty.

As she stumped forward, groping her way toward him, Martin hitched in his breath, feeling his mouth go dry. He shrank back as she reached out to touch his face, her fingers drifting like trickles of ice across his brow.

Her hand trembled, what little color she had leaching from her cheeks. "By the very devil, it is *you*. When I heard your voice, I thought I was dreaming."

"Your pardon, madame, but I don't believe we've ever met before," Martin sought desperately to disclaim, but he was silenced as her fingers moved over his mouth.

"Did you imagine I would ever forget that voice of

yours? So silken, so persuasive, it has haunted my nights these past ten years." She pressed her fingertips harder against his lips and a chill spread through Martin, a strange disturbing sensation. He remembered that the witch was reputed to have the ability to draw out one's thoughts merely by her touch.

Martin struggled to render his mind a blank. But he could tell it was already too late. Cassandra's mouth thinned in a smile of cold anger and triumph. She leaned in closer, her breath reeking of brandy. Obviously she had been sharing in the celebrations, but she had only had enough to make her a little unsteady on her feet.

"Well, my bold lover, after all these years, you magically appear at my hearth once again. It seems that the fates have finally decided to smile upon me."

"I am glad they are smiling on somebody," Martin muttered, "All I seem to be getting from them is another kick in the arse."

Cass chortled, stroking his brow with a terrible gentleness. "You cannot imagine how long I have desired this reunion. You disappeared so quickly after our one night of passion."

Martin moistened his lips. "Ah, well, forgive me. I always meant to call the next day, drop by with sweetmeats and flowers, but I wasn't sure of my reception."

"I think you know perfectly well what your reception would have been. I would have cut out your heart and eaten it."

"That would be a shame. My heart is really tough. I'm sure you could find far better cuisine in a city the likes of Paris."

He sucked in his breath as her hand moved down his throat, her nails lightly scoring his skin.

"My lone wolf," she murmured. "Do you know how much of these past ten years I have spent thinking of you?"

Martin averted his head, trying to avoid her fetid, brandy-soaked breath.

"I—I'm flattered, madame, that I should have been of such importance."

"Oh, yes. You certainly were. I have given much, much thought to what I would do if I were ever so fortunate as to get my hands upon you again."

Martin grimaced. That's exactly what he'd been afraid of. "You spent all that time thinking of me? Time you surely could have put to a better use."

He clenched his jaw as she began to undo the lacing of his doublet, but at that moment, a small voice piped up.

"Maman?"

Cassandra froze, as did all the other women in the room, Odile and the guard sank into deep curtsies, but Finette whipped around, exclaiming, "Megaera, what are you doing out of bed?"

The little voice replied. "I couldn't sleep. I-I had a bad dream. I've been worried about Carole. Is—is she back yet, Maman?"

Finette started toward the girl. "You don't need to be worried about her, Your Majesty. You need to get back to your bed."

But Cassandra straightened, her lips setting grimly. "No. Bring the child here."

As Finette obeyed, Martin's heart thumped far harder than it had when he'd been threatened by the witches.

He waited, holding his breath as a diminutive figure came closer.

She was such a tiny little thing. For a moment he desperately thought she couldn't be nine years old. She had to be younger than that. She couldn't be his daughter. He looked at the thin little creature with her angular face and her dull brown hair. Her most striking feature was her green eyes, and when they spied Martin in the chair they went wide. She hung back timidly until her mother touched the terrible medallion about her neck and turned.

"Come here, child. You've plagued me long enough with your questions about your father. I've always told you that he was the devil. It turns out I was wrong about that. It seems you were sired by a wolf. Come here, Megaera, and make your curtsy to your dear papa."

THE BREEZE DRIFTED in through the window of Simon's bedchamber, carrying with it the soft rustling sounds of the trees outside, the sweet scent of flowers and herbs from the garden, the plaintive call of a nightingale. Simon and Miri faced each other just as they had that night when they had first met amidst the standing stones. But instead of being surrounded by torchlight and the bonfire, there was nothing but the soft glow of the candles and the aching vulnerability in Simon Aristide's face.

A face far more world-weary than that of the beautiful boy Miri remembered. A warrior's visage, hewn by quests that all but vanquished him, dragons that almost slew him, darkness that almost claimed him.

But in the stable where he'd wrestled the devil for his soul, he'd won. This night. This moment. Miri could feel how desperately he wanted her, feel the wonder in him, the dread.

His voice echoed in her memory, as he huddled near the pond, the witch blade that had saved Elle's life cradled in his hands. *Have I ever gotten anything right?*

She knew he didn't want this—their making love—to be one more mistake. Something she would regret.

"Simon? Can I tell you a secret?" She reached up, trailing her fingers along his scarred face.

He sucked in his breath, as if that single scrap of gentleness undid him. His eye drifted shut at her touch, the lashes of his undamaged eye sooty dark, richly curling on his unmarred cheek. "You can tell me anything, lady."

"I think I've been waiting for this forever. From the first moment I saw you, I—"

"You were barely a child then."

"I didn't say I knew what to do with you then. But all those nights, alone in my cottage in the woods, there were times I couldn't help but imagine . . . I didn't dare admit to myself that it was you in my dreams. A dark lover, who wasn't afraid . . ."

"But I am. Afraid I'll hurt you. Afraid I'll fail you. Afraid . . . you deserve someone perfect to bed you, Miri. Someone whole, with a clean heart to offer you. There's still so much between us. I can't see how—"

"I want you," she cut in, gazing into his eye. "Only you."

"Then God help you. I'm not strong enough to walk away."

Gently she slipped her fingers beneath his eye patch, not wanting anything, especially that piece of leather he'd hidden behind so long, to stay between them.

She'd seen him without it before. Removed it, when she'd known it chafed him. But this time, it was different, so much different. A tangible acceptance of scars they had dealt each other, a tender absolution.

She pressed her mouth to the twisted flesh, her own eyes drifting shut, her whole body alive with wonder, need.

Courage. He'd shown so much courage, daring to come to her, letting down the walls that he'd battled to keep between them for so long.

She unlaced his doublet, slid her palms beneath his linen shirt. Burrowing between cloth and his warm skin.

Simon groaned as her fingers traced the planes of his chest, and Miri gloried in his response as he pulled away, ripping the garment over his head, impatient to be free. "I need to touch you . . . need to see you . . ."

He undid her clothing with hands that trembled, this man, so fearless, so strong. Powerful fingers that had comforted a simple boy, soothed a pain-wracked horse, and challenged hate-filled mobs to protect the innocent now peeled away layer upon layer of Miri's gown, unfolding the cloth from her body like the petals of a flower until she stood, pale, still, naked before his hungry gaze.

She had never felt shame in her body. Yet, as Simon gazed at her she felt a glow of something new, something different, a womanly surge of pride that she could bring such heated pleasure to the man she loved.

Simon skimmed his sword-toughened palms down the slope of her shoulders, the curve of her hip, trailed his fingertips along the slope of her breast, setting her afire with a heat she'd never known, his mouth finding the hollow of her throat, kissing her as he scooped her up in his arms to carry her to the bed.

The bed too wide for a solitary man. The bed that whispered of dreams Miri doubted Simon Aristide had ever acknowledged, even to himself on the dark nights he spent alone.

He drifted her back, atop the coverlets, following her down, his big body atop hers, the weight delicious, the contrast of his hardness against her softness leaving Miri breathless.

A daughter of the earth, she'd been nurtured on the balance of nature, had been so certain she understood the dance of male and female, the pull of sun to moon, sea to shore, sky to earth.

But as Simon's mouth took hers in a hungry kiss, his hands learning every dip and curve of her body, his hips settling, heavy against her as she opened her thighs, she knew she'd understood nothing at all of the magic that was making love.

Making love . . .

For that was what Simon was doing to her. Infusing every fiber of her being with the passion he'd denied for so long, telling her with his hands, his mouth, how hungry he'd been, starving for the taste of her, the feel of her, the welcome her body could give to his.

Miri gasped as Simon's mouth closed over hers, his tongue tracing the crease of her lips, begging entry. She opened herself to him eagerly, letting him inside. Simon groaned, arching against her, and she felt the hard ridge of his erection.

She smoothed her hands down the broad expanse of his back, trying to get closer, reach deeper into places in his heart he'd withheld from her so long. She caught his bottom lip between her teeth, teasing him with womanly instinct old as the first daughter of the earth who'd given her body in the shadow of the standing stones. Rites of fertility, affirming life, the earth renewing itself.

Simon kissed his way down her throat, her breast, his breath hot, his lips moist and unbearably sensual as they closed over Miri's nipple. She cried out as he suckled her with fierce tenderness, drawing from her every last sensation, until her whole body cried out with longing only he could satisfy.

"Simon . . ." Miri gasped. "Simon, please . . ."

He sealed her mouth with his kiss, driving himself deep.

Pain drew a cry from Miri as he pierced her maidenhead, but she laughed, a sound that startled Simon. Made him hesitate. He drew back, looking down into her eyes.

"Are you all right?"

"I'm just—just so glad that it's gone . . ." she said, smiling up into his eyes. "You made me wait . . . a long time . . . Simon Aristide."

"I'll make this night worth it, Miri. If it's in my power . . ."

He set himself against her in a rhythm that surged like the power of the sea around Faire Isle, a pulse of life that she'd felt in the earth, but never understood until now. The pulse Simon confessed he'd felt when he'd lain on the ground as a boy.

It beat against Miri's heart, her head tossing, cries wrung from her throat as Simon brought her to wonder and surrendered to his release as well.

A magic as old as time. But new. Unbearably new as Simon and Miri claimed it for their own.

Chapter Twenty

THE DARKNESS WAS SO HEAVY AND UNRELENTING IT SEEMED to press against Martin's eyes. He could feel the dank cold of the stone wall pressing against his back where he was chained, and he pulled on his manacles, gritting his teeth in frustration as he tried to wrench them out of the wall.

He knew he was locked up in some hidden underground chamber beneath the house. From what little he'd been able to see before the witches had left him chained in darkness, the walls looked old and crumbling, ready to fall down at any moment. Except, of course, the one to which they'd chained him. And that seemed as solid as a marble pillar.

He'd flexed his muscles and yanked until his wrists

were raw, but to no avail. He leaned back, panting, adjuring himself not to panic. "You've been in worse situations, Martin le Loup," he muttered. Unfortunately at the moment he was unable to recall when.

He was chained up and at the mercy of a mad sorceress who'd had ten years to plot her revenge. He'd stolen away from the farm, leaving Miri with that witch-hunter who was once again betraying her trust. And the only one with any idea at all of where he'd gone was Yves, but the boy had been so entranced with the feathered cap Martin had presented him with for helping with his horse, he might not remember much else.

It was difficult to contrive any notions of escape when he couldn't even see his own hands to tell if he'd made any progress at all in working himself free. If he had the light of even one candle stub . . .

He should have heeded his old friend Pierre, who had often warned Martin to be careful what he wished for. For at that moment the door at the top of the stairs creaked and a flickering light appeared. It was hard to rejoice at the approach of a candle when you had no idea what sort of torture might follow in its wake.

Martin tensed, squinting as the approaching light sent shadows flickering up against the walls. He heard a soft footfall of someone creeping stealthily down the stairs. He braced himself for God knows what, completely unprepared for the flash of dainty white nightgown and the tiny bare foot.

It was the witch's child. He still couldn't accept the fact that she might also be his. He'd gotten only a fleeting glimpse of her before she'd fled the kitchen after Cassandra had named him her father. She'd seemed a wild, strange little thing with wide, haunting green eyes.

She'd appeared both awed and afraid of him. He was rather surprised that she'd ventured down here alone to confront him. Equally surprised how his own heart thudded at her approach. When she reached the foot of the stairs, she froze for a moment, candle in hand. He squinted at the glow of light after the total darkness.

Once his eyes had adjusted, he watched as she set the candle down on a rough wooden table. The taper's glow haloed her solemn, thin little face. But her hair didn't look as unkempt as it had been before. In fact, it looked as though she had been at some pains to brush it and tie it back with a pink ribbon.

She came closer, her waif-like eyes fixing him with that unnerving stare. She just stood there for a long moment, saying nothing. And for once in his life, Martin, usually so glib with any female who crossed his path, couldn't think of a single thing to say to this tiny being who might well be his own daughter.

At last she clutched the ends of her nightgown and dipped down into a quaint little curtsy. "Good—good evening, Monsieur Wolf," she stammered.

Nonplussed, Martin said, "Good evening, um, Mademoiselle Silver Rose."

A small frown furrowed her brow. "My name is Meg," she said.

"A peculiar name for a Frenchwoman, if you'll pardon me for saying so."

She perched on one foot, rubbing her bare toes about her opposite ankle. "Well, my name is really Megaera. But that's not much better. Maman says I was named for an avenging fury, a goddess with snakes for hair. I don't really like snakes," she confided.

"I'm not terribly fond of them, either," Martin admitted. His remark earned a slight hint of a smile on that face that seemed all too serious for a child.

She ventured to come closer. "Is it true? Are you really my papa?"

"So your mother would have me believe."

"But . . . you don't want to believe it." Her small shoulders heaved with a crestfallen sigh. "I don't blame you. It's hard for me to believe it too."

"Why?" Martin asked.

She reached out to timidly touch the sleeve of his velvet doublet. "Because you're beautiful and I'm ugly. I'm thin and scrawny and my hair is the color of mice. I went upstairs and tried to brush it, make myself a little pretty, but it didn't help."

Martin was moved by her forlorn expression in spite of himself. "No, you're quite wrong. Your ribbon is—is very fetching. And your hair is not the color of mice. It reminds me more of cinnamon and as for being thin, I was rather scrawny myself at your age, but I grew."

Perhaps it was less than wise to draw such a comparison, say anything to encourage this child to think she might belong to him. And yet, the sadness in her eyes tugged at his heart. When his words elicited a quavery smile from her, he found himself smiling back in return.

"Sometimes I wish I could conjure up a spell that would make me grow faster, make me prettier. But I don't really like magic. It frightens me."

Martin regarded her in surprise. "But I thought you were planning to become a fearsome sorceress, rule over all France."

Meg shook her head sadly. "That's Maman's dream. Not mine. I don't want to be the Silver Rose."

"What would you like to be?"

She cocked her head to one side. "A beautiful lady who can dance and play the lute. But right now, I would just like to belong to someone. Be their little girl." She looked up at him so hopefully that Martin squirmed, his chains rattling.

"Ahem, you do belong to someone. Your mother."

The child's bottom lip quivered. "No. I'm only her Silver Rose. Her dream. Her ambition. I've never been just her child." She stole a bashful peek at him from beneath her lashes. They were remarkably dark and thick, framing her deep green eyes. "I've dreamed about you for a long time," she said.

"You have?"

"Maman doesn't like it when I daydream. But I've often thought about who my papa was and wondered, imagining that you might be a handsome prince who rides a great white horse."

"Well," Martin said ruefully, "I have a horse, but I'm afraid there the resemblance ends. It's no good, your dreaming about me, child. You'll only be disappointed. I'm afraid the angels weren't particularly kind when they gifted you with parents. A witch for a mother, and me . . . I am little more than a shiftless adventurer. I'm afraid I wouldn't make much of a father."

He tugged on his chains, displaying his manacles. "And, as you can see, my current prospects are severely limited."

She dared to come closer still. When she touched the place on his wrist where he'd abraded the skin in his struggles, her eyes welled with tears. "You must have made my maman very angry. That's not a good thing to do, monsieur."

Martin sighed. "I'm painfully aware of that, child. But it's kind of you to warn me."

"When she's really angry, she makes people disappear." She blinked back her tears, attempting to smile. "Except, if I'm going to save you, I have to be the one to make you go away." She swallowed hard. "Even if I never see you again."

"No, mademoiselle . . . Meg . . . if—if you can find a way to get me out of here, I'll take you with me." Martin blinked twice, astonished by the rash words that fell from his lips. He'd barely set eyes on this child more than an hour or two ago, and yet he already felt some inexplicable kinship with her. Or maybe it was just one of his usual impulsive urges to rescue another damsel in distress, albeit a very young one.

Her face brightened at his promise, only to cloud over immediately after. "I wish I could go with you, but I can't. Maman would never let me. You—you see . . . ." She delved into her nightgown, dragging forth a silver chain from which a medallion winked evilly.

Martin stared in horror, scarce able to believe that even Cassandra Lascelles could be evil enough to curse her own child with such a hellish burden.

"Mon Dieu," he said. "Why would your mother give you such a devil's charm?"

Meg's fingers trembled as she touched the medallion. "Maman uses it to keep us linked together and—and sometimes to punish me when I don't do what she tells me."

Despite the child's obvious fear of her mother, Meg's small chin lifted with a hint of defiance. An unexpected spark of mischief crept into her eyes. She leaned closer to Martin, whispering. "May I tell you a great secret, monsieur?"

Still reeling from his shock over the medallion, Martin managed to nod.

"And if I tell you, you swear not to tell anyone? Especially Maman?"

"I swear—" Martin started to cross his heart, but his hand couldn't reach that far. "Your secret will be safe with me, ma petite. She shan't wring it out of me, even if she threatens to . . ." Martin almost said "put out my eyes and cut off my ballocks," but he remembered just in time who he was talking to. "Even if she threatens to feed me to the most ferocious of dragons."

An unexpected giggle erupted from Meg. For a moment, her pale face and those far-too-old eyes were transformed. Martin realized the little girl had likely not laughed often enough. If she truly had been his child, he would have made sure her eyes often sparkled with merriment. That she had pink ribbons and trinkets aplenty to help make her feel pretty. Instead of that damnable medallion, a locket of purest gold. Martin checked himself, astonished and dismayed by his imaginings.

He had a tendency to stray into daydreams as heedlessly as his daughter . . .

His daughter. The words stirred a strange, poignant ache in his heart. The little girl leaned closer, her lips cupped close to his ear. She whispered. "The medallion helps Maman keep track of me, but I've learned how to fool her sometimes. I use my imagination and pretend that I'm hiding in a great . . ." The child suddenly reared back, giving a sharp gasp. She grabbed at the medallion, her face going white.

"Meg, what is it? What's wrong?" Martin asked urgently.

She stumbled back from him, her eyes widening in fear. "Maman, I—I wasn't pretending hard enough. She—she knows where I am and she's angry."

"For mercy's sake, child, grab the candle! Get out of here! Go hide!"

"It's—it's too late," she quavered.

Martin heard the door at the top of the stairs being wrenched open, the hinges screeching. Then the dread tap of the cane as Cassandra Lascelles began to descend into the underground chamber.

Meg stood, frozen in fear like a fawn caught in the sights of a crossbow. Martin grated his teeth, yanking at his chains, his every impulse to leap in front of the little girl, shield her. But all he could do was watch, helpless as Cassandra descended upon her daughter like the fury Meg had been named for.

The witch's sightless eyes seemed to hone straight in

on the cowering child. "What are you doing down here, Megaera?"

The child moistened her lips. "I—I just wanted another look at Monsieur Wolf."

"Are you sure you didn't come down here with some notion of springing Monsieur Wolf from his trap?"

"N-no."

"You little liar!" Cassandra hissed. Her hand closed, white-knuckled, over her own medallion and Meg gave a horrible cry.

She sank down to her knees, tears spilling down her cheeks while Wolf roared. "What the hell are you doing to her? Stop it!" He gave another savage wrench at his bonds. "If you want to torment somebody, why don't you pick on someone more your size? Me!"

"You'll get your turn soon enough, my lone wolf." Cassandra's lips snaked back in a cold smile. "Right now I have to teach my daughter a lesson in loyalty."

Meg doubled over, gasping and clutching her stomach. "Maman, please don't! Make it stop! I—I'm sorry!"

Martin bared his teeth, a fury coursing through him more feral and primitive than he'd ever known. If he had been a wolf, he would have ripped out the woman's throat. Meg's sobs tore through him, her pain piercing him worse than any pain of his own he'd ever felt. The witch's terrible punishment seemed to go on forever, until she finally released the medallion.

Meg lay prone on the rough stone floor, her small shoulders heaving. Martin ached to gather her up in his arms. All he could do was glare up at the witch and curse her.

"God damn you to hell! What kind of mother are you to do such a thing to your own child?"

"The one who is going to make a queen out of her despite all the bad blood she inherited from you."

Groping down until she found the child, Cassandra seized Meg roughly by the arm and hauled her to her feet. "There's no time for this sniveling, Megaera. You must come upstairs and get dressed. The miasma you translated is ready, and we have an audience with the Dark Queen."

The child whimpered. "But I don't want to go."

But Cassandra replied coldly. "It is high time that you saw what it takes to seize power. Learn to be ruthless enough to destroy all who stand in your way."

"For the love of God, woman, she's only a little girl!" Martin protested. "Do you know what horrors were visited upon Paris the last time a miasma was released? The entire city was plunged into madness and savagery that lasted for days."

"That is exactly what I have in mind."

"And what if the miasma consumes you as well? The slightest shift in wind—"

"Thank you for your concern," Cassandra interrupted with a sneer. "But my clever daughter has devised an antidote to protect me. I shall not be driven mad."

"You are *already* insane," Martin snapped. "Do you think the Dark Queen is a fool? Why would she even grant you an audience?"

"Because I have something she wants," Cassandra purred. "The *Book of Shadows*."

"You mean to offer her that terrible book?"

"Of course not, you fool. I have had a book fashioned that will look very like an ancient grimoire. The pages will even be a little . . . *dust* coated." She smirked. "The Dark Queen will not realize she has been tricked until it is too late. As for any suspicions Her Majesty might harbor, they will be lulled. How could it be otherwise when the book is presented to her by an innocent little girl?"

Cassandra draped her arm possessively across Meg's shoulders. The child shuddered, looking sick with apprehension.

Martin strained at his bonds, suppressing a savage oath. "This scheme of yours is pure lunacy. At least leave Meg out of it. If you fail, do you know what the Dark Queen will do to her?"

"Then we'd better not fail, had we, Megaera?"

The child trembled, looking stricken as she yanked free of her mother and cast herself at Martin, her wet cheek pressed close to his. Clutching at his hand, clinging to him for dear life.

"Meg," he rasped in her ear. "Don't be afraid. I'll—I'll get loose. I'll come—I'll save you somehow."

But the witch's hands had already closed over the little girl again, hauling her away.

"Damn it, Cassandra!" Martin snarled. "You can't make her do this!"

The witch gave a mocking laugh, tapping her medallion. "I can make her do anything I want, including kill you. But that's a pleasure I reserve for myself."

Her hand clamped down on Meg's arm, the woman groped her way back toward the stairs. Meg cast him one last glance, as though seeking to memorize his face before she was dragged up into darkness. The door slammed behind the two of them with a dull thud. But Meg's candle continued to burn bright enough for Martin to be able to inspect the metal object the child had thrust into his hand under Cassandra's very nose.

It was a small, sturdy hairpin.

Despite the grimness of the situation, Martin smiled. With fingers that nimble and a mind that clever and bold, Meg was undoubtedly his daughter after all.

*

ALL THE CANDLES had guttered out save one, its soft light playing over the naked planes and angles of Simon's body. Miri snuggled, drowsy and sated in his arms, but she was reluctant to surrender to sleep. She'd waited too long for this night, and now that it was here she wished it could last forever.

The peace she felt was deeper than any she'd ever known. She only wished she could be as certain Simon shared her feelings. He'd ever been a man of few words, and their lovemaking seemed to have even stolen those. He lay silent, his fingers twined in her hair, as her cheek rested against his chest, marking the rhythm of his heart.

But when she raised her head to smile tenderly up at him, his features were so grave it cast a shadow on the afterglow of happiness that had lain over her since he'd claimed her.

"Simon?" She faltered. "You—you aren't having any regrets?"

"Lord, no." He brought her hand tenderly to his lips. "But I'm afraid you well might."

When she tried to protest, he laid his fingertips gently against her mouth. "I feel like I've been damned irresponsible, taking you this way. Giving in to my own needs."

"My needs as well, Simon," she insisted.

"It's only that I've spent this past year haunted by what happens to young women when they're caught in the desperate situation of having an unwanted babe out of wedlock. If I've gotten you with child, Miri—"

"Would our babe be unwanted?" Miri asked wistfully. "Have you never dreamed of having children of your own? A son, perhaps, to teach all the things your father taught you?"

"It's been a long time since I've dared to dream anything."

"That's not what this bedchamber has been telling me."

Teasing, he said, "Are you reading auras again? What is it you've sensed about my house? Something haunted?"

"No." She folded her arms and propped them on his chest, peering up at him. "No. It's more one of waiting for life to begin. This is a large house, Simon. Perfect for a family. You can't tell me that you never thought of that when you built it."

"Perhaps I did," he said, caressing a tendril of hair back from her brow. "I just never believed it could be *my* family."

"And now?"

"I don't know. It's too fresh. It's too new. And there's still too much unsettled. The matter of the Silver Rose. How your family is going to feel about us. And then, about your suitor, le Loup."

The mention of Martin saddened her. He had disappeared from the farm and no one seemed to have any idea when or where he had gone except for Yves. The boy's account of Martin's departure had been jumbled, a confusing tale about an urgent errand and Monsieur Wolf promising to return by morning. Or maybe it was nightfall. Yves had been so crestfallen by his inability to remember, Miri had hated to keep pressing the boy for more details.

As inexplicable as Martin's departure had been, the impulsive action was so like him, Miri was far more grieved than worried by it. Resting her chin atop her hands, she said, "I never wanted to hurt Martin. I'm afraid he might have seen us embracing by the pond, and that's why he left so suddenly. I didn't even get a chance to tell him good-bye."

"I wouldn't fret over that," Simon said dryly. "If I know anything about le Loup, he's not the sort to beat a meek retreat. I predict he'll be back before morning unless he's gone for reinforcements to rescue you from my dastardly clutches. But he'd have a damned long ride to get all the way back to Navarre."

"Or Ireland," Miri said softly.

"Ireland?"

She hesitated only a moment before confiding. "That's where Ariane and Renard have been all these years. Living in a cottage, deep in the Wicklow mountains. It's so beautiful there, Simon."

He stared at her, astonished, and then cupped her cheek tenderly in his palm. "Thank you for trusting me with that."

"I do trust you. Now, if only you could learn to trust yourself."

"Perhaps you could teach me, if only we could stay here. But unfortunately, we can't."

"The Silver Rose." She frowned, recalling what he'd said earlier to Carole. "So you think the sorceress is Cassandra Lascelles?"

"I have no way of knowing for sure until we have a chance to further question Madamoiselle Moreau in the morning. But you must have met the Lascelles woman years ago when your sister mistakenly befriended her. What was your impression?"

"Ice. Evil." Miri's brow furrowed, searching her memory. "She troubled me greatly. I sensed something dark in her, disturbing, but there was one reason more than any other that I didn't trust her."

"And what was that?"

"My cat didn't like her."

He laughed in spite of himself. "As I recall, Necromancer was not real fond of me, either."

"He was the first night we met, when you helped me rescue him." She smiled up at him, her cheek dimpling. "And I think, like me, he might be willing to give you a second chance."

He sobered a moment. "That second chance, Miri. Or third, or fourth . . . I don't want to waste it. There's something I need to tell you."

Miri stilled, her heart giving a small skip of apprehension. "What is it?"

"It's about the night that I went to see the Dark Queen. There was one thing about it I concealed from you. She gave a document into my keeping, giving me full authorization, the power of life or death over the coven of the Silver Rose. It was foolish, wrong of me not to tell you. But I was afraid you would either demand that I destroy it, or it would make you mistrust me all over again." He regarded her anxiously and she could tell how much he still feared that.

"If—if you want me to tear the document up, get rid of it right now, I will."

"No. All I ask is that you wield the power that you've been given wisely."

"I'll try."

"And there's one more boon I'd ask of you."

"Anything in my power to give you."

Miri drove away the shadows the only way she knew, her fingertips trailing lightly down his chest, lower. "Make love to me again, Simon, before the sun comes up. And try . . ."

"Try what?"

"Try hard to remember . . . how to dream . . ."

*

REPLETE FROM SIMON'S LOVING, Miri nestled in his embrace, her eyelids getting heavier as she gave way to sleep at last. But even the strength of Simon's arms around her could not stay her from being pulled into the haunted world of her dreams.

Miri drifted toward the palace, but this time the towering white walls seemed familiar to her, and she could remember having been here before, and not just in her dreams. She was walking across the wide green lawns that bordered the Louvre.

The path led her past a grotto, and she saw the lizards again, but this time they were no more than carvings in the rocky wall. She continued on until she reached a grassy

area that bore signs of having recently hosted a gathering
of ladies enjoying the lazy summer afternoon. Soft stools
and embroidery had been left abandoned, a chess set
perched upon a table, but not the monstrous pieces that
had frightened Miri before. Just ordinary chessmen, the
kind that she could lift in her hand.

She picked up the dark queen. It seemed so small and
harmless, just sitting in her hand. Unlike the shadowy
figure that loomed ahead of her. Miri froze as she saw
Catherine de Medici, the woman garbed in her familiar,
unrelenting black. She was attended by only one of her
ladies, a faded blond woman. As Catherine stared at a
point past Miri, she gripped her hands together tightly, her
expression tense, eager, as though waiting.

Miri turned, following the direction of her gaze. She
saw another tall, dark woman approaching, her skin icy
white, her eyes empty and unseeing. Cassandra Lascelles.
And she was being led by a child, a little girl with soft
brown hair and frightened green eyes. Eyes the deep hue of
a forest that reminded Miri strangely of Martin's eyes.

The child clutched a black, leather-bound book under
one arm. Miri stood poised between the two women, invisible as a ghost. The little girl delivered the book to the Dark
Queen, then shrank away, trembling. But before Catherine
could open the book, Simon erupted out of nowhere.

When he lunged for the book, the Dark Queen let out
a furious screech. A struggle ensued. As Simon wrenched
the book away from her, it fell open, a cloud of dust rising
from the pages.

Simon breathed it in, choking. His knees buckled, giving way beneath him.

Miri's eyes flew open. She jerked upright with a sharp gasp, startling Simon awake. His arms tightened about her as he fixed her with a sleep-blurred gaze.

"Miri, what's wrong?" he mumbled. "Not another nightmare?"

"No, not a nightmare," she cried. "A warning. I know now what my dream means." She tugged at him urgently, trying to rouse him more fully awake. "We've got to go talk to Carole. Question her about the Silver Rose before it's too late."

Chapter Twenty-one

Despite the warmth of the afternoon, Martin drew the broad-brimmed black hat lower over his face, a dark cape swirling off his shoulders. Sweat trickled down his brow, his vision half obscured by the eye patch he wore. The leather irritated his skin and he wondered how Aristide could tolerate wearing such a thing, scaring old ladies and small children be damned.

But as Martin strode toward the gates of the Louvre, he ignored his discomforts, concentrating on scowling and looking as sinister as possible. It was a desperate ploy, trying to pass himself off as the witch-hunter. But on such short notice, he'd had no time to come up with a better scheme for getting himself inside the palace.

It had taken him until morning to pick that blasted lock, and he'd had to waste more precious time before he'd been able to steal out of the underground chamber and flee the Maison d'Esprit unseen.

He didn't know how much time he had to thwart Cassandra and rescue Meg. But it wasn't the first time he'd launched himself blindly into some wild adventure.

Yet, for once, his heart didn't pump with the familiar thrill of fear and excitement. His stomach was knotted with apprehension. Perhaps he had in his lifetime embarked on far more dangerous missions for the king of Navarre, but never had Martin set out on one whose outcome was more important to him.

As he hung back a little, he assessed the guards, trying to guess which one looked dim enough to be fooled by both his disguise and the document he had forged, making it seem he'd been summoned by the Dark Queen.

The one with the thatch of red hair, his stomach straining against his tunic, looked like Martin's best bet. But before he could swagger in the man's direction, a hand suddenly clamped down on his shoulder.

Martin's heart leapt as he was forced about to face the man looming behind him. He looked dead on into Simon Aristide's grim features, but for once the man's face lightened. The bastard actually had the impertinence to smile at him.

"If you're seeking to impersonate me, le Loup, you should at least make sure you get the patch over the right eye."

Martin flushed, a surge of fury tearing through him. He

launched himself at Aristide, going for his throat. But Aristide evaded his grasp, dragging Martin away from the gates, back behind the shelter of a broad tree.

"What the devil do you think you're doing?" Simon demanded.

"Don't you presume to question me, you treacherous bastard!" Martin snarled, struggling to break free, drive his fist into Aristide's jaw. But before he could, Miri appeared, her hair looking windblown, her face streaked with dust from the road.

Martin stopped struggling, not knowing whether he was more dismayed or relieved to see her. "Miri, I don't know what you're doing here, or how you and the witch-hunter found me, but you need to be warned about what I learned last night. This lying bastard here—he's been working with the Dark Queen."

"I know," she replied calmly.

"You know?" Martin's mouth fell open.

"Yes. Simon told me."

"Did he tell you about his mistress as well?"

That at least seemed to ruffle some of Miri's aggravating calm.

"What mistress?" Simon scowled.

"Gillian Harcourt, as if you didn't know!"

"Gillian and I parted company years ago. And what the devil has she got to do with anything?"

"Oh, not much," Martin sneered. "Only that the blasted woman is in league with Cassandra Lascelles, and she's even now helping that sorceress get inside the palace to—"

But Miri interrupted him, turning to Simon. "This Gillian—she must be the blond woman in my dream!"

"Dream? What dream?" Martin demanded. The blasted eye patch was making it necessary for him to shift his head from side to side to be able to take in both Miri and Simon. Impatiently, Martin wrenched both the patch and his hat off. "What's going on here?" He glared at both Miri and Simon. "How did you find me? I want an explanation!"

"You first," Simon said. "Where the blazes did you disappear to last night?"

"Surprised either one of you even noticed I was gone," Martin muttered, causing a bright flood of color to appear on Miri's cheeks.

"I don't have time to get into any explanations now. There's a little girl the witch has dragged into the palace. I have to help her."

"The little girl with the green eyes? Carole told us everything about Meg," Miri said. "We know that she's Cassandra's child. That she's the Silver Rose."

"There's one thing you can't possibly know," Martin stormed defiantly. "She's also my daughter. And she's no evil sorceress. So if this witch-hunter of yours thinks he's going to touch her he's going to have to go through me first. The poor child has been at the mercy of that devil woman. Cassandra's the one who's been forcing her to do all these things." He glared at Simon. "But why do I bother trying to explain such a thing to you? You can't possibly understand what it must be like for her, under the control of a madwoman."

"Perhaps not a mad*woman,*" Simon said softly. "But I can understand her fear and confusion far better than you would think. Still, you're right about one thing. We don't have time to delay. So we can either stand here and engage in another useless bout of fisticuffs or you can trust me to help rescue your child."

****

THE DARK QUEEN PACED along the secluded walk of the gardens. She had bade all her ladies return to the palace save for Gillian. The garden bench bore evidence of the disrupted afternoon. A lute left propped against the wooden seat, the chess game unfinished. Catherine toyed nervously with one of the rooks.

Sometimes she felt as if she'd been playing at chess her entire life, but the consequences of wins and losses were far more deadly than having one's pawns swept from the board. She could hardly believe that the object that she had long sought, the *Book of Shadows,* was about to be delivered into her hands.

She had been astonished when Gillian had approached her with the news that someone from the Silver Rose's coven had come to the palace, and that they were willing to hand it over to her for a sum of money.

The money was a trivial thing. Catherine would have paid any amount to have acquired that book, but after so many years of searching and waiting, the book seemed about to fall into her hands all too easily.

All of her suspicions aroused, she studied her lady-in-waiting. Catherine's eyes might not be what they had once been. But even she could detect Gillian's nervousness, smell the fear in the woman.

Catherine had been too long inured to treachery, the ways of intrigue, not to recognize a traitoress when she saw one. But Catherine was adept at concealing her emotions; not by so much as the flicker of an eyelash did she let Gillian know her suspicions had been aroused.

Gillian would have been far more nervous if she had realized that Catherine had had the forethought to have Ambrose Gautier waiting at a discreet distance, ready to arrest the courtesan at a moment's notice should Catherine's suspicions prove correct, that Gillian was playing her false.

Gillian's hands fluttered to her throat, but she summoned up a nervous smile and said, "Your Grace, I believe the woman whom I told you of has arrived."

Catherine squinted across the lawn to where a tall woman with dark hair approached. Catherine held herself tense, wary as she watched the figure approach. No, two figures. She was astonished to see that the second one was only a child. And the child appeared to be leading the older woman by the hand.

Gillian murmured to Catherine, "Poor Mistress Cassandra is blind, Your Grace. She is completely dependent upon her daughter."

"It intrigues me. How did any woman so helpless ever manage to succeed in getting the *Book of Shadows* away from the Silver Rose? A task even the formidable witch-hunter Aristide failed to accomplish."

"I—I don't know, Your Grace," Gillian's voice faltered. "The woman would explain little to me, but she has the book. Surely you can see the child is carrying it."

Catherine's eyes narrowed. The child was certainly carrying something. But Catherine had allowed herself to be fooled once before. All the same, her heart gave a flutter of hope.

Catherine took an eager step forward, only to check herself. The woman and the child did indeed look harmless enough, but she had not survived this long by taking any unnecessary chances. "I'll pay the woman whatever she asks," Catherine said. "But first, I must examine the book."

Gillian's skirt rustled across the grass as she approached the woman and her daughter. They stood some ten yards away from her, speaking in low voices.

Catherine could not hear what they said, but the blind woman murmured something in her child's ear, then shoved the little girl in Catherine's direction. With the book clutched to her thin chest, the child crept toward Catherine. She was a plain little thing, her most striking feature her large green eyes, which were filled with fear.

Curbing her impatience, Catherine attempted to speak in gentle tones. "Come closer, my dear. There is nothing for you to be afraid of. Just let me see your book."

The little girl halted in front of Catherine, dipping into a trembling curtsy. She hugged the book tighter as though reluctant to surrender it.

"Give me the book, child," Catherine demanded.

Slowly, the little girl extended the book to Catherine. But as Catherine's fingers closed over the small leather-bound text, a dark figure rushed toward Catherine. She was startled to see it was the witch-hunter, Aristide. At the sight of him, the child emitted a terrified cry and fled back to her mother.

"No, Your Grace!" Aristide roared. "Don't touch the book! It's a trick!"

Catherine hesitated for a fraction of a second, but if anything could have convinced her of the book's authenticity it was Aristide turning up to snatch it away from her. She shouted for Gautier, but he was already there, flinging himself in between her and the witch-hunter.

Before Gautier could draw his sword, Aristide felled him with one blow of his fist. When the witch-hunter grabbed for the book, Catherine tightened her grip, refusing to release it.

"How dare you!" she cried. "What do you mean by this outrage?"

"I mean to protect you, woman! Now give me the damned book before—"

Catherine clung to it with all her strength. Aristide yanked it from her hands with such force the book went flying. It crashed to the ground, flung wide open, a choking cloud of dust rising from the fluttering pages.

Too late, Catherine stumbled back, pressing her handkerchief to her nostrils. Her head whirled, webs of darkness dancing before her eyes until she sagged to the ground, oblivion claiming her.

Miri had raced after Simon, tripping over the hem of her skirts. All she could do was watch helplessly as the events of her dreams spun into reality before her eyes. The dust that flew from the book was no miasma, of that much Miri was certain.

Instead of being incited to madness, anyone within range of the book, the Dark Queen, her guard, and Simon, had crumpled to the ground. Simon had managed to fall on the book and close it up. But he had crashed against the bench, the grass around him littered with chess pieces. His brow was gashed open, blood trickling down the side of his face.

Miri flung herself down beside him, feeling frantically

for his pulse. It was thready, but still strong. She glanced toward where the Dark Queen had fallen nearby, one hand outstretched, her handkerchief fluttered to the grass.

Miri snatched it up and wet it in a nearby fountain. She applied the cool cloth to Simon's face, chafing his wrists. To her relief he moaned. His eye fluttered open.

"Miri?" he breathed, his voice thick and slurred. "Wh—what happened?"

"I am not sure," she said. "I think the book only contained some sort of sleeping powder."

Simon's head drooped to one side. "Where—where's Cassandra? The girl?"

Miri, in her concern for Simon, had forgotten all about the sorceress and her daughter. But as her gaze searched wildly around, she saw there was no sign of them or Gillian Harcourt either. And Martin . . . Miri had believed him hard at her heels. But he appeared to have vanished as well.

Simon squeezed Miri's hand, tried to rise, only to sag back weakly. "I'll be all right," he said. "Go . . . go find the child . . ."

꙳꙳꙳

MEG FELT HER MOTHER'S HANDS dig into her arm like claws, dragging her as they half stumbled down the bank toward the bend of river below the palace. There should have been a small boat moored, Finette and Odile waiting to help them make their escape. But Meg saw no sign of anyone. She tried to dig in her heels, protesting, "Maman, there's no boat. I think we are lost. We—we must have come the wrong way. We have to go back."

Cassandra drew up panting, one hand flailing out in front of her in a desperate gesture. "What! Go back where?" she shrilled. "Where is that wretched Harcourt woman? She was supposed to have helped us get away."

"I don't know," Meg sobbed. Gillian had fled at the first sight of the witch-hunter. Perhaps she had reached the river first, warned the others and they had all abandoned Meg and her mother.

Cassandra's nails dug in as she gripped Meg by both shoulders, giving her a ferocious shake. "Damn you! You betrayed me. You betrayed our cause! What was in that potion you translated? It was no miasma, that's for sure!"

"I—I'm not sure," Meg faltered. "I think I made a mistake. It was just some sort of a sleeping draft."

Her mother grated her teeth. "You made no mistake. You did it on purpose, Megaera. Damn you!"

Although Meg trembled, some fierce surge of defiance shot through her. She lifted her chin. "Yes! I did! I did it on purpose! I didn't want anyone to be hurt and I don't want to be queen and *my name is Meg!*"

Her mother dealt her a ringing slap, but at that instant a stern voice called out, "Stop, Cassandra! Let her go!"

Meg's heart fluttered in her chest as she spun about toward the sound and saw *him* coming down the bank. The man she'd never thought to see again, despite what he'd promised her when they parted. But yet he came like a warrior prince with his dark hair and his magnificent clothes, his sword clutched in his hand.

Meg's breath left her in a whisper, the name escaping her that she'd waited all of her life to utter. "Papa!"

But as he bounded toward her, her mother's arm hooked possessively about her shoulders. Cassandra's fingers flew to her medallion, and as Martin drew closer, she said, "Stay back. One step more and I swear I will destroy her. I won't let you or anyone else take my Silver Rose from me."

Meg trembled. She saw her father hesitate, not knowing what to do. And she knew that as brave as he was, there was no way that he could defeat her mother's terrible power. She looked up at him piteously.

"It's all right, Papa. There's nothing you can do. It's enough that you came."

He took another hesitant step forward, only to freeze when Cassandra's hand tightened around the terrible medallion. But at that instant a lady came rushing down the bank wearing a blue gown. A tall lady with a mass of white-blond hair. She drew up short beside Meg's father.

"Martin," the woman said.

He turned to her desperately. "I don't know what to do. Miri, she's got that cursed medallion. The other one is about the child's neck."

Cassandra's hand clamped down on her daughter's shoulder. "Who is that? Whose voice?"

Meg stared up at Miri, saying in hushed accents, "It's a fairy."

Miri came closer, smiling at the little girl. "No, I'm your papa's friend. My name is Miribelle Cheney."

"Miribelle Cheney?" Cassandra snarled. "I remember you. You're Gabrielle's sister. The insignificant one."

But ignoring her, Miri's attention focused on the child.

She knelt down in front of the frightened little girl. "Meg, I want you to listen to me carefully and keep looking into my eyes. Even a magic amulet can only have power over you if you allow it. I'll tell you something my mother told me a long time ago. All magic is, is the power that comes from your own mind." Miri touched her hand to her temple. "But even stronger is the magic that comes from here." Miri placed her hand over her heart.

"No one can have power over you unless you allow it, not even your own mother."

"No?" Cassandra sneered. "Let me show you the degree of my power."

Cass's hand tightened over her medallion. Meg clutched at her chest, giving a little cry of pain.

Martin rushed forward, tugging at Miri's arm. "Miri, what are you doing? You can't—"

But Miri pulled away, commanding him to be silent. She kept her gaze focused on Meg, engaging the child's eyes, never wavering. Though the child's eyes were filled with tears and fear, she looked back at Miri as though mesmerized.

"Look at me, Meg. Only at me," she commanded, "and do what I tell you. Take hold of the medallion and pull it off."

The little girl's fingers reached for the amulet around her neck. Her mother's breath came out in a furious hiss and Meg cried out in pain again, sinking to her knees, looking up at Miri.

"I c–can't. It's too heavy. It's pulling me down."

"Miri, stop! You're going to get her killed!" Wolf protested again, but Miri waved him fiercely aside.

"It's not too heavy, Meg. It's only a necklace, nothing more. Just pull it off."

"You try to do that, Megaera, and I'll kill you. I swear I will," her mother ground out.

"No she won't," Miri said. "She can't harm you, Meg. She has no power over you. Take the necklace off."

The little girl looked desperately back at Miri, and as Miri stared into those green depths, she could see all the fear, the pain, and the hate that Cassandra was pouring into her daughter. All this time when Miri had been dreading standing up against this fearsome sorceress, she had never expected to find herself doing battle through the eyes of a child.

Her hands itched to reach out and tear the medallion away from Megaera herself, but she knew she couldn't do this for Meg. All Miri could do was try to pour all her own strength and light and hope inside the child.

Meg sniffed, although the tears coursed down her cheeks. Her small shoulders squared with determination. She hooked her fingers around the chain and with one mighty wrench, she yanked the medallion off and over her head, flinging it down on the ground. The effort cost the child the last of her strength, and she fell to the ground, sobbing. But Martin was already there, waiting to catch her, gather her up in his arms.

Cassandra's fingers tugged futilely at her own medallion, and she gave a horrible cry. The woman fell to her knees, tears streaming down her cheeks. "No! What have you done to me? You can't take my Silver Rose! She's all that I have!"

Martin cradled the sobbing child in his arms. Placing her hand on his shoulder, Miri gave him an urgent shake.

"Martin, you have to get Meg out of here now. Before the queen recovers enough to send the guard after her and Cassandra."

Martin stared up at her. "And what of you?"

"I have to go back for Simon."

"The devil you are—" Martin began, but Miri cut him off.

"There is no time to argue. Meg is the one who is in the most danger from the Dark Queen. Get her out of Paris and back to Simon's farm. We will join you there somehow."

Martin stood, lifting Meg into his arms. The little girl clung to him, burrowing her wet face against his shoulder. Glaring fiercely at Miri, Martin said, "Damn it, Miri. You can't expect me to leave you this way. Don't ask me to choose—"

"The choice isn't yours. It's mine! Now go before it's too late."

Even now, distant shouts could be heard, warning of the palace guard's imminent approach. Martin cast Miri one final agonized glance before fleeing with his daughter in the direction that led back to the city.

As Miri hesitated, trying to decide herself what to do next, she realized that Cassandra had made her way to the river's edge. During her argument with Martin, Miri had all but forgotten the sorceress. Cass had used the interval to grope her way to the end of the embankment. Whether by accident or design, she slipped, tumbling down into the river with a loud splash.

Miri hurried to the edge of the embankment, dropping to her knees, hoping somehow to catch the edge of the woman's skirt, but the current was already pulling Cass away from shore. She flailed wildly as the water soaked her gown, the weight of the fabric dragging her down. Her frantic efforts to stay afloat were only driving her farther from the bank. She disappeared under, only to emerge, gasping.

By this time, the palace guards came rushing down the embankment. Miri felt a hand clamp down on her own shoulder. She turned desperately to the man towering above her. "We have to do something. Try to help her!" But she realized that it was already too late. Cassandra's dead white hand broke the surface of the water one last time only to sink down, and vanish beneath the sparkling waters.

⸙⸙⸙⸙

SIMON LAY STRETCHED OUT on the bed, his eyes closed. He winced as Miri tended to the cut on his brow. The room was a beautiful one with hanging tapestries and a four-poster bed that was used by some of the maids of honor of the palace.

Better than the dank dungeons of some prison, which was where Miri had almost feared they would end up. But they were prisoners all the same. She only prayed that Martin and Meg had succeeded in escaping.

Miri dabbed the blood off Simon's brow. It had been all she could do to keep the man lying down as she attended to him.

"I'm not as skilled at attending a man as I would be if you were a dog, but it looks to me as if you might still need a stitch."

"I'm fine, Miri," he said. "I need to get up." He pushed her aside, even though she tried to urge him to lie still.

"I'm not sure you have shaken off the effects of Meg's sleeping dust."

"No." He curled his nose up in distaste. "It's the perfume on that pillow that's making me dizzy. Reminds me too much of . . ."

"Of Gillian Harcourt?" Miri said in a small voice.

He lowered his hand from his eyes, looking at her somewhat guiltily. "Miri, I'm sorry you had to find out about it that way. But Gillian and I were finished a long time ago. We never even began. It was just a brief period of weeks where we were both using each other."

"Oh, Simon, you don't have to explain to me."

He slipped his hands in hers, but before she could respond there was a knock and the door opened.

Ambrose Gautier entered, the man's jaw swollen from Simon's blow. He addressed Simon with grudging courtesy, "Ah, forgive me for interrupting this tender moment, but I'm here to escort both of you into the presence of Her Majesty."

Flanked by guards, Miri and Simon were escorted to the queen's antechamber, but as soon as Ambrose Gautier had announced them, he made a respectful retreat. Simon was a little surprised to find that they had been left alone with Catherine. She looked pale and shaken after the events in the garden. He knew his own head still reeled. He realized that it was sheer, indomitable will that allowed Catherine to rise to her feet to meet them.

Simon, as ever, hardly knew what to expect from this woman. He just knew he'd rather be facing the Dark Queen without Miri. He tried to keep her slightly behind him as he stepped forward to make his bow.

The Dark Queen acknowledged them. "Monsieur Aristide, Mademoiselle Cheney, please come forward. My eyesight is bad enough these days and breathing in a lungful of that infernal dust certainly hasn't helped."

Simon made his bow, but Catherine barely acknowledged him. All her attention focused on Miri. When Miri started to curtsy, she held out her hand, saying, "Come closer, child."

Simon half started to intervene. The Dark Queen said wryly, "Never fear, Monsieur Aristide. I'm not about to eat the girl."

Miri strode forward, looking as tall and proud as any of the Ladies of Faire Isle. Although she sank into a curtsy, she held her head up proudly. Catherine caught her chin between her fingers, squinting down at her.

"Miribelle Cheney. So you would be the youngest of Evangeline's daughters. I remember you from that summer you visited your sister, Gabrielle, in Paris. Quiet young thing you were, the girl with the disturbing eyes."

"Disturbing, Your Majesty?" Miri asked.

"Yes, child. I was once very good at reading eyes. I could ferret out the darkest secrets of anyone's soul. Your eyes were always more like a troubling mirror, reflecting back one's own darkest secrets." She let go of Miri's chin and stepped back. "Oh, never mind. It's the aftereffects of that infernal potion. I'm rambling."

As Miri rose and stepped back to Simon's side, Catherine rubbed the bridge of her nose as though trying to clear her head. "Well, Monsieur Aristide, our alliance did not end up exactly as I had hoped. Of course, at the time I didn't realize that you were also receiving help from Faire Isle."

"I didn't see the need to mention it, Your Grace. After all, our aims surely were all the same," he challenged, knowing she couldn't well refute that, admit what she had really been after.

"True. All the same, you must admit the three of us made a very unlikely trinity. And now, since you have been a little remiss in forwarding your reports, perhaps you could clarify exactly what was going on in my garden today."

Simon quickly filled her in with what he had been able to piece together of Cassandra's plot. "I think the original intent was for the Silver Rose to inflict a miasma upon Your Grace. Something so powerful as to drive you to madness. And when the duc de Guise came—"

"It would incite me to murder him, which would have set all of Catholic Paris in an uproar and they would likely have come to destroy me and my son. A very clever plan."

Miri ventured to speak up. "Truly, it seems like total madness to me, Your Grace."

"No, my dear. It could possibly have worked, except for a small matter, that the duc de Guise is not in Paris. His meeting with the king has been postponed until next month. But your Silver Rose was not to know that, because Gillian didn't know it either. The woman has showed herself markedly ungrateful to me. Although she managed to flee the palace grounds, my guard is still searching for her. Hopefully she will be captured before she leaves the city and then I will deal with her disloyalty."

The way Catherine said that sent a chill through Simon. Despite Gillian's treachery, he felt a stab of pity for his former mistress, but there was nothing he could do for the woman.

Simon studied Catherine, trying to gauge her mood. She had to be angry about the trick that had been played upon her, bitterly disappointed that the text she had believed to be the *Book of Shadows* had turned out to be a fake. But she appeared to have her emotions well in hand as she demanded, "And so this Cassandra Lascelles woman, she was the one behind all of this? She was the Silver Rose? And you are certain she is dead?"

"Presumably so, Your Grace. She fell into the river."

"I—I saw her drown myself," Miri added in a quiet voice and shuddered. Despite the Dark Queen's presence, Simon reached out to take her hand comfortingly in his.

"The woman is undoubtedly dead, Your Majesty," Simon said. "And sadly, she dragged her poor child down with her. Neither of them could have survived."

When Miri started in surprise at his words, Simon gave her hand a warning squeeze. But Catherine was too absorbed by her own thoughts to notice. She paced her antechamber scowling.

"The child is of no concern to me. What I want to know is what became of the real *Book of Shadows*."

"Alas, Your Grace, that is something we may never know now that the Silver Rose is dead," Simon replied blandly.

He had his own ideas regarding the book's location. He intended to launch a thorough search of the Maison d'Espirit at the first opportunity. But he kept his expression carefully neutral as Catherine glared at him.

"It seems I placed far too much faith in your skills, Master Witch-hunter. I had expected you to track down the location of the witch's coven and that infernal book as well. Who knows how many of her members might still be at large?"

"With the Silver Rose gone, I doubt they will pose any threat to Your Grace."

"All the same, you have keenly disappointed me."

"Disappointed you?" Miri quivered with indignation. "Your Grace already seems to have forgotten that Monsieur Aristide risked his own life to foil the sorceress's plot. If it had been a miasma instead of a sleeping draft, you would have lost your reason and the entire country might now be on the brink of revolution."

Catherine pursed her lips. "True enough," she conceded grudgingly. "And I suppose he did rid me of the threat of the Silver Rose."

"For which I believe Simon told me you offered him a reward," Miri reminded her.

"He said there was nothing that he wanted. But I suppose, like most men, he has changed his mind and thought of something."

Simon only had to consider for a moment before saying, "Yes. Just one thing. I would like you to restore the Lady of Faire Isle and her husband to their property."

Miri gave a soft gasp. Even Catherine looked taken aback at the request.

"Just when I think I've grown too old to be surprised, Monsieur Aristide. A witch-hunter asking for the restoration of a witch?"

"No," he said. "A very wise woman, and her husband. I made a mistake years ago, and so did you. I believe Your Grace and I both hope this is the end of this Silver Rose matter. But with all these witches dispersed across the countryside it would be good to have the Lady of Faire Isle back on her island helping to keep watch."

The Dark Queen pursed her lips, seeming to turn the matter over in her mind. "For once you and I seem to be in agreement, Master Witch-Hunter. Ever since that raid on Faire Isle, the world has seemed strangely out of balance. But one would have to know where to find the lady."

Miri spoke up. "I believe that I could help with that, Your Grace. I would be happy to get word to my sister as soon as possible."

The queen nodded glumly, but she turned to Simon. "But what of you, monsieur? With these witches abroad, perhaps I can persuade you to continue in my employ until they are all hunted down."

But Simon shook his head. Gathering Miri's hand tighter in his, he said, "No, Your Grace. My witch-hunting days are over."

Epilogue

T HE SUN SPREAD A SPARKLING STREAMER OF LIGHT ACROSS the pond, a soft breeze blew through the trees, and Simon's farm was a peaceful haven after all the violence and turmoil of Paris. Miri drew in a deep draft of air, feeling like she could finally breathe again. She smiled from the doorway, looking at the trio over by the pond, Yves, Carole, and Meg skimming stones, feeding some stale bread to the ducks.

Her smile was rather sad as she reflected that of the three, it was only the largest, the tall, ungainly boy, who remained a child at heart. After all that Meg and Carole had gone through, they had been transformed forever, forced to grow far beyond their years.

But it was pleasant for the moment to watch them

laughing and happy and being children. As a shadow fell across her, Miri looked around as Wolf joined her in the farmhouse doorway, gazing across at his daughter. His lips quirked wryly. "Mon Dieu, she actually likes it here. What is it about you wise women and farms?"

Miri laughed. "I don't know if I could even begin to explain it to you."

Martin looked wistful. "She's happy. It's the first time I've seen her smile since—since . . ." Neither of them had to say since that grim moment the child had been told of her mother's death.

"I almost wish I could let her stay here, but—"

"I know." Miri regarded him sadly. They'd all agreed that the best course was for Martin to take Meg and vanish. Although the body of Cassandra Lascelles had never been recovered, she surely could not have escaped the river's current. Miri hoped that woman's insane plans had died with her, but when Simon had raided the house in Paris, the remaining members of the coven had all fled. Nor had the *Book of Shadows* been found, even in the hidden underground chamber. Some of the witches might still be determined to find their Silver Rose and resurrect Cassandra's dream. There was also the danger that the Dark Queen might discover that Simon had deceived her regarding the true identity of the Silver Rose and that Meg had not drowned along with her mother.

Turning back to Wolf, Miri asked, "So where will you go? I thought perhaps you could take her to Faire Isle."

Wolf shook his head. "No. Not even with Ariane returning am I convinced that my daughter would be safe there. I'm not even sure that it's safe for me to take her back to Navarre. I think that our best course is going to be to leave France entirely." He attempted to smile. "We'll get by. Don't worry about us, Miri. I think Meg is fond of England. It will be like going home to her. I've traveled there enough that I can pass myself off as an Englishman, although it makes me shudder to do so. Ah, but the sacrifices one must make for one's child." But his smile vanished the next instant. He looked wistfully at Meg. "God, Miri, I've never had anyone of my own before. When I was rescued by Captain Remy I adopted the rest of you as family, but she's—she's of my blood," he said wonderingly, as if he could scarce believe it. "I'm her father. Me, a papa. Who would have ever imagined it?"

"I'm sure you'll be a fine one."

He shook his head. "I'm terrified. I don't have the least idea how to go about it. I never had any father of my own. When I think of the mistakes I might make . . ."

"I think that you will find that children can be very hardy flowers. Just a little love and sunshine is all they require to thrive quite well. Being Meg's father . . . You must think of it as just another grand adventure."

"There's only one difference. This time I'm scared to death." But he said nothing more, as Meg had crept up to join him.

She slipped her little hand into his. "Don't be afraid, Papa. I'll take care of you. Just like I always wanted to take care of Maman, but she wouldn't let me."

As a tear trickled down Meg's cheek, Martin applied his handkerchief and wrapped his arm around his daughter. Miri hunkered down beside her and took her hand.

The little girl regarded her gravely, with eyes far too old

for that pale little face. "Do you think I am very wicked, Mistress Cheney? I'm the one to blame for Maman's dying."

Miri stroked the girl's hair back. "No, child. I believe you did your best to save her. Sometimes, no matter how much we love somebody, we can't help them. Not unless they're willing to do that for themselves."

Meg frowned. As wise as she was, it was a lot for a little girl to absorb. She ran her hands up to her neck. "I always hated that medallion Maman made me wear, but—but it's a little scary having it gone. It's like I could always feel her, know that I had someone."

"Well, now you have somebody else, and I can give you a far better charm than that medallion." Miri produced the locket from her pocket and draped it around the little girl's neck.

Meg examined it and traced her finger over the etching of the wolf. When she looked up at her father, there was a blinding smile that entirely transformed the child's face. Miri thought, she's going to be a dazzling beauty someday. Martin is really going to have his hands full. But she kept that reflection to herself. Wolf was already nervous enough as it was.

At that moment, Simon came out of the barn leading Martin's horse, and Madame Pascale emerged from the house with the provisions she'd packed for their trip. As Meg made her farewells to Carole, Martin turned to Miri and Simon.

"Well, farewell, witch—" He stopped to correct himself. "Aristide. I'm forever in your debt, monsieur. I, of course, trust that you will entirely forgive me if I don't embrace you in parting."

"Not at all," Simon said, stepping back, "I'd be far more grateful to you if you didn't."

"I would still have to be vexed with you, and say you stole my Lady of the Moon, but I'm afraid she was never mine to begin with."

"Nor was she mine."

"These ladies of Faire Isle, they follow their own hearts and make their own choices. And it's clear to me that she has made hers," Martin said sadly. "I trust I don't even have to tell you to take good care of her."

"I'd hardly do otherwise. I wouldn't want you turning up in my stable again."

Both men smiled and shook hands. Martin turned at last to Miri, his heart too full for a moment to say anything. He clasped her hand. "My dearest friend. You know if you ever need me . . ."

She nodded, tears sparkling in her eyes. "I'll be fine. You have someone else who needs you far more now."

Martin brushed a kiss upon her cheek, then he swung up on his horse, lifting his daughter in front of him. The child looked adoringly up at him as they cantered down the lane, Yves racing after, waving his feathered cap in farewell.

Carole and Madame Pascale returned to the house. There were more arrangements to be made for Carole's own journey back to Faire Isle and the babe who waited for her there.

Miri found herself alone with Simon as she had scarce been since they had returned from Paris. For a long moment their gazes met.

"Well," Simon said, "now, my lady, when do you want

to set out? I know you must be eager to get back to Faire Isle."

"Yes, I will want to be there to greet Ariane when she returns home. And of course, I have got to get Carole back to her son. Simon, I wish you would come with me."

"I hardly think that I would be welcomed there."

"But it was because of you that the Lady will be restored to Faire Isle and I want everyone to know that."

"You expect too much of people, Miri. I'm glad that I was at least able to put something right, but to imagine that I could ever be forgiven and welcomed there is just too much to expect. And yet, I know Faire Isle is your home. Where you belong. Where you've always wanted to be."

Miri shook her head. "I thought so once. I remember Ariane saying she hoped I'd find what I was looking for when I returned to Faire Isle. But it wasn't on Faire Isle. All I was seeking on the island was my past. But my future is right here with you." She held out her hand and he still looked as though he scarce dared to reach for it. So she caught his instead.

"In case you didn't recognize that for what it was, Simon Aristide, I'm asking you to be my husband."

He smiled, one eyebrow rising a fraction. "You ladies of Faire Isle are disconcertingly bold."

Miri refused to be daunted by his teasing. "One of us had to say it and I could tell it was not going to be you, my very reluctant suitor. You've never even told me that you loved me. It's a fortunate thing that I'm so very good at reading eyes."

Simon brought her hand up to his lips. "I do love you,

Miri. I always have." He smiled as he drew her into his arms.

"Because I've always been your greatest weakness?"

"No, dear heart," he murmured, pressing his lips tenderly to hers. "My greatest strength."

About the Author

SUSAN CARROLL is an award-winning romance author whose books include *The Bride Finder* and its two sequels, *The Night Drifter* and *Midnight Bride,* as well as *The Painted Veil, Winterbourne,* and most recently, *The Dark Queen* and *The Courtesan.* She lives in Rock Island, Illinois.

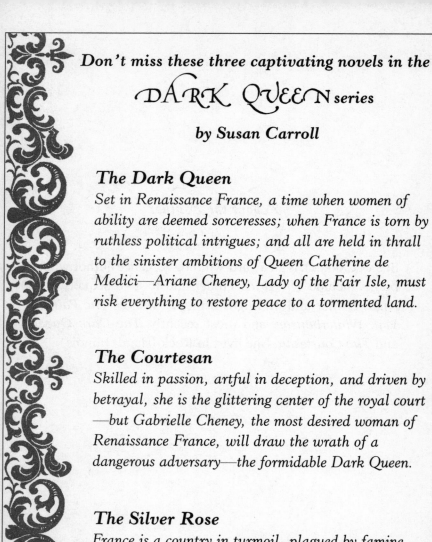

Don't miss these three captivating novels in the

DARK QUEEN series

by Susan Carroll

The Dark Queen

Set in Renaissance France, a time when women of ability are deemed sorceresses; when France is torn by ruthless political intrigues; and all are held in thrall to the sinister ambitions of Queen Catherine de Medici—Ariane Cheney, Lady of the Fair Isle, must risk everything to restore peace to a tormented land.

The Courtesan

Skilled in passion, artful in deception, and driven by betrayal, she is the glittering center of the royal court —but Gabrielle Cheney, the most desired woman of Renaissance France, will draw the wrath of a dangerous adversary—the formidable Dark Queen.

The Silver Rose

France is a country in turmoil, plagued by famine, disease, and on the brink of a new religious war. In the midst of so much chaos, Miri Cheney must face a far greater evil—a diabolical woman known only as The Silver Rose.

Published by Ballantine Books • Available wherever books are sold